RECKLESS SKIES

To my friends and family
I couldn't have made it without you.

Prologue

Wind swept the barren desert. Sand collected on the canvas sheets of the tents. A shadow fell over the dunes as skeletal dogs barked incessantly. Ghosts of men stepped onto the hot, burning sand, eyes travelling to the island floating peacefully above them. It was rare to see it so plainly, and at that notion they knew they only had now to get out.

A nomad with sun-scorched skin glanced back at the large, uneasy crowd. His eyes wandered toward the flashing lighthouse looming above him. He, his people, and his torn and battered tent town were a ruin of what once was. The majority of the people were hard, battle torn; even the children had been denied their childhood. He looked back up to the city and squinted as it flashed back. Saved! They were saved from this deadly desert!

"Gather together! Today is our salvation!" called the chief with a joyful smile. Finally, they were saved from this hellish desert, from the dehydration, the sleepless, starving nights. The people, at least a hundred or more, gathered together as the floating mountain sent ships soaring down to meet them.

Among the crowd was a young boy and his father, staring up at their saviors with flickering smiles. Heat waves distorted the gleaming silver ships, sunlight glinted off of the wings and flashed in the boy's bright blue eyes. He squinted and glanced away, his eyes shifting and scanning up the thinned form of his father. The weathered man looked back down at his boy.

"Do you see those ships Allen? They're going to get us out of here. We'll be in heaven, you see?" He dropped to his knees and pointed. Allen tilted his head and looked at his father, his long, chestnut dreads sweeping over his shoulders. He was nine, and already bore the weight of death every day.

"Heaven? Really? Will there be angels?" he asked, his voice soft and filled with questions, his eyebrows furrowed with childish curiosity. Despite the grueling pain of the desert, the ravenous men, and terrifying monsters...he still had a glimmer of hope that only children could have. His father smiled sadly at him, not exactly knowing how to respond to the boy's question.

"Angels...not ones with wings, but with caring hugs who will take care of us as soon as we get up there," he reassured, a quick nod following his imaginative words. His father had done everything to keep his boy safe, and even though sometimes it wasn't enough, he would be damned if he ever failed. A big smile of gapped teeth brightened the boy's face and he nodded.

"We'll be together in Magnus City, and we'll have a great house, and we'll play sports in the park, you and I, just like dads and sons should," said the man, frowning slightly. He read a lot of old books, books covered in dust, books from the past, books that seemed to transport them back in time to a better place. A time they couldn't get back. Now it was run, fight, survive.

At least it had been. Now, heaven, *heaven* was coming to them, and they would be safe. That perfect place, with civilized people, where war was a thing of the past; the past where the books came from. Magnus city lived in the future of peace.

"I'll like that! What do you think the city is like?" asked Allen, jumping on the balls of his feet with uncontained excitement. His father knit his brows and rubbed his scraggly beard in thought. None of them had ever been in the city. From down in that wasteland it looked so peaceful. After all, it was spared from the death that surrounded them every day.

He smiled and looked at the sky, watching as the ships drew closer. The ships themselves were like the graceful swans he saw in the pictures of the old science books. A soft smile flickered on his lips. Was this to be his new home? A better place? A better way of life? No more stinging sandstorms, dangerous mutated beasts, and horrible murderous raiders, but...heaven?

The ships alighted on the ground, enormous things they were. Fit to hold tens of thousands of people. Murmurs passed through the crowd, murmurs of excitement and hope. Saved. They were saved! A puff of steam escaped as a steel drawbridge lowered. A joyous cheer erupted from the gathering and they began to step forward.

"Halt." boomed an almost inhuman voice on a loudspeaker. The voice thundered and rolled in Allen's mind like a thunderstorm and his eyes widened with shock. The crowd stilled, eyes almost as big and confused as the little boy's. He squinted to see a line of black uniformed soldiers marching out, guns glinting in their arms. A sentry stepped up, gripping his weapon with a confident hand.

"You will proceed in orderly rows of four. Welcome aboard the Magister." The soldier's loud voice bellowed over the blazing, red sand dunes. A shiver ran through the crowd. Allen's skin prickled, like spiders crawling on his bare arms and the back of his neck. He shook himself; his imagination was getting the best of him. The sensation however, lingered.

His father grabbed his hand to make sure they wouldn't be separated. The soldiers marched behind the rows of nomad refugees, prodding any person showing a sign of disorderly conduct; much like cattle handlers.

Allen's hand was being squeezed fiercely by his father; his knuckles white with fear of the unknown. The boy frowned and his head turned in frantic jerks as he took in his surroundings.

A blast of cold air almost took his breath away as rows of blinding, white lights shone down on them icily. The walls were steel grey, and reflected the lights dully. Their feet clanged on thick, rigid steel that was almost greyer and drearier than the walls, if that were possible. Allen found his stomach was rolling, his heart thundering in his ears. His frantic eyes were desperately searching for one thing he could find familiar in this strange new world.

His father looked back down at him and nodded reassuringly, but they were both scared of what was to come. At least they were together. The seemingly endless hall widened, spilling into a giant holding pen.

The crowd immediately began spreading out, a hive of curiosity. When the sentries pushed them back, an uproar of confusion spread through the crowds. Allen spotted a man fighting with a guard in a vain and stupid attempt to assert his autonomy. A boom of thunder sounded and the man fell to the floor. The people screamed and began scurrying away from the nomad's limp form.

Allen caught a glance of blood, shattered bones...half a face that only a few seconds before had been filled with promise and hope.

His heart froze from sheer terror; the gun blast thundering in his ears, the spiders crawling on his skin, and his stomach gripped with sheer terror.

The crowd grew frantic and suddenly the grip around his hand was gone. Nothing was familiar.

"Dad!?" he shouted, gasping as another bang echoed through the hall. More guards came in to subdue the crowd.

"Dad!?" His heart quickened and it hurt to breathe. Where was he!? One moment he had been by his side and now he was gone! How? Tears welled up in Allen's eyes as he was swept away by the mob.

Allen was trampled to the ground, the air knocked out of him. He lost his vision for half a second. The floor swam left and right as he tried to regain his bearings. There was a jolt of motion. His ears rang with the pounding of his heart.

He got to his feet as his attention was captured by the alien guards staring down at the holding pen, gripping their guns menacingly, ready to prevent another riot as food and water were passed out. Allen stared up, silently thankful that the crowd had calmed to a simmer.

At least no more guns were being fired. The Dwellers must've learned their lesson. His eyes shifted and he watched as a man in a black, flowing cloak, with a shimmering, white uniform under it, approached the balcony that overlooked them. Standing beside him was a woman in a similar uniform with long braids and dark skin.

"Welcome refugees, I am Captain Sylva. I am glad to say that we are now departing to Magnus City. We expect orderly behavior as provisions are passed around. If not, we will not hesitate to dispose of you." He paused, letting the threat sink in. Allen winced slightly, mind flashing with rapid images of the man with half his face blown off. He glanced around and wiped his wet, tear streaked face. He needed to find his dad, but there were so many people, he didn't even know where to begin.

Everyone was silent as they stared up at the captain, not daring to speak while he loomed over them.

"When we arrive in the city, you will wait in the pit, gather your provided supplies, give us your information and wait for the rest of your family. If they do not arrive within the day, you will be sent to your holds, and children will be sent to The Home." The words made a lump grow in Allen's throat. The Home? What could that possibly mean for him? He let his eyes wander as the lump grew bigger and more uncomfortable. He tried to swallow it down; he couldn't cry, not now when he needed so desperately to find his dad.

"With all that said, please enjoy the luxuries of the city, and remember, *Pax est vita,"* he recited before gliding back into the hall with his entourage.

Allen shivered at the maxim. He didn't know what it meant, but he had a feeling he would find out. He found phrases he couldn't decipher glowing on the walls.

"Progressus est scientia, Scientia est pax, Pax est vita."
The last phrase was bigger than the others.

Allen glanced up as a white uniformed crew member came to his row with a hot pot of stew. He received a bowl and stared down at it greedily. His stomach ached, rumbling as he realized just how starved he was. He was reminded of the hunts conducted by the survivors, and how almost all that they caught was inedible...and then they'd starve another night.

For the few seconds of holding that steaming, heavy bowl, he forgot his fears, and remembered just one thing. He was ravenous. Immediately, he wolfed it down, spilling gravy on his ragged clothes. He wasn't the only one, as people around him all ate as if they hadn't eaten in days. That had been their lives.

Allen found he had finished the bowl in a matter of seconds, and licked the inside to get any last bits of food. He wiped his mouth sloppily and put the bowl on a tray as it was passed by. He needed more. He was still hungry and one bowl stew wasn't enough.

The others murmured. Their murmurs turned to shouts now that they felt they had the freedom to talk. Allen panted from exhaustion; drowsiness hit him like a wet sandbag. He was alone and scared. What would he do without his dad? He prayed to whatever god was up there for his father to come find him.

There was a rough lurch that brought the young boy from his dazed sleep. He looked around frantically as the black armored guards strode in. An announcement sounded at the speakers and Allen felt dizzy and disoriented at the sudden motion and sound. He stumbled to his feet as another wave of the crowd began being herded out of the holding pit and down the long narrow path that would eventually lead to the exit.

Guards surrounded them, walking on a separate walkway from the crowd of refugees. Three more heavily armed sentries stood at two different exits. One was labelled "children", the other labelled for adults. The bulkier sentry bellowed for a halt.

"Children ages nine and under, bring them now, through this ward," he ordered through the muffle of his tinted face shield. A wave of little boys and girls were brought to the front. Allen was one of them.

"Allen! Allen!" he heard a shout behind him and he turned, seeing the red face of his father. He gasped and tried to push through the crowd to reach him, but a rough hand grabbed his shoulder. He yelped with surprise and anger.

"Please proceed. You'll meet up with your family on the other side." His words were cold, and what made it worse was the fact Allen couldn't see his face past the tinted shield of his helmet.

"Allen! Son!" the shouts echoed in his mind, and he felt his grasp on control quickly leaving him as he was herded into the long, seemingly endless hallway. His father, that was his *father,* so close but so far.

The horror of his situation made him want to scream...This wasn't fair! This was supposed to be heaven! He was supposed to be with his dad in Magnus. They were supposed to be together! That had been the plan.

"Hey...It's gonna be ok...we'll return to our parents soon enough. Remember what Captain Sylva said?" whispered a small girl, her platinum blonde hair in dreads much like his. He glanced back at her and frowned.

"Promise?" he whispered. The girl crossed her heart and smiled a sweet smile that melted away his icy fear. He smiled back; he couldn't stop himself.

"Promise. This is Magnus city, I believe we're in good hands," she reassured. Allen nodded, the girl beside him calming his heart with her confidence and her sweet smile.

"I'm Allen. Allen Rosinsky." he held out an awkward hand. She grinned and took it. Her hand, much like his, was calloused from the hard days in the desert.

"Maya Hart," she replied. Allen smiled. Finally, here was someone who wasn't ordering him around or yelling at him. Their feet marched on with the others, his eyes wide with shock and alertness. He saw a break in the hall, a stream of golden light shining through...It was sunlight. A ghost of a smile brushed his face as he marched onto a landing pad.

Allen made the mistake of looking down, seeing the Earth looming far beneath him. His eyes widened. To think just hours ago he had been down there. Something about it was strangely alluring. He felt a little piece of him fall away, he grimaced and an anger filled him.

The landing pad conveyed them up into another holding pit and they were ordered at gunpoint to take seats; oldest to youngest. Maya sat beside him, her dark eyes scanning the walls around them. The walls were a soft blue that faded strangely into purple. Watching the colors change nauseated him. He watched as, one by one, they were sent to the showers. Maya was called and she hesitated before leaving his side.

'No, not again.' The bitter words filled his thoughts as he watched her tentatively step away, parting into a hallway he couldn't follow her into. Another lost person. He was losing his grasp, clawing to hold onto things that slid through his fingers.

He glowered as the guard gestured for him to go. They didn't know his name, and they didn't care, they only pointed and shouted.

Allen got up and trailed behind another boy into the showers. The tiled floor was sleek and colorful. A green light blinked, capturing his attention. A voice spoke up, telling him to unclothe and place his clothes on the metal tray. Without hesitation he did as he was told. He was shell shocked, scared of what might happen if he were to disobey.

Wall tiles blinked red and a glass door automatically slid open. A waterfall cascaded down from a sleek shower head. He hesitantly stepped inside, the hot water melting away his tense nerves.

A blue light flashed over him and a mechanical hand folded out from the wall, one of its fingers was a sharp blade. He cried out of shock and whipped away from it. Another mechanical hand grabbed him and held him still with alarming strength. He panted from the instant rush of adrenaline, eyes frantically watching as the blade began cutting away at his chestnut dreads.

He watched the tangled clusters drop to the wet floor. His hair was now cropped and soft. Stunned, he washed the rest of his lean body, his baby fat had been wasted away from starved nights and hard labor. He looked older than nine, that was for sure.

The grime of his face and body also went down the drain, revealing the soft features of his somehow still round, child's face. The shower suddenly turned ice cold and he gasped, backing away as it automatically shut off.

Allen frowned and stiffly wrapped a towel around his waist. He walked out, seeing his old clothes had been taken and in their place was a pair of black pants and a white t-shirt with a long number pinned to it. He also found a stiff pair of black running shoes on top of the clothes.

He slipped the foreign clothes on, shaking the water out of his short hair. A green arrow lit up and a small bell jangled. The nine-year-old, already feeling ages older, followed it with a bitter, almost involuntary baring of teeth.

There was something they said back on the wasteland, a phrase he hoped could've been left on that barren surface. "Run, fight, survive." This sterile city had its maxims and he had his. The wasteland's maxim stirred his thoughts. He deeply considered how he would have to use them here in this strange, new place.

The rest of the day was a blur of soldiers prodding him from one place to the next, and constantly filled with the fear of not being able to find his father. The sky grew dim, families collected as he sat alone with several other kids. Where was his dad? His heart sank like a boulder, as slowly, the other kids thinned out. At least Maya was there. Would they get sent to the Home?

The very thought sent his heart plummeting. He couldn't! He had to get out, he would rather be on his own than in an orphanage. He looked at Maya and smiled weakly.

"I'm getting a little nervous," he mumbled, rubbing the back of his neck. Maya smiled back and patted his head. Her once tangled hair had been cropped short like his

"Everything will be ok, just wait and see." she whispered. Allen sighed. Something deep inside him didn't believe her. A large glass door slid open and two guards led in a group of people.

"Maya Hart?" called one of the sentries. Maya's head perked up and she smiled brightly, her eyes welling with joyful tears. Allen looked up, and watched her reunion with her mother and father. He felt his stomach flip as she waved goodbye to him. He looked away, envy filling him, choking him. That wasn't fair. Why couldn't he have his family back? He glanced at some of the other kids waiting with him.

An hour...two hours...three hours. Eventually he was the only one left. How? He knew his dad was here, he saw him with his own eyes! He was with him. Allen stood up and paced about, a large lump growing in his throat. This couldn't be, this hadn't been the plan! He was supposed to be with his father in Magnus. Together! Four hours.... five hours...no one came. Allen's anger boiled over and he shouted with rage.

"Dad!? Where are you!? I know you're here! Please! Please come get me!" He screamed at the cameras and doors. His hands twitched and he grabbed the closest thing to him, chucking it at the wall in front of him. It shattered, and a light went off. The door opened and he turned.

"Dad? I thought I would never see you again, oh thank…" his eyes scanned the door, and all he saw were two guards. His father was nowhere to be seen.

"W-where's my dad? I know he's here!" he demanded, eyes flashing. The guards looked at each other.

"Six-two-zero, your father did not come. It's...time to go. Put on this mask," said one of the voices from the tinted helmet. The guard held out a strange device, a mask with a filter, that covered the mouth. On the side was a speaker, and it was connected all around by a tight belt.

Allen ignored the gas mask; he could hardly pay attention to any of it. His world dropped from under his feet, and his body was crushed, lungs caving in on themselves. His dad...his dad would never just leave him, he refused to believe so!

"You're lying, where is he!? The other kids all got their parents, I saw my dad before I left the ship! So... where is he?" he demanded to know. He was enraged, and the lump grew so big he could barely breathe. The guards glanced at each other.

"There are so many people...he'll come to The Home tomorrow...but the day is at its end and we need to get everyone out. Now let us help you put on this mask," the other guard said. Allen darted away as the guard reached out at him, his glare going from one sentry to the next. He snarled at them.

"You don't care! And it's Allen! It's Allen, not six-two-zero! There! I'm a real person, not a number, and I want my dad!" he yelled, his voice cracking. The soldiers shifted uncomfortably.

"Listen, *Allen*. We need to go, the bus is coming soon, and those are just the rules," said the woman, grabbing his hand. He tried yanking it away from her but she was too strong. They held him down as he kicked and squirmed, shouting unholy curses at them at the top of his lungs as they tightened the chord. He found his voice came clearly through the speaker as if he didn't have a face mask on, and it surprised him long enough for the woman to kick in his leg and force him to the ground. They pinned his arms tight behind his back. The guards hoisted him up, one stood behind just in case he tried to book it and they dragged him out of the room.

"Damn earth-dweller. Absolute savages," murmured the woman as they left. Allen gritted his teeth at the words.

The bus was there waiting, and they shoved him on, closing the doors just as he tried to barge out. Allen snarled and kicked, trying anything to force it open, but it wouldn't budge.

"Please! I know my dad is there…" he whimpered. A few kids shifted their gazes at him, eyes filled with pity, some with cruel amusement at the sight of someone else suffering along with them. He glared at nothing in particular, and his heart was torn in half, his head was pounding. There were no open seats, so he sat beside a kid near the back, but he was too torn to look at him.

"Hey mate…I'm sorry about your da', it's happened to all of us," murmured a squeaky voice beside him. Allen glanced up to come face to face with the boy sharing his seat. His buck teeth fought for attention with his sparkling green eyes, an untamed puff of red hair and trillions of freckles. Allen also noticed the boy had a gas mask on as well, hanging around his neck. He glanced around, realizing all the kids had their gas masks hanging on their necks. He took note of it, his hands reaching up to start loosening the straps, tears brimming in his eyes as he remembered the roughness of the guards.

Normally, he would've smiled, but not now. Too broken, too afraid, too enraged. The last thing he wanted to do was make a friend he would most likely lose.

"I'm Ricky…" said the ginger colored boy; his pale hand darting out awkwardly when Allen failed to speak. The refugee looked at the boy with welled eyes and slowly took his hand.

"Allen…hold on, I just…" he looked away, his body shaking as his lips curled into an ugly and painful sob. Ricky frowned with empathy and he patted his back, sitting back against the seat and wiping his own eyes.

"It's ok, we've all been there…ay, let's change the subject. You might be confused about these mask thingies; all dwellers usually are. Grandpappy told me we had to wear them or else we'd stop breathing 'cause of the air pressure," he informed. Allen raised a questioning brow at him. He didn't really care what the masks did, but he appreciated the effort Ricky had made.

"Thanks Ricky…I ought to keep you around; huh? Where are they taking us?" he mumbled glancing at the red head and offering a weak smile. Ricky looked on with remorse and sat back, waving his hand in a general direction.

"The Home…" he replied mournfully. Allen's face fell at the thought. The bus drove past a gleaming city that sparkled in the evening light. A barbwire fence, and a large shimmering sea separated the two hemispheres of the city. On one side it sparkled, the other, reeked of despair. Allen was on the wrong side of the fence, and he felt his gut go cold with dread.

Before Allen could even take in the beauty he thought he would be allowed to have, the bus turned away, driving down a narrow, cracked road and into the tight, crumbling ghettos of the Fence. This was not Heaven, and those words he thought he'd never need again came back. "Run. Fight. Survive."

PART ONE:

THE FENCE

ALLen

A whistling, icy wind drove itself through the crowded streets like a bull plowing through his unsuspecting victims. Nothing good about that crowd, the men gruff, their faces prickly with stubble that was the product of dull razors or none at all; the women were busty and improper, loud and in your face. They weren't beautiful. There was no beauty in a simple, genuine smile. Instead, there were faceless masks with hard frowns underneath as they made their commute to the looming Nuclear Power Plant. This world wasn't soft; this ghetto.

The Fence stood tall, daring anyone to cross it, its barbs shining a dull rusty red from the blood of countless unfortunates insane enough to try and climb them. Perhaps that fence was the reason there were no smiles. Barbs, coiling on the top and through the vertical steel posts buzzing with electricity. The fence made it plain that they were cattle in a slaughterhouse.

A small child or two, faces heavy with their masks, stood at the humming fence, staring out at the shimmering sea that separated the gleaming Skyline from the ghetto where they lived. Pretentious sailboats bounced above the waves like large seagulls.

That city didn't belong to them; they were denied of all its luxuries. The wind swept away from the sight of the sea, whistling down cracked paths and through markets of expired foods delivered by heavily armed provision trucks. Leftovers. The wind off the sea rushed up cracks running along the side of dilapidated buildings stacked precariously on top of each other. It hissed through the draping chains supporting flashing neon signs and advertisements for things they couldn't afford.

Along the cracked corridors, a group of men shouted, their heels thundering like a stampede of horses, running down their victim: a troublesome young man with a crooked grin. Once a stranger to this city, he now raced through its streets as if he had always lived there.

Allen was being chased along the alleys, the gang hot on his trail. His ragged breaths fogging in the crisp air. A thin tube wound around his ear and entered his nose, his mouth free of those pesky masks that dehumanized the people of the Fence.

"Ya' rat! Get back over here and take your beatin' like a man!" A muffled shout from a lean, bald man, angry red scars crisscrossing his bare chest. He leaped to snag the hardened boy's hoodie. Allen skidded into an alleyway, wind whistling in his ears. He laughed maniacally at his own situation as he hopped up a trash can, his arms darting up to reach a ladder just above him. His feet kicked off the brick wall beneath him, boosting him up. He scaled it quickly, hearing the rails clanging as more men clambered up to catch him.

This was what happened when you stole a case of whiskey from a bootlegger. That had been a bad idea, but only if he got caught! He was sure he could outrun them; it just took a bit of smarts! Something he had and they lacked. He bounced off the ladder and onto the roof, laughing as he drank precariously from one of the glass bottles in his bulging jacket pockets.

He raced to the edge of the building, skidding to a stop as he saw the sheer drop below him. *'Aw damn! Fine, I'll give 'em a fight.'* His thoughts berated him, scolding his bad decisions. A wicked laughter peeled through his brain as he panted for fresh air. He darted his head around to see the five men spreading out to surround him. He took another drink and wiped his mouth. Ten damned years in this gutter and this wasn't even his biggest problem.

"I'll jump, and the whiskey will go with me, ya freaks!" he shouted, a cocky raise of his brow daring them to challenge his sanity. The scarred man stepped forward and whipped a blade from his pocket. Allen gasped in mock surprise. A knife? He was unimpressed as silly as that sounded. Unimpressed at his own demise. He was a piece of work.

"Shut your ugly trap, and gi'me back what's mine, then accept the beatin' you deserve, Smiley!" ordered

Bruce as he held up his weapon. Allen narrowed his eyes at the nickname.

The Badgers were one of the most notorious gangs, and he had definitely run up against them too many times as he had been awarded the nickname after Ricky had invented a maskless oxygen tube for the both of them. Smiley…after he quit -quite ungracefully-from their "employment", and took some booze with him, that name carried a lot of hatred.

Allen held up the bottle and glanced around, watching the Badgers with calculating and narrowed eyes. They were approaching him slowly, and he knew his window would be sealed shut soon.

"That's bullshit! Bruce you know that I'll take you all...besides, it's just whiskey, it's probably the cheap kind! Hol' up, lemme take a nice sip to see for myself," he said coolly, his feet shifting as he brought the bottle to his lips. Bruce charged him, swinging his knife. He towered over Allen, but Allen didn't have time to be intimidated.

He swung his head back to escape the blade, his hand shooting up and grabbing Bruce's leathery skin. He pulled himself into the bootlegger, dragging him down, his knee crashing into Bruce's groin.

A loud grunt sounded next to his ear; echoing as he twisted, his hand fumbling with the buckle of Bruce's gas mask. He crashed his elbow against the mask and knocked it clean off. He spun back around and punched Bruce's nose.

Blood spurted out, splattering onto the gravel roof. Hands ripped him off the leader and a fist rammed into his gut. Air exploded from his lungs and he doubled over. Sweat poured down his face, and he let his body weight drop to set the thugs off as they tried to rip out his oxygen tube.

Allen tore his arm away from the grip of an emaciated man, Peter, who barely had a hold on him. His leg sprung back and he bounced up, swinging around and hitting the fatter one, Martin, on the side of his face with the whiskey bottle. Glass shattered over the man's greasy temple and Martin stumbled away, knocking into another goon who was in his path. Allen couldn't believe he used to break bread with these men...

Allen darted away, ducking under a punch and kicking his assailant off balance as he jumped into a run. Without a second thought, he leaped off the ledge and vaulted over to the next building. He tumbled onto his back, his body exploding with sharp pain at the impact. Without a second thought, he stumbled to his feet, his legs swinging over the ledge as he lowered himself onto a fire escape.

"Rotten bugga!" shouted Bruce as he struggled to put his mask back on. Allen laughed and jogged through the alley, swallowing large gulps of the stolen whiskey with triumph. He hoped he would never have to see them again. He may've been able to take them that time, but it had been a small assembly of the Badger gang which allowed him to create that window of escape. They'd be on his tail and better prepared if he stumbled into them again.

His lips smacked in satisfaction as he drank the liquor. This was worth it though. Good whiskey, not some cheap watered-down fake hooch he could buy at the market. He glanced behind him as he heard stomps shaking the ground and cursed under his breath.

They were relentless! He sprinted away, shoving past unsuspecting bystanders. They yelped and dove out of their path, knowing better than to get in the gang's way.

What had he been thinking!? His lungs begged for air, his legs like heavy lead. There was a break in the street, and he dashed for it, wondering when they would let up? He needed a break. At least a minute before he could continue running. God, he hated running, but he seemed to do it all the time!

He made the mistake of looking back and tripped over a curb. Cursing, he tried scurrying back to his feet, but his legs were caught and the men surrounded him. The bald man circled him as he was held down, arms pinned to his back like an escaped prisoner. They were all prisoners. He panted, internally beating himself up for his mistake. Damn, and he thought today would be his day.

"You are the biggest idiot I've ever met. You should've never crossed me Allen," snarled Bruce as he knelt down to get Allen's attention. Bruce lifted his pointed chin and bared his teeth to instill fear in his heart. Allen was too stubborn to admit it had worked.

"I'll do what I want!" he wheezed, his lungs heaving for air, his words earning him a sharp kick in the ribs. He ground his teeth in pain but refused to look weak in front of the bootleggers. Bruce boxed his ears, Allen's head spinning as the sharp slap echoed through his mind; his ears rang. The whiskey was taken from his pockets, and the one he had been drinking was poured over him to taunt his defeat. They hoisted him up and dealt blows to his face, a tooth shot from his lower jaw. He grunted, a small whimper leaving his lips at the pain. He'd feel that tomorrow.

"Okay! That's fine, just don't get my nose," He groaned, his face aching sharply. Bruce grabbed a fist full of his sweaty brown hair and sneered in his face. Allen glared back, his lips twitching into a smirk.

"Don't act so arrogant, smart guy. I could rip out your little oxygen tube right now," he hissed. Allen narrowed his eyes at him, trying to retain his fear inside of his gut. Ricky would be furious…

"So why won't you?" he asked, a fearful sparkle in his bright blue eyes. Bruce smirked smugly and ruffled Allen's hair.

"Cause I'm not a coward like you," growled Bruce, and swung his fist across Allen's cheek. He saw stars erupt in his eyes, his mind tumbling in circles, the earth about him spinning and fading from black to brightness that cut through his vision and aching head like sharp, jagged glass.

"Next time we catch you in our stock, we won't be so merciful...traitor," he snapped, letting Allen fall to the ground. He glared at the group as they began walking off, their wads of spit hitting him as a final disgrace. He scoffed and let himself fall, watching the sky flare in sparks of grey, blue, purple and red. He looked over at his tooth on the ground and groaned.

Once the world stopped spinning, he stumbled back to his feet, rubbing his head and spitting out a wad of blood. He looked back at the tooth and felt for the gap; he sucked away the blood and sighed. He knelt down and picked up the white incisor, licked it clean, and forced it back into place. He blinked away his pain, pressing it down into his bleeding gum.

"Son of a bitch," he muttered, shaking away the fiery pain streaking through his body. He slowly made his way down the emptying street, rubbing his head to dispel an oncoming migraine. He whined softly when he felt his drenched and smelly coat. Yep, it smelled like he had been bathing in alcohol. That was attractive.

He rolled his eyes at his musings and shed the bomber jacket, shaking it off and trying to squeeze the liquid out in vain. He wasn't about to let it go however; it was his only nice article of clothing. It made him a little bit angrier that it had been spoiled. With that thought he wrapped the sleeves around his waist, his shoulders hunching; every move he made tore at his bruised ribs and he winced.

"Oh Allen, it's you! I've been looking all over for you" chirped a woman as she walked by. She stopped and stared at him, looking him up and down. She frowned fiercely when she saw the sorry state he was in.

"Oh, you look awful…What happened? You looked fine last night," she murmured. Allen glanced at her and grimaced, trying to ignore the woman who had been one of his frequent one-night stands. Facing her in the daylight was kind of awkward.

"Badgers," he grunted, stretching his sore arms, before finally giving his full attention to the woman whose name he had already forgotten.

"Oh! Oh, you poor thing, do you need anything? Is there anything I can do for you?" she asked. Allen scowled in thought. That was the question wasn't it… He needed a good mix, that would get his mind off of his already swelling face. He glanced at the girl and shifted uncomfortably.

"Sorry babe, I ain't got time," he growled, skipping his feet to break into a sprint He hated this place, he hated everything about it. He hated the fact that he had been alone for ten years…Alone except for Ricky! Oh no! Allen almost kicked himself when he realized he had forgotten about their plans. He stumbled into a sprint and found himself racing time as he ran to the apartment complex he and his friend shared. God, he really was an idiot!

He glanced up, his eyes catching the glimmer of a camera flicking. His eyes narrowed and he grabbed a stone, chucking it at the mech. Light shimmered as the stork surveillance mech unfurled its wings and shot off the building, leaving Allen behind as he staggered down the busy cobblestone street.

мαчα

The stork swept over the buzzing fence, dipping over the barbed wires, its head elongated, eyes and beak replaced by a long camera. It flew back to the safety of its city, its flight slowing to a lazy soar. It passed over the docks of giant sail boats, their own wings unfurled. Twinkling lights hung over the buildings as well as neon signs displayed over restaurants and shops.

The stork drifted around skyscrapers towering in the air. The balconies with cascading flowers painted a clear picture of beautiful decadence. Trees grew tall along the streets, and the people looked bizarre.

Their clothes were sharp and new, with glittering precious metals hanging from the fabric and their bodies. The crowd was a mix of skin colors. Everyone was an individual, so much so, that it seemed as if no one was. And they all smiled...they could. They didn't have those heavy metal oxygen masks, but instead subtle, fashionable tubes. They looked... human...

The stork swooped back down, zipping past a group of young students, wearing, by great contrast to the glittering, colorful, outlandish garb of the others, clean white lab coats.

They walked in rows of four...except for one girl who walked alone, her head hung and her arms crossed close to her chest. She was part of the group, yet isolated from it. Her lashes fluttered and her dark brown eyes following the stork's flight.

Her earpiece rang and a soft sigh escaped her lips as she pressed the beeping blue button at her earlobe. She slowed down, falling further behind the group as she answered the caller, barely aware she had lagged behind.

"Hello?" her meek voice squeaked. The caller on the other end cleared her raspy throat, and the slender girl grimaced with recognition.

"Hello dahling," crooned the woman. The girl frowned with a sudden burst of anger but she kept meandering on.

"Hello mother. To what do I owe the pleasure?" she snapped, her voice trying to take on a threatening tone, but she still sounded shaky, weak; pretending.

"I just want to check on how my sweet little surgeon is doing. I heard today is the beginning of your big exam," she exclaimed. A bright smile flitted across the girl's face. She actually remembered? That was surprising... *'I wonder what she wants now...'* she thought cautiously.

"Yeah... yeah, I'm on my-"

"It's utterly disgusting they make you go to that wretched place beyond the Fence though, I mean, you got out of there, why go back?" she growled. The girl's brief smile was gone, her face melting into a hardened frown.

"Oh…" why did she expect her mother to be happy for her? "Heh, yeah…" she didn't have it in her to argue. It was as if she could feel her mom's pouty scowl.

"Now Maya, I don't want you losing your head. You know this exam will get you a fine place at the Remedium. Surgeons are the highest paid after all," she went on to say. Maya bristled. Something about that statement really got under her skin.

"Uh huh…well you know I'm not in it for the money," she said, her voice giving out and cracking. Her mom barely stifled a chuckle, clearing her voice to distract her from laughing. Maya hung her head with embarrassment.

"Well Maya, you best be, after all I did to get you in the finest medical school. I expect you to be able to look out for our family dear," she said aridly. *'Don't you mean, pay for your plastic surgery?'* Maya swallowed her words and nodded, quickly stuttering when she realized her mom wouldn't be able to tell.

"O-of course… I'll be back in six weeks." Her mother always pulled her on a guilt trip, and the worst part is, she always succumbed to it.

"Yes, you will. I don't want you to have to stay any longer than need be in that pigsty. I didn't get this family out for nothing."

"Of-of course mother, and I promise I'll make you proud." Her mother only grunted before letting out a series of coughs. Maya winced and fiddled with the hem of her lab coat.

"I uh...I gotta go." she murmured. Maya glanced around, panicking when she saw that she couldn't find her group. The crowd parted so she could see the shining white coats in the midst of the gaudy colors of the civilians and she ran to catch up. They barely noticed her when she returned, and she lied to herself about preferring it that way. She was practically invisible, purposefully making herself small.

What happened to her? The real Maya was lost in the prison of her nervous anxiety, gone, not the same. She wanted herself back, but she wouldn't let her out at the same time. Not since that day. She remembered it so vividly, it rocked her so completely to the core that it physically hurt to think about it.

The pointing fingers, the mocking laughter. God. It was the day her "best friend" found out Maya's mom had been sleeping around. She had run in circles to spread the rumor that Maya had only been accepted into Medical school because of her mother's cheap, trashy bimbo bribes. After all, how else would a Ghetto Rat be able to enter the esteemed academy, or better yet, the Skyline?

She had been so broken that day, she couldn't even count the pieces of her shattered heart, let alone try to put it back together. It was that day she locked herself inside thick walls.

She remembered her boldness before coming to this place. Her dad...she missed him. But ever since her parents' divorce, she'd never been allowed to see him...ever. He had been left behind in the ghetto. Amanda, her mother, said he was better forgotten.

She also missed her old friends, but...people changed drastically in the span of five years and she didn't know if they'd even remember her. She had never said goodbye. She tried to convince herself she didn't care, after all, she'd never see them again, even though she was returning to the poverty-stricken prison called the Fence.

Her lips twitched into a smile when she remembered that smug smirk of her old bestie...and their banter in those old times. But according to Amanda, he, much like her father, was better off forgotten.

"So, Hart. Like returning home?" sang a sauntering man in the unmistakable Stratus uniform. He was one of the three officers who were accompanying them as their armed guards, but she could already tell that he was one to abuse his authority.

She didn't know how he knew her, but the Stratus must've looked into their files. It was the only logical explanation. All the more reason to fear him. She hung her head, too scared to confront him. After all, he was the one with a gun on his hip.

"Please just go away."

veronica

"Whoa, she talks after all! What's the matter sweetheart, scared? Don't worry, I'll protect you. That is my job after all, isn't it Hart? I'm Jason," he crooned, placing an arm around her. She frowned and ducked out from under him. *'Ugh, I'd rather find my own way to the docks!'* she screamed inwardly. The elite were all horribly entitled! She felt bile in her throat as he leered at her, then pouted when she rebuffed his advances.

"Hey! Leave her alone Jason and pick on someone your own size for a change, or are you a sissy?" snapped a girl with brilliant purple hair. Maya glanced at the girl. Her skin was a lovely golden brown with a soft glow even in the grey light, and she was also in a Stratus uniform. Maya felt a sense of relief wash over her. At least someone stood up for people instead of abusing them.

Jason growled and puffed his chest up at the confrontation while the medical students looked away, trying not to draw attention or add fuel to the Stratus' rage.

"Oh please, you don't scare me!" growled Jason, and then a smug grin spread across his face. He was proud of what he believed was a clever turn of the tables on her. The girl snorted and forcefully poked his chest. The group slowed down and watched fearfully at the drama unfolding before them. Maya lowered her head, she never intended to cause such a fuss.

"You wanna find out? You know who I am, don't test me, *dirt*," she growled, shoving him. Jason stumbled back, his face twisted with shock at her intensity and he held his hands up.

"Watch who you bark at Veronica. Your mom's dead for a reason," he spat. Maya winced at the comment. What gave him the right to say something like that? The crowd gasped at the words, and Veronica rankled, lifting her chin up.

"You're gonna regret that," she seethed, causing him to laugh airily.

"What are you going to do to me, soldier? My dad would make sure you'd follow in your mother's footsteps if you laid a single hand on me!" Maya couldn't stand it anymore and jumped in.

"That's-that's enough…" she mumbled. Jason shot her a look before laughing arrogantly and shoving past the two.

"Have fun with your girlfriend, Ronny," he spat. Veronica growled under her breath and flipped him off behind his back, rolling her eyes. Maya crossed her arms, the crowd lost interest and, with a few wry chuckles, forgot about the two girls.

"Asshole," murmured Veronica, the two falling behind the group. Maya glanced up at her and smiled.

"Thanks for sticking up for me...are we allowed to talk to Stratus officers?" she said, holding her hand out. Veronica chuckled and high fived her despite the intention of a handshake, leaving Maya happily baffled.

"Well technically, no. But I'm not one to follow protocol. Besides, it'll be fine, it's not like Jason followed the rules either," she said, chuckling.

Maya snickered, glancing at Veronica with a newfound respect. *'I could give her a chance...maybe she's not as entitled as the others,'* she thought.

Finally, the shining, silver lighthouse of the pier caught her attention. She smiled in relief and picked up her pace. She had to admit, returning to the Ghetto was nerve racking. From what she heard on the news, the crime rates had gone up, and drug dealing had become a main source of income- not that the ghetto was even given the luxury of a currency. Their currency came from their quite primitive bartering system. She gulped at the thought of returning to that forsaken place.

The sad thing was, the academy used the people of the ghetto as lab rats, and sent their medical students to test their surgical abilities on them. Human guinea pigs? It took a hardened person to deal with that.

Maya used to visit the Medicum Tents at the port of the Fence. It had taught her a lot, and was the main reason she had wanted to be a doctor. They tested unrefined medicine on their Fence victims, with little indication that they would work. Even now they tested cures for radiation, which was even more beastly.

Of course, the good doctors were the reason any of the unfortunate souls of the Fence received relief from their fierce wounds and terrible diseases.

She thought it was cruel, but also...necessary, as it was a needed process. Besides, she would ace the exam. She wasn't going to fail; she was sure of it. Failure was not an option, not in this cutthroat industry. She sighed with sorrow. She had become a surgeon to help people, not for personal gain. But then there was her mother. That was a monster all on its own. Perhaps the Fence would offer her an ironic sense of freedom from Amanda's controlling reach.

RICKY

Allen hunched over at the oppressive weight of the looming grey buildings, sweat pouring down his chest and back. He scrunched his nose in distaste from his acrid smell, a terrible mix of blood, sweat, and whiskey, which had gotten worse. He walked up the stairs as he caught his breath, coming to a corridor overlooking the trash covered streets.

A flickering green light lit up the cratered path. He covered his nose with his red tank top, spotted with holes in the collar and waist. It did very little to hide the smell. He needed new clothes, everyone did. His feet stopped subconsciously at a green door, with its chipping paint and small nicks from bullets long ago. Not Ricky's doing, that was for sure. He didn't need to knock. He lived here too. But in the spirit of being late, he figured he'd be decent.

He knocked on the door softly, scared that if he pounded too hard it would crack and give way to his fist. There were muffled stomps and the door swung inward. A shrewd red face poked out; green eyes narrowed. Ricky was a lanky, rat of a man, his ginger hair always and forever a crazy mess atop his pointed head.

"You're a little late Al," he scolded. They held an uncertain stare before Ricky broke down snickering and fell back inside his house, Allen following him. It was littered with junk metal and balled up paper, but other than that it was clean and not a regular, trashy abode that seemed to be the homes of people here. An organized mess. Allen took a whiff of the stale room, the familiar smell of grease, smoke and soldering flux stung his nose.

"I really don't mind; you gave me enough time to actually get shit done. I've been working on my mechanicals, y'see. After I'm done wit' this one, I'mma sell it," he said with a bubble of excitement. Allen quickly looked over the machine.

"What is it?" he asked. Ricky smacked his lips as he readied himself to answer the question. He scurried over to the head of the mechanical and held it up.

"It's a doll, for the Scandals," he explained lightly. Allen snorted his disdain, a crooked grin growing on his face as he tilted his head to get a better look. It had an almond shaped head, a pink visor over the line where eyes would be. Allen glanced back at Ricky and rolled his eyes, laughing slightly at his friend.

"Ah, I get it...Ricky, you gotta get yourself a girlfriend, especially now, you're twenty! You're spending too much time with mechs," he teased. Ricky growled and set the head down, his eyes flicking with annoyance at his friend's lack of interest. It was then he noticed the bruises on his face.

"Hey, what the hell happened to you?" he asked, vaulting over to his friend, and room-mate, to study his wounds. Allen shrugged him off nonchalantly. He would rather not have to share the gory details, knowing he would be scolded.

"Oh...um...fight," he grunted. His friend narrowed his eyes, his arms slowly crossing over his chest.

"Why am I not su'prised?" he grumbled. Allen chuckled nervously, and shrugged, trying to act innocent, but he knew Ricky saw right through him. Ever since the boy had shown him kindness on that bus to the Home, they'd never parted. They were all they had, and Allen couldn't bear seeing his friend leave him...not after losing his father.

Allen blinked, that was ten years ago...he wasn't about to dwell on it now, even though it always haunted him, always found a way to crawl into his subconscious. Ricky stared at him expectantly, bringing him back to reality. He coughed and swept past him, trying to put distance between him and Ricky's judging eyes.

"Allen, you've got to learn to control your temper. One day, I'll be on my commute, and you'll be dead on the side of the street. Game over," he snapped, rubbing his eyes. Allen waved his hand, whisking away the scenario.

"I don't have a temper, you're talkin' nonsense. And I didn't start the fight...it was Bruce and his stupid gang," said Allen, falling onto the soft and squishy couch. Ricky came to stand in front of him, glaring at his irresponsible friend, his eyes wide with anger.

"Bruce!? I thought I told you not to mess with them! You keep messin' with 'em an' you're gonna end up dead! It's bad enough you even got involved!" barked Ricky.

Allen winced at Ricky's concern. He knew he was right, but he couldn't admit defeat so easily.

"We needed the protection! Don't bring this up again!" he shouted. Ricky scowled, crossing his arms.

"We were fine! I told you time and time again that the gangs wouldn't protect us, and you'd want to quit, and then we'd be in more trouble than usual! You didn't need to do anythin'," he retorted. Allen rolled his eyes with annoyance. He didn't want to continue arguing. Ricky frowned at Allen before his eyes narrowed apprehensively.

"You get angry over the smallest things," continued Ricky. While his words rang true, Allen hated admitting he had anger issues. He didn't have them! Sometimes he lost his temper and threw something, so what? He was human and everyone got angry, and they all had their ways of expressing it!

"Everyone gets angry, Ricky," he snapped, his almond eyes narrowing into glistening blue slits as he squinted in irritation at his friend's persistence. Ricky scoffed at him, sitting down as well, sinking into the leather cushions despite his light weight.

"Yes, but not everyone throws fists when they get a bit miffed," he retorted. Allen chuckled. He couldn't deny that, but come on, he couldn't be the only one. Obviously those ruffians from earlier took out their anger through violence. He wasn't violent all the time. In fact, Allen truly hated fighting. It was just in a world like this, it was a necessary skill to survive. It was a skill that had been ingrained in him ever since he could walk. The surface had demanded it, and so did the Fence.

"Well at least I don't hurt people who've done nothing wrong...unlike Bruce and them, they're total bastards, I really hope one of them just drops dead," he grumbled. Ricky barked with insincere laughter, before frowning coldly.

"Do you even hear yourself? I think that fight liquified your brains!" he scolded, giving a light slap to the side of Allen's temple. Allen pursed his lips and sighed. He struggled to hoist himself out from the deep ocean of the sofa's cushions.

"Fine!" snapped Allen, voice muffled as he concentrated on getting up from the sofa's embrace. With a kick of his legs he found his leverage and threw himself off the quicksand of a couch, "Maybe I do have a little temper, but that doesn't mean I'm a brute ok? I get angry about reasonable—"

"Petty—" Allen glared at him, his jaw jutting out in annoyance. Ricky held the glare, before allowing himself to sink more into the couch. He glanced down at the old, black, leather sofa and sighed in exasperation.

"That couch has no spine! Get a new one; geez!" blurted Allen, kicking the sofa with distaste. The command was rather outlandish. They'd had that sofa for years, because it was really all they could afford. The cracks in the walls that they could never repair proved that. They were lucky they even had a couch in the first place, and not a trash heap.

Ricky laughed with triumph and hoisted himself up, rolling back to his feet and pointing at him with an accusing finger.

"See? Petty!" he exclaimed. Allen groaned, and walked angrily into the kitchen, taking out a bottle of gin, vodka, tequila, rum and the last of the triple sec. He poured the mix of drinks into a tall glass, ignoring Ricky as he also entered the kitchen. The Irish scoffed at the sight, and took the bottles away.

"Stop it, that's all I got from the Understreet, you're wastin' it all!" he growled, putting the caps on begrudgingly. Allen shrugged and began drinking his half made Long Island Iced Tea. It burned his throat in a beautifully satisfactory way. His stomach warmed and his face flushed. The headache of his beating subsided as he gulped it down. Ricky stole a glance, and sighed as he gave in and poured himself a glass of vodka. There was a contented silence as the two drank together.

Allen sighed loudly and put his glass down, a sharp thunk as it hit the counter. Ricky flinched, having not expected the sudden noise.

"Ricky, my good man, I drink to you. Happy birthday!" slurred Allen, the mix of the whiskey from earlier and "tea" he'd just gulped down began to take his mind. He felt all warm, cozy, and happy.

Ever since he had started to imbibe liquor at age fifteen, he had been a hopeless addict. He loved being lost in the numbness, not needing to think hard about anything. Ricky's voice wove in and out of his mind, but he caught the last words as he focused his dilated blue eyes on him.

"We all know you drink for yourself but thanks for remembering. God I'm old...twenty already," he sighed. Allen smiled; his swollen cheeks flushed from the liquor that was finally hitting him.

"Oh, quit your whining, at least you're not thirty!" Ricky shot him an irritated look and took a slow drink from his glass, staring at Allen with his narrowed green eyes.

"You're just saying that to spare my feelings," he grunted, making Allen twitch from the small talk. He shifted and swallowed the rest of his drink. He needed to do something, *feel something*... He wasn't doing that by standing around like a fat, old married man. He glanced at the doll and then at Ricky, shifting restlessly on his feet.

"Let's go to a scandal," he said with a wolfish grin. Ricky glanced at him and frowned, placing his glass in the sink and wiping his hands on his oily khakis.

Without waiting for his response, Allen slid back into his bomber jacket and walked briskly for the door. Ricky grumbled and followed after him begrudgingly.

Ever since the former desert ghost had gotten used to the city, it had become his. He knew every Understreet market, every scandalous, red building, and every blurred face that happened to show. At least he knew their names. Names picked up from gossip and pointed fingers, dark bed sheets and giggling whispers.

Scandals were the beating heart of the Fence, and maybe that wasn't a good thing. The well off, the entitled yuppies of the Skyline, looked down on Scandals. They were counterproductive wastes of time in their scientific, educated minds. However, to a poor bum on the street, they were a cascading waterfall of pleasure to get his mind off of his back-breaking labor and constricted life of deprivation and dissipation.

Those pretty red buildings were probably the most well-kept complexes in the ghetto, an indicator of how much business they got. It was almost sad that cheap thrills and temporary satisfactions were what these people put their blood and sweat into...but the chance to see each other smile...to feel human. Allen believed that was the real reason people were so attracted to the Scandals.

Allen couldn't deny the satisfaction of seeing someone smile at him, to see it plain and simple without having to guess why, was just beautiful. Even though he knew that the elite hated the Scandals, he partook in them just as much as everyone else.

People with self-control worked hard in the factories and climbed their way into the skyline to join the ranks of the elite. If a person had self-control and determination, the Fence wasn't a permanent life sentence...but that was also a lie wasn't it? Nowadays it seemed as if the elite had completely locked those gates for good.

Allen was a waste; Allen had given up. What was the point, with no one to cheer you on? He knew if his father...if his father were here, he would be pushing his son to be better, to be *something* other than just another blurry face in the crowd. However, that's all he was, and all the Skyline was. It was a dream for the gullible, a dream forgotten as soon as he opened his eyes and got out of bed. He didn't work hard, he hardly even worked at all. Nothing really mattered to him. He had nothing that motivated him to get a life and take responsibility for it. He didn't have a wife, he didn't have kids, the most intimate he could get was a wink, a whistle, and a fleeting night. That's what he was good at. He was a has been at nineteen.

"Allen you're spiraling again," grunted Ricky, "...have you met anyone?" he asked, trying to pull him out of his thoughts. His question however, only sent his mind plummeting. He gave a wan smile in remembrance of the woman from earlier, but she meant nothing to him as rude as it sounded, and the thought put a long frown on his face.

"You know me…" he murmured. He could only see in his mind's eye: her wispy, fair hair, doe like brown eyes, and brilliant smile. His heart skipped a beat everytime he remembered her. The girl from the immigration facility, ten years ago when he was a stupid kid. The girl who had captured his heart only a few years later, and made him spend years throwing rocks at her window at insane hours of the night. Her parents always ended up chasing him away.

"Oh…still haven't gotten over her?" Ricky barked. Allen winced, running a hand through his hair…Maya's smile, her friendly waves, the aching absence when she left. She was truly a one percent. Someone with a persistence he wished he had.

"How can I, when she makes me remember how much of a failure I am, and, and, besides…Maya is too good for me, and I wouldn't want to drag her down anyway," he cursed, his jaw clenched with annoyance.

Why did Ricky have to bring that up? Allen wished he could forget Maya, move on…it hindered him, and it sounded silly. He spent nights with dozens of women trying to feel something. It was never enough and he was sorry he even tried. She climbed her way to the other side. She was probably happy and rich. He was nothing but a forgotten whim of her past. A friend if he was lucky enough. She was too good for him, always had been.

"Mate, it's been five years since she left. You have this bad habit I like to call, *dwelling on things*. Get yourself out there, and forget about her, there's plenty of fish in the sea," Ricky quipped generically. It's what everyone said, it was expected of people. Everything was fine, everything would get better, suffering was only for now, you'll find someone eventually. When were things going to stop always being out of reach and in an imaginary land called tomorrow?

"No Ricky, I'm not looking for a commitment right now, but you my good man are two decades into your life; you're the one who needs to settle down," he retorted, throwing the attention off of himself as they entered a large black door, the gate to the scandalous red buildings.

"Oi, shut up, ya wank." Darkness hit their eyes, and the dream no one wanted to wake up from began, the continuous cycle of the Fence.

ZECH

The lights flared red, and alarms began ringing. Hysterical screams ricocheted off the walls and screeched out of the testing room. The shrieks only added more heat to the fire that flickered in the beast's eyes as it began its rampage.

Stratus flooded into the room, guns raised, ready to take on the beast that had taken the last of its torture.

Sickening wails and the heavy sounds of thuds bounced inside the biologist's head and his breath shook. What had he done!? He had gone too far this time! With a gulp, he peeked out from behind his cover, gasping at the sight of the soldiers' body parts strewn across the room. Blood sprayed the walls as the creature frantically searched for a way out. It was a large, twisted, dark shadow tinged with red from both the lights...and the blood. It was a true monster! What had he created!? It was a crime against nature!

The scientist felt his heart jump as the beast focused its attention on him, and its lips peeled back in a blood-chilling snarl. Vargas' lips trembled and he reached for anything that would save him… A gun! He scurried under the large stainless-steel desk, the beast snarling at the sudden movement.

As sweat dripped into his eyes, he dove for one of the machine guns slick with blood. He aimed the gun and stumbled back as the creature advanced with a speed he could barely comprehend.

His fingers clamped on the trigger, ripping off an explosion of bullets. There was a blur, and the scientist was slammed into the wall. He groaned, his back screaming with sharp pain that sent him to the floor.

He wheezed for air, feeling hot tears spring into his eyes and he wanted to cry out for help. He heard another roar and braced himself for his inevitable death, but then heard a metal clang.

His eyes shot up as the beast yowled, and his lips quivered in relief. The Chimera, one of the most effective, fearsome mechanicals on the Stratus force had finally arrived! The mechanical would take care of the beast, his life was more important. Now there was nothing left to do but escape!

Vargas flung himself off the floor and raced to the hallway and out to safety. The beast and the mechanical wrestling as he escaped. He could hear the sick cries of the beast, and those eyes...those burning amber eyes...they'd haunt his mind forever.

THE MEDICUM

A sharp voice addressed Maya's class. She sat up to attention, listening as the captain instructed them on safety while in the ghetto, which they were approaching as they rode the submarine through the sea. The dark water surrounded them. It was evening and the sun's golden rays broke through the water around them.

"There are no ways across this sea except by ship or sub, so I advise you, when you've finished your semester, be punctual, because once the sub leaves, if you are not on it when you need to be, you are stuck here. Until provision trucks arrive, you will not be able to leave. The time from our departure and the provision trucks arrival is lengthy and by then, you might be dead. Lots of savages on the other side of that fence...*Progressus est scientia, Scientia est pax, Pax est vita,*" he recited. Maya narrowed her chocolate eyes, her body stiffening at the accusation, and the maxims of Magnus City.

'Progress is knowledge, knowledge is peace, peace is life... as if any of them actually practice what they

preach.' The constant drumbeat of maxims nobody believed left a bitter taste in her mouth.

"Those things are scary as hell. Ever seen those old movies?" asked Veronica as the two girls stared out at the sharks. Maya shook her head absentmindedly. They were huge, their daggers for teeth protruding from their yawning mouths. Maya swallowed her nervousness and stared into the liquid abyss.

"Are you sure you're allowed to hang out with me?" she asked again. Veronica glanced around at the other stratus officers who stood still near the entrances, shrugged and turned back to Maya.

"It'll be fine, I like to be a little more human than how they train us to be. Besides, I get the feeling that you want me to sit with you," she said with a small wink. Maya smiled, somehow comforted by her reply.

She looked back out the window as the sharks darted away and another sea creature swam by the window. Her eyes widened when she saw a marine mechanical up close. It was about twice her size, in the shape of the fabled mermaid. It had a blank glass face, it's tail hypnotically pulsing up and down, pushing it through the water. She stared, mesmerized as more of the mermaid mechanicals joined them, deep, glowing, blue eyes lighting up their dark, black faces.

"What are those used for?" she asked, glancing at Veronica who lit up at the chance to show Maya something she knew.

"Well they regulate the water and take care of the sea creatures."

Maya smiled at the explanation. Most Magnus city issued mechanicals were used by the Stratus. The metal mermaids fell away, the solid blue was now all she could see and not a fish in sight. A song filled the water and her mouth gaped in awe as a pod of whales swam with them, their songs carrying through the speakers overhead. Maya smiled softly at the animals and she yawned with contentment at their simple beauty.

How long was this sub ride? She glanced back out the window, choking when she saw the glaring eye of a giant mechanical Kraken. *'Oh my Goodness!'* she thought with bewilderment. Her breath caught in her throat as the Kraken quickly flowed out of her line of sight in one quick swoop of its tentacles.

She sat back, her heart thumping so loudly, it filled her ears. She loved it, the thrill. Oh, how she wanted real adventure, but that wasn't who she was anymore.

"Attention passengers, we are arriving at the Fence. Prepare to disembark." announced the captain. Maya gulped and gathered her things. Here she was again, where she was a completely different person.

She prayed that she wouldn't be haunted by the people of her past, but deep down she wished she would be. Maybe they could help her be...Maya again. That once tenderhearted, clever, opinionated girl who always spoke her mind. Of course, it had gotten her in trouble a lot with her mom, but...it was never really that bad. She always had her father to stand up for her. The windows darkened as they passed through a tunnel that grew shallower until finally the submarine broke back onto the surface, the grey stormy light beaming through the windows.

Maya stepped pensively out of the submarine. She smiled softly as Veronica walked by her side. Veronica's thick black boots clunked against the concrete sidewalk. Behind them, a large stone door closed, as a barred gate swung up to let them out. *'This place is depressing...'* thought Maya bitterly. There were two people waiting for them at the opening of the submerged walkway, dressed in snow grey and wearing clear goggles that were lit on the side rims. As the students arrived, she made out the faces of a man and woman. *'Must be the heads of the Medicum,'* she thought.

"Good afternoon students, I am Dr. Farley, your boss for the next six weeks," the hardened, grey-haired man announced abruptly. The woman flipped her brown hair away from her chic, sepia face, her warm eyes welcoming them.

"And I am Professor Anand. I'll be grading your exams," she said before they both turned away to lead them down to the Medicum. Dr. Farley immediately started to lecture; not bothering to look back for their attention. Some of the students held side conversations, which annoyed Maya, who was eager to learn.

Dr. Farley stopped dead in his tracks and pointed to a young woman with short black hair. She was a big talker, and it seemed her rowdy murmurs had earned a spotlight.

"You. Go back to the sub. You're out," he growled. She stuttered in surprise; eyes widened with shock. Professor Anand glanced back with a raised brow, but she continued walking.

"W-what? Why? You can't do that! I just got here!" she protested. Farley shrugged, his eyes narrowed, a cool distant look on his face as he addressed her.

"Rule number one: the Medicum is not the place for conversation during work. That's what your after hours are for. This is not a classroom; this is a working facility. Since you do not seem to understand that, I will make an example of your failure. What is your name?" he barked. The woman stammered over her protests, tears welling in her eyes. Maya frowned. This didn't seem fair at all! Even if she never had gotten a chance to know them, she still wanted them to succeed. People didn't become doctors for the fun of it, and that was admirable...right?

"My, um, well, my name is Angelina..." she whimpered. Farley grunted, nodding his head curtly before looking over the silent crowd.

"Well, Angelina. You are fired for misconduct. Return to the sub before it leaves you here," he ordered.

"Oh my God! You...you can't be serious!" she stammered. He narrowed his eyes and looked over the students. Maya's face drained of color. He was very serious, and that was worse. Angelina whimpered in defeat, her tears glistened on her face before she ran away in a flush of rage and humiliation. Her career...down the toilet. Maya choked, realizing that this term was going to be a very hard one.

"Now, would anyone else like to continue their conversation while I try to give important instruction?" he barked. There was a murmur of no's in the crowd and he nodded, turning back around and continuing his lecture.

"As you now know, I run a tight ship, and despite the fact that incompetent students come here with untested commercial medicine, most of my patients get out alive. Let's keep it that way. When you fail your first exam, you're out. No retakes." he whipped back around and stared down at a young man with obsidian skin who began to protest but thought better of it.

"These people here are *not* just a *test* on your ability to do a surgery. Do I make myself clear? They are living beings with hopes and dreams and families, and if you wreck their life and think the worst that can happen to you is a single failure amidst every other success, I will wreck *your* life. Do I make myself clear?" His voice lowered in volume with each word he said until shivers crawled up Maya's spine. A hushed, "*Yes sir*" fell out of the crowd and he nodded knowingly.

"Good. Now that's out of the way, welcome to the Fence. Try to stay within the boundaries. Crime has been rising and I don't need any more patients." Maya's heart pounded, but she felt an instant respect for the doctor. Someone who was part of the elite who valued Fencers' lives? Maya was secretly pleased.

THE FENCE

Allen woke up with a groan. Jesus; he felt like he was dying. His eyes pulsated with a sharp ache and he squinted, bringing his hands to his face. He could already tell this was going to be a headbanging hangover. What even happened last night? He vaguely remembered the scandal, and then, he didn't remember anything.

"Morning sunshine!" shouted Ricky, his high-pitched voice clanging in Allen's ears. He groaned in response, rolling over into the soft quicksand of the mechanic's couch.

Ricky wiped his oil-stained hands and walked over with a bounce in his step, a mischievous smirk on his face. He seemed unaffected by last night's misadventures. Allen hid his face with a pillow, a throbbing headache and a dull, pounding pain in his stomach that rolled and heated to unbearable temperatures.

"How ya feelin'?" asked Ricky, sitting down in the chair across from his friend. Allen glared at him and curled his knees into his stomach. Why did he always do this to himself?

"I feel like crap! What happened?" he asked. Ricky chuckled and shook his head.

"You happened...now get off my couch and go take a shower. You smell awful, and you're making my furniture smell bad too!" he growled mercilessly. Allen moaned, but even the horrible thought of having to move his body with too many pain sensors going off wasn't enough to stop him from rolling off the couch. He trudged into the bathroom.

"Yeah, love you too, asshole," he muttered.

"I heard that!" shouted his friend from the kitchen. Allen snickered but it intensified his pain.

The bathroom was a cramped green space, with damp rags and half-filled bottles of mouthwash. As he shed away his stiff clothes, his eyes caught the purple, green and blue scattered bruises along his side. His first instinct was to touch them, to invoke a fresh pain to keep his mind away from the dull ache in his head. His second instinct was to wonder how he even got them in the first place. Oh yeah, it must've been from his beating from yesterday.

His entire body was stiff and seemed to be tearing cell from cell at every move he made, especially his ribs and legs. When he squatted down to get the water they kept under the sink, his body contracted in pain. With a groan, he pulled out a gallon and checked how much they could use for the day. The numbers swam as his vision blurred and he shrugged. *Two quarts should be enough; I could brush my teeth in the shower...* ' he rationed inwardly.

Allen entered the crusty, old shower with the jug of water and carefully poured some over his bare body. The icy water ran down his battered skin and he trembled from the cold.

He set the jug down on the shower floor. His hands raked through his wet hair. He reached for a rag and their one bar of soap. He only cleaned his armpits, hair, and feet. He risked a swig of the cold water and got his toothbrush, the bristles bent and abused from years of use.

He dipped it into the mouth wash and began to brush and gargle. He spit the water out into the drain. He stepped gingerly out of the shower and began to put the supplies back where they belonged. He felt just a bit fresher than he did when he woke up, but there is only so much a half gallon of water can do.

He balled up his dirty clothes and stuffed them in the hamper. They'd have to take those down to the Community Wash. That meant bringing their own water, however, and Ricky was stingy with water.

Allen shook off his musings and shuffled back to the living room. He now wore Ricky's clothes, since they were clean, and a frown on his face. He looked over to see Ricky polishing the doll. At the sight of Allen in one of his many black t-shirts, Ricky snickered and rolled his eyes playfully.

"Well one of us is gonna have to change," he teased. They both chuckled before Ricky sighed and continued his thought, "Come on, let's go sell Dolly." He finished, tying the mech's wrists and ankles with zip ties. A yawn hid Allen's patronizing laugh.

"Ok, just let me get some breakfast," he mumbled. Ricky watched Allen out of the corner of his eye as Allen poured a glass of rum.

"Right...Breakfast." But he didn't move to stop him. He draped a tarp over the doll and buckled the ends to keep it concealed and safe. Allen watched as Ricky darted back and forth, getting a small hand truck for the mechanical. Allen sipped slowly and kept his eyes trained on the busy work, not offering to help.

Ricky gestured for them to leave with a nod of his chin and Allen followed behind him. His eyes drooped groggily as the two clambered down the metal stairs. Allen felt his mood drop again as his feet hit the cracked concrete. He glanced over to see several children playing stick hockey outside. A few kids, their eyes sunken, looked up at them. They were like little skeletons, and Allen couldn't stand the sight. Before the kids could beg for food, the two men hurried away.

Every step Allen took was a battle, not only mentally, but physically. The cratered street did everything in its power to trip him up. Garbage littered the sidewalks.

"Hey big boy, wanna have some fun? I can show you a great time," slurred a woman from an alley. Allen darted a look down the shadowy corridor, seeing the outline of the prostitute. His skin crawled at the sight and he ushered Ricky on.

"Oh, come on baby! We all got mouths to feed!" She yelled as they dashed away, the clanking of the hand truck's wheels the only sound as they jostled down the road. Allen hated these commutes.

The streets started to get busier, and Allen watched as some people would risk taking off their masks to smoke a cigarette. He grimaced. He hated smokers, but he barely vocalized that hatred because he knew he was a hypocrite. How can you hate smoking when you filled your liver with alcohol? Different people, different poison. Some people preferred scratchy throats and blackened lungs. Some people would argue that's better than hangovers and failed livers. At least Allen didn't do both. That's how Allen liked to measure his worth. At least he wasn't worse. He could always be worse.

He looked down at the heaps of trash, his eyes snagging on a man with torn, baggy clothes and an unkempt beard. He sniffed the fresh scent of urine and noticed the man had pissed himself...and just lay there in the puddle. Allen scrunched his nose. At least he wasn't worse. At least he wasn't like that guy.

He looked over at Ricky. At least he had him. At least he wasn't entirely alone, even when it felt like he was.

The sun had already begun to beat down on them as they made their way to one of the many scandals in the ghetto. Ricky gagged, causing Allen to look up at him.

"I wish you woke up earlier, the heat always makes the streets smell worse," Ricky complained. Allen smiled sheepishly, trying not to take a whiff of the streets that smelled like a mix of shit, piss and rotting...corpses? Allen choked at the thought. He glanced up at the sky, seeing dark clouds on the horizon.

"Let's just get to a scandal and dump this thing off. The streets should cool down soon, there's a storm on the way," he grumbled. Ricky's eyes widened and he glanced at the dark clouds rolling in from the sea. They needed to get home before the clouds filled the streets and brought the lightning.

This is how they lived. They made this commute every month or so to sell one of Ricky's creations. They were paid in booze, food, or water. They lived in their apartment because Ricky worked in the Power Plant. As long as you worked in the Plant, you were guaranteed a place to sleep. The landlord had no idea Allen lived there, too.

Then there were the gangs, which extorted from all the citizens of the Fence fees in water and food with the power of the fists, bats, knives, and collective manpower. Allen worked for them only to stop the fees. However, he quit after doing some things that he still felt remorse over.

And he couldn't just quit without pledging his life to another gang for protection from the Badgers. Ricky still hadn't forgiven him for it either. Now if the Wasps wanted anything from the two, they'd have to give it. Whether it be their labor or their resources. Thankfully they hadn't asked anything of them yet.

"Oh, if it isn't the infamous Allen Rosinsky and his big-brained lackey!" Hollered a familiar voice. Allen looked up at the wolf-like man, his dark skin almost blending into the soot-colored walls. Ricky rolled his eyes and Allen chuckled.

"Well, it's more the other way around. In all honesty, I'm the big, stupid lackey of the esteemed Patrick O'Brien!" Allen barked back, a grin filling his face as the Scandal owner, Michael King, approached them. Ricky sighed at the introduction, but he couldn't help but feel a little burst of pride at Allen's good words.

"What can I do for you two at my fine establishment? Can I take a guess that it has something to do with the tarp? Are you bringing me a body to bury for you?" asked Michael, an air of humor to his words...yet there was something that also sounded very serious. Ricky laughed nervously.

"Nah, it's a mechanical," he replied, beginning to unbuckle the tarp. King watched with eager eyes as the tarp began to fall away. Allen glanced back and forth between the doll and the Scandal owner. They sold a lot of Ricky's trinkets to him. The Scandal proprietor's eyes sparkled as he circled the doll.

"What does it do?" he asked. Allen zoned out as Ricky explained the doll's purpose, the words nothing but a buzz. The Scandal's rooms were a smoky black. The lights were dimmed red and yellow. There were cages along the walls with a single pink light that would usually highlight a dancer.

Only one stood in a cage at that moment. She was just practicing and Allen made it a point not to stare at her. Scandals were only active during the night. During the day, Michael did business. This Scandal was owned by the Wasps.

Allen backed up subconsciously as Ricky turned his mech on, the pink visor lighting up and its body humming to life. He watched as it twisted its hips and limbs. He glanced at Ricky, who was looking on with dim eyes. He looked...disappointed. Allen swallowed tentatively and continued to stare sadly at Ricky who stood there, shoulders hunching with each move the mech made. He had created this thing, this mech that brought him joy in making, but watching it do what he had made it do made Ricky's soul cringe.

Michael really liked it though. His eyes were bright, and his head nodded along. His sparkling white smile, that contrasted starkly against his black skin, brightened the room and he began to laugh giddily.

"What a wonder! This is the future of Scandals right here!" he howled, his wolf-like smile filling the room with sly enthusiasm. Allen frowned at the thought. He surely hoped that wouldn't be the case. That would take the humanity out of it, which was why people kept coming to the scandals.

"And what about us, what will you do to us?" muttered a voice from one of the cages. Allen looked up to see the woman who had been practicing.

"Lavender…" warned her owner, "We don't have time for your soapbox." Lavender narrowed her smoky, brown eyes, her ivory skin glowing from the bright, neon-pink light above her.

"Well, nothing can replace a real woman like you. It's more of an art piece, right Ricky? Besides, maybe it is better that you get out of here, you can do better things, we all want to be better right?" said Allen, a small smile lifting his lips. Lavender frowned and turned away, but not before Allen saw the depth of despair in her eyes. He knew he had gotten to her, his heart seethed at what he had seen. Ricky sighed and rubbed his head.

"Exactly, just a feature to look at," mumbled Ricky, glancing over at the mech that continued to grind and writhe to music that wasn't playing. Allen could see his eye twitch. He knew Ricky hated the degrading way his own creation now presented itself. Even when that's how he made it, he hated it. Ricky was too good for this place. Ricky belonged in the Skyline, where his work would be appreciated.

"You boys don't have to make her feel better. Shut the hell up Lavender and get back to work! I don't pay you to preach, if I wanted to hear a sermon I would've gone to church," snapped Michael. Allen and Ricky flinched as the owner stormed over to her cage and slammed on the rusty steel bars. The clang of his fist and Lavender's squeak of fear echoed throughout the rooms. Allen sucked in awkwardly on his teeth. King turned back and smiled again, trying to ward off the tension he had created.

"Alright, I'll take it. Wait here for me while I get your payment." With that, he stalked out of the room. Ricky slowly reached to turn off the mech, and the silence stretched between them. It was the longest five minutes of Allen's life. He found himself glancing at Lavender as she hid her face in her hands. He wanted to comfort her, but he didn't want to meddle with Michael's...property. That word felt wrong in his mind. He slowly began hating himself more the longer they stood silently in that God forsaken room.

"There. Now get the hell out of my Scandal! You've caused enough trouble," growled Michael, shooting a poisonous look at the woman. Ricky grunted as he shoved a large and heavy bag of goods in his arms. Before they could look to see what treasures they had been rewarded with, Michael ushered them out. Allen winced as the doors slammed, and he could hear the faint shouts inside.

"Holy shit," murmured Ricky. Allen just nodded as the two made their way back down the street. No words were shared, but it was a mutual understanding that they'd have to take the back route, or else they'd get mugged.

The two stooped down in an alley, the shadows of the cramped building looming over them. They opened the bag and took everything out, counting up their payment. A liter of milk, two gallons of water, a two-pound bag of rice, and a cheap bottle of wine that was more water than it was wine.

"Well...this will get us through next week. We can use this gallon for laundry, this for drinking...how much water do we have under the bathroom sink?" asked Ricky. Allen glanced up in thought, trying to remember how much he used that day.

"Three gallons and a half," he said. Ricky narrowed his eyes at him and sighed. Allen frowned and began to fit everything back into the bag.

"You used half a gallon?" growled Ricky. Allen's eyes widened in exasperation at Ricky's constant nagging.

"No, I did not! I took my shower and then I brushed my teeth, I didn't...Oh my God!" he protested with a seething rage, he felt his argument fall to pieces when he remembered the rule they had mutually made about water usage. Ricky groaned and rubbed his eyes.

"How many times do I have to tell you, if you take a shower, you can't brush your teeth, it's one or the other, not both! Now I can't do neither!" he moaned. Allen nodded, running an exasperated hand through his tangled hair. Ricky went on to continue lecturing his friend about water usage when a sound caught Allen's ears. A low, humming frequency that sent chills down his spine.

"Shut up, shut up now," he whispered sharply. Ricky bared his teeth at the demand, beginning his protest before Allen cupped his hand around Ricky's mouth. Then the sound got louder.

It was an aircraft. Allen crept to an opening in the alleyway to see a large, jet-black ship hovering just above the buildings. Ricky wheezed and backed up against the wall, holding his hands over his head in a futile attempt to hide. It was an open secret around the Fence about what happened when the elite decided to grace them with their presence.

No one dared step into the street. Allen watched as shutters snapped closed and doors clicked to lock. They were near the downtown plaza, which was too generous a name. It was a more open space that was crowded with bazaar shops and gang patrols. Usually. Right no... the little concrete slab of a town square was completely empty.

They were so close. Just a building to hide them from the jet-black ship that hovered menacingly above the square. Mechanicals; giant, bulky centaurs that terrorized the Ghetto, began to surround the lot. Their hulking metal arms shifted into assault weapons in case anyone attacked. No one was stupid enough to attack an elite ship, however. Especially not with the promise of extra rations. Ricky and Allen peeked out of their cover and watched as the ship lowered to the ground. Two men in black suits stepped out, a guard on each side. Allen felt his memory flashing back to the guards who shoved him onto the bus when he was nine.

They needed to get out of here, but the two were so frozen in their fear, so paralyzed, that they couldn't even move a finger. A centaur lumbered over to a large, familiar building made of cracked red brick and barred windows. The two elites followed the mechanical, and the large iron door creaked open for them. That building was the Home.

Allen felt his mind wandering back to when he and Ricky were trapped there. It was no orphanage. It was a holding pen, and they had been cattle. Allen and Ricky were lucky to have made it out. The elite came in sometimes and chose a child to their liking, then they'd take the child to the Skyline. No one knew what they did to those kids. A lot of rumors circled around. Many people liked to believe the elite wanted to raise the children in the beautiful Skyline. Allen and Ricky had always been a bit more skeptical. Still, no one really knew.

What felt like hours had passed before the two men left the Home, escorting a small child, barely six years old. The child had a happy smile on his face. He was finally leaving the Home and going to the Skyline. Allen felt a strange and disgusting feeling wash over him. He wanted to rip the child away from the men, tear his little emaciated hand out from the grip of the guards. Was it jealousy? Or was this truly just wrong?

Allen had always had a feeling that they were just lab rats to the elite, just like all the medical experiments that happened in the Medicum. His legs shifted as if he was getting ready to sprint in... but he stopped.

He could feel his heart thunder in his ears. He wasn't brave enough. He couldn't save anyone...not even himself. He slunk back down, watching as the elite led the child into the aircraft. The mechanicals stood, waiting to jump on anyone who dared step out of line before the aircraft took off.

"Come on, let's go," whispered Ricky, but neither of them moved, watching as the sleek, black ship began to lift off from the ground. There was a thud, a large pack dropping from the belly of the ship. Rations! His disturbed mind snapped animalistically at the idea of snatching the provisions for the two of them. His mouth watered. He forgot about the kid.

Allen could see the windows and doors begin to open as the hidden crowd's attention was captured and he growled greedily. He could see Ricky's breath quicken as he began to stand up.

"Allen..." he could hear him like a small buzz at the back of his mind. Allen's eyes were fixated on the large pack.

"Allen, let's go," said Ricky, but Allen felt his body lurch forward as if pulled to the pack by a string. The mechanicals unzipped the pack and laid everything out, before standing to the side, returning to the strange statuesque way they stood at the edges of the plaza. Before Allen could rush forward, Ricky grabbed him.

"No! We have what we need! Let's go," he snapped. Allen clenched his jaw and squeezed his eyes shut.

"You're right...I'm sorry," he said in defeat. The roar of the crowd filled the air as clusters of people began to race to the rations before the gangs could get there. The mechanicals sprung to life, sentient enough to know when a riot would start.

Allen and Ricky took the provisions that Michael had given them and tried to sneak through the alley. They were forced out onto the street as the alley came to an end. *'Just make it to the next one,'* thought Allen as they scurried across the open road.

Allen snuck a look at the crowd and could see fights already starting to break out. He gritted his teeth as he watched a man crush a child beneath his boot, ripping a bag of grain out of the poor kid's hands. He felt his gut wrench, his feet stumbling as Ricky tried to pull him to the next alley.

"They have rations!" howled an old woman, her spindly finger pointed at the two stragglers. Ricky and Allen froze for the briefest of seconds as a group of six broke off from the crowd to chase them down.

Then his feet carried him, weighed down by the heavy bag that Ricky and he were both lugging. They shared a look and knew they'd have to fend off the men closing in for their spoils.

As they let the bag fall and stood around it, a thick cloud of fog enveloped the street. The people let out a shocked gasp, and it was as if for a moment, the chaos stopped.

The rain didn't fall normally in Magnus, just the thick fog, wet and cold, but the rain didn't fall. That wasn't the reason storms were so dangerous. It was the lightning. The White Whip as most called it.

Allen looked around, watching to see if the white whips would strike. The lightning flashed across the clouds, like bright veins skittering through smoke. They needed to run, they needed to run back to the safety of their home! Allen saw a shadow in the corner of his eye disturb the fog and he growled.

"On your left!" he snapped. Ricky ducked, and the immediate threat of their attackers resurfaced. *'Caught in a storm, white whips everywhere and six assholes trying to steal our food...my favorite kind of day,'* thought Allen bitterly as his fist hit a man square across his nose. His knuckles stung but he didn't pay attention to his own pain, his mind preoccupied with the obstacles at hand.

Allen felt the air beginning to heat up and he yelped. Quickly, he pushed himself and Ricky back, as a bolt of energy flew through the street, burning the air around it as it struck through about a dozen people, finally finding its mark on a centaur.

Allen stooped down to get their rations as Ricky looked up to watch the Centaur. It twitched and began to run haphazardly down the main street with newfound energy, its circuits beginning to catch on fire. Allen panted as he shoved Ricky forward and pounced after him. He tried to ignore the scalding heat of the vaporized fog surrounding them and didn't realize how close the centaur had moved.

The centaur whipped about, it's horse-like legs thrashing at anything and nothing at the same time.

"Watch out!" screamed Ricky, but before Allen could react, a flailing hoof connected with the bottom of his spine. Searing pain erupted from his lungs and his back crumbled under the weight of his body as he fell limp to the ground, writhing in pain as his nerves flared; the centaur collapsed behind him and erupted into blue flames.

THE SKYLINE

He couldn't believe this. His sources said that subject 227 had made it to the Fence. How? How had it made it that far?

Dr. Vargas wrung his hands. He, the most renowned scientist in Magnus City, had slipped up. How could he have not prevented this catastrophe? How could it have escaped? He had surgeons, molecular biologists, highly trained security details, radiologists, military reinforcements, mechanicals. Surely word would get out that the monster he had created had *escaped!*

He knew he had only himself to blame. His newest formula coupled with the increased exposure to radiation had caused the appalling effects of the mutation, but he hadn't expected it to be so monstrous.

He grimaced as images of the creature flashed through his imagination. Nightmare. He had been having such severe night terrors that he was afraid to sleep. It was frightful; nothing like how it had started, weak and small, a mere child. Now it was gigantic, muscular, and animal-like; and it was all his doing.

He knew it would only be a matter of time before the thing would begin to terrorize the people. An uncontrollable beast, mutated by radiation and his own genetic manipulations. It would only increase in strength and aggressiveness. They had to find 227 before the situation inevitably escalated. After all... monsters were just that, monstrous, and they could only destroy.

Vargas clattered up the marble steps leading to the Libranian House. Above him loomed the great statue of Libra, her face etched with a judgmental scowl as she held the scales of justice, the golden chains glistening in the dull light. The fog of a great passing cumulonimbus cloud hit him. He could hear thunder in the distance. It was as if the universe itself reflected his anxiety, knew his anger, and his overwhelming fear.

He passed through the giant marble doors with his key card. Tinted windows shielded the outside from the business of the Libranian. Employees roamed the lobby of white jasper and long marble pillars. They wore neutral greys; the atmosphere was solemn. Small hums of conversation filled the vast room, but Dr. Vargas was on a mission. He passed through inspection with an easy flick of his key card, climbed into the elevator and swiped his authority card over the sensor. The elevator followed the orders, and the soft *dings* rang in his ear as he rose through the floors.

Finally, the doors opened and Dr. Vargas walked into a circular office, tinted windows surrounding him. A long desk was set at the head of the room, and a large silver and marble chess board captured his eye; that is until a soft voice demanded his attention. He looked up, seeing the Judge in all her glory, her frizzy greying hair surrounding her cool, dark face like a lion's mane.

"Doctor Vargas...fancy seeing you in my office, unappointed. What is the problem?" she asked plainly, casually. It was a cruel kind of casualness that sent a chill crawling down Dr. Vargas's back. He waited for her to scold him on barging in unannounced, but her attention was elsewhere. Her silver eyes were focused down at the chessboard as she moved a piece, a pawn.

Despite years in the city, no one knew her old country, her name or anything about her, because when she devoted her life as judge, Magnus became her country, her name and all she was. That kind of uncertainty never set well with him. Dr. Vargas nodded and stood at her desk.

"For years I have been working to cure radiation so that we may return to our home, Earth. You know of my project, as it...affects everyone in the world," he said, just a bit arrogantly, but it was true. The world was poisoned with radiation, except in a few pockets where the nuclear fallout failed to breach. If he could just get the formula right, and somehow speed up the half-life of a decaying atom, he'd be able to cancel out the radiation and restore the world. Not to mention reverse the effects of mutation.

"Of course, doctor. Where are you going with this?" she asked, leaning forward just a bit. The scientist gulped before nodding to reassure himself.

"I lost one of my test subjects, um, specifically, subject two hundred, twenty-seven. It was a... nightmarish misadventure," he said, grimacing. The Judge let out a deep sigh and stood up, her flowing grey robes falling in delicate folds around her ankles.

"Well, this is quite a problem, I'm assuming, considering you came straight to me," she purred menacingly. Dr. Vargas sighed, and nodded curtly. He explained the dangers and its possible location. He watched as she shook her head, eyes closed in disappointment.

"I've sent out my own team, and notified the programmers, and they all say the same thing. If he's in the Fence, he's probably being hidden." His face revealed his growing terror. The Judge clenched her fist and, in a moment, had made her decision.

"I'll send in the General and his lieutenant to find the people hiding your subject if there are any. When we find them, you can have them to continue your tests. Subject two hundred, twenty-seven will have a sample of its blood taken, but then you will destroy it immediately after," she paused for a moment, silence stretching between the two of them.

Her eyes captured the scientist in their predatory gaze, a lioness on the hunt, "Doctor Vargas, do not continue your work until the matter is resolved, understood?" she ordered softly. Dr. Vargas almost protested. He had just had another subject delivered to him, and he needed to get this project finished! However, he knew better than to argue. No one protested the Judge without deadly ramifications.

"Clear as crystal," he said in begrudging gratitude, flinching as she knocked over a rival chess piece. The silver piece, a knight, falling with a clink. His signal to leave.

Damon stood in the shooting range, pointing his gun and shooting multiple rounds before sighing and turning to the rookie he was coaching, only because he had seen him struggling.

It wasn't customary for an officer to meddle with the lower ranks, but he couldn't help it. He had been helping the rookies ever since his best friend left her daughter in his care, and he finally had the chance to be a father again.

"You have to line up these two rear sights with the front sight at the end of the barrel when aiming, or else you won't hit your target in the right place. And don't close your eyes, nothing's going to hit your eyes, unless your grip is absolutely horrible and it somehow slips in the drawback. Which it shouldn't, because if it was you wouldn't be here. Now shoot the target properly this time, please. I believe in you. You can do it," he encouraged, smiling sadly as he talked.

The rookie grinned and held up his gun, doing what Damon told him to do. The ring of the shot echoed in Damon's ears. The rookie gasped, exultant as he stared at the bullet hole lodged in the bullseye.

"Hey thanks, sir!" he exclaimed. Damon nodded curtly before turning and running into his partner, Matias, or more formally, General Sylva.

"Lieutenant, I've been looking for you everywhere! Come on," he said. Damon nodded curtly and followed, patting the rookie on the back as he left.

"Have you heard about our assignment, or have you been shooting?" asked the General. Damon rolled his eyes at the sarcasm but smiled anyway despite how wrong smiling felt.

"Yes, I received word of the assignment...Dr. Vargas was having trouble...what exactly was it?" he asked, catching up with his friend. Matias glowered.

"A mutated creature, he calls it subject two hundred, twenty-seven. It's anthropomorphic from his description, and seven feet tall, so it shouldn't be hard to spot in a crowd," explained Matias. Damon nodded in contemplation.

"And it's in the Fence, right?" asked Damon, a flicker of excitement glowing in the dark corners of his mind. The general grimaced and nodded.

"Right, but the Judge forbids us from actually investigating ourselves, which in my opinion, just takes the fun out of it," he explained, chuckling slightly. Damon frowned, knowing from past experience that he was speaking of the fun it took out of terrifying the people behind the Fence. It unsettled him.

"Yeah definitely. Well, all I can think to do is read the case file and send out rewards...maybe a find and seek Gorgon. Wait... I have an idea. My trainee, little Boyce, she's in the ghetto, maybe I can send word to her to be on the lookout," he suggested. Matias caught the last suggestion and tilted his head skeptically.

"Are you sure? She's Raven's daughter and... well you and I both know her history," murmured the General. Damon rankled at the poisonous words aimed at his now deceased friend.

"I'm sure it'll be fine. I trust Veronica. She's one of our best soldiers and you know she is," he argued. General Sylva merely sighed and gave his partner a feeble smile.

"Alright Damon, shoot her a message. I want results *now*!" Damon smiled at the opportunity to let Veronica shine, his surrogate daughter. However, his pale, blue eyes revealed a hole that even Raven's daughter could never fill, a pain in his heart for a past he longed to change.

Exam

It was evening, and Ricky struggled to carry his friend, blood streaming out from his back. A lump grew in the ginger's throat, how could this happen!? Why did he let it happen? Gosh, why did a nineteen-year old weigh this much?

The flapping tents and gleaming Medicum coats of the nurses and doctors caught his eye and a ghost of a relieved smile played at his lips.

"Don't worry Al, I gotcha. Hold on," he pleaded. He had been dragging his friend for hours trying to get to the Medicum. It was a very secluded place from the market square, and it was quite a distance carrying his barely conscious friend's dead weight.

Allen moaned, his eyes fluttering open. Sweat poured from his face as he shivered. It just wasn't right for him to be unable to move!

"Ricky I'mma goner!" he wheezed, every word sending him into spirals of unbearable pain. He was surprised he was still conscious.

"Help! Help us!" Ricky cried breathlessly. No one heard and he let Allen drop before grabbing his arms and dragging his limp body, belly sliding through the gravel. Allen gritted his teeth, tears of utter agony welling in his eyes.

"Someone help!" He screamed, louder this time. There were a few shouts and nurses rushed over with a stretcher, hitching Allen's body up and carrying him the rest of the way into the tents. Allen groaned at the pain, panting breathlessly. Damn mechs, there was a reason he loathed them.

"Oh my God, he's awake!?" shouted a young doctor who was standing with a group of other clean-cut young men and women. Allen snarled at them. They looked fresh-faced, not like the hardened doctors he had seen here before.

At least they had an ER in the first place. Ricky followed behind him, trying to mask his own fear and frustration.

Allen gasped and held back tears. It was excruciating to move, so he didn't. The pain in his back was like being stabbed again and again and again.

"Quick, get him one of the surgeons!" shouted a dark, complected woman. ___ Allen's eyes flicked through the crowd of doctors in a panicked flurry, blurred faces surrounding him.

The nurse carrying the head of the stretcher tripped over a rock and he roared as his body was so abruptly jostled. It *hurt,* God how it hurt. The worst part was, he was dealing with it, not blacking out into oblivion again. He needed a drink.

"You! Congratulations, your first exam," barked the woman at a girl with platinum blonde hair. The girl nodded hastily and Allen immediately realized what his luck was. Medical students. He wasn't getting out of here alive!

The girl wrung her hands but nodded, following the stretcher into a curtained-off room. One of the nurses stepped in Ricky's way.

"Hey! Let me through, that's my best friend!" Ricky shouted as the nurse shushed him to reason.

Allen wheezed and dug his head into the hard cushion of the stretcher. His legs were jerked out from under him, eliciting another growling, feral moan from his lungs. The girl's shaky hands hovered over him as she assessed the damage.

"Can someone please turn him over?" she whispered. His mind stopped- body freezing. That voice...something about that voice was so familiar, it took his breath away. Two sets of sturdy hands gripped his arms and flipped him over onto his stomach, and he cried out again.

"Definitely nerve damage, this will not be an easy procedure," she murmured under her breath, her voice shaky, almost as shaky as her hands.

"Can I have some water, and get me some anesthesia," she ordered meekly. The nurses nodded and left immediately.

"Don't worry sir," she whispered, her entire body shaking before she took a long deep breath. Allen squeezed his eyes shut, trying to focus on her voice, but the way her hands shook did not comfort him in the least. He scowled and tried to focus on anything else but his rising panic and pain. That voice...

"I know you from somewhere..." he croaked. She questioningly cocked an eyebrow, then her face drained of color. Her brown eyes stared down at him and he forced his head to look at her.

"Um..." before she could reply, the nurses arrived again and pumped anesthesia through his oxygen tube, hitting him hard with the sedation. Another nurse handed her the water. She shook out her nerves, willing her entire body to be steady and calm, as the medication kicked in and overpowered Allen's overwhelming pain.

Maya stared down at the young man, who looked a bit older than her. She had to admit he was well built, and she couldn't help but glance at his slack face that was under the influence of the anesthesia. His words rang in her head. He said he knew her, but that was ridiculous, wasn't it?

She sighed and shook away the intrusive thoughts. Wondering who this poor man was, wasn't going to save his life. She quickly cleaned up the wound and finally got a better look at the mangled and bruised flesh.

Maya gagged in repulsion. The wound, which really looked more like a mashed-up blood orange, was very recent. It was bright red, blood and skin pulverized, with dark purple and green rings already formed around it. She took another sip of water to keep herself from vomiting. Simulations had never prepared her for this. This was real.

She took a deep breath, forcing herself to a steely, controlled calm. She wiped down the wound as the nurses connected the man up to the monitors and IV.

Once all the preparations were finished, her now steady hand gripped the scalpel and cut deftly adjacent to the gruesome wound. The skin parted at the pull of the hooks in the hands of the nurses. She studied his spinal cord, wondering how this much damage had happened in the first place.

Maya reached for another tool, an instant x-ray. She scanned him, seeing the spine was cracked and twisted. She felt her gut twinge just a bit at the reality. *'Don't worry Maya, it'll be fine, ok?'* she reminded herself. She knew what to do and prayed she could do it correctly.

She held out her hand and a nurse wordlessly gave her a syringe. The solution was genetically modified growth cells that would heal broken bones. The Remedium was still working on limb regrowth, and that wouldn't come out until some time.

She could recite the history and reason behind the development down to the page in the textbook. Years of intense medical school had drilled in everything she would need to know as if she herself was a mechanical.

Her hands worked fast as she began to suture, with needle-like precision, what had been torn. God, she was nervous. It took everything she had to keep her hands steady. She had worked on dummies and virtual simulations, but this was the real deal, and if she failed, that was it for her. Her dream to save the lives of people stripped from her because of one screw up. She looked down at the face of her patient and frowned.

That face, it *was* familiar...she felt she knew him, somewhere deep inside her mind.

The curtain opened and she flinched, not letting her tools jerk inside the open wound, however, as she knew that would lead to instant failure. At that moment, Professor Anand stepped through the curtain. She seated her slim body on the chair behind her, perched like a sparrow. She pulled out a cubelet and tapped the screen silently so as not to distract the surgeon.

However, now Maya's heart raced a mile a minute, her hands trembled ever so slightly and she set the tools down to take a drink. Anand stared at her, assessing her, and Maya instantly returned to the man who seemed so...utterly familiar. Who was he?!

A small twitter breezed through, landing on the anesthetized body. It was a tiny mechanical. It looked like a dragon, but with insect wings. Its entire face was nothing but a black screen. Its tongue darting out, a little recorder on the tip.

Her breathing became heavy as her eyes glanced up every so often at the small surveillance mechanical. She reached for another sip of water, her nerves calming as she took a deep breath and returned to suturing the ghastly wound.

Finally, she cleaned the wound one more time with disinfectant and let out a shaky breath, the hard part was over, now if she could just finish.

Under the watchful eyes of Professor Anand, she stitched up the outer layer of skin. Maya patched up the incision and stepped away, a deep sigh leaving her mouth. *'I did it...wait,* did *I do it?'* She thought frantically.

Without another word, Professor Anand stood up and left the isolation of the curtain. Maya let out a deep, shaky breath and wiped the beaded sweat off her forehead. As she stepped out from the tent to gather her wits, she came face to face with a weasel-faced man with wild ginger-colored hair. He was glaring down at her.

"How is he?" he demanded. She gulped as sharp breaths escaped her lungs.

"Um...he should be a-ok..." she stuttered. The Ginger's eyes snapped to an immediate fury born of fear and love for his mangled friend before he sagged, groaning and rubbing his eyes.

"Dammit Allen!" he whispered hoarsely under his breath. Maya froze. Allen...suddenly the memory snapped into place!

Allen, the boy from the immigration ship, the one she had comforted. The one who refused to tell her about his home life but always wanted to hear about her day. The boy refused to tell her why he would always wear the same clothes, and barely accepted the jacket she gave him, but always got her things that weren't very valuable, material wise, but to her... she still had those things in her dorm room.

Allen! How had she not recognized him!? Suddenly her throat tightened and she took off her mask. Allen... the boy who she had venomously told to go away before leaving him in this prison.

"Did you say Allen?" she whispered. Ricky glanced at her questioningly, his eyes widening.

"No way! ... Maya?" he breathed in disbelief. The two stared at each other in dumbfounded shock.

creature

He had been so naive, fourteen years old and a head filled with wishful thinking. Thoughts that told him that even though he had nothing, he could be everything. He wasn't jaded to the world yet, having Ricky and Maya was enough for him.

Definitely not his father, but family. So, this turn of events wasn't something he could easily accept.

"Wait, what do you mean...leaving?" he snapped as he watched the blonde girl scrambling about her room, packing her clothes away in suitcases that were fraying at the edges. She glanced up at him, that wide, heart melting, smile dimming.

"Well...I mean...I've been working my whole life for this," she said, her brows furrowing. Her words drew a scoff from him.

"Your whole life? You're thirteen! You don't...we don't have lives," he growled. She frowned at his words, and he regretted them immediately.

"You may not have a life!" she exclaimed as she strode towards him with a fierceness that shocked him, closing the distance between them, "but I do! Why can't you just...be happy for me!?" she cried. Allen was taken aback and turned away to keep her from seeing his flushed, angry face.

"You'll be just fine without me...you have Ricky and your family." He whirled around; teeth bared at the memory of his father never coming back to him. He had never told her his grim reality. Honestly, she was such a fool for believing him.

"No! I've lost everything, my family...myself...You and Ricky are all I have left...I...my dad, he never came back and I... you can't leave me. I really do need you; I do!" he shouted. Tears brimmed in her eyes as she backed up, the flush of her face draining at his words, his tone. He stumbled back, stunned that he had suddenly revealed everything to her. Her eyes narrowed, and a cold frown crossed her face.

"Allen,"

"Don't." he sat down, defeated, his back slumping as a long sigh escaped his throat.

"No, you listen to me...we've known each other since we were kids...and you suddenly tell me your family...never came for you? How could you even hide that from me? Why would you hide that from me!? I thought you trusted me!" she cried. He stared at the ground, refusing to meet those eyes, those warm, chocolate eyes now filled with betrayal. He couldn't bring himself to see her, looking at him like he had stabbed her in the back.

"I... I just didn't want you to think I was...I don't know, I mean... How have you never noticed? Really? How has that thought never crossed your mind? You're so naive Maya. You honestly believe that you can go to the Skyline? What, because you're smart or something? They don't give a shit if you're smart! They don't care about you!" he snarled. Maya's eyes widened at his piercing words.

"Get out," she hissed. He stood with a jerk at her words, his heart thudding hard against his ribcage. He could feel it tearing itself apart.

"Wait...no, Maya, listen I'm sorry, I didn't mean it like that," he pleaded; his chest shook, his throat tightened as if it were being wrapped around by a snake. She twitched away from him and sighed.

"Get out Allen," she demanded. She wouldn't show him her face, but the small heaves of her ribs, the weak whimpering... She was crying. He had made her cry... The thought killed him a thousand times in the moment of that realization.

"Fine... have a good life," he spat bitterly, mostly angry at himself. He waited a moment, hoping that their irrational outbursts would fade away and they could move past it. He wished so much that she would turn around, but she didn't. She didn't say anything, she didn't move. Allen slunk away, climbing out the window and jumping to the ground.

Something brushed his arm... Allen's eyes flickered open as his memory was interrupted. He glanced up. Where was he? Last time he was awake, he was lying in the Medicum writhing with unbearable pain, and now he was watching dust balls float around him in his familiar living room. When had he gotten back to Ricky's?

Allen yawned, blinking hard to get his tired eyes to open and focus, but his breath caught in his throat as he glimpsed a reddish-brown form moving just on the edge of his vision. He turned, gasping as he saw a giant, hulking, hairy creature stalking through the apartment. The door was ajar against the wall, thick evening light spilling in the gaping, shattered door frame.

He tried to stand up to run, but too late remembered his back injury, and fell in a heap on the floor next to the couch.

The strange canine-looking creature jumped at the sound, whirling around and facing him. His eyes quickly went fierce, his nostrils flared.

He wasn't wearing an oxygen mask, but he appeared to be breathing perfectly... and Allen gulped at the sight of the creature's long, sharp fangs.

Allen choked as the creature let out a furious snarl, before baring its teeth and taking a territorial step forward. Its bushy red tail stuck straight out with alarm. It looked strangely human, its hands were shaped like a man's hands, replete with opposable thumbs...if you could overlook the fact that from each long, spindly finger extended a sharp, curved claw. Finally, a human torso… Allen immediately shifted his gaze back up.

He realized it must've been a fox. He could tell by the narrow snout and bright red fur…The fox barked and lunged forward, clearly not willing to give up this new found territory.

Allen shouted with surprise as the thing pounced on him, its strength alarming, and speed impossible to imagine. Allen pummeled it away giving him just enough time to stop his sharp teeth from enclosing on his neck. His fist hammered at its slender snout, the fox dragging him off the ground and tossing him into Ricky's favorite armoire.

Allen winced at the pain of the shelves digging into his shoulders, and at the fact, Ricky was going to come home to this.

"Stop it you freak!" He wheezed; despite the fact he knew it couldn't be reasoned with. The thing stood on its hind legs. It snarled and pounced toward him, again. Allen lunged out of the way by a hair and threw anything his hands could grab.

The beast was taken aback as a soft pillow slapped his face. He backed up slightly, his dog-like face a mask of confusion at the harmless assault. Allen gulped and slowly stood up, creeping out from the small space next to the armoire. The beast watched his movement and growled. Allen shushed him and rubbed his back to relieve some of the flaring pain. He clenched his jaw. A shadow of memory of the mutants on the surface flickered through his mind.

"Hey, get away…" he said breathlessly, moving to the kitchen as the fox stalked towards him, studying his retreat.

The sound of an alarm alerted both of them.

The fox glanced at the door, its amber eyes falling upon the sight of a giant mechanical Centaur galloping down the street. His eyes widened and he scrambled back, a terrified whimper escaping his lips. The creature looked at Allen with pleading eyes.

"P…p… pah…lease…" it whined in a low, barely audible but **human** voice. Allen's head shot up at the beast's words.

"You can talk!?" he sputtered, heart thundering against his chest with disbelief, his face paling. The creature whimpered, shrinking closer to the hallway. He glanced outside, his eyes skimming over the city skyline. His breathing sharpened and he turned back to Allen.

"Please…help, have survive," he murmured clumsily, bringing his paws to his white-furred chest. Allen blinked, his guard going down like a crumbling wall. *Run, Fight, Survive.* His personal mantra raced about in his head as the creature whined, looking from him to the city skyline outside.

"What the hell? What are you?" Allen gasped. The creature whined and crawled towards him, reaching his hand out.

"You need to get out of here," he ordered, backing away with distaste and anger. This creature had attacked him and now he was asking for help?

"Pl-uh-ease, th-they f-fin...find me," he struggled to say. Allen shook his head, his eyes shifting to the gaping door frame.

"Who are they?" he asked, slowly making his way to the open hole. The fox hesitantly followed him, brow furrowed and eyes wide with fear.

"Tor-tor-torturers, bad men who...who hurted me, I... I come back home, but they will take, they take m-me again..." he supplied. Allen looked at the creature questioningly and tried to move the door over to cover the hole. However, the pain in his back made it impossible for him to lift the door into place.

He knew he should keep it talking, it was the best way to keep it from turning violent again. He could feel the thin plasma of his blood seeping onto his hand and he needed to fix the stitches he'd torn wrestling with that thing or else his back would be in worse shape.

"How can you talk? You're...you're not exactly a man," he pointed out. He felt so stupid for engaging with this feral monstrosity, but...he felt it would be wrong for him to turn the creature out, even to kill it himself. Something about the creature resonated with him. Maybe it was the fact that it represented how he felt he was seen by the elite. When he was in the Immigration hall, when the captain told them to cooperate or they'd have no problem with killing them. Maybe this creature knew that fear, and Allen didn't want to be a harbinger of that feeling. Never. So, he would ask it stupid questions to keep it from tearing him apart, and he wouldn't force it back out into the streets.

"I... learned...I'm, was...like you," he responded. Allen was impressed it had the mental capacity to answer questions, and it made him wonder where it had come from, and who had created it.

His mind snagged onto his last statement. *'Like me?'* he thought in befuddlement. What did that mean? He said he had come back home. Was he from the Fence? That was preposterous, if a seven-foot tall monstrosity was from the Fence, he would've known about it for a long time.

Unless... His mind wandered to the day of the riot...when he watched the child being taken from the Home. Coming back home...no, that couldn't be. He shoved it to the back of his mind, not allowing himself to even think about it.

He looked around frantically for anything to distract him, he caught sight of the door frame and sighed in partial relief, and partial exasperation.

"Well, now thanks to you, there's a door off its hinges," he grumbled. He would fix it himself if every movement didn't threaten to tear open more stitches. He never got a break.

"S-sorry, scary noises, needed place to... to hide" whispered the creature. Allen glanced at him with puzzled irritation.

"Right. Man, Ricky is gonna hate me. Hey, you got any identification? A name? Number? Something I can call you?" he asked, limping back to the couch. The monster followed him, sniffing the scent of blood, eyes widening in alarm.

"Th-they told me I di-didn't have name anymore, th-they called me t-two twenty-se-seven...but I maybe can remember b-before...Ze...Zech...I... I don't remember..." he responded disconsolately.

Allen slowly lowered himself down, wincing in pain. He'd have to get Ricky to call for help, or ask him to sew him back together. The echo of memories of his own number from when he arrived in the city played through his mind and his heart went out to the creature. So... Zech? What names even sounded remotely close to that? The closest name he could think of was Zach.

"Do you mean, Zach?" he asked, but the beast only growled and shook his head with frustration.

"No! I... I don't remember! It hurt too much t-to remember," he snarled. Allen's eyes widened in fear that he had goaded the thing into another attack, and a silence fell between the unlikely pair.

"Ok...your name is Zech," he sighed. The fox smiled as best he could, his tongue lolling out as he sat down. He was a hulking giant compared to the man beside him. He was satisfied with the name, and that was all Allen needed. Besides some relief from his back pain, he didn't want to get paralyzed again. Allen leaned against the couch, wincing as his wound made contact with the back cushions.

"What the—!? Allen, what the hell happened to the door?!" Allen jumped as he heard the skidding of footsteps run inside. Zech vaulted to his feet, growling like a rabid dog. Ricky paled, stumbling away.

"Wha— Allen?" he whimpered. It appeared his question had been answered, although Ricky didn't really find this "answer" amusing. Allen slowly stood up, a sheepish smile on his face. Ricky glared at him, pointing at the fox with disbelief.

"No! You can *not* keep it, ya pox!" he cursed, his eyes wide in panic as Zech's hackles rose defensively. Allen held up his hands, legs shaking slightly.

"Ricky, meet Zech, Zech meet Ricky," he stammered as his friend glared at him icily. Zech huffed, stepping in front of Allen protectively.

"Bad man...?" he snarled. Allen tried to signal to Ricky that the creature was not going to hurt him, and despite the tense situation, he actually started to chuckle. He stopped when he saw the cold frown on his friend's face. Allen pushed the creature's arm away.

"No! This is my friend," he exclaimed. Ricky groaned at him, eyes twitching with dismay.

"Well, I'm about to be your enemy! What is going on!? Allen, please explain, please try to somehow explain what the hell is going on," he cried.

Allen grinned sheepishly, gesturing for the naked, humanoid fox to sit down.

"Well, you'd never believe it, pal,"

"Oh ho, don't pal me, and I already *don't* believe it," interrupted Ricky whose face was cherry-red from fury and terror. Allen rolled his eyes, waiting for Ricky to sit down so he could explain what had happened.

"Well, I was sleepin', right? Well, I was. Anyway, then this thing brushes past me and I wake up to see Zech,"

"Zech?" Ricky once again interrupted. Allen stared at him, blinking with annoyance. The fox chortled slightly under his breath at the exchange.

"Yes, Zech. He chose the name himself. Anyway, he attacked me out of fear," he said. Zech whimpered slightly and nodded.

"S-sorry," he said in shame. Allen knit his brow as he felt compassion for the creature taking over his heart and he patted the creature's shoulder absentmindedly.

"You're good. Anyway, to stop me from getting mauled I started talkin', and it turns out Zech is this lab experiment who escaped from them…the elite. So... I'm helping him," he said, crossing his arms, wincing slightly at the tearing stitches in his back. Ricky glared at him with infuriated confusion.

"How are you going to take care of it, you can't even take care of yourself!" he snapped. Allen laughed nervously.

"Well, he's a capable...good man, uh, I'm gonna teach him how to read. He can talk as you might have heard. He knows how to reason so I'm already halfway there, and he's strong, he threw me into the cupboard without even trying! That could be very useful," he said with a grin.

Ricky's lower eyelid twitched.

"This is absolutely *bonkers*! Are ye' an idiot!? You've done stupid things before, but this officially *crosses* the line! Unbelievable!" he spat, standing up. Allen gritted his teeth.

"Please, Ricky? Look at him. He needs help. Don't tell me that he's not what the elite see when they look at us. I think he's one of us...I think he... Ricky, the elite stare down at us with upturned noses. All we are to them are lab rats for their amusement. They did this to him...we can't be that way, we can't turn our back on him, and... it's just...man I don't know," he said. Ricky glanced at him.

"Well...that's a load of bullocky coming from you. Where did this newfound compassion come from? You turn your back, we all do!" he accused. Allen frowned. Ricky's words hurt. He felt his throat tighten at the accusation, a long frown growing on his face.

"I don't know Ricky. Maybe it's the fact that I'm so sick of turning a blind eye to what they do to us. Maybe it's because when I look at him, I see a little part of myself," he spat, recalling the riot, and the little child that had been plucked away by the greedy fingers of the elite. Ricky looked surprised at the first statement but didn't make a move to address it.

"Ah yes, I can see the resemblance. So, what do you expect us to do? Obviously, we can't just stroll through the neighborhood with a seven-foot fox-man," he retorted. Allen moved a hand back to his wound and clenched his fist around it.

"We dress him up normally and hide him, simple as that," he said. Zech's tongue lolled out in a canine-like smile. Ricky frowned.

"Are you sure that's gonna work? He's, like I said, a *seven-foot* tall *fox man!*" He looked at Zech with fear. Allen waved him off.

"Well...you might be right, but you feel it too...you want to stop the elite. They use us like guinea pigs. We are expendable to them... We can't keep turning away when we see someone in need," he said, standing up. The movement tore open more of his stitches and he groaned. Ricky's eyes widened.

"Tore your stitches already? You're impossible! How am I supposed to quote-un-quote, *trust you* with a giant fox man if I can't even trust you with your own stitched wound!?" he asked in exasperation. Allen tried to stifle a chuckle and waved him off.

"Seriously, I'm fine. That's why I have you, right?" he said. Zech whined slightly before his ears swiveled, and his hackles rose.

"What's up with him?" asked Ricky as Allen carefully began taking his shirt off so they could work on his stitches. Allen thought about Ricky's question and shrugged.

"In... intruder...," murmured Zech, backing away. Ricky looked behind him to see a young, familiar woman standing at the bottom of their landing. Allen winced over to the gaping door and looked over the railing of the balcony.

"Maya!?" he exclaimed through a whisper; his eyes wide in confusion at her presence. Was he seeing things!? Had he become so insane that he was starting to see his childhood crush!?

Allen did a double take, seeing the woman checking a piece of paper and looking up and locking eyes with him. He choked and retreated back inside; his eyes wide with shock.

"Oh yeah...she was your surgeon...she took off running when I noticed her, it was an out of body experience, truly... Guess she's here now...of all times," he murmured.

Allen looked at him in shock, stammering as he ran a hand through his hair, eyes wide. No! No, it was a dream! It was a dream that she was here, that would explain the fox! It had to be a dream, and he would wake up now!

He squeezed his eyes shut, but his reality remained unaltered and he groaned. He then remembered Zech was, in fact, a real thing standing in the middle of their living room and he cursed. This definitely wasn't a dream.

"Ricky, hide him...and... get him some clothes please...or something?" he ordered. Ricky faltered slightly, trying to think of any clothes big enough to fit the creature.

"Today please!" Allen snapped. The redhead jumped at the words and nodded. He looked up at the creature, sizing him up before sighing and gesturing to the hall.

"Zech... let's uh, go to the back..." said Ricky, shaking his head in utter disbelief. The fox bared his teeth at the man but did as he was told. He followed Ricky down the hall, to the bedroom, to avoid the woman who was jogging up the stairs.

Allen awkwardly turned to the gaping doorway and tried to smile; however, it came off as more of a nervous grimace.

She stopped when she came up to him, her eyes shifting to avoid looking at him. He winced as he heard a crash in the other room, coughing softly to avert her attention.

"Maya! Long time no see! What brings you here? I thought you were busy at the Medicum! Or you know, not on this side of the fence in the first place? I did not know you were going to be here, whatsoever. If I had known, I would've cleaned up...I'll shut up now..." he murmured. She stepped back, not sure what to say.

"I...am, I just...I wanted to check on you...and uh, why is your door missing, what...what's...what's that smell?" she asked, her train of thought derailing.

He gulped and stepped aside, smelling himself subtly until the scent hit him. Dog...fox. He bit the inside of his cheek and carefully walked over to the couch.

"Do you have a dog?" she asked. Allen shook his head, scratching the back of his neck anxiously.

"N-no, no I do not. Dogs, they cost too many resources to keep around. Ya gotta feed it, clean up after it...I mean, I can barely even feed myself. Besides, I don't even like dogs. If I had a pet, it would be a cat," he reasoned. Maya turned to him and frowned. He caught Maya's eyes and smiled awkwardly with the tension. *'I can barely feed myself... good going, real smooth. Get a grip, you're better at talking than that.'* he scolded.

Allen sighed, wincing slightly as his gaping stitches sent knives and needles down his back. Ok, that was enough. These things needed to be sewn back together.

"Hey, you're a doctor, right? How about you help me with this, I mean since you're here and all," he said, turning around and removing his bloodstained hand. She gasped.

"How did this happen? What have you been doing?" she asked, moving over to him in concern. He sat on the couch as she rummaged through her bag. He glanced back, watching her with silent awe.

She pulled out a portable medical kit. He began to finally let himself feel the burn in his back and he winced with pain. It was amazing how people could block out agony until it finally had to slap them in the face and force them to deal with it.

Maya cleared her throat awkwardly.

"This isn't usually the circumstances women see me with my shirt off," he joked, trying to relieve the tension in the room. She didn't laugh. He clenched his jaw. *'Not my best, definitely a miss...'* he thought.

The sting of cold antiseptic cloth brought him out of his thoughts and he sighed. He was overwhelmed with emotion. This was so strange. He was so completely taken aback by her presence; he had turned into an awkward mess. How was he even supposed to react? Burst out crying and hug her and apologize for everything that had happened. Congratulate her for her successes? No, instead he was trying to act casual and it was just making the atmosphere feel utterly wrong. He decided to just shut up.

For the first time in forever, he couldn't talk. He couldn't initiate a conversation. Nothing but icy silence bridged the gap, and so many questions and confessions burned in his mind and his heart. However, he couldn't bring himself to ask or tell any of it.

They sat in silence as she fixed his wound, and he gritted his teeth through the stinging of her stitching him back up, this time without anesthesia, until she had repaired the ripped sutures.

Allen was about to turn and address her and thank her for her help, but he was cut off by a yelp. He winced as a loud crash emanated from Ricky's bedroom, followed by a doggish bark.

"You said you didn't have a dog," she said, crossing her arms. His eyes widened and he shook his head.

"I don't have a dog," he said, gulping. She narrowed her eyes and looked past him, clearly unconvinced.

"It's not something to hide, I love dogs! I remember the old dogs from the surface. They're very rare to find up here," she said, trying to step past him. Allen frowned and looked behind him.

"Maybe the ghetto is getting to you Maya because you're hearing things, see? No bar—" before he could finish his sentence the hulking lab creature barreled out from the hallway, growling in a fit of rage, a shirt pulled over its head. Maya screamed at the top of her lungs, stumbling back.

Ricky sprinted after Zech, Allen sighing with disappointment. This was why they couldn't have nice things.

WILDERNESS

Veronica rubbed her eyes. She was exhausted. All day, pacing around the Medicum, waiting for people. Nothing had happened. *All day.* The people here in the Ghetto that she did see walking around, cowered before her like starving, stray dogs, scurrying away before she could even say a word.

As the patients came and went, she had begun to realize that these people weren't anything like how the Elite said they would be. She was certainly not surprised that they misrepresented that too.

Her mother always told her that the Elite lied. So, this was just another one of their lies. They were so...fake. Everything in the Skyline felt so plastic and false. Her mother was the only thing that was real; the only person who made sense; the only person who seemed to see the wrong in it all. This was all wrong.

Secretly, she loved the Fence. Despite all the fear-mongering and the gross smells that wafted from the streets, she felt more alive here than she ever did in the

Skyline. When she walked down those streets, she didn't know if she'd be attacked or not. It kept her on the edge.

This place didn't scheme, this place was life or death. Something about that was so thrilling, so honest, it was a breath of fresh air. All her life she had felt suffocated by their schemes. Ever since her mom was executed, she had been drowning in their intrigues.

At any moment, someone could decide she was next. Here...no one stabbed you in the back, they stabbed you in the stomach so you could look them in the eye. She appreciated the honesty. Her whole life had been lies after lies after lies. She didn't even know why her mother was executed. There was candor in the suffering here. She felt like she belonged here.

A gentle hand rested on her back, snapping her out of her reverie. She turned and caught the eyes of Professor Anand. The dark woman smiled kindly, handing her a paper cup of coffee.

"Are you doing alright Officer Boyce?" asked Dr. Anand, "I can see a vacant look on that face, nothing alert about it. Aren't you a Stratus?" she added, a small smirk playing at her lips. Veronica chuckled wryly and turned away. Was she alright? Every part of her wanted to run away and disappear into this ruin of truth.

"Why do we separate the city like this?" she inquired. A patient who sat in a rusted wheelchair near them frowned at the statement. Dr. Anand smiled sadly, observing the ghetto that surrounded them.

Veronica braced herself for the usual excuses the elite gave. '*Surface dwellers bring their savagery with them. We can't let their crime taint our sanctuary. We can't just leave them to die on the earth. Progressus est scientia. Scientia est pax. Pax est vita.*' She could recite it. The maxims sickened her, even though the words were that of hope. *Progress is knowledge, Knowledge is peace, Peace is life.* She had learned how hollow it all was. She knew that had been what her mother had been trying to show her.

"The elite are clever. They can make anyone believe what they say. You know why they're here. You don't need me to tell you. That is why it is our job to do our work as best as possible. As Vishnu wills it," she murmured, drawing closer to Veronica with each word she spoke. Veronica's eyes widened and she immediately wanted to change the subject.

"I've been hearing the patients talk about scandals. What are those?" she asked, nodding her head towards the patient to her right, who was suffering from an overdose. Dr. Anand sighed, rubbing her forehead in annoyance.

"Ah yes...the Scandals. They mark every street. We get at least ten patients with alcohol poisoning a day," she explained, pointing out into the ruins. Veronica looked down, trying to hide her piqued curiosity. They had nothing like that in the Skyline.

"Sounds wild...ever been to one?" she asked as she fiddled with her armored vest, zipping it up and down. Professor Anand chuckled, and shrugged nonchalantly.

"Of course, I have… Everyone goes eventually… Well unless you're Dr. Farley who believes strongly against them. They always intrigued me. In my home, the women were kept mostly inside. We were homemakers you know? I defied them in many ways," said Dr. Anand. Veronica nodded with understanding.

She glanced up, noting the small blue dot in-between the woman's eyes and smiled. It was rare for anyone in this age to showcase their beliefs so plainly, and Veronica admired her for her courage.

"Yeah, all the power to you...thanks for the coffee." She held her paper cup to the sky in toast.

Dr. Anand chuckled and nodded. She bowed her head in respect and then turned on her heel to continue surveying the students. Veronica glanced down at the patient with a questioning look.

"Scandals, huh?" she asked. The man shrugged, nodding timidly. She smiled at him, which took the man by surprise. Stratus officers never spoke to civilians, and they certainly never smiled at them. In fact, Stratus never went without a helmet. Those helmets that hid their faces behind black screens that made them appear like mechanicals themselves. Veronica hated it, and even though Lieutenant Rose got onto her about it, she never wore it unless she had to.

"Everyone's been to a scandal ma'am, it's the only thing to do around here, 'sides dyin," he murmured. Veronica chuckled wryly.

"Don't call me ma'am...my friends call me Ronny," she said, grinning. He smiled back hesitantly. She guessed he had never been shown kindness by a member of the elite. A pang of remorse shot through her heart.

"Thanks, I'm Peter," he said. Veronica grinned and patted his shoulder. He turned, his smile growing.

"How about you come to one? There's one near the Medicum...I'll be out in five days. I'm sure as hell gonna need a drink by then. I'll meet you at nine and show you the ropes," he said.

Veronica glanced up at him, putting his features to memory. A thin nose, scrawny, dark hair and bronze skin. She noted his eyes, blue with a ring of orange around them. She could remember those eyes. She smiled and held out her hand, and when he put his hand out, she high fived him.

"Sounds fun! I'll be there. In five days, right?" she asked, glancing toward the street. Peter looked down at his hand in awe, as if he had never seen it before. One of the doctors took his wheelchair and began to wheel him away.

"See ya later, Ronny," he whispered, waving goodbye to her. She lazily saluted him, a small smile twitching at her the corners of her lips. She looked out at the crumbling brown buildings and a thrill went down her spine. She watched as a few people wound in-between the ruins, spraying it with painted obscenities. They caught sight of her and raced away.

She wanted so badly to chase after them and spend the whole afternoon tagging with the Fencers - or at least spend it roaming the crumbling ghetto and seeing the integrity it brought to her life. She saw her spirit in those graffitied buildings.

Her ear began to ring, and she quickly put her fingers up to the earpiece.

"Officer Boyce awaiting orders," she said firmly. She smiled as Damon's voice crackled over the line.

"Don't be so formal, it's just your boss," he said. She chuckled at the kindly voice of the lieutenant. She had known him for most of her young life. He had been a close friend of her mom's, and had taken her under his wing after her mother was executed. He was almost like a father to her. It was he who convinced General Sylva to let her on the force. She softly greeted him and they exchanged pleasantries as she went to a place more private to speak to him.

"Listen, I know you were assigned to protect the Medicum interns while in the Ghetto, but I have a very important mission for you." Veronica furrowed her brows and she leaned in almost as if he were there in person.

"I'm all ears," she said. He began to explain the problem with the missing subject; subject two hundred twenty-seven. It was in the Ghetto now, and she needed to find it, or at least find the people who were hiding it. Then they could send in a find and seek gorgon and she'd be rewarded greatly, possibly even promoted.

Veronica didn't care about the last part. However, she did find the idea of a mission that could actually be exciting a lot more thrilling than pacing around the tents all day.

"I'll take it. Thank you, sir," she said. With that, Damon hung up. Veronica sighed as she looked out at the Ghetto streets, the words of Anand echoing in her mind.

Imposter

Allen shouted in an attempt to stop the noise. Maya sprinted towards the door, only to be stopped by Ricky. Word of Zech couldn't be known outside of his apartment. Allen lunged for Zech, pulling the t-shirt over his head, the frightened fox's eyes dilated as sense came back to him.

"Hey, what the hell is wrong with you!? When I say hide, you hide!" he scolded. Zech whimpered and pressed his ears to his head. Allen sighed in regret at yelling at the animal.

Maya's breathing was heavy and she shoved Ricky in vain. The girl whirled around to look at the beast, her lip curling.

"What is that thing!?" she hollered. Ricky glanced at Allen and clenched his jaw, holding the fox back.

"It's...not a dog, that's for sure," he lamely retorted. Maya narrowed her eyes and whipped her head around to look at Ricky.

"You're all insane. I honestly, shouldn't have come," she hissed, trying to step past Ricky. Allen darted up.

"Well, I'm sorry to burst your bubble, but you're here. His name is Zech... Maya," he pressed. Maya turned back, her chest heaving, trying to catch her breath.

"What, Allen?" she snapped. Ricky crossed his arms; his entire face one big question mark as his tired eyes travelled to his friend.

Allen had been rendered speechless. His entire life was in shambles, and now this? For some reason...he got mad. She graced him with her perfect presence, her head filled with promises but with no follow through, and he found himself seething with rage. How dare she come to them now! She was so blind, so ignorant to the pain they went through.

"Listen, Maya, this thing escaped a lab...if you lived here long enough, you'd realize what that means. Do you even know what happens here? Or are you too caught up in Maya world where everything is perfect and everything the elite do is right?"

"Oh, I love how you start conversations right where they left off," she barked, her eyes welling with tears at the accusation. Ricky sighed, cocking his brow at her before she looked away.

"I know, I was surprised when I saw him too...Allen...doesn't make very good decisions with his life," he said, eyes narrowing. Allen groaned and held his hands up, like a man facing a firing squad. Zech's ears were still planted firmly against his head as he covered his frantic amber eyes.

"Well hold on, he needs our help. We didn't want to drag you into this, but now that you know about him, you've walked into our little conflict, and we can't let you walk out," explained Allen. Ricky glanced at him, and seeing the true cry for solidarity from his best friend, he caved and gave a hesitant nod.

Of course, he would help his friend, no matter how much he disagreed or just how impossible it seemed. Maya, however, glared bullets at Allen, who was staring back at her, his eyes wide with both anger and hope.

"Ugh, please don't let me interfere with this weird tension ye maggots got. I don't want no part in it. Hell, I didn't want to be involved in this *giant* either! I mean, to make matters worse, I don't even think Zech's supposed to exist, and we don't have a plan!" snapped Ricky, glancing at Zech, who avoided looking him in the eye.

Allen stood up and murmured nervously. "Listen, Maya, you... You're a doctor, and... I know you don't care about us anymore...but you should care about him. If you gave a shit about helping people, you'd realize he's one of us, and your precious elite are the cause of his destruction," pleaded Allen, and he gestured to Zech.

Maya covered her eyes and crossed over to the couch. In that moment, she felt so much weight on her shoulders. She couldn't stand up under their accusations. She wasn't the bad guy, here.

"You are hiding an illegally obtained lab creation, in this slum of a city, with absolutely no plan. Helping you with this, could probably ruin my career," she groaned. She had worked too hard to let all of her work go down the drain because she got caught up in the life of ghosts from her past. She couldn't let herself be manipulated. She had dreams. She darted a look at the beast, her lip quivering. What did they mean when they said it was one of them?

"I... can't do this...I won't give you away, but I can't be part of this," she whimpered. Allen felt his heart drop to his stomach. What did he expect? Ricky clenched his jaw, but nodded towards the open door.

"Well Maya...thanks for your...help...I hope you're happy with your decision. The door is uh...open. Go ahead and walk out," he murmured poisonously.

Maya hesitated, staring at Allen for some sort of closure, but he narrowed his eyes and turned to Zech. The creature whimpered and backed away from her. Maya sighed, rushed out the open doorway and clattered down the metal stairs.

Allen turned to Ricky, the two sharing a mournful look. He sucked in through his teeth and ran out as well before she could get away.

"Where are you goin'!?" hollered Ricky. Allen ignored him, calling out to her just as she was about to get in the car. Maya turned to him, furious.

"What? What could you possibly want?" She insisted. She was so stressed; with her internship, her mother, and now this? This was all too much for her. Why had she come back? Maybe to get closure, to tell Allen she missed him, or to scream about how he was so wrong about her.

"I... You...I don't know...well actually I'm not letting you get away again, that's what. Where are you going after this?" he asked, glancing at the car with uneasiness as he scrambled down the stairs. Maya caught his gaze and shook her head.

"I don't know… We got the evening off. The first exams are over," she murmured.

Allen gritted his teeth at the word. Exams. They were just exams. Was that what Maya thought of them nowadays?

"Well...walk with me." With a dismissive shrug of his shoulders, Allen began to walk down the dreary, cracked road. Maya glanced at the car, her eyes staring at her reflection. Clean, sharp, ghostly, short hair straightened to perfection, pristine white coat without a wrinkle. It felt off. It wasn't her, but this was the life she had chosen when her mother had announced that they were moving to the Skyline. She looked back at Allen as he slowed his pace, looking over his shoulder at her expectantly, as he meandered away.

There was a tug at her heart, a longing for her past. She dragged her feet forward, like walking through tar until she met him.

Allen smiled and held his hand out to her. She stared at it for a moment, before finally caving and taking it. A wash of relief passed over her, like a warm air that chased away the cold. A smile returned to her face. She felt at home with him, despite their 'history.'

Maya's ear rang and she frowned, pressing her blinking earpiece. Allen peered over with nosy curiosity, swaying on his feet as he let her walk ahead of him.

"Hello Maya, you haven't called. I was getting worried," crooned Maya's mother.

Maya scowled, sure her mother was not worried.

"It's ok mom, I haven't seen or been around any crimes," she said stupidly, her voice growing softer the longer she talked. Her mother sighed loudly. She found herself staring directly at the ground as if in shame.

"Have you spoken to him?" asked her mom, her voice aggressive. There was no hint of care for her former husband, or the fact that he was Maya's father. She didn't need to make the distinction. Maya knew by the disgust laced in her mother's voice that her dad was the man that she spoke of.

"Of course, not mom...you told me not to, obviously," She dug her knuckle against her forehead as if to rub her stress away by force. Allen shot her a confused look as he listened to this conversation that was strangling his friend. What was going on?

"Seriously Maya. I know you hate me and you think *he* hung the moon, but I did what I did because I had too. You hear me? Don't think for a second that you amount to anything in the eyes of the Elite. You are nothing without me, Maya. If it weren't for me, you'd stay in the Fence with that vile man, you hear? That man kept our family back, kept me...*us* back, and then got mad because I was trying to save you from that filthy life!" she scolded. Maya clenched her jaw.

Again...she was never enough for the woman. She was a straggler, a burden. Her mother made sure she told Maya that every second she could. She frowned at that last statement. Saving her? As in, she committed adultery.

She'd rather have stayed in the Fence than have a bad reputation in the Skyline. Everyone she went to class with knew about her and her story. How her mother had slept with elitists to get into the Skyline. How she was just a poser compared to all the perfect little elite children. *'Hang up on her! That'll show who's in charge!'* her eyes widened at the alarming thought. Her mom would just be angrier, and she didn't want to deal with her. It was better to just avoid stirring the pot.

"I know mom...I promise I won't see da-...I mean...*him*," she muttered. She could hear her mom purr with contentment on the other end.

"Good girl," she buzzed, before the line cut off and Maya was once again left to her own thoughts.

Allen caught up with her, his eyes narrowed, *'What's going on with you? What are you thinking?'* he wondered. "What...what was that?" he asked.

Maya stared at her feet, before she sniffed and kicked a rock dejectedly. The sun painted the sky a stark red, scars of navy clouds running across the expanse.

"That...Allen...Allen, I need to see my dad," she said quietly. Allen nodded slowly. He felt a twinge of jealousy. She was so lucky. She was so *lucky*. She was so incredibly *lucky* that she could say that. That she could see her family. That she *had* family. Allen would give anything to have such a broken family if it meant he could have one.

"I'll walk you, someone like you can't walk around in the open without some kinda bodyguard. I'll be your guard," he said. Maya smiled softly at him, and he couldn't help but lose himself in the depth of her eyes. So warm, reflecting the red sky, glowing, shimmering, capturing the evening star. Her eyes were as big as the dark night sky. He missed them so much. He had missed those eyes.

"Allen?" she asked, and he realized he had moved closer to her. She backed up and he smiled sheepishly.

"My bad, I just uh...haven't seen you in so long. You're just...so perfect," he murmured. She frowned, looking away from him. A silence stretched between them. *'Dumbass, why do you always have to run your mouth?'*

"Well come on, let's go see your old man," he snapped, marching forward. He glanced behind to see Maya begin to trail tentatively behind him.

*'I'm an idiot. She doesn't care about me. She's an Elite now. She's an **Elite** now, don't I understand what that means? She's not ever going to love me, or care about me, or anyone. They don't care. The Elite don't love, or care. If they did, Zech would be happy, I would be happy. Allen, let her go.'*

Fear

"I really can't believe he left me alone with you...to go follow that stupid girl. What does he see in her? Pulled him on a string for so long. Used him, I say. He never stops talking about her. She's...she's, oh forget it, you wouldn't understand." Ricky harrumphed as he gathered his tools. Zech watched him with a wary frown.

"Pulled him on string? Like chain?" He gasped, "Is she torturer!?" he barked, his hackles rising. Ricky's eyes widened and he held his hands up in alarm.

"Of course, she isn't! I mean, emotionally, probably, but she's not... You don't have to worry about her. Why don't you do something useful ya walnut for a brain, and help me fix my door," ordered Ricky. Zech let his tongue loll out in a dog-like smile and nodded.

"Yes," he replied as he plucked the door up with ease. He held it up where Ricky indicated. Ricky noted how easily he held it; his arms weren't even shaking.

"You're pretty strong, aren't you?" asked Ricky as he began to screw the hinges back in.

Zech lowered his eyes, and let out a whine that was barely audible. His tail sagged to the ground; something was clearly wrong with him, but Ricky ignored it.

"Well, we gotta find out what to do with you mate," he mumbled as he worked as quickly as possible. Zech glanced outside.

"I am not welcome here anymore. I went back to Home, but I never let them see me. I see myself in windows, I am scared. I don't want to scare the other children. Are you scared?" asked Zech, his piercing amber eyes trailing down to fall on Ricky.

Ricky didn't know how to answer that. He was terrified all the time. Terrified of the gangs, terrified of the Elite, terrified of losing resources, of losing his job, and of losing Allen.

Zech *was* terrifying, and Zech *meant* all of those things could happen. Zech's existence could be the catalyst of the gangs attacking... because the elite are attacking, and sending inevitable rewards, and that meant he'd lose everything, and that meant Allen could get killed, that Ricky could get killed. He *was* scared. He was *always* scared and more so now that Zech was a part of the equation.

Ricky looked up and met those eyes for a brief moment before he went back to focusing on the hinges. Yes, he was scared, but no one needed to know that. He fumbled one of the rusted nails, the small nail falling clumsily to the floor with a quiet clatter.

"I... I ain't scared. Not of you, anyway" he lied, clenching his jaw as he tried to fill his mind with handy work instead of thought. Zech sniffed in, his eyes narrowing.

"But you are," he growled. Ricky bounced up after stabbing himself with the screwdriver, and let out a groan of both pain and annoyance.

"And what are you? My therapist? I'm... Yes, I'm scared of a lot of things. I'm not scared of you... Unless you give me a reason to be. But you won't, right? Because if you did, then we'd have a problem," he snapped. Zech let out a dog-like whine, lowering his nose in thought.

"We do not have problem, I... also scared," he whimpered. Ricky sighed and rose on his tiptoes to fix the last hinge.

"Well, seems like we're in the same boat. We 'ave to get rid of you. We can't keep you around Zech, as much as Allen thinks we can. You're too..." he trailed off, narrowing his eyes as he scrutinized the monstrous being that towered over him, the tips of his ears touching the ceiling.

Zech tilted his head, studying the man before him who literally reeked with fear. His eyes went wide. He wanted to get rid of him? For the first time, Zech finally felt safe, even just a little, and he wanted to get rid of him? He felt a stirring in his chest, and the beast let out a low growl, his eyes dilating.

"You...get-get rid of m-me? You...you give me back to-to them? To the tor-torturers? I will rip-I will rip you to pieces!" he snarled, letting go of the door and slashing the wall with his claws.

Ricky shouted, lunging away from the monstrous beast snarling at him. As he hid behind the counter, he began to try and explain his motives before Zech did what he intended to do.

"No! I don't wanna give you back to the Elite! I... We're going to save you! You can't stay here. They'll find you here. We have to get you out of Magnus, that's the only way you'll be safe," he cried as Zech lumbered towards him. The fox poked his ginormous head over the counter, and Ricky screamed as his huge claw grabbed his shirt and heaved him over to face him. Ricky glanced at the ground, which was one foot below him.

Zech's snarling captured his attention again and he winced, staring straight into the eyes of the beast that was threatening his life because it was nothing more than... scared. Zech's eyes softened at this new understanding, and Ricky watched as those striking amber eyes filled with tears.

"I sorry," he whimpered, his claws slowly unclenched and dropped Ricky, who landed with a thud. Ricky wheezed, and ran a hand through his hair as he comprehended what had just happened.

"We're not going to hurt you, Zech. We're going to help you escape this place," he promised. Zech's ears flicked as he thought. Before Ricky could protest, Zech engulfed him in a hug, then spun the little man around. He squeezed Ricky so tightly he could barely breathe.

"You are- you are good friend to Zech. I will...pro...protect you with my...with my life. I sorry I scared you. I pr-promise no-no hurt will co-come to you, or to Allen," he thundered. Ricky wheezed, his legs flailing as he tried to reach the ground.

"Let...let me go!" he cried. Zech glanced down, and grunted with surprise at how purple Ricky's face had become. He dropped him. Ricky hit the ground once more, and doubled over as he coughed pathetically on the floor. Zech helped him up, chuckling a little as Ricky pushed him away, and stumbled to his couch.

"Thanks...thanks Zech. Really appreciate it," he wheezed. Zech stood awkwardly, his shoulders hunched. Finally, Ricky sat up, and rubbed his face.

"Ok. How do we do this? How do we get *you* out of the city? We'd need a ship, and I don't know how to fly one. There aren't any ships in the Ghetto either. All of them are in the Skyline...Oh...no! No, no, no! There's no way," he moaned. Zech's hackles rose at the mention of the Skyline.

"I no go back," he whimpered.

Ricky rubbed his eyes. "This is impossible!" He cried.

Zech whined and crouched on his knees. He moved over just enough to plop his head on Ricky's lap. Ricky pursed his lips and absentmindedly began to scratch Zech's ears. The corners of his doggish lips flicked upwards.

"Unless...the Medicum students, they're the only ones who come and go. We'd need to somehow smuggle you, a seven-foot-tall monster onto that submarine by the end of the term," he murmured.

Zech whimpered, flattening his ears to his head. "I no go back," he whispered.

Ricky nodded solemnly. "I know Zech, I know. We don't really have a choice though. If we're to get you out of Magnus, we need to go through the Skyline."

Zech sighed. He knew it was true, he trusted Ricky and Allen. They were sheltering him, of course he trusted them. Anything they said was right. Right?

Ricky scrunched his nose and began to pace around. Zech watched him, grinning goofily and following behind him like a shadow. He copied Ricky's gestures, putting his hand to his chin and running his hands over his head in exasperation.

"If only Maya would agree to work with us! This would be so much easier...what, what are you doing?" He asked, finally noticing the way Zech was copying him.

Zech smiled sheepishly, his ears falling back. "Nothing…" he giggled. Ricky frowned, but could not contain the laughter rising up from his belly.

Zech panted, laughing as well, but it sounded like a strange mixture of heavy breaths, barks and whines. His unusual laugh only fueled Ricky's cackle and he dropped to the floor, holding his stomach.

"What kinda...What kinda laugh?" He wheezed. Zech hovered over him, grinning practically from ear to ear.

"I have made it across water once, if you say it is best, I will do again," he uttered. Ricky stared at him, his grin growing as well. The two got up, and as soon as Ricky's feet landed on the ground, his eyes lit up in excitement.

"I've got it! If I disguised you as a mech, you'd be able to walk about in the Skyline unscathed, and if Allen and I disguised as Stratus, you could smuggle us onto the submarine!" He whispered with barely contained excitement.

Zech barked, and wagged his tail.

Ricky bounced on his feet and sprinted to the supply closet. He ripped out a sheet of blue paper and white charcoal.

Zech watched with growing excitement as Ricky swept everything off the table and draped the paper over it. Immediately he began to draw up plans for some kind of mechanical. An exo suit for Zech, who whined in bubbling joy.

As Ricky worked, he brought his hand up and rubbed Zech's back with newfound affection. Allen was right...he was one of them.

TEa FOr TWO

The house was shabbier than Allen expected, considering it was part of the Diamonds. Ivy grew up the walls, giving the weary looking house a breath of life.

Maya glanced around, amazed that the windows were still in good condition, but were stained with fingerprints, which threw her off. This place could do with a bit of spring cleaning, but something about that filled her with joy. Finally, she wasn't surrounded by plastic perfection.

She ran to the porch in a bolt of happiness, and Allen smiled as she pounded on the paint chipped door. There was a shout.

"I'm...I'm coming!" croaked a cracked, old voice. The door creaked open and out popped a slender face, eyes deep and tired, grey hair cropped, nose a bit bulbous, but still small, much like his daughter's. Their eyes met, and tears welled in the old man's eyes.

"Dad..." whimpered Maya. For too long her mother had kept her from contacting the "crazy, old man," demonizing him beyond belief. She couldn't believe she had finally made it here.

Her father pulled her close to him, hugging her tightly as he sniffled. Allen watched as the two embraced for what seemed like ages.

He scratched the back of his neck and smiled at the sight. At the same time as he smiled at their embrace, envy and the old sorrow of having never found his father filled him. He wanted more than anything to reunite with his own old man, and seeing Maya happy in the arms of her dad only made that old, but still bleeding wound in his heart hurt worse.

"I'll...see you later Maya," he said, frowning. Maya waved dismissively and he grunted, walking away. He felt bad, but then again, she wasn't really paying attention, so it didn't matter. He slid out the bottle of vodka and screwed off the cap. He needed to wash this awful day away.

"Maya...what are you doing back in the ghetto?" asked the slender old man. Maya felt a pang in her heart at the fact that he never even knew she was studying to be a surgeon.

"I'm an intern here...at the Medicum," she explained. Her father, who went by Tony, only nodded, his lips pursed.

Maya took in the old house she had grown up in and felt her heart wrench as her eyes welled up. So many memories...so many bad and good memories. Everything was mostly white except for the hardwood floors and a large fireplace that had been her favorite spot for stopping to think about things.

It was a much nicer house than Ricky's hole in the wall apartment, with hanging plants and candle light. The Diamonds were always so much nicer, and even had a taste of the Skyline. She never knew why her father had gotten this far, must've been years of working at the Medicum, which had definitely taken a toll on his health. Tony had always been an honest man. The weight of silence that hung between them was heavy.

"How's Amanda?" asked Tony. Maya winced at the mention of her mother. That woman was the last thing she wanted to talk about with her father, of all people.

"Oh...she's...Amanda." was all she could say. Her father knowingly nodded, that was the only answer he needed. He knew exactly what that meant.

Tony was in so much shock he had forgotten simple hospitality. All he could do was stare across the room at his daughter who had been taken from him for so long. He shook himself out of his stupor and quickly went into the kitchen.

"Do you want a drink? I have tea, I can make us some tea...We have a lot to talk about," he rambled, going to his white cabinets and digging through them to get tea bags.

Maya smiled softly and sat down at the dining table as if she had been called to supper. She had missed her father so much, yet being in his presence right now felt so wrong. She should've kept in touch with him. It felt so strange and yet filled her heart with a lightness just to get to be with him. However, the air was heavy and she didn't know what to talk about. All she wanted to do was cry in his arms, but she wasn't five, and she was trying to be strong.

"What's the Skyline like?" he asked after another moment of silence passed between them. Maya glanced up at him and frowned, deep in thought about how best to answer that question. How was she supposed to explain to him that it was nothing like she had wanted it to be?

It was beautiful, yes. It was a magnificent example of mankind's ingenuity. However, it was empty, it was cold, and no one cared about anything except for themselves.

It was empty without her father, that's what it was. She endured the Skyline. At least here she knew people actually cared about her; like her father... and Allen... A deep guilt settled on her heart. She had been so cold to them. The Skyline had gotten to her.

"Numbing," she replied, rubbing her temple. Tony chuckled wryly as he sat near the stove, watching the kettle with a close eye.

"Is it not everything you hoped it would be?" he asked. Maya shook her head. It was everything one could expect and hope for. It held all the promises Magnus had offered...but it was desolate.

"No, it's amazing. I just... It's empty. There's nothing, except my career there, that makes me happy. Every second mom is barking at me like some...I don't know. I just wish you could've come with us. I've been struggling to make my way. The only thing that's kept me going is knowing that you would be proud of me," she admitted. Her father blinked slowly, the tea kettle whistling behind them.

He quietly took it off the stove and poured them both the steaming water, before plopping in the tea bags. Maya sat, anxiously tapping her fingers.

"I see...you're a surgeon?" he asked, a shimmer of pride in his eyes. She smiled up at him and nodded. Her father carried the mugs of tea to the table and set them down. She watched as he paced from the dining room to the kitchen with milk and sugar.

Finally, he sat down and the two shared a content moment of nothing but sipping the tea. It was nice. She was beginning to grow accustomed to the silence.

"I remember my days at the Medicum...I always knew you'd follow in my footsteps. When your mother just up and left with you...I didn't know what to do...I figured I'd retire. I just didn't feel like...I wasn't inspired to go the distance to save lives anymore, because, I really just wanted to fall off the edge of the earth...So I left the Medicum. They replaced me with a new, fresh faced surgeon, Farley," he said as he sipped his tea.

Maya listened intently. Farley? Dr. Farley replaced her father? She smiled at the thought that her own father could've been teaching them. The smile turned into a frown the longer the thought lingered.

"Maybe you could work at the Medicum... I could provide you with a room and we could get back all the time we lost together," he said, his smile growing. Maya grinned and stood up. That sounded beautiful and perfect. Her eyes welled at the very thought. She could be with her father, and not live in a stale, stainless steel society. She wouldn't have to deal with the rumors, or her mother, and she could spend time with Allen...

She frowned. Allen... he wanted her so badly to join them in whatever they were planning. She could feel it. Some part of her heart tugged in that direction and she wanted to...but she had worked so hard to get to where she was now, to help them was to throw it all away.

"Dad...if you had to choose between your career or saving a life, what would you choose?" she asked, her voice quivering. Tony's eyes filled with thought at the question. He took another pensive sip of tea.

"It all depends on who's life is worth saving to you," he replied. Maya frowned at her father's response, staring down at the table as she ran the words back in her head over and over. Allen had told her that Zech was one of them. What did he mean by that?

"Dad, how do the Elite test their science?" she asked. Tony's eyes darkened and he looked away, refusing to meet her eye.

"They do what they have to do," he said curtly. Maya nodded. Of course. They did what had to be done. It was all necessary for the betterment of mankind. The Medicum tested on patients, people were exams… but it was a needed part of society. After all, how else would the city return to the surface? Zech…

"He's one of us…" she murmured. Of course. She had always known they used the Fencers as lab rats…maybe she had just hoped it was just her academy, and untested medicine. No, no it was so much more than that. Oh God.

Tony looked up, shooting her a quizzical look. She shook her head and stood up. She felt…dizzy. The ground swam beneath her, and she suddenly wanted to run as far away as possible.

Feral

Allen woke up with a jerk as he felt something prodding at him. His back was still healing four days after the incident with the mech. The poking brought a groan to his lips. Four days dealing with Ricky's feverish planning and Zech's slow moving education.

As his eyes opened so he could smack the living alarm clock, he came face to face with those bright amber eyes. Allen sat up, and ran a hand through his tangled hair to express his frustration.

"What do you want?" he asked, clearly irritated. He rubbed his eyes of the heaviness of deep sleep. Zech wagged his tail, his eyes bright with excitement.

"Morning, Ricky want us to go to junkyard" he stated matter of factly. Allen grimaced, but noted that Ricky must've decided to jump his plan into action. A wave of guilt washed over him as he realized he hadn't been much help. *'Typical, good job Allen,'* He sighed and nodded, rubbing his back as he went into the kitchen.

"Ah...I see. Well, wait for me to get ready, I guess," he grumbled. Zech followed him like a happy puppy, bent over so his head wouldn't hit the door jamb.

"Get ready...?" he asked with confusion. Allen rolled his eyes and yawned, turning on the lights and hissing slightly. He squinted, looking at Zech and grumbling under his breath about how this was *too early* to deal with so many questions!

"Yes! After I get a change of clothes, I'll help you get dressed a'ight?" he said, sticking his palms over his eyes so he wouldn't have to face the glaring kitchen lights. He sighed as he thought to himself, *'Taking care of this thing is like taking care of a toddler.'*

"...A'ight," Zech repeated, smiling. Allen glanced at him and chuckled softly, nodding his head with a small sense of happiness as already Zech had begun to take his mannerisms. He stooped down to get some food, frowning as the ice box was empty. They needed to get more food from the market, but the trucks wouldn't return until Wednesday. Guess he'd have to get a snack along the way.

Allen blinked as he felt eyes boring into him. He turned around, seeing Zech staring at him, waiting for him to do something.

"What?" he asked, clapping his hands awkwardly. Zech threw a skeptical look at Allen that he must've learned from Ricky and crossed his arms.

"You're not *getting ready,*" he accused, looking Allen up and down as if sizing him up. Allen shrugged nonchalantly.

"Of course, I am, Zech. Staring at the icebox is everyone's way of getting ready in the morning. Give it a go...but not for too long, the icebox gets insecure about people staring at it for too long and loses its chill," he lied, gesturing for Zech to look in the fridge. Zech's eyes brightened and he replaced Allen's spot with great enthusiasm.

"Ok!" he yipped, staring intently into the icebox in an attempt to *get ready* for the day. Allen grinned and nodded with amusement. That would get the fox out of his way for now, then off to the junkyard.

"Nice, keep it up!" he encouraged. Zech nodded slowly as Allen backed away into the bathroom. He began to brush his teeth, sacrificing the shower. He reached down for the water and carefully poured some on top of the brush, before quickly putting it back in the cabinet, then he glanced over as Zech poked his nose in.

"Go, get out!" He groaned, nudging Zech out from the bathroom and closing the door. He could hear Zech begin to walk away.

"Do you want me to keep staring in icebox?" he asked. Allen rolled his eyes and smiled wryly, waving his hands.

"Give the icebox a break. Go sit on the couch, or better yet, wake up Ricky," he suggested. *'It'd be nice if*

Ricky had to suffer this early wake up along with me.' he thought in amusement.

"Ricky?" asked Zech, making sure he had heard correctly. Allen groaned and nodded, opening the door and pointing down the hall in exasperation.

"Ok, get on with it," he ordered. Zech nodded and pointed down the hall, before scampering like a happy dog. Allen rolled his eyes playfully before going to get the brush to comb through his unkempt hair. He needed to cut it, but that cost resources. *'Why can't things just be free?'* he wondered.

"Ricky!" called Zech in the distance and Allen chuckled. Both men hated waking up early, especially considering they mostly stayed up at night talking about depression and drinking. Ricky hated to admit that he almost had the same knack for alcohol as Allen. There was a loud groan from Ricky's room and Allen snickered.

"Morning sunshine!" called Allen in a mocking sneer. Ricky stumbled out into the bathroom and narrowed his eyes.

"Oi, after you're done makin' yourself less disgusting, the both of you get out and do something useful, aye?" he grumbled, hitting Allen on the shoulder; careful to stay clear of Allen's still healing back. Allen laughed. Ricky's accent was thicker in the morning and Allen thought it was hilarious. He sighed playfully and nodded, pulling his shirt off and lumbering down the hall.

"That's the plan, bucko," he called, going into his hallway closet picked out a clean shirt. Ricky leaned against the doorframe and grunted.

"Shut your gob. Do we got any food?" he asked, looking curiously into the kitchen. Allen shook his head, slipping into a shirt and pulling his favorite brown jacket on.

"Nah, icebox is empty, at least with things you can make immediately. I'm sure the pantries have something," he informed, kicking his old pants off and hopping into a pair of ripped jeans. Ricky turned his head away.

"Damn. Ok," he grumbled. Zech lumbered over to him and dropped to all fours. He rubbed his head on Ricky's hip, Ricky sighed and scratched behind his ear. Zech closed his eyes in contentment, before he stood back up. Allen gestured for him to follow, and the beast gladly trailed him.

"Come on Zech, put this on," he said, going to the closet and pulling out one of Ricky's "kilts." Zech raced into the room, sniffing the skirt and scrunching up his nose.

"How?" he asked in confusion, putting his arms through it like he had done his shirt. Allen rolled his eyes and pushed his arms away.

"Stick your legs through it. It's what Ricky calls a kilt, but it's really just a fancy plaid skirt," he said slyly, a smug smirk on his face as he threw a look at his friend. Ricky gasped and dove for the kilt.

"It was passed through my mum's side of the family for generations. It has serious traditional value! Don't give him that," he growled, grabbing the kilt and jerking it away. Allen clenched his jaw as he remembered how important Ricky's heirlooms were to him. He sighed and looked at Zech.

"Yeah, well, he can't wear either of our pants," he pointed out, gesturing to the burly, long legs of the fox. Zech whined and bent his knees just a bit, thinking it would help him somehow fit into the smaller pants.

Ricky sighed and reached into his closet, digging for an article of clothing he was willing to give up.

"Here, wear this," he said, throwing something at Allen's chest. He caught it and held it up, his face one big question mark.

"What is it?" he asked, waving the obviously women's clothing in the still air. Ricky rolled his eyes, poking it, the fabric rippling like a disturbed puddle.

"It's the maternity skirt," he replied with a shrug. Allen shot him a puzzled look.

"Why in the world do you have a maternity skirt?" he asked, laying it on the bed. Ricky rolled his eyes and grabbed it, pulling it out.

"Cause it's stretchy and I was going to use it for another mechanical," he reasoned. Allen smirked and chuckled, grabbing it and throwing it over to Zech.

"Excuses, excuses," he mumbled playfully. Ricky growled under his breath and dug through his coat which had been lying on the floor.

"Shut up, it's true! Get him all dressed and then out ye go!" he said, giving Allen a halfhearted shrug.

"Fine! Fine," he said, holding his hands up in surrender. He glanced at Zech as he struggled to maintain balance on one leg and put the other one through the skirt.

"This is weird," he muttered. Allen burst out laughing. Zech pressed his ears to his head and laughed along, losing balance and steadying himself on the wall. Quickly he pulled it up on his waist and looked down. Allen chuckled slightly at the look.

"Tell me about it. Are you comfortable?" he asked, digging through the closet to find one last thing. Zech looked up and nodded.

"I'm ok," he said, jumping up just a bit. When Allen couldn't find anything, he turned and tore down the black curtains Ricky had put up. The move caused Ricky to shout in protest, but his words trailed off into a grumpy murmur. *'That should work.'* Allen thought matter of factly.

"Cool. Here put this on, I got you," he said, draping the curtain onto the fox and wrapping a sash around the neck. He tied it loosely, forming a crude hood. Zech looked unsure and glanced back.

"Cloak?" he asked. Allen chuckled and nodded, pulling the makeshift hood over the fox's head. The cowl hung low over his nose and Zech whined, lowering his head even further so he could see. He looked like a little, well huge, gremlin.

"Yeah man!" exclaimed Allen, glancing back at Ricky, "he's getting it!" he called. Ricky glanced up and rolled his eyes with annoyed endearance.

"Whatever. You're both ready, now leave me to my peace!" he ordered. Allen patted Zech's cloak, sticking in any indication of the fox, his tail, his long snout, any tufts of fur. He stepped back to observe his handiwork and grimaced. Zech looked like a hunchback. Ricky nodded and walked over to the two.

"Ah yes...The Hunchback of Notre Dame. Glad to see you're incorporating your literature of the surface into his snazzy, new look. I think we should call him Quasimodo." Allen punched playfully at his shoulder.

"Yeah, yeah, I'm working on it," he said with a wry smile. Ricky chuckled and shoved the two out of his room, Allen laughed under his breath.

"Come on Zech, it's time to take you to the junkyard."

Zech barked and pointed at a hastily written list Ricky had drawn up last night. Allen reached over and grabbed it

"I'm ex... excited!" he exclaimed. Allen smiled and rubbed Zech's back. He couldn't blame, they hadn't been out of the apartment since Zech first graced them with his terrifying presence.

"Hey, I promise bud, while Ricky's working on your exosuit, we're gonna work on your syntax," he said with a determined nod.

Zech immediately focused on Allen's face, the hood slipped down again. Allen rolled his eyes, but chuckled anyway.

"What?" he asked, tilting his head. Allen waved his hand as if trying to reach for the things he wanted to say. Once he grasped it, he huffed and looked at Zech.

"We'll start slow. Hopefully we can find some nice children's books in the junkyard. Sometimes you can find those kinds of things," he explained with a grin. Zech copied the grin, but growled in irritation as his hood flopped off.

"What do you like...like read?" He asked, trying to piece together the right words. Allen glanced at Zech and shook his head. One way or another, he had to help Zech sound more normal. Maybe it was selfish for him to think that, but if selfish pride was what it took to teach something, it'd have to work.

"Like *to* read," he corrected. Zech nodded in understanding and took a mental step back to reform his sentence.

"Ah...what do you like *to* read?" he asked again, smiling as he got it right. Allen grinned softly and patted Zech's back with a heartwarming joy at being able to share with his new friend what his father had so painstakingly taught him so many years ago.

"That's a good question. I haven't read much of anything in a while. I think I'd have to say...this old book of poems...Road Signs. It sounds stupid but, it was everything to us. When we lived on the surface, my old man had this collection of books, and he would read that one to me every night...I had one special poem..." He trailed off, remembering the poem his dad had book marked: "Dreams of the Child." It used to remind him he could do anything. He could be anyone... Now it just reminded him of who he had actually become, and the people he had lost in the process.

"Poem?" The fox's question pulled Allen from his depressing thoughts so he plastered a fake smile on his face.

"I'll show you later. Let's just focus on what we're doing...Put your hood up man!" he groaned when he finally noticed Zech's exposed face. Zech grunted and flipped the grey hood back over his head, flattening his ears.

Damon walked around the warehouse, observing the Stratus mechs. His ear began to ring and he tapped his earpiece.

"This is Lieutenant Rose speaking," he said gruffly. Damon found himself staring into the black mask of a gorgon, it's mechanical strands of snake-like hair slumped neatly along its stark, silver shoulders.

"Hey Damon, it's me," said Veronica. Damon smiled and began to type in an access code into the gorgon.

He greeted her and the two exchanged familiar pleasantries, before a silence hung between them.

"Is there a reason you're calling me?" he asked, the Gorgon's face blinking to life, a white screen ready for orders.

"I've been scouting the ghetto… You know these people...they're really, they're really...suffering," she whispered. Damon clenched his jaw. He remembered the way Raven would speak to him. *'These people, they're suffering. They need our help. We should help them.'* It had been that mindset that had brought about her execution.

"Careful soldier," he murmured. He held up a barcode from his watch and the gorgon scanned it. Its face lit up with a wanted poster, the words a bright blue, a holographic outline of subject two hundred twenty-seven popping up. More physical data about the Fence's coordinates downloaded onto the mech's program. The gorgon's hair came to life and writhed about, testing the air.

"Have you found anything worth reporting?" he asked. Veronica was silent for a moment. Damon then saved the information and powered the gorgon down. It was tagged, it's screen a dark sea-green with a tag number instead of completely black. It would soon be shipped out.

"Veronica?" he whispered, leaving the warehouse and walking out to the landing pad where his ship was waiting for him.

Veronica sat on a fire escape, looking down at an alleyway. A mangy rat was rummaging through the garbage, and as it dug out trash, she saw the outline of a human face. She grimaced in disgust as she watched the rat begin to pick at the man's rotting flesh.

"How did it get this bad for them?" she asked. Damon sighed, and she could tell he didn't want to talk about anything other than her mission. She knew why. They were both under harsh scrutiny due to her mother's mutiny and execution.

"Well, Veronica, you can help them by finding subject two twenty-seven. Who knows what kind of terror that creature will wreak upon them," he reasoned. Veronica shook her head as she swallowed down bile. She felt a burst of compassion and grabbed her pistol, aimed, and shot. The rat squealed as it slumped over dead.

"What was that?" asked Damon. She sighed and began to walk down from the fire escape, and made her way to the dumpster.

"I was just taking care of a rat, don't worry," she grunted. She grabbed a silicon pipe and moved the rat away from the man's face.

He was an old man, his face wrinkled and pale. He smelled like he had been dead for a few days, but she could still see his humanity, who he once was. She didn't know what kind of life he lived, but people were often products of their environment. It just wasn't fair.

"Listen, Ronny, I need you to focus and find the subject. I'm sending a find and seek gorgon to take care of it, but I need you to find out where it's hiding. Can I trust you with that?" he asked. Veronica stared at the old man and clenched her jaw. This was so unfair.

"Yes sir," she murmured. Damon fell quiet, and she heard the hum of the ship as its engine started.

"Ok...I'm trying my best to keep you on the force, but you have to do your part," he grunted. Veronica nodded and looked away, packing her pistol back in its holster.

"I know, I know." She sighed and hung up, clenching her fists. Was this subject even that much of a danger?

She began to think about Dr. Anand's words. She knew that the Medicum was using untested medicines like guinea pigs. These people weren't treated like people, they were treated like lab rats. What if this subject was just another lab rat? Would her mother be proud of her? *'No. No she wouldn't be, and you know it,'*

"What are we finding?" asked Zech as they walked through the indicated paths of the junkyard. After trekking through the Fence, they had to climb through the Drop Off, a barricade of sharp volcanic rock that gave way to a steep hill of gravel. Below that was the junkyard, well technically. It was a landfill for the elite, but to the Fence people... Well, one man's trash was another man's treasure. It was basically a supermarket where everything was free. An all for one department store.

Allen grunted and looked down at the list Ricky had given them. His eyes scanning the land fill.

"Um, let's see. Ok. So, we need steel parts. You'll find them on that side. There on the old automobiles. Rip them apart," explained Allen, and he pointed at a cluster of old broken-down cars. Their paint was chipped away, and their metal was rusted. It would be easy to tear apart. Zech's eyes widened as he studied it.

"How we carry?" he asked, glancing at the vehicles. Allen stopped to think about it and shrugged, digging through the piles of trash.

"Um...good question...too many questions and not enough answers...Oh!" he exclaimed, jerking up as his eyes caught the glimmer of a shopping cart. Zech followed his eyes and squinted.

"Hm?" he grunted, looking back at him. Allen gestured for him to follow. He led Zech over and grabbed it, smiling.

"Go find another one of these," he ordered, looking around, and chuckling as he brought down the front basket. He slipped the paper on and balanced it. *'Perfect,'* he thought with triumph. Zech looked around and whined slightly.

"Is it safe?" he asked with apprehension, gulping as he sniffed for any intruders. Allen glanced at him and frowned, nodding his head curtly.

"Of course. Don't worry you'll be fine. If anything tried to attack you, you'd probably rip it in half," he reasoned. Zech froze at the words, flashes of his escape from the lab playing in his mind. He closed his eyes and shook it away, willing himself to move forward and away from the haunting images of the carnage he'd left. Zech focused on the shopping cart instead.

"Right..." he muttered. Allen smiled and hunched back down, digging through the junk. Screws, wires, pistons. He would probably find those items in the vehicles. With a huff, he went to the wreckage and glanced back as Zech climbed up a hill of garbage.

"Alright get to work!" he called, holding his fist up with excitement. The fox in the distance held up his fist as well and barked. Allen chuckled, grabbed a baseball bat and then opened the hood of the first wreck.

He smiled as he remembered playing in the junkyard with Ricky, when his best friend had found his love for building mechs. Back then it was still semi-safe to roam in the junkyard. Nowadays, gangs fought over the territory like wolves. In this place, he was the muscle and Ricky was the brains. The day was...

...crystal clear. The sky was a piercing blue, like a tropical sea above them. Allen and Ricky were playing tag in the crumbling piles of discarded metal and glass. Allen was it, and that meant Ricky was in trouble. Allen launched himself over a car hood, pouncing on the scrawny ginger.

"You're it!" Ricky tumbled, the shove throwing him off balance as Allen stared in shock.

"Oh my God! Are you ok?" Allen found himself bubbling with laughter despite his concern as he went to help Ricky- who had landed in a pile of scrap metal.

Ricky stared to the side; his eyes had caught something. Allen looked at him questioningly and held out his hand to help him up. Ricky smiled brightly and took it, shaking off his pain.

"Are you...good?" Allen asked, looking him over for any signs of blood. Ricky waved him off, stooping down and grabbing a metal claw. Allen looked curious and watched as he tried to tug it out of the pile.

"Yeah, I'm fine. Help me get this," grunted Ricky, pulling with all his might. Allen ran a hand through his short-cropped hair. It had finally started to grow past peach fuzz from when they shaved off his dreads.

"Get what?" he asked, studying the mass of tarnished metal that Ricky was playing tug of war with. Ricky sighed in exasperation and looked at him with growing irritation.

"Just, pull it out with me!" he groaned. Allen cocked his head and smirked. He patted Ricky on the back and squatted down, putting his hands on the arm Ricky was pulling at.

"I don't think you're ok. You took a hard fall," he began to tease. Ricky rolled his eyes.

"Just stop being stupid and help!" he demanded, trying to take control back from their bicker. Allen rolled his eyes and did as he was told with an exasperated sigh.

"Alright, alright! Geez..." he grunted. The two heaved until the scrap flew out, the boys falling onto their backs. Allen came face to face with the dead, big, light bulb eyes of an old rusty mechanical. He wheezed and shoved it off of him. Ricky jumped up and turned it over, smiling.

"This is so cool!" he exclaimed, wiping some of the dust away with care. The mechanical was rounded, with a bell-shaped head and a copper body under heavy green tarnish. Allen shrugged, not understanding his friend's fascination.

"What's so cool about it?" he asked with genuine confusion. Ricky studied it with a glimmer in his eyes, a soft smile growing on his face as he stared at it lovingly.

"It looks like one of us..." he murmured. Most of the mechanicals resembled animals, and they didn't have a face; but Allen knew for sure that the one in front of them looked nothing like them.

"Are you tripping?" Allen grunted, snickering quietly. Ricky rolled his eyes and stood up, looking at his best friend. Then he picked up the bulky mechanical.

"I- just- just help me carry it back to the Home," he pleaded, making a failed attempt to charm him with puppy-dog eyes. Allen pushed his face away with a sigh of exasperation.

"What? No. No way. I'm sorry but what would that bat say to us if she saw us carryin' this hunk'a garbage?" he asked, gesturing to the mechanical at their feet. Ricky groaned.

"It's not a hunk of garbage Allen! I... I want to fix it up. I can do it," He insisted. Allen looked concerned. He'd never seen Ricky work with mechanicals. All he ever did was make wooden turtles for some of the kids.

"What makes you say that?" asked Allen skeptically. Ricky looked back at the mechanical and frowned.

"I... I just want to do this Allen. Don't be a jerk. Help me." he grumbled, wiping off more dust. Allen rolled his eyes but shrugged, finally giving in to his friend's wishes.

"Fine, but if we get in trouble, it's your fault." he stated unequivocally. He circled Ricky and grabbed the Mechanicals feet. Ricky grinned and nodded happily.

"Fair enough." he said with a nonchalant shrug. Allen smiled as the two heaved it away.

About two months had passed and Allen had completely forgotten about the project, until Ricky shot through the door, running in with a swoop of his arms. Allen shouted in shock at the unexpected visit; not even a knock at his door!

"I finished!" cried Ricky with triumph. Allen's eyes widened and he glanced around, skeptically.

"The...machine?" he asked to jog his memory. Ricky nodded with excitement and held up a remote control. He began pushing buttons and pulling a joystick. At first, Allen was a bit annoyed and didn't believe him, until the bronze and copper, round little mech waddled into the room, bright eyes shining with a sense of promise. Allen's eyes widened and he grinned, patting Ricky on the back.

"I always knew ya' had it in ya!" he exclaimed, grasping his friend in a celebratory hug. Ricky wheezed, laughing slightly and shoving him away; a proud smile on his face. He ran to stand beside his new and improved mech and patted its head.

"Yeah! Say hello to Tod!" he introduced. The two boys laughed and began to play with the mech...

Ricky never stopped building after that. Even when Tod had been destroyed by bullies in the Home, he kept at it. Allen always admired Ricky; the man never gave up. He smiled softly before glancing over at Zech who was staring at him expectantly.

"Got the shopping cart?" he asked, tossing a set of buckles and belts into the basket. Zech smiled and nodded, gesturing to the cart that was just a bit bigger than Allen's. *'That will work perfectly.'* he thought with approval.

"Yes… what you got?" asked Zech, sniffing at the basket filled with scraps. Allen frowned, shaking his head at the incorrect speech.

"What *have* you got...I gathered some of the items from the car, now all I need you to do is rip it apart, can you do that?" he replied, gesturing to the automobile. Zech whimpered slightly but nodded in cooperation.

"Yes," he said cautiously before gripping the rusted metal and heaving. His muscles bulged. The steel groaned and ground in a hiss of metal that made Allen glad Zech was so big and strong, before it finally gave up and ripped off in chunks. Allen grinned in triumph at the destruction.

"Hey thanks, pal," he said, patting his back. Zech smiled triumphantly before going to tear the rest apart. Allen nodded and left him to it, walking around and rummaging through the garbage.

He grunted and dug out a cuckoo clock, the little silver bird stripped of its white feathers, its little body mottled with dirt and rot. Allen frowned and gently stroked the small metal bird with his thumb. He was sad it had ended here. With a sigh, he opened the clock and began jerking the gears and straps out. He pocketed the bird and set the wooden clock down. It was rotten, falling apart, and therefore useless. He carefully wiped his hands of splinters and went back to Zech.

"Hey, are you done with that?" asked Allen, gesturing to the car with impatience. Zech glanced up from his perch on top of the car, in the middle of tearing off the roof.

Allen cocked his head in expectancy, and Zech ripped off the rest, another screech of metal tearing through the silence and sending Allen's ears reeling with the loud cacophony of metal being shredded to manageable pieces by the beast. Once Zech had finished tearing off the last piece, he hopped down and tossed the sheet of metal in the cart.

"Yes, I am," he grunted, smiling sheepishly. Allen grinned and nodded, walking around the mostly naked skeleton of the car, the inside still intact. He kneeled down and pointed to a cluster of engine parts.

"Awesome. A'ight, let's get the pistons and head out. I don't want to be here too long," he mumbled.

Zech nodded and split the chassis apart, ripping the pistons out and setting them in the cart. He tilted his head, catching onto the last of Allen's sentence.

"Why not?" he asked, his ears pressing to the back of his head in worry. Allen sucked through his teeth and shrugged dismissively.

"This isn't exactly public turf anymore. We need to leave. Let's go. We got what we came for," he explained, pulling on Zech's coat. Zech nodded and pulled up his hood. Allen grimaced, feeling a strong sense of curiosity and dissociation. How in this God Forsaken universe had Zech ended up on his doorstep?

"Zech, how did you get here?" he asked, wiping his eyes slightly in regret for asking an intrusive question, but he thought it would be useful to know. Zech frowned slightly.

"I...I, I was chased by monsters, scary night. I don't want to think about it," said Zech, his eyes welling up. Allen frowned and hesitantly reached out to the fox, his hand resting on the giant's shoulder.

"I understand not wanting to talk about something. You never have to tell anyone anything if you're uncomfortable with it. I get that, I've been through scary nights," he admitted. Zech looked at Allen in amazement.

"You...you do?" he asked. Allen chuckled as they walked slowly through the junkyard, heaving the heavy carts was a bit of work.

"Well sure, everyone does. You're never alone. 'Sides, I'm your friend." Allen nodded at his statement. He wanted so badly to help this creature, it tugged at his heart and sobered him. He wasn't used to being sober. Zech smiled and put his hand on Allen's shoulder as well.

"We are friend. You are best friend to Zech," said Zech with a grin. Allen smiled back and the two walked on in contented silence.

Allen looked around, hearing a few gruff voices and pointed. Zech growled under his breath and turned as shadows played along the stacks of junk.

The fox's hackles rose and he bared his teeth, taking a few shuffles back before locking eyes with Allen.

The man stood with a scolding look, and Zech shook away his caution, grabbing his cart. Allen followed suit and the two sprinted, the wheels rattling on the gravel.

"Hey! Who's ova' dere?" barked a gruff voice. Allen cursed and glanced up at the hill as they approached. The Badgers! He couldn't believe his luck.

He stepped off, holding onto the back and riding the cart down the uneven path. Zech looked startled as he flew past.

Zech glanced back before mimicking Allen and pushing off. The two sailed down the hill, Allen having to use all of his strength to keep the cart on course. The large cart swerved and almost flipped over, but Zech grasped it and dug his foot into the ground.

There was a blast of heat and Zech cried out in terror as his cloak caught on fire! The men behind them were chucking flares at them! Zech grabbed the flame and yowled as his hand cupped the heat. He put it out, but seared off some of his fur in the process.

The hill levelled out and Allen grabbed Zech's cart.

"Come on!" he exclaimed. Zech heaved for air, and the two sprinted to the Drop Off. Allen clenched his jaw as he looked for the best way to climb. With a burst of strength, Zech heaved his cart over his head and charged up, switching it over his back and hobbling over.

Allen took a brief instant to admire Zech's strength, but looking back, he saw the gang was getting closer. Zech hopped back over, grabbed Allen's cart and started sprinting. Allen followed behind, grabbing a stone and tossing it, the rock struck one man in the face.

Zech and Allen sprinted, pushing the carts away as maneuvered around the potholes. Finally, they dipped under the cover of another street.

Allen could hear the gang hollering and pounding after them. He peeked out, and saw them prowling around the entrance of the Junkyard.

The majority of the Badgers backed down, satisfied they had chased them out, except for one straggler who began to chase after them. Allen smirked and looked at Zech.

"We can take 'im," he grunted, rolling his sleeves up. Zech flipped his hoodie up in preparation to walk through the crowded streets before looking at Allen in confusion.

"You sure?" he asked, tilting his head. Allen glanced up and nodded, not only was Allen strong enough to take on one guy, he also had Zech to scare the guy lifeless.

"I'm positive. Let him come to us. On the count of one...two…" he counted, looking over and seeing the man approach. Zech growled in impatience, his muscles rippling as he shifted.

"*Three!*" he snarled, launching himself into the street and grasping the man, slinging him into the intersection where Allen had hidden himself. Allen, however, was so taken aback by Zech's eager attack, he was knocked down, the guy falling on top of him.

"You!" breathed the man as they sat tangled together on the cratered street. Remembrance flickered through Allen's mind. It was one of the men that had beaten him for the whiskey! Peter! The two had never gotten on well, even when Allen was a Badger.

Allen sneered and despite his position, knew he'd win. He wouldn't allow himself to lose to this asshole again. His arm shot up, elbowing the guy in his nose, blood spurting out. The man, scrawny and drenched in sweat roared in pain, punching blindly as tears welled in his eyes. Already, his nose began swelling.

Allen's head flicked away, grinning as Zech's shadow hovered above. The fox suddenly whipped into action, dragging him off and swinging him into the streaked glass of a closed down business. The glass shattered around the criminal and Allen rolled onto his feet, hopping up the ledge and heaving the man up, pinning him to a wall and sucker punching him square in the jaw. His tooth shot out and Allen laughed triumphantly.

"It's an eye for an eye and a tooth for a tooth as they say," he snarled. The man panted, shaking his head in pain.

Allen wriggled his loose tooth that had been knocked out weeks before and the man gagged slightly, blood seeping from his mouth. Zech growled and approached them and Allen glanced up, his eyes widening as he saw that the fox's pupils were thin slivers of black against almost glowing amber irises. His fangs were bared, and for a second, Allen was terrified. He stumbled away as Zech flexed his hands.

"Enemy…" he uttered as the man slid down the wall. His paws, which seemed covered in soot despite the fiery red of the rest of his body, shot forward and grabbed him by his shirt, heaving him back up. The man's eyes flashed with sheer terror and Allen shot a questioning look at his giant friend.

"Zech?" he asked, shuffling forward, and right then and there, it was like he was paused and the rest of the world was put into slow motion.

His senses proved useless, and his legs betrayed him, and all he could do was watch as Zech, his arm a blur of speed, punched through the man's chest. Allen was too shocked to even question how that had been possible!

The sharp slap of flesh gave way to a crunch and blood spat out, spilling onto the shattered glass covering the floor. Allen's eyes widened with absolute horror at the gore. He wanted to stop Zech, but he didn't know how. Besides, it was too late. His feet caught and he stumbled forward. Time sped up again and he found his voice once more.

"Zech, no!" he cried in vain, losing his footing on the shards of glass. His hands planted themselves on the filthy floor, and he looked up, immediately regretting it when he saw Zech begin to jerk his hand out, the man's chest making a sickening sucking sound as his heart was ripped out of his chest. Allen felt his stomach convulse, as a shudder ran up his whole body.

Zech's fist was clasped around something that was shooting blood, leaving a big gaping hole in the man's chest. He dropped a beating heart on the floor, Allen's eyes widening in horror as it rolled over to him.

He choked and closed his eyes, hearing the body slump on the ground. Allen looked up to find his body sprawled out like a rag doll. He flung himself away from the spurting organ in disgust and terror, scowling to fight back the bile building in the back of his throat.

"Hell! What!? We weren't supposed to kill him!" he hollered, voice cracking, as he looked at the man; a bloody mass on the floor.

Zech's ears flicked, his tail stiff, the end tipping ever so slightly. Allen leaned over, his stomach rolling at the sight of the internal organ still beating and gurgling blood. His eyes squeezed shut as he felt the contents of his stomach erupting from the back of his throat, and he puked in horrified disgust, eyes welling from the stress. He coughed, wiping the dribble of stomach acid from his lips with a shaking hand.

He grew suddenly alert as he heard a growl emanate from the fox. Zech spun around to him and barked, his eyes still slits of hatred and anger.

"Zech! It's me, Allen!" he exclaimed, stumbling back, his legs still weak. Zech stared at him for a long moment that seemed to stretch in time, and Allen suddenly began to realize just exactly what had escaped from the Skyline. Ricky was right, this was insane!

Zech blinked, his ears drooping and he backed away, his pupils dilating as he shook his head, bringing his hand to his face. He glanced at the blood and whined, scurrying away, his entire body racked with tremors.

Allen's eyes widened at the reaction and he hesitantly stepped over to the fox, his shaking hand cautiously outreached in compassion.

"I'm sorry, I didn't...I didn't *mean* to! I- I don't know *what* happened!" he sobbed, Allen nodded and reached over to put a calming hand on Zech's head, cautiously scratching his ears. The fox closed his eyes and took a deep breath.

"It's ok... you're not in trouble," Allen reassured, putting his hand on the fox's broad shoulders. Zech gulped and looked down, gasping slightly as he saw his bloodied arms.

"My hands..." he croaked, his voice shaking, flashes of his memory replaying in his mind. The Stratus, the blood, the Chimera! Zech squeezed his eyes shut, trying to ward off the painful memories.

Allen clasped Zech's hand in his and looked down at it. He didn't do it on purpose, something came over him. If only he knew what it was. This definitely complicated things.

He glanced back at Zech; the fox's amber eyes wide with morbid fear. Allen gulped and shook his head, smiling to ward of the horror.

"We'll wash them, you'll be fine," he consoled. Zech looked doubtful and glanced at the man, squeezing his eyes shut and looking away immediately.

"I don't want that happen again," he whimpered. Allen clenched his jaw slightly, he had to make sure Zech was going to be safe.

"It's ok, alright?" he repeated, smiling softly again. Zech shook his head, covering his face in shame.

"No...it not," he breathed, his body shaking with sobs. Allen shook his head and stood up, looking around at the mess. He swallowed his disgust and fear. He looked down at Zech and clenched his jaw. *'He's scared... just think about what he's gone through to escape. You and Ricky are the only ones who have shown him kindness. You have to be there for him, you're all he has,'* thought Allen, his eyes softening with understanding.

"Here, get up, don't look at him, cover your eyes. Help me get this stuff home and we'll clean you off. It won't happen again. We'll work on it," he swore.

Zech glanced up at him and blinked hard, slowly standing up, covering his eyes again. "Promise?" he whimpered, hiccupping from the uneven breaths in his chest. Allen frowned, but nodded, patting the giant's shoulder.

"Promise," he muttered, leading Zech out from the horrifying scene. They got their carts and went down the road, passing through a thick cloud and entering the busy streets of the ghetto. No one asked questions when someone walked through their midst covered in blood. They kept their heads down...and maybe that was a good thing.

The Power Plant

Ricky sat tiredly at the assembly mech, his toolbox sitting beside him as he opened one of the gear boxes. He had worked the overnight shift and the large warehouse was filled with a cacophony of noise that bounced around in his skull. Mechs blew out steam as they performed their necessary functions. Workers droned on, quiet murmurs passing through them.

The Plant powered the entire city of Magnus with Nuclear Energy, and was an extremely risky place to work. It was in the Ghetto because the workers, *Fencers*, were expendable.

The blueprints for Zech's exosuit were stashed in his toolbox. For most of the day he had secluded himself to write them. It would've been easier to do at home, but he was a responsible working citizen...with a warning for already having been late, so he wasn't about to raise any more suspicion. He was already on the gossip radar. To make matters worse, he had gone through old prints of the Stratus mech designs, trying to find any weaknesses that could possibly help them, which could also, potentially, earn him a higher spot on the watchlist.

While he had tried to hide out to work on the blueprints, the stress of the time limit ate away at his mind. He was supposed to be fixing the faulty machine, but he had different ideas.

He glanced around and scratched his plume of red hair anxiously, looking for someone who could've been watching him. Anyone, that's who, but he saw no one around him, so he decided now would be his moment. He knew Allen wouldn't be able to find everything he needed.

He opened the circuit board, his hand reaching for his pliers as he found the disc; a circular coding made to fit every mech, with a hollow glass ball in the center, and two coils on the inside that would spark electricity. He slipped the disc into his box, digging around to find the replacement disc the shop had given him. Apparently, the one he had taken was faulty. He was supposed to return it so it could be sent to the programmers. He knew he could fix it though; despite the fact it could get him in trouble.

He got off the floor, smiling triumphantly as the mech hummed to life, and continued with its program.

Ricky patted the Mech, a proud smile on his face for pulling it off. He glanced around, the Power Plant workers performing their duties mechanically. He jogged over to one of his colleagues, trying to think of an excuse to leave that didn't require too many words.

"Patrick! Hey, I was wondering if you could help me with some calculations?" asked his coworker. Ricky glanced at her, stuttering and rubbing the back of his neck. He was never good at talking to people. It wasn't that he was shy, no, just awkward.

"Luna, uh...actually, um...I... if I help will...will you tell them that I'm taking a lunch break?" he fumbled through his words, keeping his head down as he tried to think up a good excuse to leave. Luna arched an eyebrow at him.

"Uh...sure? Why can't you do that yourself?" she asked, holding up her calculator and the equation she couldn't get quite right. *'Uh because if I tell them they'll demand the disc I just took from that faulty mech, and then I'll have to give it to them, and I'm trying to steal it, but I'd never tell you that, so can you please just do what I ask?'* he thought with growing frustration. He looked up at her and shrugged, taking her problem from her hands.

"I don't really like talking to the supervisors," he murmured as he punched in the numbers after rewriting the exponential equation. She nodded in understanding. Ricky awkwardly jerked his hand up to give her the paper, the answer circled haphazardly, his numbers a bit hard to read.

She squinted, trying to decipher what he had written, looking up at him in confusion. He wasn't very popular among the other Power Plant workers. Most just knew him as the loner mechanic. The only time anyone ever talked to him was when they couldn't do something math related. Ricky knew it too, but he tried to not let it bother him.

"Eight thousand, sorry...my...my handwriting is kinda all over the place, you accidentally forgot to multiply the exponent, which is really important, so just keep that in mind next time you do inventory. Alright thanks; bye!" he rambled, his voice cracking as he left.

She frowned, looking after him as he sprinted away. Luna only shrugged, and immediately forgot him.

Ricky raced down the street, the giant Plant growing smaller and smaller as he pushed himself further into the Ghetto's streets, his toolbox bouncing lightly in his hand.

He completely lost his footing when a slight body barreled into him. He went flying, his back hitting the ground hard as he fell, his face scrunched in shock and pain. He groaned, rolling to his stomach.

"Ricky? Oh, my goodness, are you ok? I didn't see you!" said Maya, her face wide with concern as she held out her hand to help him up. Ricky waved her off, kicked his legs under him and lumbered to his feet.

"I can tell..." he grumbled bitterly. He wiped his hands off, picked up his tool box, and checked to make sure the disc was ok. He sighed in relief when he found no scratches or breaks.

He shot Maya a look of contempt. He wasn't exactly fond of her after their last encounter...or any other time for that matter. Allen complained too much and Ricky was loyal.

"What...what's that?" she asked, gesturing to disc. He glanced at her and shoved it back inside, closing the tool box.

"It's nothing, don't worry about it," he murmured. She looked at him questioningly. Ricky stood up and rolled his shoulders as he avoided eye contact. Why was she even here?

"Well...what do you want? You wouldn't be walking over here without a reason. What is it?" He asked. He shouldered past her and Maya stuttered. She stumbled after him, and tried to keep up with his long stride.

"W-what did Allen mean when he said Zech was one of us?" she asked tentatively, as she toyed with the hem of her coat like she so often did.

"I don't know Maya, what do you think it means?" he asked, cocking a bushy, red brow at her.

Maya scowled at his response. Ricky couldn't help but find a bit of amusement in it. He had never really liked her. She always seemed like she thought she was better than everyone. He hated how much Allen talked about her; if he could count all of their conversations, eighty percent of it would be about Maya. How perfect she was. How much better she was than them. How much Allen hated that she left, a void in his heart. It was so stupid! *She* was stupid!

"I don't know! Why does everyone talk in riddles with me! I'm being kept in the dark!" she cried. Ricky groaned, rubbing his forehead. He didn't have time for this, and she was really beginning to irritate him.

"Maybe it's because you've always been in the dark! You've never seen the Ghetto the way Allen and I have! You lived in the Diamonds! Your father was the head surgeon of the Medicum. You had everything, and then you moved up in life and went to the Skyline to party it up!"

"You don't know anything about me!" shot Maya. The two faced each other, Ricky glaring at her with a cold scowl. He narrowed his eyes as he watched hers well up.

'Oh God; don't pull that shit on me,' he thought. He could feel his annoyance boil over and spill out into hot anger.

"I know enough," he hissed. Maya pursed her lips, blinking away her tears. She would not show weakness in front of this asshole.

"You have no idea what I've been through, what it took to get me out of this… You know…I was coming back because I wanted to help; but no! I'm not dealing with this," she breathed, and with that, she turned away, brushing her tears from her away.

Ricky rolled his eyes, letting out an angry puff of laughter. "Good! We don't need you anyway! Go back to the Skyline, Elitist!" he hollered, his jaw clenched in rage. He watched with a sick kind of satisfaction as she stormed away. With a smug roll of his shoulders, he turned and jogged the rest of the way home. He bounced up the stairs to his apartment with a spring in his step and swung through the door, remembering to brace himself for-

"Hey Rickle pickle," greeted Allen absentmindedly-yep there it was. He and Zech were sitting on the couch together with a journal. In the center of the living room were the two carts filled with scrap; the landfill items on the list. Next to the carts was a bag of produce. So, they'd had the entire two days to themselves and they didn't even bother to clean up?

"And here he is, to wreck my day!" grouched Ricky in annoyance, already pissed from the fight he'd had with Maya. Allen chuckled obliviously, and patted Zech's back, who continued to read as Allen stood up to speak with his friend.

"Love you too. Blueprints?" he asked, looking around. Ricky sighed and set his toolbox down.

"I only got so much written, you know I have to work, too," grumbled Ricky as he unfurled the large sheets, and set them down on the table. He took his reading glasses from his pocket and propped them on his nose as he readied himself to work again. Allen chuckled playfully and walked over to him.

"Hey...Ricky, I was thinking about the plan...and I mean when you look at him, he's not very robotic, and the metal we gathered is very old. We need new metal...I think we should fight in the arena. I heard they captured that centaur that took out my back. They rebooted it to fight in the Understreet. If we fight it, we can bet to keep the mech for parts," rambled Allen.

"Are you crazy? Ya wanna die, ya pox?!" Ricky smacked him with the blueprints. Allen held up his hands, batting the papers away. Zech looked up, barking timidly at the attack on his best friend.

"If you don't kill me first! Calm down! Hear me out," he said, Ricky groaning and running his hands through his hair from the thought of fighting a mech in the arena! He was already on edge; this was just making everything worse.

"Zech and I will fight in the arena together. For extra efficiency, I'll be there for him if he...never mind, but it's the easiest way to get a mech. You know it. We can't just steal one off of the street! That would be the fastest way to get put on the watchlist," explained Allen, crossing his arms as he stood firm in his plan.

Zech stood up slowly. "But, Allen, you promised it won't happen again," murmured Zech, his ears pressed against his head anxiously. Allen frowned as he turned to Zech, walking over to him and rubbing his arm comfortingly.

"It won't Zech, but these are the things that have to happen before you can be free, ok? I'm sorry. It's ok though, I'm going to be there with you, I won't let it happen again," said Allen firmly, nodding his head. Zech stared at him before sighing, nodding as well, a little surer of himself with his friend's comfort.

Ricky looked at him questioningly, completely in the dark. He stepped forward and gestured to Allen and Zech.

"What are you even talking about?" he asked. Allen lifted his chin and shook his head in denial.

"Don't worry about it. Besides, that was an A-B conversation...so *C* your way out of it," grumbled Allen protectively. Ricky grunted and went back to the table, shaking his head. Allen could tell Ricky wasn't going to talk more on the subject. He also noticed that he was on edge. What had happened? *'Bad day at work, probably.'*

"Come on Zech, let's continue," said Allen. Zech smiled and joined him on the couch. He picked up the leather-bound journal, which was torn at the seams, the pages stained and wrinkled from years of use.

Almost every old yellowing page was covered in smeared markings of graphite, with childlike doodling. Allen had written countless poems in that journal, both original and copied from books. He'd never admit it to anyone though, and in fact had stopped doing it a few years back.

Surviving in the Ghetto took too much time and energy and he couldn't waste it scribbling nonsense on old paper. When Zech had asked about the writing, Allen had just waved him off and told him not to worry about it.

Ricky sighed, turning to his blueprints and sketching the last bit of the exosuit in white chalk, then finished off some equations for the programming in the margins. He clapped, and went to the cart of scraps, setting out everything with heavy grunts.

"A... child dreams...b-big or small, to a grown-up it means, nothi-nothing at all," stammered Zech as he fumbled through the written words. Allen smiled and nodded. He had committed some to memory, having written them down the first chance he could get in that old journal he had bought from the Understreet. He was ardent about teaching Zech his favorite poem. It somehow made him feel closer to his father, and unlike the nights of booze, broads, and loneliness, it was a good feeling. For once, remembering his father didn't send him spiraling into despair.

"The worl- the world is cru... *cru*-el, and lif-life's u... what's this word?" he asked, Allen leaned over and read it.

"Unfair," he said. Zech nodded and reread it, saying the word he had struggled with. Allen watched with a glimmer of paternal pride.

"Th-that's what they say, until you're beaten down and... Allen this poem is mean," said Zech, interrupting himself. He looked up at Allen who had his hand covering his mouth to hide his smile while Zech had a bleak frown on his maw. Allen snickered.

There was a clang as Ricky set down the final piece of scrap from the carts. The noise didn't break Allen's focus, he was used to the sounds of Ricky building.

"It gets better, just keep reading. You're doing great," he encouraged him with a grin. Zech grunted and returned his attention to the poem.

Ricky got up to get the welding equipment that he had bartered for in the Understreet. He sighed, the whole conversation with Maya digging and biting at him.

"I ran into Maya…" he murmured. Allen raised a curious brow and turned to him with piqued interest.

"Oh yeah? What did she say?" he asked. Ricky just shook his head. He shouldn't have brought it up. Allen was latched onto the conversation now, however, and one look at those narrowed blue eyes caused Ricky to cave.

"Well, she wasn't very pleasant. She was just… *entitled*; expecting me to just bow down to her every whim because she's just so great. God, I don't know; it pissed me off, so that's why I'm a little on edge right now," he said, practically pulling out his hair. Allen grimaced as he studied the situation. What was Ricky saying? How had she been entitled?

"Are you sure? What did she say?" he asked. Ricky caught Allen in a cold stare, calculating his next response so he wouldn't step on Allen's toes. He didn't know if Allen would be mad at him or agree with him. Ricky was a little scared he would defend her.

"I don't remember, all I remember is that I really hated it. I got her to leave me alone though. She ran off. We won't have to worry about that elitist," he grumbled. Allen frowned. He had lived with Ricky for a long time, and he knew when he was hiding something from him. Zech glanced up from reading and he lowered his ears. He sensed the tension.

"Why was she even trying to come with you if you had to get her to leave?" he pressed. He was sure there was more to this story. Ricky glared at Allen and just shook his head.

"I don't remember, I was too angry. Forget I said anything, I shouldn't have brought it up in the first place," he grumbled.

Allen let out a sigh of frustration as he came to a slow realization of what was going on. "But you do remember...she wanted to help, didn't she?" he asked, growing angrier at his friend by the second.

Ricky rolled his eyes and groaned, but didn't try to deny it. That was stupid of him. He couldn't believe he would bring that up. Had it really bothered him that much to where he had to run his mouth? God he may have been intelligent, but he damn sure lacked social sense.

Zech whined as the tone slipped deeper and deeper into fighting words.

"I can't believe you Ricky, why would you do that? You know Maya isn't a bad person! If she wanted to help, you shouldn't have chased her off...We need her!" he groaned. Ricky sighed in exasperation.

"We don't need her, Allen. I have a good plan. *We* have a good plan. Fighting the centaur is fine, we can do that. We don't need Maya. You just want her around because you want her to fall in love with you! Newsflash pal, she's not going to. She's one of them!" he hissed. Allen clenched his jaw at the reminder.

"Why is that so bad that I want to be with her? She's perfect. Of course, I'm in love with her, and if she wanted to join us, we should've let her!" he shouted.

Zech barked as the energy increased and Ricky glanced at him.

"Why do we need her, Allen?" he asked, "I have a plan, and it excludes Maya Hart! Besides, why drag her into our mess, eh? She's happy, Allen. She's successful. Do you want to take that from her? Do us all a favor and just stop being selfish!" he exclaimed. Allen growled, and shoved Ricky away from him.

"Hey!" barked Zech, who was loyal to both of them and he didn't understand what was going on. Allen sighed as Ricky balanced his stance, eyes wide from the push. He pursed his lips.

"You're unbelievable. I'm going to go talk to her," stated Allen.

Ricky rolled his eyes, he waved him off with a dismissive hand. "Go on then," he grumbled.

Allen scowled and stomped towards the door, slamming it shut.

Ricky sighed, letting his head hang in defeat. Zech whined and came to stand beside him, rubbing his back.

"There I go again, makin' a mess of things...God, that was such a dumb move," he murmured, rubbing his eyes. Zech whined and shook his head.

"You have kept house very clean," he said. Ricky looked up at him and smiled wryly.

"Thanks pal," he whispered, his eyes trailing to the door.

Allen raced through the streets, darkness descending. He couldn't believe Ricky would drive away the girl of his dreams so easily. Why would he do that? Maya, she meant everything to him, and no matter how much he tried to move on, something would always remind him of that.

For instance, he knew she had wanted to help them, and he could already feel his heart break...again. He saw the horizon of the fence, and quickened his pace. As he passed the crumbling apartment complex, just before he could see the shining white tents, he stopped.

The reality of his situation slapped him in the face, his breath frosty as he stared ahead. There she was, glowing in the soft white light of the Medicum as if she were an angel. She looked up and he could've sworn she had spotted him.

What was he doing? Was he really selfish enough to take away Maya's success, her dreams, just so he could have the slimmest chance of being around her?

He *was* being selfish. Ricky was right. Ricky was always right. He needed to trust in his friend. He had always been there for him, no matter what, and as he stared at Maya, haloed in white light, he remembered that she hadn't been there for him.

She had left him and chosen a life worth living, and good for her. He realized he didn't want to take that away from her. He loved her more than he loved himself. With that sobering thought, he turned to go back and with one last look over his shoulder, he saw Maya disappear into the folds of a tent.

He looked ahead and sighed. He had come all this way. He was a bit too prideful to go crawl back home now. Not after the fight he had just had. *'I... I need a drink,'* he thought, and with that, he began the fool's walk to those gloriously awful, red buildings.

THE SCANDAL

Veronica looked around, sitting alone at the bar as people danced. Well, the more she watched the more she realized they had no idea what dancing was.

She sighed. She'd been waiting there for a full half hour, and was starting to think that the man had stood her up. She scrunched her lips in annoyance. What a rotten thing to do. She thought about those blue eyes, the fiery orange ring around the pupils, and she imagined those eyes covered with a black bruise. No way would someone stand her up and get away with it. After all, she was putting her mission on hold for this.

"Bastard," she grumbled, swallowing her shot of tequila and looking around. She could use a cigarette. She wasn't a smoker, but the enticing sense of rebellion she felt by lighting one and breathing in its fumes seemed right for the occasion.

She got up and bought one from one of the dispensers in the corner and quickly went back to her seat with a creeping uneasiness. She would have a smoke, then leave. As she sucked in the scratchy smoke, she knew she needed to get on with her job.

She glanced up as news began to play in the background. A creature, *the creature*, had escaped from Vargas Biotech and had made it to the Fence. Of course, there was a public outcry for the authorities to capture it before the creature could hurt people or damage property. She groaned a bit, her responsibility haunting her everywhere she went.

She shook away her thoughts as the channel changed to the weather. She had put it off: the mission. Something about it just didn't seem right to her. Something about that dead old man in the garbage dump kept coming into her mind's eye. She let out another puff of smoke with a cough. She definitely wasn't a pro at *this* particular skill.

"Jesus, do you know how bad cigarettes are for your lungs? God they're disgusting, and they smell bad too," grumbled a man who had sat beside her. Veronica lifted the cig off her lips and looked at him with an icy stare, before she turned her whole body to face him. She blew out a puff of smoke in defiance, even though secretly she knew he was right.

He coughed, and chuckled wryly as he waved it away. She studied his face; square jaw, roguish, brown hair, and bright, blue eyes. It was always the blue-eyed folk who seemed to find her. She couldn't deny his looks, but she shrugged at his words, sniffing her nose in contempt.

"Yeah, well neither does alcohol, but you reek of that shit," she said with a smirk.

He grinned at her response; his stomach warm from the alcohol she had just called him out on. He blushed slightly at that, and bit the inside of his cheek.

"Tough girl, huh? … My name's Allen," he said, extending his hand to her. She glanced at it, and took another drag of her cigarette.

"Did I ask?" The two fell into an awkward silence. Allen shrugged, bringing his hand back in. He grinned and glanced back at her.

"I'm gonna guess you got stood up," he said. Veronica coughed awkwardly and put out her cigarette.

"What makes you say that?" she asked. Allen laughed, gesturing to the crowd of dancers hypnotized by the music.

"Because no one stays at the bar by themselves." She pursed her lips, turned to him, and lifted her chin.

"Maybe I'm just that kinda girl," she said. He shook his head, chuckling as he studied her closely. She had clean clothes, a clean face, a stern eye. Something about her was inviting, but guarded. She radiated with power.

"No, you're not, and here's how I know. Gold hoops, crop top, eyeliner wings, and… high ponytail, *straightened.* You're here to party, and you're here to party with *someone* and that someone didn't come. You can't fool me," he replied with a cheeky grin.

She shifted uneasily at his uncanny assessment of her. "Well, so what if I was stood up? What makes you think you can talk to me?" she asked. She was starting to become intrigued by him. She noticed that he looked a bit cleaner than the other fencers, despite his ripped clothes and stain-splotched collar. His brown bomber jacket was probably the only thing that looked well kept on him. Still, there was a freshness to him, like some kind of hidden potential.

"Well...I'm not shy, and I like meeting new people. I've never seen you before at a scandal, and I've seen everyone," he said.

Veronica bit her lip and took a sip of her tequila.

"No way! Are you one of the medical students?" he teased. She glanced around and shrugged.

"Why should I tell you?" she asked. She didn't think telling him anything about her would be a good idea. He laughed and let it go.

Veronica chuckled nervously along with him. He seemed relaxed, not ready to pounce at a moment's notice. She'd humor him; it was better than being here alone, after all.

"My friends call me Ronny," said Veronica, holding out her hand as an acceptance of his presence. Allen grinned and reached out before she snatched her hand away, a mysterious smirk on her lips that dragged him deeper.

"But *you* will call me Veronica," she said confidently.

Allen shrugged and took a sip of his drink. "I'll take it over the nickname I had in mind," he mused. She raised an eyebrow and leaned in curiously, the tilt of her head all he needed to see to know her question waiting on her lips.

"Cigs, or newbie," he joked, laughing. Veronica rolled her eyes and put the cigarette out.

"Funny. If you call me cigs, I get to call you liquor-breath," she teased. Allen smirked at her and nodded. He took his drink and gulped it down. Veronica finished hers as well.

"Touché! I'll just be Allen, and you can just be Veronica."

She chuckled and held up her hand for a handshake. Allen smiled and studied it, before the both of them swung their hands and high fived. Veronica looked at him with widened eyes, a smile growing on her face.

Allen got up and she glanced at him curiously. He gestured for her to follow.

"You came here to party, right? Dance with me." A welcome smile on his face.

She considered his offer, before grinning and taking his hand. The music ran through their veins, and she began to enjoy its effect. The sharp picks of guitar strings intertwined with a smooth, bass saxophone as a women's husky voice belted a love song into the air.

The room was packed with swaying bodies. Two laughed as the general atmosphere of the Scandal hummed through their bodies.

"So uh, what's so appealing about medicine?" asked Allen, his grin expressing his interest. Veronica scrunched her nose in thought. How would she lie her way out of this one?

"I don't know. I was going to be in the Stratus," she murmured, half-truths weren't necessarily lies. Allen chuckled, and glanced around nervously at the mention of the Stratus.

"Well...what made you not choose that?" he asked. Veronica frowned; how would he even understand the kind of scrutiny she had to deal with? Even now, since they had installed a camera in her eye, she couldn't really do anything treasonous.

All the time Damon had spent buttering up the Judge, just so she could continue her training in the academy, just so she could join was extraneous. All because her mother had gone against the status quo. She had never even been told what her mother had done. Damon had basically adopted her and kissed the Judge's ass to keep her safe. She owed everything to him. How would this guy understand any of that?

"Well, I was going to go with the Stratus because I believe strongly in justice, and my mom was a commander...but... It didn't end well for her...and I'm really not supposed to discuss it. Basically... I decided it would just be better if I could still help people but, be further from the power," she explained, the mention of her late mother causing a lump to swell in her throat.

Allen smiled sadly and nodded with understanding. "I see where you're comin' from… What happened to your mom?" the question slipped from his lips and he instantly regretted it as Veronica glanced away.

"I'm sorry, that was bold of me," he said, smiling to relieve the tension. Veronica nodded but waved it away.

"Yeah...you're gonna have to be at least a level five friend to unlock my tragic backstory," she joked.

Allen snickered, as he quickly thought of the best way to phrase his next question. "What's that gonna take?" he asked. She grinned and simply shrugged; her eyes narrow with mystery.

"That's for me to know, and you to find out," she said, spinning on her toes and laughing as her ponytail swept around her.

Allen smiled, and he glanced around. He pursed his lips at how cramped they were. Normally, it was fine, but he just wasn't quite there yet. He glanced back down as she swayed, her eyes closed, heart thumping along to the bass.

For a second, his mind wasn't focused on Maya. He could feel his stomach heat up with something more than alcohol. He didn't know if it was the coyness, she surrounded herself with -a chase was always exciting- or if it was just his broken heart and the vodka. Maybe it was a mix. Whatever it was he needed a bit more of it, and what better way to do that than get more drunk?

He leaned down and told her he was going back to the bar, and Veronica glanced around, watching as he slipped through the people.

She watched as the lights dimmed and everyone in the crowd started cheering like crazy. A screen rose up, revealing a runway. What was going on? She watched as scantily clad women walked down the stage, and the crowd hollered vile and lewd things at them. The last one on the stage was a mechanical...a woman shaped mechanical. She scowled as she watched with disgust.

Her eyes widened at the concept of being left alone at this place, in this crowd. Suddenly, it wasn't so glamorous anymore. Her mind filled with dark thoughts, and it was then she remembered she had left her gun with her stuff back at the Medicum. *'Rookie mistake, you idiot,'* she scolded.

She knew not all of the Fence fear mongering propaganda was true, but there was a fear that she couldn't ignore. She didn't feel safe anymore now that all the men in the crowd were getting more and more rowdy.

"Allen," she whispered in a second of panic, and began to shoulder her way through the increasingly aggressive crowd.

"How much are you?" two thick hands grabbed Veronica from behind, the cold callouses gripping her exposed stomach. She let out a panicked yelp, her elbow shooting back instinctively and hitting the man's soft stomach. He groaned in both pain and annoyance.

"Hey, listen bitch-" growled the man, before he went quiet. Veronica glanced up to see Allen with his hand on the man's shoulder.

"Back off! She doesn't work here, and even if she did, that's unacceptable," he growled, his fist flexing. The man was taken aback for a second and Veronica took her chance. She ripped herself out of his grasp, and punched him across the face. As he moaned with pain, she shot her elbow back across his ugly mug.

Allen's eyes widened with surprise at her skill. The man tried to slap her, but she grabbed his hand and twisted his arm. She kicked him in the crotch, the man wheezing and beginning to fall to his knees. The crowd began to circle around the three, shouting as they watched the smaller woman take down such a large man. She pushed him over and stood over him.

Her breath was heavy and she glanced around. Allen's eyes were wide in shock. He had never seen anything like that from the women in the ghetto. The crowd went silent in awe, and Veronica lifted her chin in defiance.

Allen glanced down at Veronica and he smiled, the heat returning. Maybe it was her coyness, or her courage, or general moxie, or maybe it was his broken heart and the vodka. It was definitely a mix of all five of those things and he felt his heart skip a beat as he continued to smile goofily at her.

"I should probably go," murmured Veronica. She turned and rolled her shoulders, looking around for the exit. Allen stumbled after her, the overwhelming emotions of his stupid, drunk brain subsiding as he actually began to try to think. Did medical students know how to fight like that? Her mother had been in the Stratus. Maybe she had been taught a few things? She had been so fast and precise, and took no hits at all.

"That was somethin'...where did you learn how to do that?" he asked, opening the door for her. She looked at him in pleasant surprise, clearly shocked that a Fencer would even know to open the door for a lady... She reminded herself that *that* was just an unfortunate stereotype and not to be so discriminatory.

"Don't worry about it," she grunted, as she looked back at him. Allen tilted his head in curiosity and pocketed his hands.

"Alright, I'll let it go...Oh, here's a simpler question. Why'd ya color your hair purple? It's a good look, just wanna know the method behind the madness."

Veronica's lips twitched at the question. She had personal reasons, but it felt too weird to tell him. He wasn't, of course, at a level five yet.

"Because purple is the color of royalty...and I'm a queen," she stated. Allen grinned at the answer. It was a good one. She was a force to be reckoned with, and he couldn't help but feel drawn to her.

"Hell yeah you are... Hey, do you know a girl named Maya?" Allen asked, tilting his head, realizing that was the first time he had thought about Maya since he had met Veronica. She looked at him questioningly.

"Uh, actually, yeah. I, she's sweet...why?" she replied, looking at him, brows high with questions. Allen shook his head, smiling a bit at the coincidences that surrounded him.

"Ah, no reason...but uh, if you see her can you tell her that I'm sorry?" he suggested. Veronica studied the request. Did they know each other? She thought back on Maya, and remembered she had been a rare transfer from the Fence. It was quite possible they had been friends before. *'Small world,'* she thought.

"Yeah I can do that for you..." she said with a smile. Allen grinned and saluted her. The two walked backwards for a moment as they began to part ways.

"Thanks chief... Hey be careful. You're cool, and cool people should stay safe," he said with a lazy grin, skipping as he turned around and launched into a run. Veronica smiled softly at the statement. No. The propaganda didn't include everyone in the Fence.

She had half a mind to run after him, and she had a strange feeling that if she let him go now, she'd miss the chance of a lifetime. She went to move, to chase, but her feet were glued to the ground.

Veronica glanced around, the world swaying slightly and started the journey back to the Medicum. She was going to hate herself tomorrow morning, but how could she regret such a fascinating encounter? She looked behind her, hoping to see him again, but he was gone.

BETWEEN TWO SURGEONS

Maya's confidence had grown by leaps and bounds the last few weeks. Her hands no longer shook when suturing wounds, and she had grown more comfortable talking to patients and other doctors. She felt like she was becoming herself again. Maybe seeing her dad had finally broken her out of her shell; reminding her of herself.

"Doctor Hart," a gruff voice barked. She snapped to attention, her bob of platinum blonde hair bouncing as she whirled around to address her superior, Dr. Farley.

"Sir! Is there something wrong?" she asked, trying to straighten her white uniform. Dr. Farley glowered furiously, and even though his eyes were cold and the wrinkles showed his stress, his lips twitched into a smile.

"No Doctor Hart, you're not in trouble. I actually wanted to compliment you. You are one of the best student surgeons I've ever had intern here. You're a good doctor. I can tell you're in this to help, not for the money, or status," he said, his severe frown softening into a smile. Maya's eyes widened and she couldn't stop herself from grinning from ear to ear at his praise.

"Oh! Uh, than-thank you," she stammered, his words taking her by surprise. Dr. Farley nodded curtly and fixed his tie.

"I recognized your name. You're Tony Hart's daughter!" he exclaimed.

Maya smiled and happily shook her head, yes. Dr. Farley grinned at the knowledge that his old boss and friend's daughter was following in his footsteps.

"Tony was a good doctor. I looked up to him... He really fell apart when you left, but you're here now, I see," he said.

Maya swallowed at the guilt of that fact. *'I shouldn't be guilty of that. It was mom's fault; not mine.'* she reminded herself.

"I was a bit upset at myself when I didn't recognize you at first. Tony talked about you all the time. You live up to his name," said Dr. Farley.

Maya smiled at him. "Thank you, it's good to hear, I've always looked up to him. Obviously, he was one of the reasons I became a doctor," she said.

Dr. Farley nodded in understanding. "Hey. Doctor to doctor, I came from the Fence too... I know what it's like to be looked down on by the students due to our background," he said.

Maya's eyes widened. "You? ... How?" she questioned. Dr. Farley frowned and rubbed his eyes. There was an awkward silence as the older doctor ran a hand through his pepper grey hair.

"I was taken by the Stratus when I was ten…from the Home. It was years ago, but it fills me with anger to this day… But that's why I'm here- to help the people of the Fence." he said.

Maya tilted her head as she listened. "Zech…" she whispered to herself.

Dr. Farley shot her a confused look. Maya glanced over Dr. Farley's shoulder when she caught a flicker of movement. Was that? No!

"Well, in that regard, I guess we have a lot more in common than I thought we would," she said. Dr. Farley nodded and smiled at her. The two shared a moment of silence, Maya's eyes shifting behind him every once in a while. What were Allen and Ricky doing here?!

"Well I should probably get back to work, but you're doing good, and... I'm glad I get to work with a Hart again." He smiled and turned away.

Maya waved goodbye to him as a big smile grew on her face. Being noticed by someone she admired as much as Dr. Farley, felt good. She thought back to his story, about the fact that they both came from the Fence in bad situations. She thought about Zech and remembered Allen and Ricky were here. *'Crap,'* she thought bitterly, stepping to march after them when a voice caught her.

"Typical of someone like you to cozy up to the superiors, isn't that right, Hart?" sneered Jason as he came up behind her. Maya clenched her jaw and turned on him, crossing her arms. She didn't want to deal with him, right now... or *ever* for that matter.

"What are you talking about?" she asked, waving her hair out of her face. Jason leaned towards her and smirked.

"Well come on Maya. We all know how you got into the Skyline. Mommy slept around with a couple of officers, secured you both a place with a man that would take you two skanks, and then she slept with the Dean so you could get into school. Now you are flirting with the boss so you won't get suspended. Very smart Maya! You Fencers are so very crafty, aren't you?" He moved in too close for comfort.

Maya rankled, and she lifted her nose in contempt. "How dare you. I'm not like my mother," she hissed.

Jason chuckled and grabbed her arm. "Sure, you're not. You're a Fencer, and I heard that they'd do anything to cozy up with superiors... Guess what I am?"

Maya's eyes widened as he pressed his lips against hers. She shoved him away, and stumbled back.

"Don't touch me you sicko! I'm not a... you know what? I *am* a Fencer, and we're a lot tougher than you can imagine, *asshole!*" she spat.

Jason's eyes widened in shock. He had never seen the usually quiet girl talk like that; *and* he had never been opposed. He growled and advanced on her.

"I could get you fired! I could accuse you of being the one hiding that monster out on the loose! I could make you lose your degree, your life… No one would care, because you're one of *them!*" he hissed.

Maya lifted her chin. "Yeah? Well...screw you! I don't care! Don't touch me. Just because you're an elite, just because you're *Stratus,* doesn't mean you're entitled to treat people like that, so screw off jerk!" she snarled.

Jason scowled at her and stomped away. Maya wiped her mouth and felt a small wry chuckle bubble up from her stomach. She pumped the air and danced in a small circle.

"Hello Ms. Badass, how are you today?" she asked herself as she straightened her coat. Pride burst from her heart and she grinned. She was back! She was back. She felt a small ounce of dread leak through in the midst of her celebration and she swallowed.

"Oh crap," she sighed and sat down. What had she done? What if she lost everything? She didn't want to lose this career opportunity, she had worked so hard, and… She had chosen this over helping Allen.

"Oh Allen…" she whispered… He had always been there for her no matter what, helped her through all of her problems, and never complained about his own life. And, his life had been awful. She had been too self-absorbed to even realize it. She still was. She clenched her fists in resolve. She had to do this. Her head perked up when she remembered they were here. She had to catch them before they left!

She began to race through the Medicum, her eyes searching for her once best friend. As she turned the corner of the white tents, she ran right into a man who was stooped over. She glanced down and felt her heart drop when she saw the puff of red hair. *'Oh God,'* she thought.

Ricky looked up at her and clenched his jaw. "Hello Maya...here to report us?" he asked. She rolled her eyes as he stood up. *'Two jerks in one day, how perfect.'*

"Of course, not Ricky," she said, and crossed her arms.

Ricky sighed and ran a hand through his hair. She frowned.

"Where's-"

"Listen. I'm sorry, ok!? For...how I acted last week, I'm sorry. I was just looking out for Allen..." he said, his face flushed a bright red.   Maya flinched at his aggressive apology, but the corners of her lips lifted a bit.

"Well shit, say something," he grumbled.

Maya huffed and looked up at him. Ricky gulped, his Adam's apple bobbing as he swallowed.

"Where's Allen?" she asked. Ricky pursed his lips and looked away. He nodded and gestured for her to follow.

"Well let's look for him...Why? What do you want?" he asked, his tone laced with venom.

Maya sighed in exasperation at having been stuck with him. *'He apologized, that's good,'* she thought, but part of him clearly still felt a strong animosity towards her, and she couldn't deny she felt the same for him.

"I want to help," she said firmly. Ricky turned to her; his eyes wide with a hot annoyance.

"Why do *you* want to help? Don't you have everything? Wouldn't this just ruin everything you've worked for?" he asked hotly. There was something personal in his voice, and it wasn't directed at her. Maya stood straight and lifted her chin.

"I did, but it stunk. It was just...I hate it. I'm not doing anything right. I want to help Zech. What kind of doctor would I be if I didn't help someone who has obviously suffered so much? Besides, Allen's always been there for me—"

"—Uh-huh, ya think?" snapped Ricky.

Maya huffed at the snarky interruption, but shrugged it off. *'I'm so sick of taking everyone's crap today,'* she thought.

"I want to be there for him," she said. Ricky stared down at her and sighed in defeat. He continued to lead her, walking quickly and dodging anyone they encountered. He must've been here to do something illegal.

"Ricky what are you two doing anyway?" she asked. Ricky looked back at her and grinned.

"Tasers, it's for an exosuit." he explained. Maya nodded, before tilting her head, a small smirk coming to her lips.

"If you want some real electric power, I could get you some defibrillators. They're very powerful," she said.

Ricky glanced at her and furrowed his brow. "Uh...Really!?" He was excited, and for the time they were on the same page.

Maya turned to him and raised an amused brow at him.

"Yeah I am sure, besides, you guys look really suspicious sneaking around like this," she said. Ricky grunted.

"Ok. Fine, get defibrillators," he mumbled. Maya smirked and poked his shoulder teasingly.

"And what's the magic word?" Ricky glared at her, before running a hand through his hair.

"Please…" he groaned. Maya smiled and stood up, gesturing for him to continue looking for Allen. Ricky moaned in exasperation.

"Ricky!" a harsh whisper came from inside a tent. Ricky looked over and rolled his eyes, pulling Allen out.

Allen held a taser and looked up, his eyes falling on Maya and widening in surprise.

"M-Maya!" he exclaimed. Maya smiled softly and waved to him. Ricky sighed and looked at the taser.

"I'm...I want to help," she said. Allen felt his stomach flutter and he grinned. Ricky rolled his eyes and the two shared a look of contempt. There was still tension that rankled from last week. Allen had gotten home late, which didn't lead to a lot of making up, and then the two had given each other the silent treatment. Ricky had thrown clothes on him in the morning and barked orders at him, and the two had not made much conversation on their way to the Medicum.

Allen walked past Ricky and smiled at Maya. "Thank you, oh God, I knew you'd change your mind!" he said. There he was, falling for her all over again. She always found a way under his skin. He pulled her into a tight hug. Ricky rolled his eyes.

"Hey, you guys need to get out of here though. I'll get you defibrillators… My boss was from the Fence...I think what happened to Zech happened to him, but he had the privilege of escaping. I'm going to try to help smuggle you, work some things out over here...We leave in two weeks, after that, the window is closed," she said. Allen and Ricky glanced at each other, and Ricky pursed his lips.

"Allen there's no way-"

"We can do it!" interrupted Allen. Ricky huffed, but rolled his shoulders back. Maya smiled at them, glancing at Ricky as he crossed his arms.

"I know, we all can," she said firmly. Ricky grunted in surprise as she pulled the two of them into a hug.

"The whole lot of you and your affinity for hugging will be the death of me," grumbled Ricky. Allen chuckled and ruffled his hair. The two friends smiled at each other, letting some of the tension between them dissipate.

"Tell Zech that I'm on his team. I bet he could use the good news," she said to Allen. He followed her as she led them into a tent and went through some cases.

"Will do...hey, Maya...It really is so good to have you with us," he said. Maya looked up at him.

"Well, Zech needs help, we're doing this for him," she stated. Allen nodded.

"I'm glad you've come around; I knew you would."

She popped open a metal case. Two defibrillators lay side by side and she snapped the case back closed.

"Take these and go, I'll make arrangements here... Good luck Allen," she whispered, and the two hugged.

"Luck was never on my side...until now of course. Good luck to you too," he said with an affectionate smile. He saluted her before jogging after Ricky, who was scowling at him for taking so long.

Maya giggled and sat down, running strands of hair through her hand. She was doing this. She wasn't going to stand by and be another pawn for the Elite. No matter how hard she worked they'd never respect her. Jason's actions proved that.

But Allen, he had always respected her, and her dad had been one of the best doctors. She'd be damned if she wouldn't fight for something. She'd fight for Zech.

THE UNDERSTREET

Veronica made her way through the ramshackle streets. She picked her way through a destruction zone where a building had collapsed. Large steel wires stuck out of cracked concrete, and shattered glass littered the crumbling asphalt.

She kept an eye peeled for anything suspicious, trying to find a Fencer that was too tall, or too wide.

The streets were filled with fog, and she wiped her face, careless of her makeup. She had decided to lose her Stratus uniform, instead; donning a leather vest, tank top, baggy, ripped jeans and combat boots. She kept her gun holstered at her hip, which she periodically reached for when she saw shadows bouncing on the walls. This part of the street however, wasn't as inhabited. A couple of men in ripped clothes stood around a garbage bin glowing with licking flames of fire.

Veronica watched them. She swallowed and turned down another street. She looked up to find it was a dead end. Her breath caught as she stared at the tall brick wall that was cracked and about ready to come down. However, what it presented was too beautiful to let fall. The largest mural of graffiti she had ever seen. It showed the Skyline in bright colors, with gardens, waterfalls, tall, gleaming skyscrapers. It was everything the Skyline was supposed to be, all behind dark barbwire, the black paint streaking down in angry dread. Below the fence, looking out, were thousands of spray-painted rats, reaching for the city, longing, but trapped.

Veronica walked up to the wall and gently placed her hand along the painted brick. She stared at the rats, a long frown growing on her face.

"What...what am I doing?" She whispered. Her mother raised her better than this. She was better than to be what she was, a *Stratus*.

Loud voices resounded through the alley and she wheezed, hiding behind a cracked lump of concrete. She watched as gathering shadows bounced off the walls and listened intently.

One of the men was a bit rough with his English, and had a mix of accents from the other men, which she found weird. However, one voice was strikingly familiar.

She poked out her head, seeing the forms of the people. Her eyes widened when she saw the man in the middle. He was a giant! She had never seen a human that tall before!

She watched them intently as the shortest, but more athletic man pulled open a grate, and the other, lankier man stood with a gallon of water. She saw a glimpse of the shorter man's face and her eyes widened.

"Allen?" she whispered. The monstrously tall man perked up, and turned to study the wall she hid behind. As she peered over the stone, she saw a strange box like mask that hid the face behind it. However, there was something inhuman about the way he moved. She gaped, slowly easing back behind the rock and tapped her watch.

A small holographic image of the wanted poster popped up. She checked its data, looked for the size, the weight. '*Oh my God! That's subject two hundred twenty-seven!*' She didn't have to see its face!

A small guttural growl emanating from the creature brought her back from her research and she clenched her jaw, heart racing with terror. She had not expected to just run into the damn thing! And Allen! Allen was with it? Was helping it!?

"Zech, what are you doing? Come on," said Allen in a hushed voice.

She peeked her head out again to see the men climb down a hole. Subject two hundred twenty-seven stared at where she hid, but turned away and slipped down the grate as well. Veronica let out a heavy sigh and gulped.

"Well Ronny...what's the plan?" she asked herself. She looked up at the mural and bit her lip. She cursed under her breath, and counted to ten before she ran after them. She jumped down the grate and climbed down into a dark sewer tunnel. She followed the bouncing shadows as dim, flickering lights hung above them.

Allen, Ricky, and Zech walked into the Understreet, the dome of the abandoned metro-hub towering over them. Erratic graffiti sprawled across impossible to reach places, hanging over them like a warning.

Zech knew he had seen something, something watching them.

The Understreet was a large community of contraband "retailers" who took residence like an infestation of rats under the streets of the Fence. Murals of graffiti covered the gritty, brick walls, and the lights flickered almost rhythmically. Shops were carved out from the wall where stone had crumbled and they distributed homemade weapons, booze, and other necessities and niceties. Usually things that were illegal in the eyes of the Stratus. Mechanicals...stolen contraband from the Skyline found near the Fence, and, probably the most illegal of it all… the Arena.

It stood in the very center, a stand of bleachers, a large hexagonal cage of chain-link fence, and two long boxcars jutting inside, where fighters would enter, and where mech's would be caught and retained until released for a fight.

"Allen! What a pleasant surprise! Oh, I thought I'd never see you again, you cutie patootie!" bellowed a slender girl with short black hair that curled around her ears and flicked distractingly at every word she spoke due to her nervous, jerking motions.

He glanced up, chuckling nervously as Ricky and Zech eyed him. He looked back at the woman, tilting his head as he studied her, trying to recall her name.

"Oh...hey there Susan...?" He guessed. Ricky stifled his laughter at his friend's cluelessness while Zech was completely confused. Were they supposed to be friends with this woman? The woman frowned at his words.

"Eleanor," she grunted. He smiled fakely and jerked his head in a nod, opening his arms to her with pretend sincerity.

"Right! Sorry. You really look like a Susan, must be the hairdo. Is it new?" he paused to watch as her unamused frown melted slightly.

"...but now that you corrected me, I see now that yes, you are indeed an Eleanor. By the way, Eleanors are the cream of the crop, can't go wrong with an Eleanor." He grinned and held up a finger gun, winking at her in an attempt to keep her from becoming angry at him. She blushed and swayed on her heels, obviously flattered by his charm, or insanely drunk.

"Alright lady, we've got to be on our way. Come on prince charming," Ricky grunted. Allen immediately turned and darted away to avoid any more awkwardness that any further conversation with the woman would bring him.

Eleanor frowned but turned away. She blew a kiss at Allen, which he pretended to catch. As she walked away, he mimed tossing the said kiss away from him. Ricky rolled his eyes, snickering at the gesture. Zech also laughed, pointing in the direction he threw it, a smile on his maw.

"She was nice," he said, his eyes shining happily, blissfully ignorant of the situation. Ricky cackled as he began to make a joke, only to interrupt himself with more laughter.

"Oh, she's very nice, when ya buy her a couple drinks, right Allen? And then you bring her into my house and screw around when you knew I had to work and then you keep me, you know what? Never mind." he grumbled.

Allen rolled his eyes playfully, shuddering at the memory. "Eh, shut up." He grinned wryly at his friends as they laughed. Ricky chuckled and patted his shoulder. Allen watched him leave to go to Trisha, the ticket taker's cage.

Allen usually came into the Arena to fight for resources so his name was already on the list. All Ricky had to do was highlight it and add a plus one. After he pushed the paper through the slot, he heaved the gallon of water onto the bar, his payment for entry. The dark, tattoo-covered woman, Trisha, took the tablet, and smiled at the name.

"Well if it isn't our favorite boxer. Who's the plus one?" she asked. Ricky sighed and pinched the bridge of his nose.

"Our tall friend. A real beast in the arena, or at least, he will be," he replied. Trisha smiled at him, intrigued.

"Well, you know what? *His* entrance is on the house," she said. Ricky was clearly surprised by her generous gesture.

Trisha smiled at him and leaned forward. "Us rats have to stick together, right?" she asked, and winked. Ricky smiled and took his gallon of water. He thanked her with a simple bow of his head before he made his way to his friends.

An usher directed them to enter the empty box car, giving them a disclaimer on safety, which was basically an optimistic approach to death. Allen reached into the inside pocket of his jacket and pulled out a flask. He knocked back a hard shot of vodka. Ricky merely grunted at the move.

"I don't know about this Allen," murmured Zech. Allen frowned and patted his back, flashes of Zech going crazy and murdering Peter by ripping his heart out of his chest flashed into his mind.

"Hey, hey buddy, I'm gonna be right there with you, and I'll be more prepared this time, alright?" he promised. Zech swallowed the lump in his throat and nodded, hugging him.

Allen pulled the thin and battered armor, that was provided by the arena, on over his clothes. The dented helm was once an old motorcycle helmet. He flexed his gloved hands, and stood waiting for the announcement. Zech looked at him and whined.

"This is too much," whispered Zech. Allen sighed and grabbed him by the elbows, since he couldn't reach his shoulders.

"I'm here. Just remember we need to do this, and we can, Zech. You're awesome," he whispered. Zech gulped and looked out as Trisha's voice came over a muffled speaker that crackled with almost every word she said.

"Welcome you dirty sewer rats, to the Understreet Arena! Tonight, we have a very special fight. One of *their* evil centaurs was struck down and we have relocated it here to be further demolished! A win against the Elite! We have a big fight against their fearsome mech, with none other than your favorite, Allen Rosinsky and a mysterious plus one! Joining the fight are; Lavender Hamato, Malik Indra, and the Geminis! The one to deal the last blow wins the parts to the mech, which they can either trade out for resources, make into weapons, or whatever the hell they want to do with a Magnus brand mechanical. Don't die!" she chirped, before the speaker cut out with a hiss of static.

"Ricky should come in here and fix those things," grumbled Allen as the gate of the boxcar opened with a clang. He thought over the words, taking in the realization they'd be fighting with people. Did Trisha say the name Lavender? For some reason...that name sounded familiar.

Allen fought down here when he and Ricky ran out of resources. This, of course was the first Mech he had ever fought, but thankfully, he wasn't doing it alone. With those four other people, plus Zech, this should be easy...that is if the other candidates would be civil and focus on taking out the mech and not each other.

Allen looked over, keeping a firm hold on Zech's arm, his helmet mask completely covered his foxlike face and his exoskeleton kept his tail out of sight as well.

As he walked into the Arena, the crowd burst into an uproar of cheers. He locked eyes with Lavender and he choked in realization. It was the dancer from Michael's Scandal! What was she doing here? She lifted her nose and nodded to him, flipping down her helmet.

The centaur mechanical trotted out, it's cold black face staring dead at him and he shuddered. His spine tingled with phantom pain where his back had been crushed, and since this was the same mech, it was personal. He wouldn't lose to this heap of garbage again.

Zech clenched his jaw and stood behind Allen, whimpering quietly. His eyes raced around the arena, trying not to look at the mech. Allen made a move to unsheathe the plasma sword he had been issued when they registered, but before he could, Lavender shouted and pulled out a gun.

The centaur sprang into action, its arms unsheathing heavy machine guns that ripped off rounds of ammo with fast flashes of light, bullets flying. Lavender raced away and shot. Allen ground his teeth as Zech yipped in fear. He grabbed Allen and dove out of the way with uncanny speed. Zech had already been fast, but the exosuit gave him even more strength and speed.

The crowd booed loudly at the centaur, and Allen moaned at the unfairness of the situation. He took a risky move and aimed with his left hand, throwing the sword at the centaur's abdomen. It sliced through the first gun, sticking into the ground on the other side. He could almost hear Ricky groan at the move.

Before the crowd could react, Malik, an ochre man with his long, black hair tied back, his beard already dripping with salty sweat, threw several knives from the wings of his suit. The knives lodged themselves into one of the Centaur's back legs. Allen took the chance and raced across to grab his sword.

"Not so fast Allen, that centaur is ours!" snarled the two siblings, the Geminis, in unison. They're voices were a slight mix of both masculine and feminine, and really, no one could ever figure out what the gender of the twins was. The residents of the Fence all mutually agreed to never ask.

Allen sighed as he dodged their plasma blades, batting them away with his own. One of the twins jabbed at him with an elbow when their sword didn't strike. He groaned as it crashed against his nose.

"Come on guys!" he yelled, tripping the one closest to him and kicking the other in the stomach, pushing them back. He looked up when Zech let out a loud bark as the Centaur charged him.

Zech jumped up and kicked off of the Centaur, racing to the other side of the small hexagonal arena. He looked at Allen with pleading eyes, gulping as he turned his attention back to the centaur with terror.

His mind flashed back to the night he had run away from Magnus city, how the mechs chased him down, the sound of their joints and gears whizzing as they tore after him. He couldn't do this.

Zech turned to the wall, banging on the fence of the ring and whimpering, begging to be let out.

Allen glanced at him and groaned; this couldn't be happening now! Before he could console the fox, he was grabbed by the helmet, the centaur's hand firmly wrapped around his head. With a jerk of its arm, Allen went flying, his body hitting the ground with an ugly thud.

The crowd groaned, laughing a bit as the tall one tried with all his might to escape. Allen moaned in pain as he stumbled from the ground, having rolled across the rocks and dirt. He looked up as the centaur focused on the Zech, another set of guns unfolding from its abdomen.

Malik and Lavender were engaged in hand to hand combat, as the twins groaned on the ground. Lavender shoved Malik away and shot two bullets into his head before marching towards the centaur and ripping off a barrage of firepower.

"Zech, get a grip!" shouted Allen across the ring. Zech looked back at him and wheezed in terror, jumping out of the way of the Centaur's bullets that cracked through the arena with power. He went to Allen, tears in his eyes.

"Can't do Allen, it...scares me." The crowd roared with laughter, but Allen's eyes widened with understanding. He frowned and grabbed Zech's shoulders.

"It's just a machine, and if you don't do this, we'll die in a fight club! That's not how I wanna die, Zech! We gotta take it down! You can do this, it's just a stupid machine!" he shouted. Zech gulped, and squeezed his eyes closed. The centaur slowly advanced on them, its guns poised, as it clicked back into gear.

Zech growled and whipped around, fueled by Allen's words. "You're just a stupid machine!" he snarled, jumping off the wall in a blur of shiny, green metal. The crowd roared! Allen grinned. Finally, the fight had really started.

Zech grabbed one of the centaur's guns and twisted its fist as it shot. The other contestants looked up in shock as Zech moved with mind boggling speed and pounced on the Centaur.

Allen dove to the ground, rolling to his feet and slashing at the Centaur's leg. A burst of air blasted into his face, the large gash exposing the wiring in its leg.

The Centaur reared up to stomp Allen under its steel hooves, but Zech crashed back on its shoulders and pulled at the mech's neck until he was able to throw it off balance.

With Zech's massive strength, enhanced and increased by the exosuit, he reached around and snapped off the gun, with a ferocious snarl.

Allen spun on his feet, his sword blocking one of the Twin's blows. Lavender climbed up on the cage fence to get a clear shot at the centaur's face. Zech kept pulling at the mechanical's shoulders until it reeled and fell over onto its back.

Zech launched off one side of the fencing and grabbed the chain link on the opposite side. The crowd roared with approval. The Centaur kicked wildly as it tried to stand.

"Not again!" roared Allen as the centaur gave him a weak kick -which was still pretty strong considering it was a mech- to the stomach. Thankfully, the armor provided just enough protection to prevent any internal damage. His lungs heaved as he tried to catch his breath.

The Twins grinned and ran to finish him off while he was down. Zech watched his friend struggle to them fight off while still wheezing for air, and a roar ripped from his mouth.

"No one hurts Allen!" He jumped down behind the Twins. He swiped at them, sending both of them flying against the chain link on the opposite side. Then, he turned his attention to the centaur dove underneath it. He hoisted it up over his shoulders with a great roar.

Allen shook his head to regain his wits and his breath. He looked up to find Lavender standing over him, her hand outstretched. He took it and she pulled him up. His stomach ached, but he shook it off.

"Thanks," she said. Allen tilted his head, still wondering why she was helping him and she sighed, "For standing up for me back at the Scandal… You were right. I can do better than that pigsty."

Allen flashed her a quick smile just as Zech heaved the centaur against the cement wall. It cracked from the impact and his eyes widened. The crowd stood in a wave of amazement; cheering and whooping.

"Good God…" he mumbled, as Lavender came to stand beside him. They could do nothing but watch.

The crowd roared as Zech punched the glass mask of the centaur twice before it shattered completely. He clapped his hands together as he had practiced with Ricky, activating the defibrillators. Sparks of blue electricity hissed and crackled threateningly.

Allen grinned at Lavender before he sprang into action and sprinted to the centaur as the Twins jumped at the opportunity to kill the mech before Zech could. Allen swung his sword sloppily to distract them.

The first twin turned to him and kicked his knee. Allen groaned and fell down, before the other twin kicked him across the face.

Zech charged his tasers once more, his claws diving into the mech's open face wiring. The electricity of the tasers zapped into the mech's command center, and its legs kicked wildly. It short circuited, and began to topple as its lights blinked out just before it crashed to the ground, defeated.

Allen groaned happily, still lying on the ground from the Twins' assault. The Twins looked at each other in disbelief and cried at their loss.

Allen looked up to see Zech's shadow towering over them. His face dropped when he saw Zech's menacing posture. It was all too familiar. His mind returned to the day when he watched Zech snap. He forced himself up and stumbled to his feet. He grabbed the Twins and pulled them behind him.

"Zech…" he said quietly. The crowd hushed, and leaned close to see what would happen. The mutant growled at them and stepped forward. Allen put a hand on him, a risky move, but he couldn't take the chance.

"Zech, we won," he whispered. Zech continued to snarl at the Twins, who were wide eyed with fear. He snapped his fingers and smiled, putting his hand on the fox's shoulder in triumph.

The mutant jumped, and barked, clearly still in his bloodthirsty daze. Allen clenched his jaw, and he grabbed Zech by the mask and forced him to look into his eyes.

"Zech we did it, the fight is over," he said, his heart racing at the fear that Zech could go rogue again. Zech blinked, took a deep breath, and Allen sighed with relief.

Zech whined in doggish happiness and held up Allen's hand as the crowd cheered. Allen smiled. He was right. Zech had made fighting a mech almost too easy. He shouldn't have been worried.

Veronica watched the fight from beneath the bleachers, her eyes wide. This creature had fought alongside Allen against a mech!? And not only that, but won? She watched, completely hypnotized as the electricity raced through the mech.

She watched as Allen put his hand on the mutant's shoulder and told him they had won, and how the mutant held Allen's hand up in triumph, Allen's feet dangling.

Veronica smiled as they celebrated in the ring. They looked like total dorks...the mutant cheered and gave everyone in the ring a hug, even the two ruthless twins who had relentlessly beat on Allen.

Was this the monster they were supposed to kill? This...was everything Magnus hated...and Magnus had killed her mother. *'Do what mom would want,'* she thought, her fists clenching.

She looked down at the gun in her hand with the Magnus symbol, a Mountain with a rising sun above the peak, and a silver M stamped on top, and she growled with disgust. She reached for her ear and felt for the micro piece that was pierced in her cartilage. If Veronica took it out it would set off a small alarm in the mainframe… With a sigh she left it in place.

"I'm doing this...sorry Damon," she whispered. With that, she crept out from the bleachers and went to find

Allen. She stood in a crowd as she watched a man with ginger hair hug him, jumping up and down in excitement.

Allen and the mutant celebrated with him, before Allen took the beast and led him away. The red head turned and walked down a tunnel. She swallowed and shuffled over before skipping into a jog. She followed close behind him until he came to a dead end, a ladder on the wall.

"Hey you! What's your name?" she barked, grabbing him by the collar as he tried to dart up the ladder in panic.

"Oye! What's the big idea, lady!?" he asked, as Veronica pulled him off of the rungs. She looked around to make sure no one could see her.

"Do you know Allen?" she asked. Ricky's eyes widened and he shifted on his feet, trying to subtly get her hands unpried from his collar in vain.

"Why, did he screw you? Literally? Figuratively? Take that up with him, I'm just the roommate," he rambled nervously as she stared at him with her intense, hazel eyes. She scoffed at his implication.

"No, I... I'm from the Skyline, I know Allen from the Scandal-"

"Whoa, whoa, whoa, you're an *Elite?*" he asked. Veronica scowled, her lip twitching in disgust. She looked behind her and sighed.

"Not anymore. I want to help… You'll need me, I can offer a lot to your scrappy little team," she said, with an arrogant tone. Ricky narrowed his eyes at her.

"We're full..." he trailed off as she stared him down, unimpressed by his words. Veronica gave him a fierce look and then she laughed.

"That's nice. Anyway, I'm offering you my complete training in armed combat, piloting skills, and the fact that I can get you through the fence, no problem," she said with such sureness, she almost convinced herself. Get people through the fence? That was impossible, but she wasn't about to doubt herself. Ricky was, however.

"Oh yeah? Have you ever smuggled anyone out of the fence before?" he asked, crossing his arms. Despite the fact she was shorter than him, it didn't stop her from towering over him, well, in his mind's eye at least.

Veronica pursed her lips. "First time for everything," she stated, setting her feet to show him she meant business. Ricky weighed his options. Did he really want to tell her no? He wouldn't be surprised if she hit him if he did. With a forced smile, he nodded in agreement.

"Yeah, guess so," he breathed. Veronica smiled sweetly and patted his shoulder, Ricky flinched under her touch.

"Glad we came to an understanding. What's your name?" she asked, grinning. Ricky smiled wryly at her and gave her his name. Veronica smiled at him, trying to be a little sweeter after her initial audacious introduction.

Ricky glanced over her as Allen and Zech came down the tunnel, a group of people helping them push a trailer behind them.

"Allen! You've got a friend! You take it up with him," he said. Veronica smiled at Ricky and bowed her head. She let go of his collar and brushed it off, mouthing the words '*sorry*' to him. Old habits die hard.

Allen jogged up, Zech trailing cautiously behind him. When he saw Veronica, his eyes widened with shock. How was she here? How did an Elite find the Understreet? At the same time, *why* was she here?

"Veronica! Wow, I wasn't expecting to see you so soon! You look great!" he said. Zech came up behind him and poked his head out from behind his friend's back.

"Friend?" he asked, pointing his finger at her. Allen chuckled and nodded at Zech, who then barked cheerfully, his shoulders shivering with innocent enthusiasm. Veronica smiled sadly. Was this the quote-un-quote "beast" they had been searching for? She felt sick to her stomach.

"Allen...I want to join you, um...you know...my mom would want me too. She'd try to protect Zech, so *I'm* going to. Besides, I saw you fighting and, I must say...I could do a thousand times better," she teased, a cocky grin on her face.

Allen snorted in derision at the statement. He wasn't very tall, only two inches above her, and four below Ricky. It was hard to stare someone down when they were almost the same height.

"You do, do you?" he challenged. She smirked and nodded, turning away from him.

"At least I wouldn't throw my sword at a mech...I mean come on...Can anyone say, *"amateur?"* Also, you totally let those twins get the best of you!" she teased. Ricky snickered, agreeing with her statement. Allen shot a cold glance back at him and Ricky straightened. He turned back to Veronica and crossed his arms; a smirk on his face.

"Well, maybe you and I should have a little brawl, see who wins then-"

"-I will-"

"-You will-" Allen chuckled as the two spoke in unison. Ricky rolled his eyes, but chuckled despite his firm rule about hating every time Allen flirted with a girl. Veronica also laughed and punched Allen lightly on the shoulder. He smiled at Ricky as Zech wagged his tail, always happy when his friends were happy.

"Well, Veronica, now that you're part of the group, can I call you Ronny?" he chuckled, giving her a sideways look. Veronica studied him, grinning. She wasn't about to give him that sort of satisfaction yet.

"Don't kid yourself," she said. But she flashed him a big, toothy smile to show her joy at the fact she had been let in. She caught Zech in her eyes, his head tilted curiously. She circled him, the fox staring at her purple hair in awe.

"Can I call you Ronny?" he asked sweetly. For the first time since they arrived in the Understreet, he lifted his helmet, catching her eyes in his amber ones.

Veronica looked up at him and Allen clenched his jaw. He was unsure of her; there was so much about her that was hidden behind her high wall of caution...and... pain. Who was she, really?

"Of course *you* can! And you're Zech?" she asked. Zech accepted her friendship without question and Allen wished he could be so childlike and unguarded. He was actually amazed that Zech could be that way after all he'd been through. Allen went to stand by Ricky, who was also smiling quietly, in spite of his natural caution around strangers.

"Yep! I... am... Zech!" he struggled to get the words right, but smiled with triumph at the end. Veronica looked him in the eye and accepted his wholehearted, unguarded offer of friendship gratefully. Allen grinned at Zech and nodded with approval.

"Awesome...Anyway, I'm going to assume we're using the centaur for something, so... let's get it back to your place, and we can discuss Zech's escape. He obviously can't stay here, which I assume you know," she said with a smile. Veronica waved to the people helping move the centaur and they got up and began to move, the hum of their own conversation silencing.

The way she had barged in and taken control was surprising, it was like she already knew exactly what to do. It was a bit intimidating, but Allen didn't mind. He crossed his arms, his jaw set as he tried to think through all that had happened tonight, falling back with Ricky.

"This...is going to be interesting," he murmured, a bemused smile on his lips. Ricky snorted at the magnitude of such an understatement and nodded in agreement. Allen watched Ronny with a lingering grin. He looked at Ricky.

"What do you think?" he asked. Ricky's eyes widened and he chuckled wryly at the inquiry.

"*Now,* after we're knee deep in it you ask my opinion?!...I don't know Allen. I'm getting nervous."

Allen nodded with understanding. He was nervous too. Zech had been revealed, not completely, but definitely exposed to the Fence in the Arena. If anything came up, they would turn on him in a flash for a bite to eat. But maybe that small fact was why Veronica's involvement would help.

He had seen her fight in the Scandal. He knew that she could help them. He just hoped she really was on their side.

Damon sat in the control room when he looked over to see Veronica's camera. She was talking to Fencers, and as she turned, he watched as she spoke with...

"Holy...It's Subject..." he looked around; the room was empty. He grabbed a pair of headphones and put them on, tuning into what she was saying. Was she arresting them? It didn't seem like that.

"Awesome, anyway, I'm going to assume we're using the centaur for something, so... let's get it back to your place, and we can discuss Zech's escape. He obviously can't stay here; which I assume you know." His eyes widened. She was going rogue! He knew this would happen if they sent her to the Fence.

"Just like your mother..." he whispered. He looked around and scrolled through her memory.

Damon then did something that would've gotten him killed if anyone ever knew. He recorded all of her accounts of walking through the Ghetto and edited it together before he put it on repeat. He deleted the files of Veronica's memory of the subject, the audio of her agreeing to help them... and then, when he was finished, he sat back. He let out a deep sigh and hunched over the desk.

"Oh Raven..." he groaned, and ran a hand through his pepper-grey hair. A small smile twitched at his lips. Typical of a Boyce to become insubordinate. He'd guard this secret with his life. He had given up on Raven, but he wouldn't give up on her daughter.

He wasn't about to lose another kid, blood or surrogate, just to keep a job he had never wanted in the first place. However, as he looked through her files, again, something kept eating at the back of his mind. The shorter man looked so...familiar, and he couldn't put his finger on why...

He didn't have time to think about that right now. Veronica had changed sides...and Damon was almost tempted to follow. No... she'd need him more here, with the authorities, guiding them away from her trail. Hopefully he wouldn't get executed for it.

"Be smart Ronny...you're up against the Judge..." he whispered. He looked over his shoulder and clicked out of her camera.

The centaur was strapped to a large cart. Allen tossed Zech his cloak and he wrapped it around his body and flipped the hood up to completely hide his face. He was used to this drill by now. Stay hidden, or be exposed to the Stratus.

Zech was assigned the duty to push it, which he accepted happily. They spread a sheet over it to keep it safe from prying eyes; people who would rat them out for a gallon of water.

All who entered the Understreet were sworn to secrecy knowing if one person made an accusation, the accused could make one right back. Everything about the Understreet was illegal, so there was a thieves' code of honor that kept the Understreet cloaked from the prying eyes of the Magnus mechs and Stratus.

Outside though, with the more honest Fencers, those who won resources in the Understreet had to be careful. They had to take a vow of silence before they were allowed to leave.

"I think that went rather well...you know what Allen, I think your plan's gonna work," muttered Ricky as they climbed up the rusty service ladder. Veronica snickered under her breath.

"Ah, y'hear that? A genuine compliment," said Allen with a grin. Veronica chuckled and nudged him.

"Hey dude, it's good to see you again in the daylight," she said. Allen glanced at her and nodded. His heart skipped a beat as she looked up at him, like an electric shock. He had only known her for that one evening, and for some reason it seemed like he had known her for forever.

"Totally...you know, it'll be nice having you around. When we were in the Scandal, you were...awesome... Got any moves you could show me? I mean, since I apparently got my butt kicked," he rambled. Veronica rolled her eyes playfully.

"Dude, I've been trained in combat by some of the most elite soldiers... you know, because of my mom... How did you learn to fight? Did you just figure it out?" she asked. Allen blushed and shrugged coolly.

"Yeah...yeah pretty much," he murmured. He grinned wolfishly and nudged her. Veronica looked up at him and narrowed her eyes playfully.

"You haven't seen me fight for my life though, like actually. Arenas are a bit different than the streets. Besides, how many times do you have to fight a day?" he said, with a little shrug. Veronica snorted with laughter and gave him a playful shove.

"I mean, I guess you got me there...but I think I kind of proved myself in the Scandal," she said. Allen grinned smugly.

"You had the element of surprise on your side. What if you were facing a group of-" Veronica grabbed his hand before wrapping her arm around the back of his head and throwing him over her shoulder. Allen shouted in surprise as Zech let out a bark.

Allen shot up as Zech moved forward, and he waved Zech off. He growled under his breath but when he saw Ricky cackling with laughter, he wagged his tail, and let himself relax. Allen looked at Veronica and chuckled as she completely cracked up laughing.

"Ok, ok, you got me. But, again, element of surprise," he said with a cool shrug of his shoulders. Ricky rolled his eyes to the sky, a sly grin on his face.

"Alright, well the two of you ain't fighting in my house. If you wanna spar, you gotta take it outside," he grunted.

Veronica saluted him. "Of course, that would just be stupid," she said. Ricky nodded, and his face flushed red as she winked teasingly at him.

Allen rubbed his back, which ached dully from being thrown over Veronica's shoulder, a big, stupid grin on his face.

The four made it to Ricky's apartment without incident. Zech and Allen heaved the mech up from its platform, and Veronica pushed the dolly out of their way. Ricky and Veronica joined them as they carried the heavy machine up the metal stairs leading to the flat. Allen's foot caught on one of the steps. He tripped and it was like watching someone fall in slow motion. When his rear hit the stairs, he yelped, arms stuck up as he held the mech.

Ricky and Veronica burst out laughing, Zech asked if he was ok. Allen chuckled, and blushed as he laughed at himself. His arms were shaking as he held up the mech, which hovered inches away from crushing him as his back stung with dull pain.

He lumbered back up, which wasn't easy with that big, dumb machine weighing a ton threatening to topple on top of him! They finished their climb, but after fighting in the arena, getting thrown by Veronica, and falling on his butt on the stairs, Allen was ready to call it a day.

"I swear I'm fine. Do you know how many times a day I do crap like this? That was nothing," he rambled, and his friends laughed harder. Allen smiled as they made it to the door, he couldn't help but feel a sense of community around him. It was the first time in years people he really cared about laughed with him, or worked together to accomplish something he believed in.

Ricky unlocked it, and shoved it open. They set the mech down. Allen shook out his hands and let out a relieved groan.

The four entered Ricky's house, and as they glanced around at the cramped space Allen suggested, "Here, let's move everything out of the way and set this in the center," pointing at the couch.

The group nodded and pushed the big black sofa against the back wall of the living room. Veronica slipped on the old rag rug and it was Allen's turn to laugh.

Zech glanced at them and saw them struggling with the couch. He grunted, moved with his incredible speed and picked it up.

Allen glanced at Ricky, who wasn't used to having this many people in his house. However, he was smiling and enjoying the company; usually they never had visitors. It had always just been Ricky and Allen. This turn of events felt good.

"Alright, I'll take everything apart," Ricky announced as he grabbed his boxes of tools from the shelves. Allen chuckled and wandered into the kitchen, leaning over the counter and watching everyone.

"Anyone want instant noodles?" he queried as he drummed his hands against the counter. Ricky lifted his fingers absently as his mind zoned in on his work.

Allen got out as many packs of the easy and cheap food as he could. They usually came with the provision trucks. They were flavorless, requiring people to spice it up for themselves.

He was no expert in the art of cooking, but he made do. Usually he just dumped in vegetables and whatever seasonings were handy and it suited the two bachelor roommates perfectly fine when they didn't feel like going out to eat; which was most of the time. It's not like the food out on the streets was any better.

Zech took one of the books off the shelves and sat on the couch, determined to learn as much as possible before they had to leave.

Allen got to work on their fast food dinner and Veronica stood by the impromptu chef; draping a casual arm around his shoulders. The sound of Ricky's work and Zech's clumsy reading filled the silence as Allen sparked under her touch.

"Why does it feel like I've known you forever?" she asked. Allen glanced down at her and smiled.

"You know, I was thinking the same thing. Maybe I should unlock some friendship levels so I can learn more about you," he suggested with a wink.

Veronica smirked and sat on the countertop. She looked down at him and tilted her head. His nose had a bulbous tip that hooked like a hawk's beak. It was a little thing that the elite would've seen as inferior, but she found that little imperfection attractive, in its own way. Something about it was also familiar. The way his eyes squinted apprehensively at people, or his bushy brows were almost always furrowed. She knew that face…

"Well…what about you? What happened to you?" she asked. Allen went to the fridge. That pressure weighed down on his chest, that feeling of uncertainty, of an unease that almost felt like anger. Ricky dropped his screwdriver and he glanced up, before he scrambled to get his tool.

"If I tell you my story, you gotta tell me yours," he retorted, waiting for the water to boil. Veronica sighed and the two shook on it. With a wry smile, Allen leaned against the counter and began to recount the details of his past.

"Well… you know, it's complicated. It was ten years ago, but I still feel the pain. My dad just disappeared, left me alone out here. I guess instead of mourning him like a normal person, I've somehow convinced myself that he's still alive, that I wasn't good enough for him or some bullshit. Or that he's locked away somewhere. I guess it's just, I can't imagine him dead. I guess I'm just stuck in denial, anger and, wow, you really have that effect on people, don't you?" he rambled.

He got a bottle of tequila and triple sec from one of the shelves and grabbed a glass. She watched as he looked from the glass to the bottle, shrugged, and just drank from the bottle.

Veronica frowned at him and slid off the counter. She placed a hand on his shoulder and smiled sadly.

"I guess you just want to tell your issues to anyone who'll listen. My *thing* is quite recent. My world fell apart just three years ago… The sick thing is, my mom's execution was live streamed. Everyone saw it. Magnus used it to make an example of rulebreakers or whatever the Judge is pushing these days. I was at the...in class, and...I saw my own mother getting beamed through the head," she murmured, biting her lip as she mimicked a laser beam going through her ear and her head exploding.

Allen's eyes widened and he hesitantly reached out, wanting to hug her as he saw the tears well in her eyes.

"God, that really is horrible! Jesus, I'm over here belly aching and, damn, Veronica," he stammered quietly. Veronica waved him off, a sad chuckle escaping her lips.

"We all experience these things differently, it's not a contest... The point is, I guess we have a lot in common. I mean, I guess that's why we can connect like that."

Ricky coughed and jumped into the conversation. "Look at us, a ton of sad saps. I mean, what kind of happy, content person offers to give up everything they've worked for to help a, no Offense Zech-"

"-Offense?"

"-An extremely dangerous mutant escape the *flying* city? No one!" he exclaimed. Zech glanced at Ricky and tilted his head in confusion.

"Do you also want to share a sad story?" he asked. Ricky looked questioningly at Zech before he laughed wryly.

"No, I'm fine, I'm fine!" he grunted, and with that, Ricky turned back to the mech. Allen laughed and leaned into Veronica.

"He's not fine," he whispered.

Veronica rolled her eyes playfully and giggled. The two smiled at each other, their gaze lingering.

Allen cleared his throat and went to the liquor cabinet. He pulled out a half-full bottle of vodka and poured some into two glasses. He handed her a glass out of consideration before gulping his own down. Veronica arched an eyebrow as she studied the alcohol with narrowed eyes.

He refilled his and coughed, a goofy smile on his face. "To being more alike than we thought," he said. Veronica grinned and clinked glasses with him. They both shot back the alcohol with a swift jerk. Allen refilled the glasses and got another glass out to give to Ricky.

"Let's toast to being so unstable that we want to help a dangerous mutant with a heart of gold," said Allen. Ricky took one of the glasses and they cheered. The three knocked back the drinks as Zech snapped shut the book to signal he was done.

"I want drink!" he barked. Allen shook his head firmly. Zech whined, his ears pressed to the back of his head.

He didn't question Allen's authority, so he didn't ask again. Ricky, Allen and Veronica chuckled. Things just felt so perfect in that moment. Allen frowned when he realized just how much this meant to him. He couldn't lose this.

Veronica and Zech had fallen asleep on the couch after hours of working on the suit. Bowls, once filled with ramen were scattered around the living room as well as shot glasses and beer bottles—most of which were consumed by Allen.

Allen sat with Ricky on the floor, holding things in place as Ricky put screws in place. The scritching of Ricky's tools, and the light snores of Zech and Veronica were the only sounds.

Allen could already see the mech suit coming together. The light was dim, provided by one lamp in the corner of the living room and, of course, the curtains were drawn.

"So, what do we think of Veronica?" he slurred. Ricky glanced up at Allen and a small smile played at the ends of his lips.

"I don't not like her. She's cool...but can we trust her?" he asked. Allen glanced behind him, smiling softly at the sight of Veronica slumped across Zech. The fox was sprawled across the couch, his soft fur the perfect pillow for the muscular girl.

"Yeah...I do," he said. Ricky shrugged, satisfied with his friend's answer. He didn't sense any malice from her. It was surprising to him how a person of the Elite could be genuine. She was a rarity. The two sat quietly after that for another moment.

Allen wiped his eyes with exhaustion as the day's events caught up with him, but he continued to help. He knew his friend had been up all night the night before getting Zech's exoskeleton ready for the arena. He couldn't help but admire his best friend's work ethic. If it weren't for him, the idea of getting Zech out of the city would merely be a pipe dream, and they'd probably already be busted.

"Hey, I just wanted to say thanks," Allen yawned. Ricky glanced up at him, the words dragging him from his work induced daze. He smiled crookedly, and rolled his eyes.

"Shut up...I knew you'd be lost without my genius," Ricky replied playfully. Allen snickered.

"All that genius and yet you still can't figure out how to talk to women," he teased. Ricky looked down at him and scowled.

"Well not everyone can be a Rosinsky," Ricky responded with a chuckle. Allen grinned and lay down. He swallowed nervously as he came to a realization.

"We have one more week...I'm kind of nervous, like, actually terrified." His voice riddled with anxiety. Ricky glanced down at him and clenched his jaw, nodding. They were all scared. In the pleasant comradery of the evening, he had almost forgotten the Herculean task ahead of them.

"Don't worry, I got your back," Ricky answered him with a reassuring smile. Allen patted his friend on the shoulder, before finally giving in, slumping down to the floor and closing his eyes. He pushed his fear to the back of his mind. At least here, with his friends he was safe.

MEDUSA

Ricky stood; his shoulders hunched over in exhaustion. He needed sleep, good sleep. Last night, he and Allen had stayed up until their eyes had been practically burnt out of their heads. He stared with exhausted confusion at a holographic wanted poster with Zech's face on it.

This wasn't good. Things were getting harder. It was like all the cards had been stacked against them from the beginning. It was only a matter of time before things got completely out of hand.

He growled and with a hammer from his toolbox, he smashed the cubelet that was showing the sign. No more of that to distract him. One less problem staring him in the face. Problems...there were a lot of those.

"O'Brien!" shouted an angry man. Ricky flinched, with shoulders immediately hunching up and he held up his hands, as if expecting a blow. He glanced up; his head defensively bowed as his supervisor stormed towards him.

"I'm sorry, I'm sorry... Wait... I mean... What do you need?" he asked, trying to straighten, but his own body wouldn't allow it. His supervisor scowled at him, clearly irritated.

"What do you mean? The faulty disk, do you have it? You were supposed to report back to me and deliver it, where is it?" His anger was palpable.

Ricky froze, he knew this would happen. "I uh, left for a lunch break...and I was mugged," he murmured. His muscles tightened; his body began to shake with anxiety. The supervisor clenched his jaw, his face turning a bright pink.

"You left the building with a valuable disk!? Those things are worth a fortune, do you know that?!" he roared. Ricky let out a breath. Dammit, he could already see his inevitable resignation. All for some mutant!? He had a good thing going, and now it was gone!

"I'm sorry sir, I-" he muttered, but was cut off with a groan. The supervisor waved his hands.

"You fixed the assembly mech, correct?" Ricky gulped and nodded. At least that wasn't a lie. The supervisor let out a breath and nodded.

"Well *at least* that is done," he muttered, rubbing his temple. Ricky watched him trying to calm himself down.

"Are you firing me?" he asked hesitantly. The older man looked up and crossed his arms with a sigh.

"Listen, you're a good mechanic… and I wish I could let this slide, but I just can't. We're already low on finances, and losing that disk will set us back severely. I'm sorry Mr. O'brien. It's not personal." Ricky nodded and took off his ID badge, shoving it in the supervisor's hands.

"Don't worry, it's not like I needed a place to sleep anymore anyway," he grumbled. The supervisor blinked and looked at his feet in remorse. It was never easy firing someone, especially when they knew how hard it was to live in the Ghetto. The Powerplant was, of course, what controlled housing. They'd let Ricky stay in his house long enough to pack everything up, and then he'd be on the streets.

The Powerplant's security was gone now though, and Ricky couldn't draw up any emotion other than a cold, controlled fury. He knew this would happen. He knew it was a bad idea from the start. Why had he ever let Allen talk him into this? Why couldn't they have just turned Zech away!? His hands curled into balls and his body shook.

Losing his job...Ricky couldn't shake the chills it had brought him. It reminded him of Granda. He shuddered, his skin tingling in phantom pain. Although he didn't want to go back, his anger and his trembling forced him to remember.

"Filthy, hybrid pox!" yelled the old man. Ricky flinched; his green eyes wide with fear as he hid underneath his cot. His two buck teeth protruded from his trembling lips as he curled up.
"Where are ya, yee feckin rat!?" Ricky flinched, pleading for his mother to save him, for his father to

intervene... but neither would come. After the house fire, he was stuck with the miserable old man he called Granda. He hated times like these, when the smell of beer, sweat and cigarettes consumed the small home.

"There you are!" growled the old man as his large calloused hand ripped Ricky out from under the meager bed. He shrieked, fighting at all costs to break free.

"I didn't do it! I didn't!" he cried, tears streaming from his puffy red eyes. Granda held up a broken, wooden deer figure.

"You broke my stag! How do you break a stag!?" hollered Granda, fire in his cold, blue eyes. Ricky sobbed, his arms aching at the rock-hard grip.

"It fell- I tried to catch it!" Ricky had been playing with it. He thought it had been a toy, and when the door had slammed shut and the loud belch echoed from the rickety hallway, he panicked. He had practice from the warning of that noise. In his flight he had knocked it down and then he hid.

His face stung as the loud slap of Granda's knocked him across the room. He slumped, wheezing out cries for help, cries for his mum, for his da, for anyone, but they were lost in flames.

"Never touch my carvings again you wee cumstain!" hissed Granda. Ricky sniffled, wiped his nose with his arm as a white, hot anger took over his whole body. He promised himself he'd never be like that man.

Ricky rubbed his cheek, and he shook his head to clear it of the painful memory. That same year Granda had died all yellowed with liver failure, and that's when he was picked up and sent to the Home. He had been ten then, and on the bus ride there, he met Allen, and his new life began. His new family was found, one filled with just as much trouble and angst as the last, just without the beatings.

"And here we go again. Me takin' the brunt of this dumbass, little shite. Gettin' me fired..." He let out a tense sigh and ran a hand through his hair. Maybe it was a blessing in disguise, not that he really believed in blessings.

Zech smiled as he held up a dragon fruit from the cartons of old produce that was set up in the market.

"This fruit pretty!" Allen gave him a look and Zech smiled sheepishly before correcting himself.

"I mean...this fruit *is* pretty," he said. Allen chuckled. He took the fruit in his hands and held it up to the light.

"Yeah, it's something else. Definitely not the occasional apple... Good find...but uh, I don't know if it's ripe, it's kinda hard to tell. I don't see enough dragon fruit to know the difference." Allen tossed the fruit back in the carton, grabbed Zech's hand, leading him on.

Allen reached into someone's waist coat and slipped a bottle out. He popped it open and drank the liquor inside. When he saw Zech watching him with curious eyes he frowned.

"Do as I say, not as I do," he grunted, a cheeky grin spreading across his face as he took another drink.

Zech grinned and followed his father figure dutifully, his cloak wrapped tightly around him, his gloves covered his paws.

Everything about him was off. He was inhuman, but Allen knew that, compared to the world, to the Elites gorging themselves in the skyline or the gangs that fought and pillaged mercilessly, Zech had more humanity. The thought made him both proud and sad.

They picked through the market one stall at a time, until Allen was satisfied. This time they had gotten milk. It was a week away from the expiration date, and still smelled good, so he had taken his chances. It was so hard to get fresh dairy. Allen took one last drink of the bottle before tossing it in an overflowing trash pile on the side of the street.

"Allen, where does food come from on Island?" asked Zech. Allen made a vague gesture to the fence.

"Ricky told me they grow the food from cells in like...meat breweries. Crazy biology stuff. I'm not well versed in it...but the idea sounds cool," he explained simply. Zech nodded, content with his answer.

He went back to the list of produce in his mind. Milk? Check, Ricky would be happy about that. Instant pasta? Check. Beans? Check. Rice? Check. Canned veggies? Check. Cheese that had touches of mold? Check, he would have to cut off the mold though. Bread?

Check...mold free, thankfully. Peanut butter? Check. This would last them at least three weeks if they rationed it... But of course, he had to remind himself, they didn't have three weeks. They'd be leaving in less than two days.

"We ought to have a feast, eh Zech?" he said, wriggling his brows. Zech laughed and playfully pushed Allen away. As he turned, he caught a glimpse of three, familiar, burly men... One way too memorable for comfort. Bald, scarred, and disgusting. Bruce.

He gulped and walked faster in the opposite direction. Zech glanced at Allen and took one stride to catch up. He asked no questions. He had grown accustomed to Allen picking up his pace in public places. He never asked why. He had learned to trust Allen's instincts.

Allen was grateful for this. He didn't like explaining himself. They escaped the market as quietly as they had come, the crowds of people giving out to trickles here and there as they made their way. Allen glanced around, pulling Zech into an alleyway, a shortcut he had found ages ago that led back to Ricky's apartment.

Their step echoed, bouncing between the buildings. Puddles of mud filled potholes, and the stench of garbage piled everywhere stung Allen's eyes but Zech had no problem with the stench. He jumped in the puddles, Allen chuckling, dodged the muddy splashes.

"Careful man, you're gonna drop the produce!" said Allen. Zech smiled sheepishly, before kicking mud out of his way.

"No, I'm not! You drop produce!" he protested with a cheeky grin. Allen smacked his lips in disbelief and kicked mud back. Zech laughed, before freezing, his ears sticking up and forward, hackles raised. Allen froze as well; it was always alarming when Zech got that look.

"Zech?" asked Allen, that's when he heard it. A subtle, clicking noise, followed by a slide across concrete. A quiet hiss shook him to his core and he whipped around. Zech growled menacingly.

Allen's eyes widened in dread at the sight of it. The size of a man, the terror of death, the silhouette of a Gorgon. Its snake hair writhed, its eyes glowed with turquoise intensity, as the dim light in the alley caught the sheen of its metal. Where legs should be, a snake body slithered ever closer.

He felt his mouth go dry, his heart pound. It suddenly hit him. He was staring a Gorgon straight in the eyes!

"Run! Zech! Run!" Allen stumbled, twisting his body and taking off in a dead sprint, bags of produce weighing him down. Zech followed, his eyes wide with horror.

The Gorgon shrieked, taking off in hot pursuit after its prey. It unfurled its gliders, and swooped up a wall, launching itself up and over them to block their path.

Allen skidded to a stop, covering his eyes. Zech squeezed his eyes shut as well, one glance at Allen to confirm. The gorgon shot its poison, the silvery liquid landing on Zech's cloak with a sizzle. Allen pushed him away, the both of them falling to the ground, bags of groceries tumbling. He cursed.

Zech glanced down at his cloak, his eyes widening as the fabric petrified. He glanced up, seeing the Gorgon approaching them. Allen scrambled to the garbage, and grabbed a crowbar.

"Zech, get out of here!" He pulled the fox up by his hood. Zech jumped to his feet.

"It will just follow!" he cried, holding his hands away from the stiff poison on his cloak. Allen cursed when he saw it.

"Take that off! Run! I'll hold it back." Allen gave a firm nod. Zech frowned. He didn't believe Allen could take the Gorgon on by himself, but Allen looked at him with such raw intensity and care he was moved to submission. He whimpered, lowered his ears and loped away.

He turned to the Gorgon, as it pounced after Zech, who was its true target. Allen jumped in the way, swinging the crow bar with all his strength. The Gorgon crashed to the ground, a shrill shriek screaming from its audio.

Allen jumped away from the snakes as they spat poison his way. He looked over, seeing a trash can lid. He reached for it, the gorgon's arms grabbed his waist and pulled him down.

Allen kicked it off, grabbing the lid and holding it up in front of his body like a shield as he advanced. The poison sprayed against his shield with stinging pressure. He hit the lid against the snake hair, bringing the crow bar down on top of its crown of writhing minions until no more poison assaulted the shield. He brought it up and the gorgon swiped at him, slapping it out of his hands. It went tumbling two yards away and the coiled gorgon sprang on top of him.

Allen held up his hand haphazardly, almost out of habit, covering its mouth as a spray of poison spewed out. He screamed as his hand erupted in fire, his skin turning bright red as it began to puss and sizzle, the blisters quickly hardening into solid calcium.

Tears spilled out of his eyes as he writhed, willing his hand to stay on the gorgon's mouth as he brought his left hand up with the crowbar, hacking at the nape of the gorgon's neck. His entire body was on fire as more poison dug into his flesh, his hand became a blanched white that sickened him. He wailed, mind numb, his arm a blur as he cleaved through the neck, sparks of electricity flying!

The poisonous onslaught stopped and the Gorgon's head fell, *clang,* at his feet. He jumped away, screaming in pain and watched his hand sizzle as it turned to stone.

The calcification slowed at his wrist but the pain and the horror of what had happened was unbearable! He stumbled to his feet, rocking himself as his hand burned with unrelenting fire, squeezed like iron and throbbed with the force of pounding ocean waves.

He roared with the excruciating agony, hot tears blinding him. Allen choked, waving his calcified hand in the air to relieve it. All in vain, it only hissed and burned, fossilizing before his eyes. He shot a furious glance at the body of the Gorgon, growling under his clenched jaws.

Using his good hand, he pushed himself back onto his feet. Already his hand had hardened completely. It was a statue, and numb. He had lost all feeling to it. A choking sob escaped him. He wiped his eyes roughly on the sleeve of his good arm as he turned away from the smoldering monster.

Allen carefully slipped his stone hand into his pocket, fearing that if he hit it against something, it would shatter into a thousand pieces. He had lost all physical connection to it, which was terrifying. What was even worse was now he couldn't even feel the pain -all feeling left him and now it was just dead weight.

It was his writing hand, and writing had been his one connection to his father. Poetry was his connection to humanity... He groaned. Guess he had to work with what he had left. He glanced at his left hand.

"Shit! It'll have to do..."

The reality of his situation grew worse. Where was Zech? He hoped he had done what he ordered. As long as Zech was safe.

He whimpered, stumbling along the rutted and garbage lined street. Ricky was going to freak out. He was going to finish the Gorgon's job and kill him completely. He sighed, thinking hard on the events, as each new brick of reality was laid on his shoulders. A Gorgon had attacked them.

That meant one thing. They were wanted -for real. His heart skipped a beat and he clenched his jaw. He needed a drink. He needed...to cut off this hand. His stomach rolled at the thought. It was a miracle that Ricky was an expert on mechanics. He'd be lost without him.

"Allen!" Allen looked up, not expecting such anger to come from the voice of his best friend. He flinched; Ricky furiously bore down on him.

"I got fired! I got fired, and you wanna know why?" He was still red faced and angry, as he stomped up and prodded a rage filled finger into Allen's chest.

Allen grimaced, processing this new information. He looked at his friend questioningly, his lip trembling just a bit. He felt like this was somehow his fault, and he wouldn't be surprised if it was.

"Yeah...yeah, I got fired because they knew I stole that disk for Zech's bloody exosuit. I got fired because you couldn't just leave things alone! How am I gonna survive in this hellhole now?" snarled Ricky. Allen swatted Ricky's hand away from him, his bad arm aching dully in his jacket.

"That sucks, I'm sorry," he said, and he meant it. He never wanted Ricky to lose anything. Ricky didn't deserve any of the disaster Allen had brought on him.

"I knew this was a bad idea from the start! We should've never gotten involved with this!" Ricky raked his hands through his hair. Allen frowned, cheeks flushing with new anger.

"Don't say that. We're doing the right thing," Allen replied vehemently. Ricky groaned, pacing in circles; his hands up, his hands clenched, his hands in his hair. He shook his head, his fury growing.

"No. No we're not! We're doing something - we're doing something that's going to get us killed! We should've never helped Zech. We're in *way* over our heads Allen, and there will be hell to pay!"

Allen shoved Ricky with his good hand, his teeth bared. He couldn't bear the words; he couldn't bear the thought of giving up on Zech.

"Don't ever say that again! Zech deserves life, and I'm willing to do anything to help him," Allen snarled. Ricky snorted, shoving him back. Allen strained to keep his hand in his pocket and not stumble.

"Really? You're gonna sacrifice everything? What about me? What about what I wanted? Do you care more about that monster than you do about us? I'm your best friend, you asshole! God, you're so selfish!" Ricky shouted.

"Well you could've left a long time ago, but you chose to stick with us. You're in this."

Ricky clenched his jaw; he knew Allen wasn't just talking about Zech when he said that. No. Those words carried the weight of a thousand arguments and depressing nights of booze, and the years of friendship that teetered and tottered precariously on the thin line of the baggage both of them carried. His words were stolen, and all he could do was react to his rage.

He threw a punch. Allen swiveled out of the way, grabbed his arm and tripped him. Ricky caught himself; kicking Allen hard in the shin. He seethed, slapping his friend hard on the back. Ricky threw a punch for Allen's stomach. He took the punch with a grunt. He pushed Ricky away from him and grabbed his collar.

Ricky felt his throat tighten as tears filled his eyes. His breath hitched and the two glared at each other with tear-filled scowls. As he was about to tell Ricky to stop, they heard a whimper.

"Why you two fighting?" asked Zech. He had been wandering the streets, stressed and worried for Allen, and what did he see when he finally found him? The two people who took him in, loved him when no one else would, fighting each other.

Allen and Ricky looked up and hung their heads in shame. Ricky cracked under Zech's hurt gaze. He looked away and wiped his eyes roughly, his face flushed with guilt.

"We're just...playing," said Ricky with a nervous frown. Allen nodded in agreement.

"But we're done now...right, Ricky?" asked Allen.

Ricky looked from Allen to Zech and he sighed, his anger breaking and letting sadness out like a burst dam. His green eyes flooded with tears and he crumbled to the ground. Zech watched him as Allen rushed to his side and pulled him into a hug.

He desperately hugged him back, a million soft sorries slipping from his clenched jaw. Allen swallowed as his own tears fell freely now. What were they doing? They were falling apart.

"Allen, what happened to the monster?" asked Zech, his ears pressing to the back of his head. Ricky looked up in confusion as Allen let out another sob. The reality of his situation was tearing him apart as fresh pain stabbed in his arm in remembrance. He stood up slowly, helping Ricky up with his good hand.

"Well it's dead...but uh...this happened." He didn't know how to describe it, so he pulled his hand out of his pocket. Ricky gasped, his face lost all its color and Zech barked with shock.

"Jesus Christ! See this is what I'm talking about!" exclaimed Ricky. Allen pursed his lips and nodded, looking at Ricky and wincing as phantom pain shot through his body.

"Gorgon...I need to deal with this," he groaned. Ricky gagged, looking away from the horrid sight, his eyes squeezed shut.

"By all means...Jesus...I saw wanted posters..." said Ricky. Zech's ears drooped and a small whine escaped his maw. Allen paled at the thought. That confirmed the Gorgon. He cursed under his breath. Zech hung his head.

"I'm sorry Allen… This my fault," he whimpered, overcome with guilt. Ricky frowned, hearing it from him was too heart wrenching and he couldn't handle it.

"No...no, it's not. It's the Stratus' fault. Come on Allen, let's get you fixed up," he said, the storm in his mind calming. Allen was right. He couldn't just leave. He was tangled up in this mess whether he liked it or not...and he'd rather be with Allen than alone. After all, they were all they had.

Ricky was furious as he examined Allen's ruined hand. He knew who could help...but the mere idea of dealing with Maya made him feel sick. He led Allen up the stairs and back into his apartment. With the Gorgon's mark, they didn't need to be exposed.

"Allen...we need Maya," he said. Allen looked up at him, his eyes glistening with new tears as he understood. It was in Ricky's eyes. It's got to be amputated...

"I can't let her see me like this," he groaned. Ricky growled and slammed the door behind them.

"Look at your damn hand, mate! She's the only one who can help us! I would if I could; I just... you're not made of bolts and wires. I'm gettin' Maya," he barked. Allen lowered his head.

"You're right. You're right. I need a surgeon. Get her," he said. Ricky nodded and dashed out the door.

Allen paced to the kitchen and grabbed the remaining bottle of vodka. He pulled the cap off with his teeth then chugged the entire bottle. He wiped his eyes. Everything. He had lost everything.

As if Zech had read his mind, he whined and nuzzled Allen's cheek. Allen smiled sadly, and blinked away the tears in his eyes.

"It's not your fault, Zech."

AMPUTATE

Maya left the surgery tent, peeling off her bloody gloves. A contented smile on her face. A successful heart transplant. It felt good to have saved one of her own.

She shed her white coat and took her supplies to the wash tent. Mist began to fill the streets as the clouds descended as fog. She remembered too many patients who couldn't afford an oxygen mask...and how they contracted altitude sickness. It had been hard to save them.

She left the wash tent to make her way to the living quarters, when a puff of red hair caught her eye. She turned to see an all too familiar, weasel-faced man sprinting down the street toward her. When he was aware that she had noticed him, he shouted and waved his arms. Maya's eyes widened with alarm and she jogged over.

"Ricky? What are you doing here?" She asked. Ricky doubled over to catch his breath.

"We need your help. You have to help us," he gasped. Maya shook her head with confusion. What was wrong?

"Why? What's going on? Where's Allen?" Ricky held up his hand for her to wait, as he gasped to regain his breath. As his panting slowed, he planted his hands on her shoulders.

"Allen's at my apartment. We *need* you. You have to amputate his hand," he blurted out, his voice strained. Maya's face drained of color at his request.

"Why didn't you bring him here? Ricky what happened? You're not making sense! Is Allen ok?" She rambled with growing panic. Ricky grabbed her hand and pulled her away from the Medicum.

"Wait! I can't just leave! I could get in-"

"It was a gorgon mech, Maya! He was protecting Zech from a Stratus mechanical, and he got marked. If I brought him here, he would've gotten executed on sight. Gorgon's only mark the most wanted criminals...and Allen and I are associated with Zech," he hissed into her ear. Maya's eyes widened as her jaw dropped. Ricky rubbed the bridge of his nose.

"Ricky...I'm...I'm coming, I'm coming. Just let me get some equipment," she breathed, before jogging back. Ricky followed her.

"I'll help," he murmured. Maya looked back at him and noticed the glisten of tears in his eyes.

"Are you ok?" She asked. Ricky clenched his jaw and avoided her gaze.

"I'm fine," he grunted. Maya shook her head as she strapped an emergency supply belt on and began to pack equipment into it. Her heart was thundering, and she could barely breathe at the thought of the task being thrust upon her. Any conversation, even with Ricky, to distract her was a conversation worth having.

"No, you're not," she said as she shouldered into a clean, white coat that draped down to her knees and hopefully hid the emergency supply belt. She smoothed her collar and grabbed Ricky by the forearm, leading him out before anyone could stop them.

Once they were away from the Medicum and hidden by the ruins around it, Ricky jerked away his arm and marched ahead of her, embarrassed by his tears.

"Yeah, maybe I'm not… This whole thing is getting so overwhelming. I've never worked this hard on anything...I lost my job at the Plant, today, and for what? This is a suicide mission...and you wouldn't know because you've been at the Medicum. It's been awful, just so...so *impossible*," he groaned.

Maya frowned at his words. She found herself silently agreeing, despite the little jab at her. By making the decision to help them, on a whim, she could be risking everything: her life, her career, her family. Ricky had just spoken the same fears. Although his were a little closer to home. Maya didn't feel like she had the right yet to say she understood. She barely even knew Zech.

"We are really giving up everything but...when I decided to help you guys, I did based on the fact that; I was a slave to the elite. You were too. Think about it-" she began to smile an almost crazed smile -the smile of freedom- "we're choosing liberty."

Ricky looked down at her, and for the first time he felt respected and understood. "When you put it like that…" he murmured.

Maya sighed softly as the two skipped into a jog to make good time. Maya frowned as she realized freedom came at a great price, and she knew she was about to be thrust into a terribly costly freedom.

Veronica went through her patrol, combing the streets for nothing. She couldn't return to the Medicum for fear the other Stratus officers would grow suspicious. She had just disappeared. That's what she was going to do anyway. She was a pretty bad deserter if she couldn't even take out the earpiece that was the leash that tied her to the Elite.

As she meandered through an alleyway, mist obscured the ground as it floated through the buildings, and her foot caught against a slumped figure. She yelped as she tripped.

She quickly regained her balance and whirled back. What was that? She cautiously stepped towards the figure and prodded it with her foot. It was metal and silicon. As the mist cleared her eyes widened. The hulk of a Gorgon mech. It's poison, now dry, covered the ground and on the other side of the alley, was the mech's head, snake-like tendrils drooped in defeat. Her eyes widened when she remembered what Damon had told her. They had sent a gorgon… Zech!

She sprinted away to Ricky's apartment, her heart racing with the possibility that Zech had been hurt...

"Allen! I saw the Gorgon!" she screamed as she banged on the door. It swung open, Zech's ears back, eyes wide. Veronica sighed in relief and embraced the fox. Zech whined and hugged her back.

"Thank God you're ok," she breathed. Zech whimpered, looking back into the room as Allen stumbled in from the shadows, a newly opened bottle of whiskey in his good hand as the ossified hand dangled uselessly at the end of his right arm. One look and Veronica's face dropped. Her lip curled into an angry scowl.

"They did this to you?" she snarled. Allen swallowed and roughly wiped his mouth. Veronica marched into the house and gently took Allen's hand, despite the fury in her eyes.

"You should see the other guy," he slurred.

Veronica shook her head. "This is all my fault," she muttered. Allen frowned at her and grasped her shoulder.

"What are you talking about? Of course, it isn't." Veronica brushed his hand away and paced into the kitchen.

"I was in the Stratus! God, I knew Damon had sent a Gorgon! I could've warned you, but it didn't even cross my mind! I'm so sorry, Allen," she said.

Allen's eyes widened at her words. His mind moved at a million miles a second as he processed this information. She was Stratus? Wasn't she a medical student?

"You...lied to me?" he asked, his fist clenching the bottle. Veronica shook her head and went to him. Allen was in shock, stumbling away from her as she grabbed his arms.

"Allen, no. No -well- I did about the Stratus, but we were in the middle of a Scandal. I would've been...that's besides the point. I haven't betrayed you, I'm still on your side," she rambled. Allen was paralyzed with a fear and an anger so strong he couldn't name it, so he just took another swig of the whiskey.

"Allen, I'm so sorry. I should've told you sooner... but, but... that doesn't change anything, the Elite are-"

"It's fine,"

"-What?" Veronica looked at Allen with shock at his acceptance. His shoulders crumbled and he sagged into the couch, as he cradled the bottle to his chest.

"You don't...ya don't have to explain yourself... it's-it's fine. I know what the Elite have done to you, and if you weren't loyal to us, you would've gotten us sooner right? Right?" He wanted so desperately for Veronica to be on his side. He wanted so desperately to have anyone on his side, because for too long, he'd been so alone. He was tired of losing people. He couldn't lose Veronica too.

"Right," she sighed, and she curled onto the couch beside him. She would do anything for this cause, and to prove she was loyal to it. This mission wasn't like the Stratus. There was heart. There was love. She held her hand up to her eye and her lip curled at the knowledge she still had that camera recording her every move. She had to get rid of it one way or another, or else they would all be doomed.

Her eyes landed on the bottle he clutched and she pried it from his hands. He whimpered but she set it down, away from him.

Zech circled around and sat on the floor, his ears back with guilt and fear for his best friend. Allen looked at Veronica, with a firmness she hadn't seen on his face before.

"I trust you… You're a good friend, but if you do anything-" he mumbled.

"I won't, I swear." They shared a look of understanding, and then sat in silence. Allen rested his head on her shoulder, his body heaving with silent sobs.

"Thank you, I can't lose any more people I love," he whispered. Veronica hesitantly embraced him and brushed away his tears. She had never seen someone look so vulnerable before. The Stratus did not allow emotion.

"I bet I look pathetic," he grumbled. Veronica chuckled wryly, looking ahead at Zech, who whined like a hurt puppy.

"No, Allen. There's nothing weak about what you're doing," she said, "My God! You bested a gorgon!" Zech smiled softly.

Allen sniffled and continued to cry. It was then as he stuffed his hand in his pocket that he fingered a little wooden object. He furrowed his brow and took it out. Veronica eyed him curiously as he stared at none other than the small little cuckoo bird he had taken from the junkyard. A ghost of a smile crossed his face.

The door swung open as Ricky and Maya barreled in. Veronica and Allen both sat up. He quickly wiped away the tears streaking his face, but no matter how much he tried, he couldn't wipe away the red stains and puffy eyes.

Maya took him in, her face falling, and when she saw his hand, she tasted bile in her mouth. She would have to amputate his whole forearm, elbow down as the ossification had continued to move up past his wrist.

Veronica's eyes widened when she saw Maya and a smile graced her lips. She had no idea Maya had joined their gang, and she felt a swell of happiness at the sight of her.

"Hey...long time no see," she said. Maya smiled at her, but the mood quickly turned to focus on saving as much of Allen's arm as they could. She shifted and walked to the kitchen behind Maya.

Ricky helped Allen as Maya set up a sterile station. Zech stood up and wagged his tail at the sight of her.

"Are you here to help?" he asked. She smiled sadly at him and nodded. Zech grinned doggishly and went to where Veronica was.

"Allen lay down. I'll give you a dose of anesthesia. The rest of you need to clear the room and give us some space. You won't want to see this," she said. Ricky shook his head.

"I'm not leaving. No way," he growled. Veronica glanced at Zech and understood she would be the one to keep him calm. She gave one last look to Allen, who smiled at her, before leading Zech down the hall.

"Maya...have I ever told you that you look like an angel?" mumbled Allen through his alcoholic haze. Maya pursed her lips and glanced at Ricky.

"He's drunk... That's a serious risk," she growled. Ricky groaned and rubbed the bridge of his nose. Allen scowled but then lit up and said, "I'm sure you can handle it angel, you can handle anything." Maya guided him down, onto the kitchen table.

Ricky stayed by Allen's side as Maya gave him the anesthesia.

Allen whimpered. He knew that when he woke up, his arm would be gone. He almost didn't want to do the procedure, but this was a necessary evil. He couldn't have the Gorgon's mark, and he definitely couldn't have a useless, stone arm. As the anesthesia took him, he listened to the slosh of water as Maya washed her hands.

Maya set out all of her tools. She booted up a small, handheld cube and put it on the table as well. Ricky watched as she connected chords from the cube to Allen. He flinched as she whipped a metal rod into place and set it up, before she rolled out an IV to hang onto it. She found a vein and expertly put a needle into it, then connected the IV tubing to it.

Ricky looked away as Maya monitored her equipment and connected more things that Ricky didn't comprehend. He hung his head and swallowed with anxiety.

"Have I ever said thank you?" He asked as he handed her the tool she motioned for. Maya looked up at him as she pulled up her face mask. She sat down, now confident she had everything set up. She sterilized the scalpel, then started to cut away at his skin, and peel it back. Ricky blanched and looked away.

"No…" she murmured.

"Well then, thank you. We'd be dead without you," he said. Maya glanced at him.

"I would be wrong not to help, so…I guess you're welcome," she said. She cut away all the ossified and damaged flesh and exposed his unimpaired muscles. She liberally sprayed solvent over the exposed flesh to irrigate and clean it so she could get a better view.

She couldn't mess this up. She pulled magnifying glasses from around her neck and placed them over her eyes, then hunched over as she sutured the blood vessels and began to shave away at the muscle. Where nerve endings were, she cut and tied them off above the amputation site so they wouldn't bunch up and cause him pain.

Finally, she made it to the bone and wrapped cutting wire around them before sawing away until it snapped off.

Ricky gagged at the noise. Maya carefully set the infected forearm on her table and placed a drainage tube in his open flesh.

It was almost cruelly hypnotic as Ricky watched her colderized the blood vessels. The weight of it all crashed onto him as her careful stitches closed up the last of the amputation.

Things would be so much worse now. How could he fix this? Ricky knew he had always worked through his problems. There had to be a solution. He blinked hard when he felt tears brim in his eyes.

"You really do care about him," murmured Maya. Ricky shot her a glance, before touching his forehead to Allen's shoulder.

"Bastard's been with me since the beginning. Of course I care...and what of it?" He retorted.

Maya shook her head as she turned the drainage back on to clean out any last bit of debris, before she snipped the end of the stitches. The surgery was complete. She gave him a shot of a pain reliever and antibiotics.

"I meant nothing negative. He's lucky to have a friend like you. I wish he could've come with me you know. I never stopped mourning the loss of our friendship,"

"-Until you did… Sorry, what I mean is, it matters more that you're here now. You know uh, how long should he wait before he gets a prosthetic?" He asked. Maya glanced up at him and pursed her lips in thought.

Ricky tilted his head watching her face, deep in thought. God, no wonder Allen had been so obsessed with her. She made the sweetest faces. He shook away the thought and bared his teeth at the notion.

"I can get a microbio that speeds up the healing process. It's kind of a new thing," she said. Ricky smiled; his interest piqued.

"That's cool...What does it do? How does it work?" He asked, the engineer side of him surfacing to escape the hard reality.

Maya smiled at the chance to explain her work.

"Well, it helps the body speed up in creating blood clotting cells. It should only take around three weeks, give or take. I'd need to get it from one of the university labs though," she explained. Ricky grinned at her.

"Well, we know the first thing we're doing once we get to Magnus then, right? ...I could build his prosthetic and you could...help me make it work with his body, how's that?" he mused. Maya grinned at his proposal.

"Are you saying if you build him a prosthetic, you'd want my help?" she asked. Ricky scratched the back of his neck as she gazed enthusiastically up at him. He felt a bit flustered and yet pleased to have someone to collaborate with.

"Didn't you hear anything I said? I mean—sure, why not? How's that smugglin' plan going?" He asked, trying to change the subject. Maya scrunched her nose, a signal that it hadn't been *going* at all.

"I think I have a plan for that," said Veronica as she stepped into the room. Ricky and Maya jumped in surprise at her entrance.

"Veronica! Oi, ya scared the shit outta me," breathed Ricky. Veronica cackled, before she looked down at Allen and frowned.

"I'll sabotage the other stratus guards, steal their uniforms and give them to you. Then...well then, we'll just walk into the subway with the rest of the medical students," she said. Ricky and Maya nodded.

"That's...a good plan," said Maya. Veronica smiled at her.

"Oi, that was my plan!... Although I guess you're the one who could actually make it happen…"

"Mhm," hummed Veronica. Zech joined them from the living room and as soon as he saw Allen, he chuffed with both sorrow and confusion.

"His hand…" murmured Zech, bending over him protectively.

"Will it grow back?" He asked innocently, his ears pressed to the back of his head. Ricky clenched his jaw and turned away as Maya hesitantly explained the consequences. Zech whimpered and nuzzled Allen.

"Allen, I am so sorry," he whispered. The room grew silent. Veronica closed her eyes and looked away.

"Veronica, we should probably go back to the Medicum," murmured Maya. She sighed and nodded. They needed to work on the plan.

"Ricky, I'll be back early," she said. Ricky nodded at her.

"Well, we're not going anywhere yet," he said. The three glanced at each other before Maya took down her set up and left. It wouldn't be long before everything they had been planning crashed together in a violent collision.

Soon they'd be on that submarine, and if they truly made it out, it would be a miracle. The way things were looking now, however; their mission was impossible.

"It's ok Allen… Yeah just, it's ok," murmured Ricky as he stood near the door. Allen clutched the toilet seat. He hadn't eaten much, but the little he'd had, he'd puked. It was probably the alcohol and anesthesia mix.

"No! No, it's not ok! God! Look at me, I've lost everything," he paused as another violent vomit stopped him. He couldn't look at the stub of his arm. It was disgusting, and a reminder of his failures. He gasped for air as he clenched the unmoving toilet seat.

"You haven't lost everything! Stop saying that!" Snapped Ricky. It was too early for this. The clock read two a.m. and Ricky couldn't even think straight, let alone comprehend what was happening.

"Shut up! Just shut up. I'm sorry. I'm sorry about all of this," whimpered Allen as his body trembled. Ricky swallowed down his tired annoyance and sat down next to him.

"Yeah...it's a mess...Allen...it's going to be okay. We'll get out of this. We'll start over. You're going to be fine." He patted his friend's back.

"If there's a god...somewhere out there...and he's listening to me right now...I'd want him to know that I hate him. I hate him!" He snarled. Ricky only nodded solemnly as Allen reached for their ancient dull razor and chucked it at the wall.

"Yeah...what did I say about that temper?" Ricky responded, chuckling wryly. Allen looked over at his best friend, his eyes drooping, tear stained and glassy. More hot tears streamed, unbidden down his face, dripping off his chin.

Allen curled into Ricky, letting out another sob. Ricky nodded and wrapped his arm around his broken friend, combing his free hand comfortingly through Allen's matted hair.

Zech poked his head in and whimpered, crawling over to them and laying his head on Allen's lap.

There were no more words...just Allen's quiet sobs.

OBSTACLES

Ricky had stayed up all night welding the metal in the armor he now stood over. Not only had it needed to get done, but it was a good distraction from the amputation. Allen had left this morning with Veronica to talk over the plan, and set it into motion.

He felt his stomach roll at the memory of the stub. Allen had puked and cried in the bathroom till around three. It had haunted him all morning. He glanced at the journals he had started writing around five. He couldn't bear the thought of Allen having to go through this. It would be so hard. So, he had drafted plans for a prosthetic. He would save the pieces of the mech he hadn't used for Zech. Use all parts of the kill was the old wisdom born of necessity.

Ricky had never felt worse for Allen. He'd lost his father, and now his arm and hand. Ricky glanced up at Zech who had stayed up with him all night, his eyes bright. He didn't seem at all tired. Ricky was jealous of Zech's superhuman abilities.

"I think it's done mate," he yawned, his face felt like a stale muffin. He ran a hand through his hair and sighed, plopping down onto a chair and gazing around the room. He'd have to move the old sofa back.

Wait a minute! What was he thinking? He wouldn't even be here much longer.

He gazed tiredly at the piles of metal, electric wires, and mech parts littering his floor. He sighed. That'll be a lot to clean up, which filled him with dread. In his anxiety didn't care about his inconsistent logic.

Zech smiled brightly, his teeth sharp. Ricky had to admit, the fox-man was growing on him, and he felt guilty about his anger yesterday. Allen was right, he deserved life, they all did. The factory was just a job. They came and went like storms. He smiled back at Zech begrudgingly.

"Can...me, can *I* try on?" he asked, pointing down. Ricky shrugged and stood up, wobbled on his tired legs, and then fell back into his chair. Both Zech and Ricky laughed deliriously at the move, Zech grabbed Ricky by the shoulders.

Ricky wheezed as he was unceremoniously jerked to his feet, his eyes wide. He stumbled slightly, balancing himself against the kitchen bar.

"Give it a go," he said. Zech grinned and hoisted up the helmet. Ricky gasped and ripped it from his hands.

"What the matter?" asked Zech, his eyes wide, afraid that he had done something terribly wrong.

"Not like that! You have to be delicate with it, ok?" Ricky carefully opened the helmet's face mask and slid the metal over Zech's slender head. His tufts of puffy white fur stuck out through the front and Ricky sighed. He walked around, gesturing for Zech to lean down so he could reach the top of the helmet.

Zech did as he was told, looking up as Ricky adjusted the hollow points at the top that were for his ears. Zech whimpered as Ricky pulled his ears into place.

Ricky looked down at the fox, apologizing under his breath. Zech shrugged, watching patiently as the helmet was readjusted to fit him more comfortably. The points had speakers so he could hear, and Ricky had stretched out the helmet farther in the back to make room for Zech's elongated head, considering Ricky couldn't reshape the flat glass face piece to accommodate Zech's snout.

The rest of the armor was easily put together after that, and by the time they were done, Zech looked less like an abomination of science, and more like a common mechanical. Ricky glanced down, proud that he had even made that bushy tail into an almost whip like weapon, like a mechanical would have.

"Where it go?" asked Zech, looking down at the tail that he didn't recognize anymore. Ricky grinned and held it up. He admired his handiwork before explaining himself.

"It all has to do with nanowires, electricity from the battery packs, and magnets!" Ricky paused, watching as

Zech only looked more confused. Ricky frowned and shook his head.

"Of course, you wouldn't know...don't worry about it," he mumbled. Zech smiled and jogged to the bathroom, the armor was amazingly modern and light. He wanted to check out what he looked like now. When he looked into the cracked mirror, he flinched. The sight of an unfamiliar face made his heart rate rise. The black face of the mechanical still struck fear in his heart, but he steadied his breathing and shook away his terror. He was stronger than those robots, he had already defeated one! Zech grinned behind the tinted glass and held up his arms in a flexing motion, having seen Ricky doing so earlier that morning. Zech chuckled.

"Good!" he complimented vaguely, turning to look in the direction of the kitchen. Ricky yawned and smiled before he gave him a thumbs up.

"What happened to your eye?" asked Allen as they picked their way through alleyways so as not to draw any unwanted attention. His head hurt viciously from the usual culprit, alcohol. Why did he let himself drink so much? He was lucky the anesthesia mixed with the alcohol didn't kill him.

Veronica glanced at him, a sharp, painful, ghastly memory replaying in her head.

"Maya, I need you to do one more, itty bitty, surgery. Can you do that for me?" Maya looked up at her, confusion and exhaustion in her eyes.

"So, you remember that little problem, uh, me being Stratus? We all have a camera inserted in one of our eyes...I don't know how the feedback from my camera hasn't already gotten us all killed. So, you've got to take it out."

Maya was horrified at the thought.

"Ronny, I can't do that! I've already chopped Allen's arm off today, I'm not, I don't think I have it in me to do that."

Veronica narrowed her eyes, grabbed Maya's collar and hefted her up to her feet.

"Listen here. If you don't do it, I will! I don't quite feel like biting a belt, sticking a spoon in my eye and ripping it out Kill Bill style!"

Maya didn't even know what she meant by that, because unlike Veronica, she didn't watch the old movies. However, she couldn't just dismiss Veronica's threat. Maya groaned in exhausted resignation.

Veronica tried not to think too much about it. It was more of a liberation than it had been a loss.

"You lost an arm; I lost my eye. It was another way for the elite to control me, and I had to prove to myself and to you all that I had your back," Allen's eyes widened, and he cupped her face.

"You didn't have to do that,"

Veronica shook her head and brushed away his hand.

"Well I didn't need your permission. I knew I had to. It's fine, it's just an eye. Anyway, I think the eye patch looks cool," she said. Allen merely shook his head.

"You've got more balls than I do, babe," he murmured. Veronica chuckled.

"Hey, you're the one who befriended a mutant who's supposedly an awful killing machine, so I think you're pretty brave yourself! Besides, Maya gave me anesthesia too so it's not like I bit down on some wood and cut it out with a knife...I don't think I would've been able to do that," she said. Allen grinned at her. It still came as a shock to him that she was so all in despite her background.

"Well, you're still pretty badass," he said, punching her shoulder. She shrugged him off, laughing.

"We have to be badass in a world like this," she said. He nodded and leaned in.

"That's what we do. We run, we fight, we survive," he said, echoing the motto of the surface. Their gazes lingered; mutual respect sparked between them. Allen cleared his throat self-consciously and they continued into the bazaar.

Veronica hummed lightly as they walked out into the market square. She wondered how it could be that, under their dire circumstances she could feel so...happy. It was such an odd feeling...one she hadn't felt since she was a little girl playing at her mother's feet.

The two skirted around the edges of the bazaar to make themselves invisible to the crowd.

"So... you were a Stratus officer. What was that like?" he asked. Veronica glanced at him as they meandered along.

"Mentally as well as physically strenuous. No one really trusted me except my commanding officer. He was really the only friend I had there, after my mom was executed," she said. Allen tilted his head in confused surprise. His eyes wandered, searching for something to quench his growing thirst. He needed something besides conversation to help him numb the full, throbbing pain in his arm.

"I can't believe that. You're too likable," he said. Veronica cackled as his hand snaked into the pocket of a woman and pulled out her flask.

"What's likable to a Fencer is very unlikable to an elite, so, you can see the problem. Although, let me tell you a secret. They were all boring anyway." She frowned when she noticed he was suddenly drinking. Where had he gotten that flask?

"You do that a lot..." she murmured. Allen shot her a flustered look. He screwed the cap back on.

"What are you talking about?" he grunted. Veronica rolled her eyes.

"I've noticed, you smell like alcohol and you drink a lot...you should stop," she said, grabbing the flask. Allen wheezed and reached for it, but Veronica pushed him back with one hand while she threw the metal flask into the pile of garbage at the back of the alley.

"You need water, not alcohol." Allen grimaced. He wanted to tell her to mind her own damn business but...the way she looked at him, with hope; the way she just had faith that he was brave. He didn't want to let her down.

"Ok, from now on, I'll try to go clean," he murmured. Veronica smiled at him, and he couldn't help but feel a flutter of happiness at the sight of that smile. It was so bright and full of life, and capped by that rakish eyepatch. She just had a charm that captured him. The two walked in contented silence as they made their way through the marketplace. Veronica was leading him to the Medicum to initiate her plan. They were going to the Medicum to gang up on some Sratus there and steal their uniforms. That way Allen and Ricky could go under the fence without being detected and detained.

"Hijabs! Half price today!" barked a saleswoman. Across from them a man hollered,

"Salvaged books from the old world! Here's "To Kill A Mockingbird"! "Life of Pi"! "1984"! The last one coulda been written yesterday! Get your books today!" Another barker joined the fray, yelling for people to buy his jewelry, carvings, fruit, or somewhat fresh meat. The competitive cacophony went on, like big, loud crows cawing, competing for what little wealth could be gleaned from the gaunt people of the Fence. Allen chuckled, glancing at Veronica.

"It's a zoo in here!" he joked. She laughed. He could see she was at peace here in the ghetto. She was like him. Alone in the world but for one person. She had a commanding officer, he had Ricky, and now they all had each other. Allen smiled at the thought.

"Hey, uh, I don't mean to sound weird or anything, but uh, you're not alone, alright? I sometimes feel alone, a lot and... I wouldn't want anyone to feel how I feel, so...just know I'm here for you," he murmured. He really didn't know the right way to get those words out. Veronica looked at him and smiled softly.

"Same to you," she said. Allen watched her for a bit as she glanced around, her eyes scouting for something.

"Hey, I'll be right back, I need to use the bathroom," she said. She grinned at him before jogging toward one of the portable restrooms on the outskirts of the plasma. He swallowed, watching her go. He had only known her for a week and yet they had connected so fast. He wasn't complaining.

Allen kicked a rock absentmindedly, his body buzzing with aches and pains that nagged at the back of his mind. He focused on other things to get his mind off of it. Better things, like Veronica. He didn't know why he felt so...unguarded around her! It was just like anything he said she would understand. She might joke about it, but she'd get it. He had no reason to think that way, but she had something genuine about her that he had seldom encountered.

He glanced around, feeling stripped without her company. Something wasn't right. He frowned at a sudden sensation of fear, feeling the chill move up his spine. He was being watched.

The crowded plaza was noisy, but one particular sound caught his attention, and it wasn't good. He glanced behind him, seeing...Bruce. His eyes flickered in remembrance of the swelling, the bruises, and his loose tooth ached with phantom pain. *'Not this guy again.'* he thought, glancing around.

Before he could react, he was grabbed by his hoodie and pulled, his feet scrabbling to regain his balance, as the tightened fabric choked him. He looked up, seeing the face of the fat man, Martin.

"Bruce, 'ere he is! The bastard that killed Peter!" shouted Martin. *'No, no, no!'* he thought, his feet kicking frantically as he was thrown down. The crowd ran to make a circle around them, intrigued and spoiling for the entertainment of a fight. Bruce burst through the crowd and sneered.

"Kill 'im." Allen's eyes widened as he struggled to wrest his good arm, and his stump out of the jacket, kicking up and swinging his fist into his captor's face. As he swung, another man came behind him, wrapping his arms around his neck. Allen jabbed him with his elbow, turning into the man and elbowing him in the nose.

He missed having two hands to fight with. These goons all had two hands and murder in their eyes. It wasn't fair! He still had both elbows though, even if he probably shouldn't be using it while it was *still healing*. But he didn't have time to think about that right now.

The man stumbled back, and Allen took the chance to kick in his knee cap. There was a loud crack that made the bystanders groan with a mixture of distaste and amusement. This was entertainment for the masses. The joy of suffering.

Allen stumbled forward and grabbed a rock. He did his best to aim and fire, and although the rock wobbled, it struck the man on the side of the head. He was doing his best to fight through the agony growing in what was left of his right arm.

"Oi! Smiley's only got one arm! We should call him Gimpy," snarled one of the men as he threw a punch. Allen wheezed as he stumbled back, his vision swirling.

Two more men, Drake and Marco, emerged from the crowd, bringing out knives. They howled with cruel laughter, before they vaulted forward.

"Got any shit to say to us now?" snarled the bigger man, Drake. Allen ignored him, groaned and pivoted to go for the smaller one, Marco. He grabbed his knife as he thrust the sharpened blade forward. Allen dragged him in, and kneed him in the crotch as he ripped the knife out of his hand.

Drake sliced his knife down on his back, Allen's shirt ripped loudly. He winced, hissing from pain.

Allen thrust the knife forward in a mock jab at Drake. With a quick decision, Allen head butted him, and the big man slumped over him: unconscious. Allen panted heavily from exhaustion.

He had to get out of this fight before they beat him to death and looked for a part in the crowd to make his escape.

Somebody grabbed his hair and he grunted as he was pulled down to his knees. Allen fell forward, kicking his assaulter in the ankle, temporarily freeing him from his grip.

He fell back, crawling away to get a better aim. Another man punched the back of his head, and Allen stumbled forward into the grasp of another attacker. The crowd rumbled noisily with excitement as they chanted for the kill.

Allen stabbed the knife into his assailant's thigh, bouncing back to his feet and kicking it in deeper. The man howled in pain, screaming curses. The men groaned as they stood back up, each of them exhausted.

Allen gritted his teeth; he would not yield to his growing exhaustion. Bruce approached him, a murderous fury on his face.

"You bastard. You think you can leave my gang, steal my day's earnings, and then kill Peter?! You disrespectful lit'le prick!" he roared. Allen rolled his eyes and doubled over to catch his breath. The groans of the men he'd taken down filled the plaza.

"I didn't kill Peter, ok? And the whole stealing ordeal happened a long time ago." Bruce scowled and shook his pale pate, a small smirk lighting his lips.

'I need to get out of here, but...Veronica! I can't just leave her here. I need to get Veronica, and then we need to leave—' his thoughts were interrupted as Bruce laughed.

"Oh, believe me, I know it wasn't you. You don't got the balls to kill. It was that beastie. Turns out, that thing is the most wanted in Magnus city at this very moment, a high reward that would bring anyone from this shit hole into the Skyline." Allen's eyes widened. There was an excited murmur through the crowd at the mention of a most wanted, of a reward. It seemed those reward posters were beginning to attract a following, which was inevitable but oh so inconvenient. He needed to shut these mercenary bastards down.

"If he's most wanted, why would you kill me now, when I'm the only one who can tell you where he is?" Allen reasoned, trying to buy some time...

Bruce shot him a hard look and then snorted, "You and I both know you won't weasel on your friends...You're not going to talk your way out of this one!" He straightened to his full height to finish him.

"No. No. Listen, listen. I'll tell you-just come closer and I'll whisper it so no one can hear. We can be partners again, ey Bruce? What do ya say to your old buddy, Smiley?" Bruce eyed him warily as he slowly approached. His fists clenched, but a tentative smile grew on his face, a smile of hesitant trust. He leaned in so Allen could relay the information.

Veronica was coming back from the restrooms when she saw the crowd and heard the now familiar noise of a ghetto fight. She moved closer. The crowd went uncannily quiet and she heard something about a lab creature being on the top wanted list from a man in the center of the ring of ghetto spectators. *'Shit, where's Allen!?'*

Veronica boldly shouldered through the crowd, her fingers dragging her gun from her thigh holster. Her eyes widened as the crowd gasped in shock, and she heard a loud gasp.

Instead of giving up Zech's information to the man, Allen spat in his face and drove the knife through Bruce's shoulder, a calculated blow not intended to kill. Allen couldn't bring himself to murder. That's why he had left the Badgers in the first place.

Veronica saw the flash of blood, and the glimmer of a knife. Her eyes widened in horror.

Bruce only laughed wickedly. "You still haven't killed me...you're weak and you'll be sorry," he hissed.

Her eyes flickered up and she saw Allen, his eyes wide, his mouth in a taut scowl. He angrily pushed the big man off him and turned away. In a blur the man hoisted himself up and lunged after her friend.

"Allen!" she screamed. He turned at the warning but not in time to prevent the taller, heavier man from catching him in a vice-like headlock.

Allen gasped, kicking back as the hold tightened. He felt Bruce's massive hands contract on his chin and head. He struggled as he fleetingly imagined the twist and then the snap.

The gunshot nearly deafened him but brought him back from his panic-stricken state. His neck intact, blood covering his head. He watched as Bruce slowly fell to the ground, a bullet hole between his eyes. The crowd panicked and began to stampede from the market as centaurs charged in at the sound of a Stratus gun. In the chaos, Allen looked behind him at Veronica, her shaking hands clutching her gun. She was still hidden in the crowd, but he could see her, standing firm as everyone raced frantically around her. She lowered the gun, her eyes locked with his and he could feel his heart rate rising.

He let out a breath and stumbled away, Veronica quickly sheathed the weapon and ran after him. The two sprinted through the market, people making way for them.

The other members of the gang had scattered after the gunfire.

They needed to leave the ghetto. Everyone would be looking for Zech now, and the gang would be after him relentlessly now that he was the cause of their leader getting killed. They needed to go!

Allen and Veronica swung into Ricky's apartment, panting. Ricky startled awake at the commotion and Zech bounced into the room, still dressed in his mechanical disguise. Allen saw him, not realizing it was Zech and screamed, stumbling back outside, his back hitting the railing as he fell.

"No! Allen, it me!" Allen had never felt more relieved to hear that disjointed syntax.

Ricky jumped up in surprise at seeing Allen splattered with dried blood. He gritted his teeth at the sight.

"What the hell happened to you!? Again!?" he kneeled down, examining his friend as he caught his breath.

"It's not mine. The-the Badgers, it was them! They got me in the market, but you should see the other guys, I really messed them up, and with just one arm." Ricky shook his head in dismay, blinking hard to sort his thoughts.

"I shot the man and we got away," explained Veronica breathlessly, her eyes wide with fear. She had killed a man; she really had done it. Ricky groaned. Allen had already lost an arm, he didn't need to be fighting straight out of surgery, yet for some reason, nothing stopped him!

"They know about Zech," he breathed, picking his way through the metal and plopping himself down on the saggy leather couch. Ricky clenched his jaw and backed into a chair, trying to take it all in.

"Everything ok?" asked Zech, tilting his head curiously. Allen glanced at him and frowned, sighing.

"Get your stuff together, we're going to Magnus," Allen announced, jumping to his feet. He tried to run a hand through his hair, spiked stiff with Bruce's blood. He began packing his backpack, Ricky hesitantly following him. Veronica stood at the doorway and frowned.

"I'll go to the Medicum: get Maya ready, and get the suits," she offered shakily. Allen nodded; his heart went out to her. He knew how she must've been feeling. Having blood on your hands was never easy. She closed the door and jogged off, too intent on her mission to take time to sort out what just happened in the Market. Zech watched her go, and smiled contentedly as he played with a spring: the coil of wires bouncing as he pulled it gleefully.

Escape

Maya hummed softly as she packed her bags in the community tent. Soon her time in the Fence would be over...and truly, her time in Magnus. They wouldn't be able to stay in the city. She heard footsteps approach, and she smiled, expecting Veronica to be there. As she stood up and turned around, she met Jason. Her eyes widened as he glared down at her.

"There you are," he growled, taking her by the arm. Maya squeaked as he dragged her towards him.

"What do you want?" she snapped, trying to pry her arm out of his armored clasp. Jason smirked down at her.

"No one's ever fought against me before...I like the moxie...isn't it obvious?" He murmured in her ear as his hands roved across her body. Maya struggled to free herself.

"Stop!" She cried, pushing against him. Her body crawled with revulsion and panic as he shoved her onto one of the cots, his lips hungrily attacking her neck. She began to cry and she hit and kicked him as he trapped her.

"Get off me! Help! Help!" She screamed. Jason only laughed as he looked down at her. Her eyes sparked with rage as he pinned her hands down. Maya kicked furiously with her feet and he slapped her; hard. He grabbed her ankle, and now with her arm free, she punched- her fist curled against the pain. She hadn't expected punching to be that painful! She just wanted to be away from his revolting touch.

"That's enough!" He barked, grabbing her hair and slamming her head back. She screamed as frustrated and terrified tears streamed from her eyes.

"Stop, please!" She begged as she grew exhausted. As he pulled her towards him, she heard a shout, an electric crack and Jason screeched with agony. She bolted up as he released her.

Veronica stood over him, her outstretched hand holding a taser as Jason twitched and writhed.

Maya pushed him over and grabbed him by the hair. She cursed at him as she slammed his head into the concrete, and he was finally out cold.

"Are you ok!?" Veronica asked as the shock finally drifted away from them. Maya let herself break down and she let out a choked sob.

"I was so scared! Oh my God, thank you," she wept. Veronica pulled her into a comforting embrace and stroked her hair. She soothed her with comforting hushes and rocked her.

"It's ok, I got you," she whispered. Maya choked and hugged Veronica tighter.

"I couldn't fight him off, he overpowered me and I didn't know what to do, I wasn't strong enough, and he came out of nowhere," she cried. Veronica nodded.

"You weren't…" she asked, letting the question hang in the air. Maya shook her head.

"You held him off long enough then," she said. Maya smiled at her and hugged her again.

"Thank you," she whispered. Veronica nodded and hummed quietly.

"You *are* strong," Veronica insisted and Maya smiled softly.

"Thank you." The two sat in silence before Maya pulled away to grab a towel to wipe her eyes. Veronica stood up and looked down at Jason.

"Go on and get packed. I'll take care of him. Don't worry, he won't ever bother you again," Veronica snarled. Maya nodded, before catching something in Veronica's eyes, a glimmer of unease and terror.

"Hey are you ok?" She asked. Veronica laughed wryly as she kicked Jason lightly in the ribs.

"You're the first to ask...today I killed someone. Shot someone right in the head. I only did what I had to do. He was going to kill Allen. I could clearly see he was about to snap his neck. If I was the only one that would stop it, I was ready to do that, and I did. It's not...it's not a big deal," Veronica turned away, a lump growing in her throat. Maya pensively frowned. Veronica killed someone? It sounded serious, and she began worrying about Allen's safety, especially since he shouldn't have been fighting with his stump. She also worried about Veronica's mental health. What had happened?

"It doesn't matter. You're the one that got attacked. Go take care of yourself. You worry about other people too much." Maya sighed and nodded wearily, before taking her bags to the dock.

Veronica looked down at Jason with a glower of disgust. She grabbed him by his wrists and dragged him to the back of the tent, slipping the both of them under the flaps. She pulled off every asset of armor he was wearing and stripped him of his uniform.

He groaned as he began to awake again, but she quickly hit him in the head with the butt of her pistol. She handcuffed him to one of the tent poles then she dragged a heavy tarp from a stack on the floor and covered him, before folding the uniform and shoving it in her backpack.

"What are you doing soldier? And where the hell have you been?" Barked one of the Stratus as he came through the tent flap. He was on a facility check. Veronica had to cut that short.

She shouted, launched herself up and wrapped her legs around his helmeted face. She twisted and pulled him to the ground as he tried to punch her.

"Officer Boyce! I order you to stop!" he shouted. She ripped off his helmet, her legs straddling his hips as she held up her gun. His eyes grew wide with alarm as she brought the butt of her pistol crashing down onto his temple. He yelped, trying to wrestle her off, but Veronica continued to pound her gun into his head until he finally stopped fighting and slumped over. She quickly removed the armor and stripped off his uniform just as she had done with Jason.

"Sleep tight boys, I got a mutant to smuggle," she grunted, before sauntering away.

Veronica went to the crumbling ruins just outside of the Medicum and waited. They were running out of time. Finally, after what felt like an eternity, even though it was probably less than five minutes, the guys raced into the ruins. Veronica tossed them the bag filled with their disguises. She looked up and studied Zech.

He definitely didn't look like a real animal anymore; it was almost uncanny.

"He looks convincing, doesn't he?" Allen asked, dragging her from her thoughts. Veronica chuckled and nodded. The guys strapped on the last bit of their uniforms and Veronica led them to the Medicum.

"The students are being loaded up right now. We should probably hurry," she whispered. Allen nodded.

Allen glanced ahead to see Maya with the other medical students, getting their bags checked before getting cleared to enter the submarine. He glanced at Veronica. He had never been inside a Stratus suit, and never he'd never had his face obscured by the infamous black tinted mask that made Stratus so terrifying.

Veronica looked back at him and smiled ever so slightly. But that smile faded as she flashed back to the plaza, and the jolt in her hand when the gun went off. To the tent as she tased Jason. But it wasn't the death of the thug that shocked her so much, or the appalling intentions of her Stratus coworker. It was the memory that resurfaced alongside Bruce's demise and Maya's assault. The night was...

...quiet, the moon was bright, and it kept the little girl awake. Ronny, lay in her bed, blinking up at the popcorn ceiling above as it glimmered with pale moonlight. She rolled over looking out from the large windows.

That's when she heard something, a light padding of footsteps. Not those of an animal either. Was it her mom? She slowly got up, her frizzy black hair crowning her head like a lion's mane. She tiptoed to her closed bedroom door and cracked it open as quietly as possible.

She stifled a giggle as she thought she might catch her mommy sneaking some ice cream. That happened sometimes, especially when she tried a new diet. Her eyes widened, however, when she saw the masculine figure padding through her dining room. That wasn't her mom. She quickly closed her door, her heart racing. She took a deep breath and listened against the door. Silence, then, a creak. She whimpered and looked over at her dresser. Her breath grew shaky.

There was a scream, gut wrenching, blood curdling. Ronny jumped up, racing to her desk in a blur of subconscious movement. It was as if her muscles had a mind of their own. As her hand clutched the little metallic purple pistol, her fingers curled around the trigger. It only had practice bullets, but she knew where to find the real stuff.

"Get away! Stop!" screamed her mother, sobs racking her body as grunts and whimpers resounded from her mom's room.

"Shut up!" boomed the loud and scary voice. Ronny slowly opened her door; one wrong move and she could endanger her mom. She heard a thud, glass falling and her lip curled in fear and fury. Her hands shook, but she had to be strong. Her small hands delved into the drawer and she grabbed the box of bullets, loading a few into the small magazine. Her ears were filled with the sound of struggle; thuds, cries, curses. She ran to the door, tears streaming down her face as she pushed it open.

"Veronica, hide!" screamed her mother even though she was pinned down, a knife to her throat. Veronica lifted up the gun and shouted.

"Let go of her, or I'll shoot you!" she ordered, her voice cracking. The man laughed and tightened his grip on her mom. Veronica cocked the gun, fiery determination in her eyes. She was scared, but her mommy always told her

*that she needed to have courage, that she needed to be
prepared.*

*"Your mommy and I are just playing, go back to
sleep little girl." Veronica held up the gun, glancing at her
mom, the two sharing a glance of fear, of hesitation.
Ronny's eyes hardened and she stared up at the man. Her
mom's head shot back, her elbow connecting with the
man's nose. He refocused on the woman, punching her in
the face. Veronica let out a sob and her fingers clenched,
her hands jerking up as the gunshot boomed in her ears.
The man slumped down and her mom shoved him off her.
Ronny cried, fumbling the gun and dropping it. She
stumbled to the ground and stared at the man.*

*Her mom rolled him over, gasping and holding her
hand over Ronny's eyes as she saw the sight.*

*"What mommy, where did I hit?" she asked,
crawling over. Her mom quickly picked her up and carried
her, crying, away from the dead man.*

*"Where did I hit!? He's dead, oh my...I'm sorry, I
didn't mean to kill him, I'm not a killer. He was trynna hurt
you mama, I couldn't let him hurt you! I'm sorry, am I
gonna be in trouble!?" she sobbed. She was shushed, her
mom's bronze hand combing through her hair lovingly.*

*"Oh honey, you're not in trouble. He was a bad
man, he was going to hurt mommy, he was probably going
to hurt you too. You did what you had to do...did you aim
for his head, baby?" she asked, her voice shaking, tears in
her eyes as she tried to calm her daughter. The woman*

ignored the fact her nose was bleeding. She wiped off the blood so she wouldn't frighten Ronny. Veronica hiccupped, sniffling and wiping her eyes. She shook her head frantically.

"No, I... I was aiming for his leg, I didn't mean to, I know we could've kept him until the Stratus came, that's what you say to do, I'm sorry, I didn't mean it, I'm not a killer!" Ronny squeezed her mother as she hugged her, her sobs filling the house. She just killed someone! She was nine and a murderer, her life was over!

"Veronica! You're not in trouble, now dry up your eyes right now. You did what you had to do. You're not a killer. We needed direct action. They will understand that it is in no way your fault, I'm proud of you," said the woman. Ronny sniffled, her brow furrowing. She looked up at her mom's wet eyes.

"Why? Mom! He's dead!" she cried. Her mom nodded, putting firm hands on her shoulders, forcing Ronny to look up at her.

"Yes, he is dead, but I would've been dead if you hadn't done that. You're not a murderer, you're a hero, and I'm proud. I'm proud that you acted in the face of danger, you didn't freeze up...you're going to make an excellent warrioress. I love you Ronny, don't you dare forget that. Ever. Got it?"

"...Got it," breathed Veronica, her eyes welling up at the memory. Allen glanced down at her, trying to gauge if she was alright after her long hesitation.

"Got what?" he asked. She shook her head and the four marched forwards as the last of the students were cleared to enter. Dr. Farley held Maya back with a smile.

He nodded to her and glanced at Anand. Maya felt a warm comradery with him.

"You made the top score on your exams...hopefully you can work here for me soon. We could use someone with your skill and intelligence down here," he whispered. Maya smiled at him and glanced at her friends as they waved their fake IDs to a computer chip and entered.

Zech moved oddly mechanically in the suit, and she was a bit surprised to see him, he looked so...cold. Nothing like his usual self. It probably had everything to do with the tinted black screen that hid his face. She would now dedicate the rest of her life to making sure this creature would be safe from the elite...and really, that she'd be free. She looked back at her boss.

"Thank you, Doctor Farley, it's been a real honor," she said. He nodded curtly before he let her board the ship. Maya glanced at Dr. Anand who smiled at her and waved. The two shared a mutual understanding. Liberation was near. She could tell by the twinkle in the Hindu woman's eyes. With that, she boarded the submarine.

PART TWO:

THE SKYLINE

CHeSS

The Judge sat in her ivory office; her chess board parted two ways. She moved a knight and slid it into a rook's spot. Her delicate fingers plucked the rook off of the board and set it firmly aside.

Her doors slid open and General Sylva stepped in. The Judge sighed with irritation at having been interrupted and looked up with disinterest.

"This better be good," She intoned with a small, menacing hum to her voice. Matias cleared his throat and approached her, his knees shaking in her presence.

"Two of our soldiers were found naked and unconscious in the Medicum. When revived and questioned they said that...well they said officer Boyce attacked them," he explained. The Judge stared up at him with icy coldness. A smirk graced her lips and she sat back. Matias shot her a puzzled look and obediently sat when she gestured for him to sit.

"Do you play Chess, Matias?" she asked. Matias shifted uncomfortably at the question.

"I am familiar with the game, yes, but I don't under-"

"-To win a game of chess, one must think three moves ahead of your opponent. You must see your opponent's mistakes before your opponent even makes them. Before they know you've caught them, you have their king surrounded -*checkmate*." Her voice was cold and calm, mimicking the hushed swish of an ocean tide. Matias swallowed as he processed her words.

"Yes...but how does that-"

"-Isn't agent Boyce under Lieutenant Rose's unit? I think you should test your loyalties. Both the lieutenant and agent Boyce have been affiliated with Raven, and we can't have that kind of chaos again," she said. Matias nodded curtly.

"Yes, your honor...What would you have me do?" he asked. The Judge sighed and looked out her office windows, a perfect predator's perch over the city.

"You're a smart man, I'm sure you can figure it out...I want you to think three steps ahead. Like a game of chess," she purred. The two shared a look of understanding.

one Good shower

Zech stood motionless beside Ricky and Allen. He was so scared that if he moved, the elite that surrounded them would catch on and rip him apart.

The armor that clung to his body was too tight, and rubbed his fur the wrong way. His helmet was suffocating him and he could barely see past the black mask that covered his face. But Ricky was a genius, and he had done the best he could with the time and materials he'd had to work with...

Zech looked at Allen out of the corner of his eye. His leg was bouncing nervously as he fought the urge to puke. Veronica sat with her feet on the table, glaring at anyone who so much as dared to glance at her. Maya couldn't sit with them. It would've been too suspicious, or at least that's what Veronica had told her.

Zech's heart was beating a mile a minute, and the way the water played with the lights and shadows of the submarine was too terrifying for him. He was going back... he didn't know if he could do this. What if they found him? What if they killed him? What if they killed his friends? They were the only ones who had reached out and given him a chance at life. What if everything was stripped from them? Zech swallowed back a lump in his throat. No, he had to trust Allen.

As the submarine broke surface and an announcement blared over the speakers, Zech lowered his head. His nostrils flared as he tried to hold onto his bearings. No one had suspected him yet. Zech followed behind Allen as Veronica led them out from the submarine in front of the students. Some of those students were applauding their safe return home. His tail twitched with his growing anxiety. He was back...in this awful place.

However, no one even gave them a second glance, disguised as Stratus and marching alongside the Medical students through the city. Zech glanced warily at Allen. Their face masks were void of any emotion and Zech whimpered. Were Allen and Ricky just as scared as he was?

"We're here..." whispered Ricky to Zech. Allen nodded slowly, as his head lifted to take in the massive skyscrapers and floating gardens. Bubbles of color and lights sparkled and danced above them. Large jumbo screens of News Casters and advertising of Vargas Biotech played across the massive screens in dazzling colors. Zech's eyes dilated with a raw hatred fueled by the fight or flight adrenaline pumping into his body. His heart raced in his chest and he kept having to remind himself to breathe as he stared at the scientist who was speaking on a late-night talk show. Then, his profile popped up, and a warning flashed.

The public around them murmured as they walked by. Zech could pick up tiny snippets of their conversations.

"They haven't caught that monster yet," whispered one.

"It's in the fence, who cares?" his companion mumbled. Zech bared his teeth as he glanced at Allen. Well...he was here now.

"Allen..." he murmured as they rattled up a glass staircase to a metro station with the rest of the medical students. Allen glanced at him.

"What is it buddy?" He questioned him quietly. Ricky glanced at the two, and Allen could tell he was on the verge of hissing, "*Shut up,*" at them.

"I'm scared..." he said. Allen looked down. Zech couldn't see his face.

"Me too Zech, I can't breathe." Zech smiled at the reassurance that he wasn't alone. That he wasn't the only one who was feeling trapped.

"We'll escape right?" He asked. Allen glanced at Veronica; whose helmet was off. She was chatting cheerfully with Maya. The two looked just as uneasy, but at least comfortable. They had lived here after all.

"I hope so Zech," he muttered. Zech swallowed and flinched as a bullet train flew into the station, shifting to a stop with an easy wheeze. The doors slid open and a walkway silently slid to meet it. The medical students stepped on, and Veronica led her posse of imposters on as well. Zech looked around at the train.

Sleek, white, shining. The windows glowed with an iridescent tint of pink. On a screen up ahead was a soft, pretty woman. All white; her skin, her hair, her clothes, even her eyelashes. And she wasn't white like how Allen or Ricky were, she was blanched white. Like a primrose petal.

Zech shivered with unease. She gave instructions on train etiquette, and when the next stop was. Her voice was too soft. It was a softness that made his hackles rise. It was the way the scientists tried to talk to him when he was obtained and became the subject of their experiments. It was too fake. Too nice. Too painful.

Allen glanced up at him as he heard a low growl. He tapped Zech on the arm and Zech looked away. Maya glanced at them from her corner and she smiled. Zech liked to think it was a smile just for him, to soothe his nerves. His tail wagged ever so slightly.

Allen's stomach wrenched and twisted. They were here...they were *actually* here. It didn't feel real. At any moment he could wake up, and he'd be back in the ghetto, he was sure of it. Yet here they were, and with each passing second, he stayed. the city around them sped by in a blur, nothing but flashes of color, and the skyscrapers in the distance seemed to shift with them as they sped through.

The city was beautiful indeed. It seemed to glow with an effervescent shimmer. It was like they were in heaven. Heaven indeed. They passed through those pearly-barbed- gates and now they were here. Yet he felt like he was still looking through the fence. He was a filthy hell bound soul and he had intruded on the golden grounds of God. And he felt bitter, because wasn't God supposed to be love? He had never felt love from this "heavenly" city. He was reminded just how rotten it was, just how hellish it was. Allen grew angry at the injustice, at the beauty.

He hated this city and all of its fineries. He hated this suit he was forced to wear. These suits had spread so much fear in the Fence, abused so many innocent people. Terrorized, stole and took him by the arms and forced a little boy onto a bus against his will. Called him a savage. Called him by an ID number instead of a name. Allen gritted his teeth. He itched to rip the Stratus helmet off.

The train silently slid to a smooth stop and Allen looked up to see a row of dormitories; all sleek glass. Large floating bubble-like lanterns hovered over the smooth glass path. A giant statue of two winged snakes wrapped around a flag post. Further up, loomed a huge marble building with large holographic banners. The medical academy. So, this was the luxury Maya had lived in for so long.

Allen glanced at her. She didn't look excited to see it. The students shuffled out of the bus and Maya gestured to them. The "Stratus officers" followed behind them. Maya fell back from the medical group and walked with Veronica. The two talked low under their breath, and Allen glanced at Ricky.

"What do we do now?" he murmured. Ricky shrugged, neither of them had really expected they would've gotten this far. Allen seethed, hating that he had to put all of his trust in Veronica. He mentally kicked himself when he realized just how lax his plan had been. They'd have to come up with something soon. Any extra time spent in the city was a risk, a chance they could get caught. His nerves twisted in his stomach as the students peeled away one by one.

As Maya ducked away, Veronica gestured for them to follow her. They couldn't just follow Maya back to her room. That would be too suspicious. Allen let out a shaky breath as the last student entered into a dormitory. Veronica circled to the back of one of the buildings and nodded to them. They passed an elevator and clattered up glass stairs. The hall rippled with color as they passed.

"Jesus," breathed Allen when it finally felt like they were alone. Ricky let out a sigh of relief at the slack of not being surrounded by the elite.

"I can't believe we did that!" Sang Veronica as she hopped on her feet from pent up anxiety.

Maya stepped out of her room and pulled them in. Zech barked in the excitement. They all let out a collective and heavy sigh. So, relieved they could finally breathe.

"Oh my God!" Allen shouted. Ricky dragged him into a tight embrace and they jumped about together in complete joy and maniacal excitement. Maya laughed as Zech scooped her and Veronica into a bear hug.

"We did it! We did it!" Chanted the small group as they ran around Maya's small dorm room. Allen flung a pillow at Veronica and she laughed and pushed him onto the couch. Ricky rolled onto the floor and lay there, breathing heavily and covering his helmeted face.

"Can we take these awful helmets off now?" he grumbled. Maya nodded and went to draw the curtains over the large windows that filled the wall from the floor to the ceiling. She went to lock her door and sighed as she slid down the wall and hung her head.

Ricky and Allen ripped off their helmets. Allen threw his helmet against the couch and lowered himself to the ground. He punched the air. Zech whined as he tried to take his off, but failed.

"Here mate," said Ricky as he lifted the face mask. Zech smiled doggishly.

"Thank you, Ricky," he said. Ricky nodded and walked around.

"Nice place ya got here Maya," he said. Maya stood up and went to him as he admired her stark white room and potted succulent plants. There was a trendy wall covered with cascading, green plants. Her dorm was clean and seemed to glow, just like the city itself.

"Um, thanks," she mumbled. Veronica rolled to her feet and pulled Allen up as well.

"Alright, party's over. We need to map out our next plan of action," she barked. Allen nodded in agreement.

"My plan was to hijack an aircraft and fly it right out of this city," he said with a shrug. Veronica looked at him quizzically.

"I can fly those...and I can get it for us too," she said. They glanced at her; Allen nodded slowly as he took in her information. It still shocked him sometimes when she said things that proved she was Stratus. He couldn't help it. She was so different from all the other Stratus. She cared.

"I'll help you," said Allen. Veronica shook her head.

"You can't, you'll get caught and you should be here with Zech. In the meantime, I think this would be a good time for you both to freshen up. Has anyone told you two that you smell like garbage?" Allen frowned.

"We're only doing our best," he said. Ricky snorted with laughter as Veronica chuckled.

"You can use my shower. I'll cook something, and when I say cook, I mean having it delivered from the shoot," quipped Maya. Ricky and Allen cocked their heads with confusion.

"Shoot?" asked Zech. Maya pursed her lips at the realization that they had never been able to experience the luxuries of the Skyline. Her heart ached for them.

"You stay here. Lay low. Do not leave. I'll be back later with the aircraft. They should know we're gone only after we're past the city limits and diving to the surface. I'll bring the aircraft to the Academy yard. We'll make our escape there," Veronica ordered as she saluted them. Allen darted to her side and grabbed her arm.

"Wait! Before you go-" He slipped something into her pocket as he gave her a fierce hug. Veronica hugged him back before they both pulled away with a solemn sigh.

With that, Maya, Ricky, Zech and Allen saluted her back and watched her slip out. Allen bit his lip, what if she gave them away? No, she wouldn't do that. He trusted her.

Zech whined and went to sit on the couch. Allen glanced at him with sad curiosity.

"Hey what's up buddy?" He asked as he came to sit beside him. Zech glanced at him.

"I'm so scared," he whispered. Allen nodded and wrapped an arm around Zech's hunched back.

"Yeah me too, but we've made it this far and you've been so good. I'm so proud. We're going to make it through this," he reassured him. Zech smiled.

"You promise?" Allen clenched his jaw. Of course, he promised. Of course, he did but...what if something happened? Would Zech hate him if those promises were shattered?

"I promise I'll fight every second to make it come true. If we fail, we went down swinging, right?" He said. Zech nodded solemnly.

"Yes Allen," he said. Allen patted Zech on the back and got up but Ricky shot up like a bullet.

"I call dibs on the shower!" Allen chuckled. Ricky for once didn't have to worry about conserving water.

Maya smiled at him. The two stood in content silence. Allen came to stand at the counter and watched as she placed an order for food. She glanced at him and raised a dark brow.

"What?" she asked. Allen shrugged and took a seat.

"You're really giving all of this up…" he murmured. Maya came to stand across from him and frowned.

"I never really belonged here…I was always the Fencer whose mother slept her way past the gates. I never really had a chance, and I would've ended up in the Fence again. Working in the Medicum," she replied with a self-deprecating shrug. Allen pursed his lips and drummed his fingers on the counter in thought.

"It never occurred to me until now...but we're just going right back to where we started; back to the surface," he said. Maya's lips flickered, trying to decide if she wanted to smile.

"You know when I met you, back on that ship, I thought you were very brave. I look at you today and I know that's still true," she said. Allen swallowed the lump in his throat. Every single day she still gave him reasons to fall head over heels for her. Why was she so good? So perfect? No matter what he did, she just dragged him back in. He laughed wryly.

"Shit, there you go again," he said, standing up and pacing away. Maya frowned at his reaction.

"What do you mean?" She asked. Zech glanced at them, his ears perked up as he felt the sudden shift in atmosphere.

"Nothing, I'm just-" he groaned. Maya, nonplussed, turned away.

"Nothing, thank you, Maya. And, and, you're still the most perfect person I've ever known, I know this isn't the time but, ever since we were kids-"

"-Allen-"

"-No, please let me finish. I've always been in love with you. You were always the best thing in my life, you were the reason I wanted to wake up. I tried, I tried so hard to move on, but I was always so mad and infatuated that there was always some part of me that wouldn't let me forget. And usually I don't have a problem saying these kinds of things to people but you've always been so different…" he turned away and scratched the back of his neck. *'Dammit Allen, you just ruined everything,'* he scolded himself. When Maya didn't say anything, he knew he had to play it off. Act cool, like usual.

"But it's cool, it's fine, and you probably don't feel the same way, and that's ok, I don't care," he murmured as he shrugged off everything he had just revealed. Maya hesitantly walked to him and put a hand on his shoulder. He let her turn him to face her, like a ragdoll. He was weak against her, always had been.

"Allen...I'm-" she stuttered; "-We can't think about that right now."

"Yeah, I know," he sighed in exasperation. Maya bit her lip and walked away. Zech looked up at her, tilting his head in innocent confusion. She smiled at him sadly, before her ear started to ring. Her heart jumped and she quickly answered. Allen glanced at her with a questioning look.

"Hello?! Oh...hey Mom" she sighed. She could almost hear her mother grin.

"Hello darling, I know today is the day you got back, so how about you come over for dinner," suggested her mother. Maya swallowed.

"I don't know...I'm kind of tired," she said softly.

"You'll come to dinner Maya, I want to see my little doctor," she crooned. Maya narrowed her eyes. Her mind was racing, too many things had happened that day, too many emotions danced violently about in her heart. Maybe she *should* go to her mom's house, if only to escape the awkwardness and tension that was building a wall between her and her once best friend.

"Yeah, ok. I'll be on my way," she said. Allen sighed and went to sit on the couch. Zech leaned his head against his shoulder.

Maya hung up on her mom and grimaced. She and Allen shared a look before quickly looking away.

"My mom wants to see me. I won't be long, I promise," she said. Allen nodded and sucked in through his teeth.

"See ya later, alligator," he murmured. Maya smiled softly and left, closing the door behind her.

"Ah shit, Zech. Did I just ruin that?" he asked. Zech looked at him, his eyes blinking as he tried to piece together his thoughts.

"I think it fine Allen," he said with a cheeky smile. Allen rolled his eyes.

"You said what you needed. Can't keep feelings hidden away," he said simply. Allen smiled at the creature.

"When did you get so smart?" He asked. Zech grinned at him.

Ricky sighed as he sat on the shower floor, letting the water run over his backside. Back in the ghetto, he had never had running water. He just wanted to let it rain down on him. The grime had been rubbed away, but not the feeling of disgust that seemed trapped inside of him.

It just wasn't fair. This couldn't be the pinnacle of humanity, yet apparently it was. Every other kingdom had been stripped away. This was all that was left of the world. What even happened? How did things get this bad? Why were humans so cruel?

A mechanical could be programmed. A mechanical never acted a certain way unless made to do so. Humans just *did* things. They just did shitty things...they started wars...they favored the rich...they pushed the perceived "lessers" down.

Ricky pushed his bitter thoughts to the back of his mind with a resolved sigh. At least he could have one good shower before the worst was to come.

Red Alert

Veronica walked cautiously into the Stratus headquarters. It was a heavily fortified, dark building. Shaped like a hexagon, four stories tall. It was surrounded on every side by dark black glass that matched the black face masks of the Stratus uniforms. Statuesque centaur mechanicals stood on each side of the iron gates.

She had to get in and out before anyone knew she was here...even Damon. It shouldn't be so hard, what with the sun dipping past the horizon and shrouding everything in shadows. Her heart ached at the thought of never seeing Damon again. He was a father to her who had stepped up and taken her in when the Skyline turned against her and executed her mom. She regretted that she would never get to say goodbye.

She crept through the field and over the training tarmac. The cadets were getting ready for bed. The Air Stratus launch pad was just ahead and would require a pilot or captain's ID to get into an elevator. The shipyard was perched on one of the mountain cliffs that bordered the city and the headquarters were right below it.

She toyed with the ID card of the Stratus Captain she had cut down in the Medicum, a smirk gracing her face. She kicked herself into a run and raced up the steepening escarpment. She hopped up on the granite stairs that protruded from the ground.

Above her loomed a large black corridor that connected to the main headquarters and attached to the edge of the cliff. It was easily accessed from the inside but Veronica knew if she went inside the headquarters, she'd probably never come back out again.

Finally, she reached the cavern that the elevator shaft was nestled in. She jogged to the big steel doors and pressed the card to the scanner. A light blinked green and the doors slid open soundlessly. Veronica grinned and entered the elevator.

Her heart thudded in her ears as the elevator climbed up the cliffside. Then her heart stopped when the elevator doors slid open too early. She clenched her jaw, until she saw the face that greeted her.

Damon. He quickly stepped inside and the two stood shoulder to shoulder. Veronica swallowed back a lump of anxiety as the two stood in silence and waited as the elevator climbed.

"You shouldn't be here," he said finally. Veronica shifted and glanced at him. He was frowning, his eyes shifting about uneasily. What could she even say? Did he know? Well of course he knew.

"I see you've become a pirate... I was wondering when you'd take out the camera," he murmured. Veronica flinched at the mention of her eye.

"Are you going to arrest me?" She asked, her voice shaking. Damon looked at her, his face capturing the essence of his pain.

"Are you kidding me, Ronny? I've been covering for you...I would never do that to you, you're like a daughter to me...and I've already lost a son," he sighed. She was overcome by a mixture of love and relief. She embraced him in a tight hug.

"Thank you," she whispered. Damon nodded and hugged her back. Veronica tilted her head as she processed his words. Her eyes widened.

"You lost a son...what was his name?" She asked. Damon sighed and shook his head.

"His name was Allen...I failed him, and I can't fail you," he stated. Veronica gasped as she connected all the dots. Allen? He had said he had lost his father, and...

"Damon...I think I know him...I think I met him, Damon," she breathed. Damon shot her an utterly shocked look, his face marked with questions. His eyes were wide as he stared at Veronica.

"No... what are you talking about? My son, he's-"

"He's here! I... Allen and I, we're working together! We have Ze-" Damon cupped her mouth and looked around. She could almost feel his heart racing at this news, and sweat was beginning to form on his forehead.

"Where is he? Can you take me to him?" he whispered as the elevator slid to a stop and the doors rolled open. The launch pad stood before them, the waiting aircraft standing stark and tall. They both stepped out of the elevator enveloped in a tense silence.

"We're leaving the city...come with us," she said. They stared at each other; their eyes wide with shock as their minds raced with the danger; the possibilities. Damon glanced at the headquarters and swallowed back his fear.

"You are your mother's daughter," he said softly. Veronica smiled at him. Damon gestured for her to follow, a look of determination on his face as he led her to his ship.

"I wasn't there for Raven...but I'll be damned if I'm not going to be there for you," he growled. Veronica jumped into the ship and laughed as the engines roared to life. They were going to finally be free of the Stratus...of the Skyline.

It was then that the Stratus headquarters' dark black body lit up with a threatening red glow and an alarm sounded.

BOTOX

Maya sat across from her mother in her lavish gold dining hall. The woman across from her didn't look like herself anymore. Her lips were too big, as was her chest, and no matter how hard she tried and how much Botox she injected into herself, she could never hide the wrinkles. A large mane of leopard print faux fur surrounded her velvet blouse's collar.

However, despite all this, Amanda was still beautiful. But who was to say what she looked like on the inside?

Her new husband sat beside her. The two didn't share a single word.

Maya cleared her throat, her brows were knit together from the tension of the growing, almost living silence. Amanda looked at her with an uninviting spark in her eyes.

"Are you glad you're out of that hell hole?" Asked her mother. Maya wiped her mouth, her legs bounced, communicating her growing anxiety.

"Sure, yeah," she said. Amanda shot her a skeptical look. They scrutinized each other. Maya couldn't hold her stare and looked away.

"How is everything, Charles?" Her mother's new husband perked at the question and he smiled at her.

"Everything is exquisite!" he chirped. Maya stifled a groan and instead smiled stiffly at him. Amanda grinned and touched her husband's arm as if she didn't really want to touch him, but had to.

"Did you know Charlie was a conductor?" Maya rolled her eyes and sat back. Of course, she knew Charles conducted the Imperial orchestra, but her mother never failed to repeat things about how great her life was. Never failed to rub it in her face. She lived vicariously through everyone in her life! Maya clenched her jaw. Why had she come anyway?

"Yes, mother," she said. Amanda smiled and gave a stiff kiss to Charles's cheek. Maya scrunched her nose at the exchange. She shouldn't have come. She should've stayed with Allen, Zech and Ricky. Her heart began to fall. She had completely run away. She shook her head in remorse. She had just freaked out and run away. What was she doing here? What if they got caught? Her face drained of color as her mind raced.

"You look like you've seen a ghost," said Charles. Maya stood up and ran a hand through her hair.

"I need to go, I'm super tired from the whole week and I just wan-"

"-Maya, sit down," her mom commanded sternly. Maya eyed her and the two were once more locked in a vicious staring battle. Usually she crumbled to the stare, did as she was told. But there was too much at stake. She couldn't do that anymore.

"I have class tomorrow, and I need to go," she announced with all the courage she could muster. Charles shifted uncomfortably as Amanda slowly stood up.

"You'll be fine Maya, now sit down and spend some time with your mother, who, must I remind you, hasn't seen you in a whole week," she ordered. Maya narrowed her eyes.

"Oh, stop pretending you care about me, it's always been about you. I have to go back to my dorm, I need sleep, I'm tired!" Maya hissed between clenched teeth. Amanda shot up and stormed over to her.

"What did you say to me? Maya, I have done everything for your good," she spat. Charles grunted and slipped out of the dining hall.

Maya glared at her mom coldly.

"No, you haven't. You just took me along for the ride. You reap all the rewards."

Amanda snarled at her and clasped her bony hand around Maya's arm.

"Oh, the entitlement! Who got you into medical school? Who got you past the damned Fence? Who got you onto that immigration ship!? I did! That was all me!" she whined, her volume and pitch rising to her own defense. Maya wrenched her arm away from her mother's iron grip.

"I never asked you to do that!" Amanda let out a wry laugh.

"Oh please! Don't pull that on me!" she hissed. Maya shook her head and turned away.

"You've never asked what it's like for me, I'm the daughter of the *woman who slept her way to the top*! I was almost...I was assaulted by an elite because of those rumors! My whole life there has been nothing but whispers about how much of a sellout I am, how much I don't belong here! They're right, they're right! I don't belong here Amanda!"

"You think you're the only one getting whispered about? You ungrateful little bitch!" Maya gasped at her mother's words and backed away. She hadn't meant for this to blow up, she had just needed to leave.

"You don't care. Nothing they say affects you. All you have to do is get lip injections and sit in your golden dining hall with your important, wealthy husband. It doesn't even matter because I'm not staying in Magnus City!" She let out a bubbly, wry laugh at the exhilaration of finally having said what she'd wanted to say for a very long time! Amanda's eyes widened.

"What are you talking about?" She growled. Maya raised her chin defiantly.

"I'm not staying anymore, I'm freeing myself of you and this city and these rumors, and the elite!" She screamed before grabbing her bag and running out of her mother's mansion. She could hear her mother running after her, screaming for her to come back. Maya didn't listen, she kept running until her feet flew past the marble front courtyard and she left the expanse of her mother's control.

Amanda stopped at her doorway, her chest heaving from the chase.

"Charles! Call the Stratus and get a search on Maya's dormitory! Now!" Amanda furiously screamed at her husband...

Allen, Ricky and Zech sat at Maya's kitchen island, all three wolfing down a large bowl of creamy pasta. Zech had taken off his armor in favor of a bath, despite Ricky's protests.

"Oh my God, I've never eaten this well before," mumbled Allen as he shoved noodles into his mouth. Ricky gave a muffled moan of agreement as he practically choked down a slice of chicken.

"I didn't know I could be this hungry!" he breathed as he reached for a pint of water. Clean fresh water! *From the tap!* Allen chuckled a bit as he sucked in a noodle, the tip flicking his nose. Zech giggled childishly.

"Like the bones sticking out of your ribs didn't give a hint," Allen quipped as he grabbed a buttery, warm roll. Bread! It was so buttery and fluffy! It was real food! Too long he had survived on rotten cheese and spoiled milk.

"Yeah right. Well even after your fifteen-minute shower, you still got grimy hair!" The two snorted with laughter. Zech huffed and licked his bowl clean.

"Is there more?" he barked, his tongue lolling out with a contented doggish smile. Allen tossed a roll and Zech caught it gleefully. Allen and Ricky's eyes widened as he swallowed it in one bite. They were eating like they had just got out of prison...and they had! Allen scraped the last bit of creamy sauce out of the bowl with his fingers and belched contentedly.

"If the food is this good, I wonder what the booze tastes like!" Ricky grinned at Allen's musing and tossed a straw at him.

"Only one way to find out," he grunted. Allen's eyes lit up before he stopped, his hand clenched into a fist.

"No, no... I promised Veronica I'd stop drinking," he said with a firm nod. Ricky's eyes widened and he groaned. Allen grimaced at the reaction as Ricky reached over the table and smacked him.

"After all the times I've asked!?" he barked. Zech looked up from his bowl and lowered his ears. Allen sighed and chewed on another roll.

"Are you mad?" he asked. Ricky scrunched his nose, before he sighed and sat back. Something of a mix between a smirk and a scowl twisted his face. Allen watched as Ricky melted into a proud acceptance.

"Nah... this is good for you, I'm glad you're finally holding yourself to a standard," he said. Allen smiled at his friend and shoved the rest of the roll into his mouth.

"Well, thams for the supporth," he said past the bread stuck between his teeth. Ricky snickered and rolled his eyes. The two looked to Zech and smiled.

"How are ya feelin' mate?" Ricky affectionately inquired. Zech glanced at him and grinned, his tail wagging joyfully.

"Happy!" he said. Allen and Ricky shared a smile for the creature they both now considered a collective son.

They froze when there was a knock at the door. Ricky shot Allen a look and he shook his head. Zech's hackles raised and he stood up slowly. The knocking repeated, louder. The dorm shook from the force and noise. Allen's heart leaped into his throat and he held a finger to his mouth. Ricky shifted on his feet, his face going white with terror. No... this couldn't happen. Not right now! Not when they were this close!

"Stratus! Open up!" hollered a woman from the other side. Allen and Ricky shot each other a terrified look, before they raced to Zech and pulled him near the windows. Ricky jerked the curtains away and looked down.

They had to escape! This was the only way out other than the now blocked exit.

"Open the door now or we will use force!" shouted the Stratus once more. Allen seethed as tears pricked his eyes. This can't happen! This was unfair! How had they found them?

His mind flickered to Veronica. Had she betrayed them? He could feel his heart slowly rip in two as he thought about the possibility. No, no, it couldn't have been… There had to be another reason…but she was Stratus… Why had he allowed himself to trust her!? It was all a ruse! It had to have been! Now they were trapped!

"Allen, we have to break the window! Snap out of it," Ricky urgently hissed as Zech began to whimper. Allen looked from Ricky to Zech, his mind and heart racing.

"Allen, please don't let them take me," whined Zech. Allen couldn't catch his breath. He shook his head.

"I don't...I don't-" before he could finish his sentence, the door cracked open and a mechanical snarl filled the dorm. Allen snapped out of it.

"Zech! Break the window!" He ordered. Zech snarled and grabbed a chair, before he hurled it at the glass. It cracked under the force but didn't break. Zech's terror increased as he continued to hammer the window.

Allen darted to the Stratus uniform he had so foolishly stripped off earlier and grabbed the gun. The chimera snarled. His eyes caught the sight of the mechanical and his heart dropped. It was terrifying, with a sleek black body, and a whip-like snake tail that darted menacingly. Allen reacted just in time and rolled out of its way.

Ricky screeched and jumped onto the counter. As the two Stratus agents filed in, he pounced on one before he could lift his gun. The agent wrestled him away and threw him back.

The chimera launched itself at Allen, its goat head spewing flames. The Stratus began to shoot. Both Allen and Ricky ducked under cover of the counters and couches. Zech yowled as a bullet struck his back.

"Zech!" hollered Allen. The chimera roared, it's tail whipping forward. Allen dodged and fell as he tried to break his fall with an arm that wasn't there anymore. The chimera pounced on top of him. Zech snarled and grabbed the mech. He wrestled it off of Allen and slammed it into the window; the final blow needed before the window shattered.

"Don't let them escape!" ordered the woman. Allen jumped to Zech; and the three, without thinking, leaped out the window.

Zech grabbed them midair and took the fall, the trio crumbling and rolling.

Students began to gather outside, having been attracted to the noise like moths to a light. They shouted with shock at the sight of the Fencers...and the monster before them. The chimera ran to them and pounced on Zech as he tried to stand.

He yelped as the mechanical sank its razor-like teeth into his shoulder. Allen shouted and stumbled to his feet. He shot the mech in the face; Zech grabbed it and tossed it off. As Zech turned towards the students, they screamed at the sight of his face and began to run.

The soldiers came to the edge of the window and began to shoot. The trio scattered as they jumped over a ledge and onto one of the walkways.

"We need backup at the Medical Academy!" shouted one of the Stratus. They sprinted through the campus as they heard the metallic wheezing of the chimera behind them. As they flew past, the glass walls surrounding them lit up in a vibrant red and captured picture of them.

Allen watched as their photos displayed on every glass wall throughout the campus. Ricky grabbed his shoulder and pointed at a distant skyscraper. It had gone completely red, and a large picture of the trio was flashing.

"Allen! We're... we're famous!" he spat wryly. Allen shook his head and pulled Zech down as just above them a bullet exploded into a glass wall and it shattered over them.

"Now is not the time for sarcasm Ricky!" he retorted. His lungs were working double time, his legs ached and begged him to slow down. He could feel his vision going black around the edges. He wouldn't let himself stop.

A squadron of Stratus shot out of nowhere. Zech, in a split decision, shielded Allen and Ricky, bullets digging into his back. He screeched and Allen pulled him away under the cover of a granite wall.

"Zech! Can you hear me!?" asked Allen, his eyes wide with panic. Ricky gasped for air, his head slamming against the rock wall as bullets chipped away around them. Zech groaned and looked at Allen with wide amber eyes. His red fur was slick with blood from his shoulder, and his back. Allen clenched his jaw.

"You're going to be ok," he assured him. Zech whined.

"I should've kept armor on," he whimpered. Allen shook his head and pressed his hand over Zech's shoulder, only to discover he wasn't bleeding. Before he could process that information, the Stratus were upon them.

They grabbed Allen and pulled him up over the wall. Ricky darted off to the side and Zech stood to his full height, looming over the guards as they were about to put the final bullet through Allen's brain. He snarled and grabbed the executioner by the head; he flung him aside, the soldier tumbling violently across the path. Allen shot up and ripped the helmet of another soldier off, crashing his fist into his face.

Ricky kicked another in the groin before knocking the gun out of the soldier's hands. Another soldier swung her leg and kicked Ricky in the face, sending him to the ground.

Zech yanked the soldier whose gun was raised and swung him into another Stratus as they tried to get a shot off at Allen. Ricky screamed as the bullet cut through his side.

Allen dodged as a soldier sent a flurry of punches, each punch controlled and sharp. His good arm didn't lend much to blocking the blows and he succumbed to the onslaught. One connected with his jaw and then his stomach in a rapid succession that he couldn't keep up with.

Before Allen could fight back, the Stratus swung the butt of his gun across his head and he stumbled to the ground, his vision swimming and spinning.

Ricky cried out as a soldier pinned him down, her knees pressed forcibly against his backside. Zech tried to reach out and protect him, but soldier after soldier kept piling onto him, shooting stun pellets at him.

Their orders were to subdue, not to kill. That didn't mean that they wouldn't beat them until they were practically a mass of pulp, though.

Allen watched in horror as Ricky screamed, the Stratus bringing down a heavy whip over and over.

"St-stop!" He breathed as another soldier grabbed him by the hair.

"Leave him alone!" cried Allen as blood spurted out of Ricky's mouth. This was all his fault!

"Ricky! Ricky!" Allen screamed. He fought against the Stratus agents, his fist swinging as he tried to make it to his friend, his brother!

"Patrick!" he cried as they pinned him down. Ricky sobbed and reached weakly out to him.

Zech's eyes widened when he saw this. No! Not Allen! Not Ricky! What were they doing!? His heart thundered, his eyes dilated and he roared with rage. The soldiers looked up for a split second as the mutant shot forward with a speed they could not fathom.

Without warning, Zech ripped a soldier's head off, and bit down on another agent as he flung him against another like a ragdoll. His heart beat faster and faster as screams filled his ears. He couldn't tell which were the soldiers' and which were Allen or Ricky's.

As bullets pelted him, he snarled and whipped about to face them. He grabbed two agents and pushed them against the ground. He tore apart one's body from the torso and crushed another soldier. The crack and spatter of their bones and blood filled his head. The screams were like music, loud, grating and only served to drive him on.

Zech targeted the last one, his amber eyes glistening with rage; he dropped his gun and sprinted away. Zech was about to pursue when Allen and Ricky's pained sobs brought him back to reality. He blinked and looked at his friends.

"Allen...Ricky!" He gasped, stumbling towards them. Allen crawled to his best friend. Ricky clenched his jaw as his entire body shook rapidly, blood seeping from his wounds. His shirt was soaked and Allen's heart broke for the terrible shape his best friend was in.

"Patrick," he gasped as he clutched Ricky's face.

"It hurts," he whispered. Allen crumbled, pressing his forehead to Ricky's.

"It's ok, you're gonna be ok," he cried. Zech kneeled beside them and barked softly.

"Ricky…" he whimpered before trying to pick him up. Ricky groaned with pain, before trying to plant his feet beneath him. Allen stumbled to stand and looked around him to see the blood and soldiers' body parts strewn along the ground.

"I got shot," said Zech. Allen looked up at him, his eyes widening when he saw the shrapnel littering Zech's chest. Blood trickled down his body. He breathed a curse as Ricky hung, barely conscious on Zech's arm.

Allen's world swayed. His body ached, his legs wanted to give up and his vision blackened at the edges. As he took a step forward, he stumbled to the ground. Ricky choked and slid to the ground as well, his head leaning against a wall. Zech whined and tried to pick both of them up.

His adrenaline however, had waned and all that was left was the screaming pain of the shrapnel, the pulsing of his veins as his body throbbed and ached.

"Zech?" A familiar voice called out, her voice weaving in and out of his consciousness. Zech turned slowly, his ears pressing to the back of his head.

"Maya…" he murmured. When they locked eyes, Maya choked with realization.

She sprinted down the corridor as Zech tried to walk towards her. They met and Maya let out a choked cry of shock and terror at the sight of her friends slumped over on the ground, surrounded by bloody masses of Stratus soldiers. More would come. Zech stumbled to his feet and she let him down slowly, wheezing at his weight.

Maya darted to Ricky and held up his head, tears welling in her eyes.

"Oh my God, what did they do to you?" she asked, choking on the lump in her throat as her vision blurred. Ricky groaned, his head falling forward limply. He had passed out from the shock of his many wounds and loss of blood!

Maya checked him for any extreme fatalities, any head injuries that may have damaged his brain. His head was fine, but it was his back that was a bloody mess. He had at least two broken ribs. She let out a sob.

"I'm so sorry, I'm so sorry," she whimpered. She went to Allen. He gasped for air; his eyes squeezed shut. She lifted his eyelids. She had left them. How could this happen? She dragged him over to Ricky and kneeled beside both of them. How could she have let this happen? What was wrong with her? Why had she run away? Why had she been such a coward?

Zech crawled over to her and put his head into her lap. Her body wracked with sobs. What could she have even done? What could she have done against the Stratus?

Mechanical whirrs filled the air and her head shot up. Her eyes came into contact with a Chimera. It let out a low, somber snarl, before its tail whipped out and struck her shoulder. Her scream pierced the air and she fell limp to the ground.

LaDY JUSTICe

Veronica looked out over the Academy campus, her eyes searching for a landing spot. As she searched, she found the campus roiling with Stratus.

"Damon...tune into the radio," she breathed. Damon nodded and swiped his hand over the control panel. They listened as captains spoke over their headpieces.

"We've arrested the fencers...God it's a bloodbath here...Is that monster dead? ... No, The Judge ordered we take them unconscious, not dead. Professor Vargas wanted to conduct examinations...Damn Fencers. How did they even get in? ...They impersonated Jason and Monique... Typical...What did the monster look like?... Terrifying. It got shot fifteen times, but it's still breathing. It's not even in critical condition. It's been subdued though... there was another suspect found at the scene, a student of the Academy... She was housing them in her dormitory... Name? Maya Rose Hart... Oh, I'm looking into her record, she was from the Fence too... must be one big conspiracy from those animals... Whatever. They can barely read, let alone unite together..."

Veronica slammed her fist against the window, her stomach dropping at the news. Damon turned it off. Her skin crawled at their words, each one filled with bigotry and ignorance. She hated it here.

"We're too late...no, no, we can still save them...they're still alive. Damon, where are they being taken?" she asked. Damon glanced up at her and frowned in thought.

"They're probably being taken to the brig," he said. Veronica nodded and glanced out the window. She fought back the tears that threatened to spill.

What if Allen thought she was behind this? What if he believed she had betrayed them? Her heart ripped in two, and she pressed her head against the window. She had to fix this, she had to save them. They'd be slaughtered if she couldn't get to them in time! Just...Just like her mother. She couldn't let that happen, not when she had the power to stop it.

"Under the Libranian... well then let's go," she said sternly. Damon nodded and guided the ship toward the Libranian, the big grey building standing tall on the mountain side, the statue of Justice daring them to go on.

"Alright I'm turning on the cloaking device. I'm going to go with you Ronny, you won't be able to make it alone, and as far as they're concerned, I'm still on their side. I'm going to act like I caught you and am escorting you to the brig, and then we act," he schemed. Veronica nodded her head, a knowing glisten in her eyes.

"Is this why my mom hired you?" she asked. Damon glanced at her and rolled his eyes playfully.

"No, she hired me out of pity," he said truthfully. Veronica sighed and tilted her head.

"What happened to her? You always say you failed her, how you weren't there for her in the time of need… you know, I'm tired of bein' left in the dark, so tell me…" she whispered. Damon swallowed back a lump of nerves at the request. He had been dodging this. He had so much shame.

"You're right…your mother was always a compassionate woman…I mean, she saved my life, and she wanted to save countless more… the Judge had just passed the law that stated we'd no longer be accepting immigrants into the city…

"Come with me." Raven slammed her fist on the bar where he sat, Damon glanced up at her, a tad startled from her abrupt entrance.

"How did you find me?" he asked. Raven rolled her eyes, crossing her arms as she stood firm in the mostly empty bar, red neon light from the counter painting their faces. The darkness of night outside crowded through the windows and spilled into the dimly lit bar. The shadow of the bartender flickered near them, as he mechanically dried various sizes and shapes of carafes and serving glasses.

"Come on Damon, you know you're not hard to find at these hours," she said, a playful smirk on her lips.

"Don't you have a daughter to worry about?" he asked, rubbing his eyes. Raven snorted and sat down, tapping the counter.

"Ronny is more than capable. You forget she's sixteen...and don't try to change the subject, I need you to help me. You still owe me," she said, a playful grin on her face. Damon frowned.

"What? Raven haven't I done enough for you? ... What is it you want from me?" Raven pursed her lips and leaned in as the bartender left the bar and headed to the back. Raven looked around to check the angles of the cameras and pulled him closer so that his body would block the cameras from being able to determine their whispered words.

"I need your help with immigrants. I was able to get in touch with a tower and-" she whispered, Damon gritted his teeth and shook his head furiously.

"What? Are you, insane? ...You can't smuggle in dwellers; the stratus will kill you," he remonstrated, keeping his voice low to prevent the cameras' microphones from picking up what he was saying. Raven frowned.

"That's a risk I'm willing to take. Come on Damon, I need you, this is a two-man job at best," she pleaded. Damon glared at her, hiding his face in his hands.

"And what if we get caught? I've already dealt with prison; I've already lost the chance of finding my son. Your daughter needs you," said Damon. Raven sighed and stood up, running a hand through her hair.

*"Listen, it'll work...but I can't do it alone. Please...
it's important. We need to help these people, no matter
what the law says! You should know; you were a dweller!"
she hissed. Damon glanced around him and grabbed
Raven's arm, dragging her out of the bar.*

*"I can't do this...you shouldn't either. We must live
to fight another day," he pleaded, looking around him as
they stood on the street, each moment that they continued
this conversation, his paranoia grew. He was sure they
were being spied on. Raven scoffed and jerked her hand
away from his grasp.*

*"I can't believe you...so you won't help?" She
didn't need an answer, his decision was in his eyes. He
looked up, extending a hand.*

*"I heavily advise you to do the same," he
suggested. She winced and shook her head, turning away
from him.*

*"I hope you find your son...really, but will he be
proud of his father? You have no fight in you...you're a
coward." the words hit him hard, like a fist to his gut, and
he watched as she walked off, her mind set.*

"I never saw her again after that...until I found out
she was caught. I saw the livestream of her execution...it
was the worst day of my life. I couldn't help but think
about how if I had just...helped her, she would still be here
today," he said. Veronica sat silent; pondering, unbidden
but unstoppable tears streaming down her cheeks. She

couldn't help but smile. Her mother did what she knew was right. It had always been her way.

"If it means anything...she'd be proud of what you're doing now," she said. The two smiled softly at each other and Damon clutched her hand.

"Thank you," he said. They turned back and began to arm themselves. They had arrived, the Libranian's grey walls... Lady Justice stood. That statue was more threatening now than it had ever been in their lives.

Ricky's vision swam, and his wrists ached from the cuffs locked tightly around them. Blood streamed from his nose and his body ached, every pain sensor sending out alarms. He coughed, and as he coughed, a sharp, screaming stab of pain shot up his chest and he writhed.

"Allen?" he moaned, his blurry eyes searching for his friend. The room was dark, pulsing a red color. There was no opening in the room, no clear door, but there had to be. There had to be some kind of escape. Ricky let out a slow groan, his eyes brightening at the relief of air, no matter how stale. He could still breathe, thank whatever higher powers had spared them. He struggled to get his feet beneath him and crawled near one of the dark, pulsing walls. He pushed himself up against it, trying delicately not to hurt his ribs that sent sharp stabs of pain with every move. Despite his delicate treatment of his ribs, his bruised and beaten back throbbed with pain so insistent, he gasped.

His legs shook as he slid up the wall, but once he was standing, he wouldn't allow himself to sit back down, despite the shaking of his legs that begged to give way. His vision blurred but he shook his head. He couldn't be weak now.

"Allen!" he shouted hoarsely. Ricky leaned against the wall, despite the protests of his body. He couldn't sit down.

Where were they? Was Allen dead? No! He couldn't be dead! If he wasn't dead, surely Allen was still alive. However, he knew it wouldn't last long.

Ricky whimpered, his hands pulling against the metal restraints in vain. They had failed, utterly and completely. Ricky hit the wall with the back of his head in rage at the fact. He knew this would happen; he knew they'd never have a chance.

He bit his lip and fought back hot, angry tears. Was this worth it? Was everything they did worth when this was their end? He knew Allen would say yes. Was Allen right though? Was Zech worth all the trouble Ricky had forced himself to endure for his friend? He found in his heart...the answer was yes.

He looked around, sliding along the walls as his fingers behind him ran along any crack they could find.

What had he done in the ghetto? Make mechanicals to be used by filthy perverts in Scandals? His precious creations soiled and dirtied by people who gave them nothing but a jug of water for the next week? A jug of water… He tortured himself working in a factory that provided him a shabby apartment with no running water and heating that only worked in the summertime.

Now he had broken ribs, he was shackled, and he was imprisoned...in the Skyline. His life would end here, but he had lived more fiercely here in the Skyline than he had ever lived behind the Fence. Allen was right. This was worth it.

He cursed the elite defiantly, screaming the words at the top of his lungs. Curse this city, curse the elite, and curse this prison cell! This wasn't the end!

"Allen! I'm not giving up. If you can hear me, which you probably can't, I have two broken ribs, you don't have an arm, Zech is all shot up with bullets, but we're still alive, and I'm not giving up. Neither should you."

Veronica and Damon stealthily made their way through the Libranian. She knew that she was in huge trouble with the Stratus. Ever since she took out her eye, and rebelled against her fellow officers in the fence, she would surely have been arrested on sight...but thankfully Damon was there, already having "arrested her" and was taking her to the brig to, "rot with the rest of those filthy fencers," as Damon so delicately put it.

Veronica shifted uncomfortably at his words and act of shoving her in front of the other guards, but she knew that's all it was. An act. And soon they would be out of here with her friends.

It suddenly occurred to her that this meant they'd be living on the surface. What terrors awaited them below? Her mind was flooded with both fear and excitement. Excitement because it finally meant she'd be away from the Judge's iron grip that had destroyed her mother. Veronica was ready to be free of it.

A man shouted down the hall, giving both Veronica and Damon a start. They looked up to see General Sylva striding angrily to them.

"Lieutenant! I was looking for you! Why didn't you answer your headset?" he turned a spiteful look to Veronica, "Defected." He let it sputter from his mouth like the word itself was poison. Damon shook his head curtly.

"Quite the contrary, I caught her red handed and am taking her to the brig with the rest," he said. Matias nodded thoughtfully before looking at Veronica.

"No, she has to come with me...the Judge requested an audience with her," murmured Matias as he eyed them both skeptically. He knew their history and he didn't trust Damon not to side with his once best friend's daughter.

"Oh?" murmured Damon, this was news to him, but Veronica kicked herself for not seeing it coming. The Judge had always had it out for her ever since her mother proved insubordinate.

"Well what of the other prisoners?" he asked. Matias turned and looked at him quizzically as he began to lead the two conspirators down the halls of the Libranian to where the Judge had asked to meet. It was not in the Hall of Justice. It appeared the Judge didn't find her worthy of a trial.

"In there; Damon. I'll take over from here," he said, dodging Damon's question. Damon set his jaw into a hardened determination. Veronica looked up at him and Damon snuck her a quick wink that went unnoticed by the General.

"I'll go around up the other rodents and get them sent to their execution then?" he offered. Matias scrutinized him before whistling. He didn't want to distrust his old friend, but the Judge had planted seeds of doubt and he just couldn't uproot them.

"There's a truck waiting to take them to the Biotech's lab as we speak. We already sent the monster over there. Decided we needn't waste time holding him in a cell." Veronica's heart dropped and she looked at Damon with pleading eyes. Damon tried not to show any sort of panic.

"Well, why are the others here instead? Weren't they supposed to go too?" he asked. Matias shrugged.

"The Judge didn't say," then he glanced at Veronica. Damon nodded.

"But she did say to wait for a signal to take them out. I think she has something planned," he whispered out of Veronica's ear shot.

Veronica stared into the white room General Sylva had brought them to. The heavy metal doors blocked off any possibility of escape. In the center was a pillar.

"Ok...I'll leave her in your capable hands," murmured Damon. He had quickly debated taking down the general...but he couldn't afford to be hasty and this was too important. He could spare one moment to save Veronica from an encounter with the Judge and risk both of them getting arrested, or he could save his son, his friends, the creature, and Veronica. Veronica set her jaw, her eyes sparkling with understanding, even though her heart skipped a beat as it thundered in her chest.

Damon let her go and turned to leave the room. He walked purposefully down the hall until he rounded the corner and broke into a sprint. He had to move fast. He had no idea what the Judge would do to her.

Matias took her into the white room that seemed to glow and handcuffed her to the column

"Why are you doing this? You're just the Judge's lap dog. She'll dispose of you if you make one miss step. She won't think twice about replacing you. You could join us too you know," she made her appeal. Matias ignored her. He searched her and took all her weapons.

He did spare Veronica a glance, a sad frown on his face as if he knew what was to come next. What was behind those eyes? What was he hiding...what did he know? Veronica could hear her heart thunder in her ears as he left and the door slid noiselessly closed behind him, disappearing beneath the white light.

Veronica immediately began to struggle against the cuffs that chained her to the post, bending and twisting in any way she could. It only tired her and caused her wrist to chafe and bleed.

"No use in fighting against them Veronica, it will only cause you more pain." Veronica gave a start when she heard the Judge behind her. The Judge circled around the pillar, her flowing grey robes flowing around her ankles as if she were walking through storm clouds.

"What do you want!?" Veronica snapped. The Judge sighed at the girl below her, she really was just a girl compared to the old woman. She still had her mother's face, her mother's spirit.

"I want to speak some sense to you, perhaps bring you back to the path of light. There was a time when you admired me Veronica; before all this," she said, waving her hand as if waving away a pesky mosquito.

"You mean before you executed my mom?" Veronica spat at her with all the venom she could muster. The Judge sighed and circled her, and Veronica began to feel how a rabbit must feel when an eagle was descending upon it. She let out a shaky breath.

"You must understand Veronica...your mother was not the saint you know her as; she did not hang the moon. I know, I knew her longer than you ever could have," said the Judge. Veronica glared at her.

"Why should I trust anything you say? My mother said you were a snake. A snake beyond saving," she hissed. The Judge nodded thoughtfully at the statement.

"I'm sure, I'm sure...we never really agreed on things. She wanted to open the doors of Magnus to everyone. She thought it was the humane thing to do. I'm sure she has poisoned you too child, hasn't she? There is nothing humane about bringing that filth into this city. They pollute it. Just look at the Fence. Wasn't always like that, used to be, long before you, the elite and the surface dwellers shared the same luxuries. And what did that bring, child? Murder, rape, exploitation...I wanted to stop these things, save the city. So, I worked to come into power, while your mother did everything to sabotage my efforts. She said everyone deserves a chance, even rapists, even pedophiles. Tell me Veronica, do those things, the lowest of humanity, deserve a chance? Do they even deserve a voice?" She spat. Veronica felt helpless against the onslaught of her spite. She didn't know how to answer, but she knew that it was still wrong to do what the elite did to the Fencers. Allen and Ricky weren't rapists or pedophiles, but they were still imprisoned.

"Well not all of them are bad, they deserve an equal chance," she said. The Judge smirked and turned to face her.

"Well how would you root out the evil? How do you when the thorns strangle the wheat? You don't know what is in someone's heart, therefore, we have our laws to protect us," she said. Veronica shook her head.

"You're wrong," she growled. The Judge let out a hissing laugh. Veronica began to think her mother's words were more literal than figurative.

"Oh, am I? How am I wrong?" She teased, her eyes flashing as she circled Veronica like a bird of prey.

"Because Allen, Allen isn't like that, and neither is Ricky or Zech or Maya." The Judge rolled her eyes. The girl, obviously, was too young and too simple to see the bigger picture.

"You must love them; you even took out an eye to make sure you could serve them effectively… You are too much like your mother… She would be proud of what you've become: a martyr for the lowest of humanity. A martyr for those who don't deserve compassion… You truly disgust me Veronica...but not for long," she said. Veronica shook her head and began to pull at the handcuffs.

The words were vile, but she glowed with the joyful thought of having her mother's pride bestowed upon her. Then she grew terrified in anticipation of what was to come next. What did the Judge mean? Why was she here? What was she going to do? She had to get out, but how? Why did Damon leave her?

"Your mother tried to take everything away from me...she tried to ruin my city, and now I will ruin everything she ever cared about," spat the Judge.

Veronica's eyes darted about as she processed these new words.

"She's already dead, so what does it matter?" snapped Veronica, lunging at her in fury. The Judge didn't flinch. She brought her finger to Veronica's face and stroked her chin.

"You have your mother's spirit, in fact I'd say you were a reincarnation of her, so I intend to destroy *you*," she said with a wicked grin. Veronica's face dropped and her heart thundered with panic. The last hurrah against Raven Boyce. She had to get out. Where was Damon?

"No! No!" she screamed. She felt like a rabbit thrashing about in a cage as her huntress padded easily around her. Her hands revealed something from the grey folds of her robes. It was a syringe of dark, thick, amber liquid. Veronica thrashed and screamed, a terror beyond anything she'd ever known filled her.

Icy, paralyzing, painful terror. Her attempts were useless, the Judge merely stalked and waited as Veronica kicked and thrashed, trying with all her might to not get touched by whatever the Judge was holding.

"That's quite enough girl," the Judge commanded. She clicked a button in her other hand and the pillar seared Veronica with a hot electric shock. Veronica screamed in agony.

"And guess what else? I'm going to make your filthy scum friends watch before they're taken to their death," she hissed, before she grabbed Veronica by her hair.

"Allen!" She screamed as another painful shock tore through her body. Veronica looked up to see a large screen that had once been white was now showing him.

He sat in the corner of a room, his body bruised and bloody. Veronica choked at the sight. He stood up when he saw her. She heard nothing but saw his wordless shouts.

Veronica screamed again as the shock stabbed at her seemingly cutting her limb from limb before finally she couldn't fight anymore. She slumped over against the pillar, shaking and sobbing as Allen shouted voicelessly.

He began to bang on the wall, trying desperately to escape to come to her rescue...but what could he do? How could he help her? He couldn't. He was weak against the elite. They were both powerless.

As Veronica looked up helplessly, the Judge knelt down. She tapped the needle, letting the air bubble out before jabbing the dripping needle into her thigh.

Veronica screamed. The Judge shushed her with the sibilance of a snake.

She felt sweat beading on her forehead as her vision began to grow cloudy. Every movement felt muddied and already the drug began to tear viciously through her.

It felt as if trying to wake up from a long slumber, just about to open your eyes, feeling heavy and groggy. She sank down, the light from her eyes dulling as the drug spread through her veins. The Judge stood over her, a proud grin on her face at her accomplishment.

The perfect way to ruin Raven's legacy was to turn everything Raven loved and nurtured against the ideals she had tried to instill. The Judge would destroy Veronica and remake her into her image instead. It was just too bad Raven couldn't watch with her own eyes what the Judge had in store for the girl that now lay slumped at her feet, her eyes half lidded, her body hanging limp against her arms, still shackled to the column, drool sliding down her cheek.

open wounds

Allen sat huddled beside the pillar that stood in the center of his cell, the wall switched off slowly, the last of Veronica's struggle replaying in his mind. He didn't have the energy anymore to handle what was happening. He couldn't do anything. Like all the other times in his life: he was powerless. Powerless against the elite. He was powerless when they forced him onto the bus to the Home, he was powerless now, watching as Veronica fought in vain against the Judge. His heart filled with hatred for that woman. How could she!?

His lip curled and he let out an angry wail. He had lost Veronica. He had begged that they be spared, that they leave together unscathed, he had been so stupid!

Why didn't he go with her? He knew he should've gone with her, to protect her. He could've...no, he wouldn't have been able to. He was weak, he was nothing. They were all doomed to die. The injustice of it all clawed into him and he could feel himself choking on the stale air of despair that surrounded him.

A line in the wall formed and a heavy metal door slid away. In the frame was a stiff looking man, his pepper grey hair cut short, wrinkles faceting his face in a stern frown, but when he saw Allen's eyes, Damon melted into a sob.

Veronica was right, she saw every similarity, and even though the man before him had grown almost beyond recognition, he still had the same awe-filled blue eyes. The sight of those eyes that had once belonged to his little boy broke him.

Allen paid no mind to this, but instead growled at him, and sprang to his feet.

"What have you done to Veronica?!" he snarled, his voice hoarse from screaming his impotence, his rage, and his pain.

Damon's face fell at the words. What happened to Veronica? He almost bolted out the door to go to her, but here in front of him was his son... he suddenly became very torn. He had to get his son out first, that was final.

"Allen...it's me." Damon went to undo his handcuffs, noticing his son was only sporting one arm, which was chained to the pillar in the center. He had allowed his son to face so much pain. Allen stared at him, this man was all the sudden helping him, and he didn't understand!

"What's that supposed to mean!?" asked Allen, jerking away from the lieutenant and stumbling to regain his balance. He was scared, and angry, and this man was calling him by his name with such tenderness. It was the way his father used to say it, and that made him angrier. His father was gone!

Damon held up his hands, sighing, and it was then Allen could see the tears running down Damon's face. What was going on?

"Veronica...she said you were...my son, you were my Allen...you are my son," he said softly, squeezing his eyes shut. This news slapped Allen across the face and he found himself at a loss for words.

This was so wrong; it shouldn't have been like this. Allen backed away, shaking his head in disbelief. He wanted so badly for it to be wrong. This man couldn't be his dad, but everything made sense the longer he thought about it, and the longer he thought about it, the angrier he got. His father...was a Stratus officer? He left him alone in the ghetto, and became a Stratus officer!?

"What? You're my father? Wha-...well, where the hell were you!? Why didn't you come back for me!?" his voice cracked and he turned away, hiding his tears of rage. Damon clenched his jaw, reaching out hesitantly.

"Allen, listen to me, -"

"No! You left me! You left me alone, I was nine! I thought, maybe you were dead, and to be honest, I'd prefer if you were, but...here you are! On opposite sides of the court. You work for them! They want to kill Zech, they ruined Veronica! And they tortured me, my entire life. How dare you come to me now!"

"Who are you to assume I made the choice? Do you think I wanted to be here? I would have given anything to go back and change what happened," Damon cried in anguish. So much was happening. Allen glanced over his shoulder, his face red and wet with the tears of his rage and sorrow. His mind swelled like a storm at sea, waves of anger crashing against cliffs of guilt and regret. He should've been happy, but after watching Veronica get taken by the Judge, knowing what had happened to her...he felt nothing but rage.

"Ten years..." his voice quavered, and he stifled a sob before swallowing to continue, "I survived, I ate out of dumpsters. I was beaten, and, and I ran my entire life. I lost myself; you were gone, I... why didn't you come back? Why didn't you look for me?" He spoke slow and low, his voice quivering, on the edge of breaking down. Damon stepped forward, reaching out his hand, which Allen shied away from.

"Allen...I'm sorry, I'm so sorry...There was a fight on the ship,"

Damon was filled with anxiety, his son was separated from him, and while he knew *they'd be ok, it wasn't anything he had expected. What if they hurt him? He wouldn't be able to live with himself if something happened to his son.*

He had promised him heaven, but already it was starting to feel like hell. He could get through this though, so he got in line. So many lines. He answered their questions, so many questions.

He thought he would shrivel up and crumble by the end, but his determination pushed him on. A hand gripped his shoulder and he turned back.

"Back of the line, pal," said a gruff man, a beard puffing out down to his chest. Damon grimaced as he glanced back at the yards of people. He looked back up and bared his teeth.

"This is my spot," he said, anger biting his tone. He had been standing here for hours, and he wasn't about to give it up. The man sneered at him and grabbed his arm.

He threw his fist into Damon's face, a loud shout filling the hall. The crowd gathered around them, chanting for some action, their bored minds hungry for stimulation; entertainment.

The man grabbed Damon's arm and kicked into his gut; Damon wheezed for air. He reached up, tangling his fingers in the man's beard and yanked, his head going down as Damon's knee went up.

The man cussed loudly, holding his nose in pain, his nose spurting blood as he leaned over. Damon growled and turned away, heading back to stand back in line. He gasped when he was barreled over, the man tackling him to the ground. Then the burly, bearded man shot up, throwing his fists at Damon in rapid succession.

Damon whimpered as he took several blows, his hand darting up and clawing at the man's eyes. He curled into himself to try to ward off the barrage of fists and knee blows the man was throwing at him. Finally, there was a short pause in the onslaught; just long enough for Damon to knee the man with all his might in the groin; a grunt escaped the brute's mouth. Damon tried to roll away but the brute reached out his long arms and took Damon into a choke hold.

Damon turned into him, his elbow hitting the attacker's ribs sharply, before immediately following through with a fist into his neck, and finally a solid punch to his face, knocking the man off of him.

His breath was ragged and as he looked up, he heard the boots of Stratus guards coming to keep the peace. He glanced down at the man who had attacked him and suddenly realized his position, the victor in a fight; his opponent knocked on the ground, bleeding. It was almost as bad as it looked, especially to anyone who hadn't seen the whole fight.

"He fuggin' attacked me," said the burly man with muffled and almost unintelligible words. Damon's eyes widened as the officers glared up at him.

"Wait no, it's not what it looks like!" But the officers spared no care for his side of the story, all they saw was a man who was standing victorious. They grabbed him from both sides and took him out of the line he had fought so hard to be in.

"No, you can't take me, I need to get my son! He needs me! He's only nine, please! It wasn't my fault; I was defending myself! Allen! Allen!" He cried, his legs kicking, his arms punching against their superior numbers and force.

Damon sat shaking in the prison cell, looking up at the glowing glass window, the walls surrounding him made of hard steel. He watched as guards passed, and he kept his head down. It had been three days...he had failed his son.

"Damon Rosinsky?" asked a soft voice. He looked up at a woman, her hazel skin shining in the bright florescent light. She wore the uniform of a Stratus officer, and for that he shied away.

"Yes, what do you want?" he asked, he grimaced as he forced his eyes to look away.

"I'm Raven Boyce...I heard what happened to you, and what they're planning on doing with you... It doesn't look good. I want to help you...I looked over the footage, I know you are innocent, and you're a promising fighter... I want to offer you a chance to be part of my squadron...I could use someone not poisoned by this city on my side," she offered, her hand hovering over the glass. Damon raised his eyes and he stood up, walking to her, the two separated by glass that radiated heat.

"If I accept, will you help me find my son?" he asked. Raven clenched her jaw and the two stared at each

other. Her dark eyes searched his, and all they saw was
agony.

"I'll see what we can do, but it's either come with
me, or stay here...I'm already risking my neck by helping
you," she said. He didn't have much of a choice.

"I'll take it," he muttered. Raven smiled brightly
and swiped her key card over a thin box outside of his cell.
The glass retreated into the walls. He stood there in awe
and Raven held her hand out.

"Welcome aboard!"

Allen slowed his pace, as Damon told his story
while they had been trying to find the others. Allen looked
up at him, tears still streaming.

"Well...what happened? Why couldn't, why *didn't*
you come for me?" he asked, still angry and bitter.

Damon glanced at him and frowned at the question.
He finally had his son back after ten years, and all he got as
a welcome was rage. He couldn't blame him though.

"Listen, Allen...you have every right to hate me, I
hate it too, and I would've gone after you, but, Raven, she
had erased my entire past so I could get out of prison, and
the Judge was...suspicious-"

"-What an amazing excuse, please make another
one!" Damon eyed his son and winced. Allen sighed and

glanced away. He needed to change the subject. This was going to have to wait.

"That *viper* drugged Veronica...made me *watch*," Allen croaked. Damon's face paled. What had he done? He had left Veronica with the Judge, how stupid could he have been! Too eager to reunite with his son, he left Veronica to her doom!

His hands shook as he opened another cell door. There was Maya, sobbing as she whispered Veronica's name over and over.

The disturbance caused her to look up, her face stained red, her lips pulled tight in a grimace of pain. Allen crumbled at the sight of her and rushed forward.

"Allen!" gasped Maya as he enveloped her in a tight hug. He buried his head in her soft, blonde hair as Damon moved over to unlock her handcuffs.

"It was awful Allen, the drug, Somnam, it's a comatose drug. She has no chance! It's highly addictive, one shot is enough to get someone hooked, and if over consumed, can cause a long brain-dead coma...Allen she's gone, Veronica, she's gone," Maya sobbed inconsolably. Allen bit down on his cheek, enraged, as he pulled her to her feet and led her out.

Damon charged ahead of them. Maya had not even questioned his presence; her mind was so filled with dread for her friend.

He opened yet another wall and they moved in quickly to steal away Ricky from his confines. Maya gasped when she saw him, crumpled over on the ground, his eyes wide as he played the events over and over in his mind on repeat. He didn't even see the three come in.

Ricky made no struggle as Damon unchained him, and only groaned with pain when both Damon and Allen picked him up, his arms draped around their shoulders.

"Ricky..." murmured Maya. He only smiled weakly at her as they hobbled down the hall.

"Aren't we just the picture of conquering heroes," he murmured as he tried not to think about what would happen to them.

"Come on! I have an aircraft outside. We just need to make it out without getting stopped, and then we need to save the mutant before it's too late. I just hope Dr. Vargas is still preoccupied studying him," said the lieutenant, a hard frown on his face. Ricky and Maya shared a confused look as they finally seemed to realize who was leading their escape; a man they didn't know at all. Was it a friend of Veronica's? Had she gone to fetch help before she was captured? Allen glanced around at his broken friends and clenched his jaw.

"So there's nothing we can do for Veronica?" he croaked. Damon grimaced with guilt and regret.

"Zech doesn't have much time...I need to get you all out first...I don't doubt for a second that Veronica will fight tooth and nail," he said softly. Maya, Ricky and Allen looked away. They had watched with horror what had become of their friend, helpless to stop the Judge from injecting the Somnam. Damon's words did little to comfort them.

The group started down the hall only to encounter a group of elites, garbed in grey robes, laughing at their conversation and oblivious to the escape. Damon skidded to a stop as he quickly plastered an authoritative scowl on his face.

"Oh! Mr. Rose, I mean," stuttered the woman, her long auburn tresses trailing down her back. The other court members glanced around, alarmed at this unexpected encounter with the despised prisoners.

"What are they doing out?" he asked imperiously. Damon glanced back and scowled, stomping toward the courtiers.

"What do you think? Hm? I'm taking them to their executions!" he barked, crossing his arms to emphasize his point. The woman gulped and nodded.

"But wasn't-" she stopped herself and nodded, deciding it was none of her business to question the Stratus officer's authority. The courtiers shuffled around the fugitives, the air heavy and tense between them. As soon as the courtiers turned a corner the rag tag band of escapees broke out into a hobbled jog again.

"Gotta love it when a bluff works!" he muttered and somehow, they felt a ray of hope.

They made their way through the maze-like hallways, avoiding elites by taking empty halls and racing upstairs instead of using the elevators. Damon led them to the roof, bursting out from the top floor stairwell. He clicked a button on his arm band and his aircraft seemed to ripple into existence from an invisible slumber.

Damon hurried them into the hovering machine, Allen helping Ricky up with a wheeze and a groan. That had been too easy, but Damon didn't stop to question it. They didn't have the luxury of time to think it over.

Maya huddled in the back with Ricky. He was in immense pain, and she felt powerless to help him without her equipment. But she'd have to do something, even if it was just finding a way to calm him down.

"Hey, Ricky! Breathe! Take some deep breaths." Ricky nodded and followed her instructions. He stifled a cough as he inhaled and exhaled shakily, as if the very act of controlling anything was almost beyond him.

"I'm going to be fine; it's going to be okay," he murmured. Maya lifted her head as she watched him and she glimpsed a first aid kit in the corner. She almost jumped for joy as she moved to retrieve it. He watched her, listening to the muffled conversation in the cockpit between their mysterious savior and Allen.

There was something strange about this man. Ricky could see it in the way Allen fidgeted nervously next to him. He was sure it would be revealed to him, but he guessed he'd stay in the dark for now. They were still in great danger. They still had to rescue Zech...and then cross the city border...and then fall like a raptor to the surface.

"Here we go. Help me take off your shirt; I need to dress your wounds," she said softly. Ricky blushed in embarrassment, but he didn't protest as together they peeled the black t-shirt off. He sucked in his breath at the searing pain as the dried blood from his many cuts were torn open again when they took off his shirt. His embarrassment forgotten; all he could think of was the pain that pounded throughout his body.

Maya whistled at the damage and gestured with her finger for him to turn his back to her. He shakily moved, despite the screaming pain of his broken ribs. Maya dipped a cotton swab in alcohol. He winced at the cold, burning touch, and clenched his jaw. He found he didn't want to seem weak in front of her, so he soldiered through the burning pain.

"They got you good," she murmured. Ricky swallowed, closing his eyes as if it would block out the memory from replaying in his mind.

"Really beat the ever lovin' shit outta me, didn't they?" Maya frowned as she patched up the bigger cuts that ran down his back.

"I guess I was easy pickin's." They shared a moment of silence. He looked back at her to find she was closer than he thought and he involuntarily flinched

"I know how that feels...I'm jealous of you and Allen; at least you two have the skills to defend yourself...I can't do anything like that." Her eyes hid a secret that she wouldn't share, but Ricky could see they were more alike than he'd like to admit. He had definitely misjudged her, and he hated the fact that he had been so mean to her in the beginning.

"Well then...we ought to stick together," he said softly. Maya smiled at him, and for the first time, she felt he had accepted her.

"I don't know how to deal with this...I don't know if I should be happy or not...I don't know if I should forgive you, I don't know if you even deserve that. You had power, you're a damn Lieutenant. You could've done something," growled Allen as he sat disconsolately in the co-captain's seat.

Damon sighed and nodded. He didn't know what to say. He had been stupid to believe their reunion would be happy. After all, Allen was right, it had been ten years. He'd have to earn his own son back.

"Did you even try?" Allen spat in the pain of those long ten years without his father. Damon nodded solemnly, but neither he nor Allen really wished for an explanation.

"There's Dr. Vargas's lab." Allen sat up, his heart pounding as he abandoned his anger for his father and replaced it with fear for Zech. He fervently hoped beyond all reason that they weren't too late.

This place again. The smell was too familiar. It sent blood curdling shivers up his spine. He didn't know if he could take it, this *place*. Zech shuddered at the memories that plagued his mind, memories he couldn't quite piece together.

It was all one big nightmare, a nightmare that left screams and chills in the night, never imprinting a memory, but still there. It lurked in the back of his mind. The pain. The heat, the needles. The voices of doctors. Alarms and snarls, hissing, mechanical clanking and steam. It was vivid, and sharp, and yet, when he reached for it, it shied away in the shadows of his consciousness.

He shoved against the doctors, but he was helpless, shackled in glowing cuffs, that shocked him with every rapid movement he made.

 Zech let out a shaky whimper as the scientists softly pushed him into a room surrounded by glass, and he sniffed. He knew this room. His eyes flickered about, staring at the gawking faces. His eyes caught on one face as it entered and stared back at him, like a challenge.

"Subject two-twenty-seven. Welcome home. We've missed you," Dr. Vargas crooned triumphantly, as he stood at the glass, staring him down. Zech shook, glaring into the eyes as pain filled him, his shackles lighting up as he fought against his bonds. He whimpered, crumbling to the ground.

"Why?" asked Zech, his voice shaking, eyes squeezed closed as he curled up. He wanted Allen, but Allen wasn't here. No one was here. Would they come? Were they trying? Dr. Vargas looked on in scientific curiosity at the changes in his "experiment."

"So, you can talk...it doesn't matter. You can't live, you were never supposed to...your entire existence is an error, and you should've been put down the moment you mutated." Dr. Vargas glanced at his employees and waved his hand as they pressed buttons. Zech stumbled to his feet.

"My friends don't think I am error! They will come for me," Zech spat out in challenge to the doctor's smug arrogance.

"It's a little too late for that. Enrique, get a sample of his blood first. Go," ordered the scientist. He needed to study it; see how he could manipulate the serum to not do the same to another of his guinea pigs. Zech seethed and screamed as another zap of electricity ran up his arms. He begged for his friends...they had to come; they *would* come.

He snarled at a man in white as he came at him with a syringe, but as he tried to fight against the man, his chains sent another jolting shock running through him. He shook with fear at his helplessness; the man drew his blood as he squeezed his eyes shut, almost believing if he couldn't see them, they would disappear.

Zech watched as the scientists left, holding up the tube of his glittering red blood. Dr. Vargas took it and swirled it thoughtfully, before he looked back up at him. He handed the vial back as he cleared his throat.

"Hopefully you will be the last," he said with a sad sigh. Zech latched onto the words. More children have been put through this torture? Others had endured the same torture, the same pain and terrified nights? How many had come before him? How many would come after?

Unlike him, they would not have the chance to escape, they wouldn't find someone as generous as Allen or Ricky to take them in. He had to stop this- but, he whimpered, hopeless, as he looked down at the glowing, yellow chains. He clenched his jaw, his ears straightening with alert as a machine whirred to life. He looked up, seeing a contraption lower, and his eyes caught the needle.

His skin tingled with phantom pain that still haunted him. Needles injecting him with pain inducing serums, serums that kept him shaking, howling, torturing him. Needles that pricked and prodded. He looked at Vargas, his eyes flashing with hatred, a burning hatred. A fiery anger that seared his flesh even more than any he had ever felt. His friends hadn't come, he was going to die, and it hit him even harder that *more* would follow him in this man's insane search for cures that would torture and control others!

His heart beat steadily increased as the needle drew closer and another surge of electricity ran through his body, but his anger only grew. His breathing only quickened, and his eyes could only see red. This time, he didn't try to stop it.

His claws unsheathed, clasping the chains and lunging back, despite the crippling shocks. Pain was temporary, and his hatred and anger for this place couldn't be stopped by pain. His anger was paramount.

They had marked him with the unfixable mutations. His paws burned as he ripped the chains off of him, and the fur around his wrists shriveled up. But they snapped under his strength, and he threw them aside; his breathing coming out in heated puffs. He glared at the contraption and snarled.

"Kill it! It's snapping," ordered Vargas as alarms began to ring. The sirens fueled 227's rage and he roared, clasping the machine and ripping it off its stand, slamming it into the wall. He tore off the needle and caught the twinkling glass. Dr. Vargas backed away in sheer terror as his arrogant disregard and triumph of a moment ago dissipated in the heat of Zech's fury. Subject 227 pounced forward at a speed unmatched, tossing away a Stratus that tried to stop him; the man crashing into the wall and falling limp.

The subject grabbed the needle, stabbing the glass repeatedly until it shattered around him. He stepped into the lab, tossing aside the needle, his eyes locked on Dr. Vargas and he snarled. Gone was the whimpering shrapnel strewn creature, in its place was the true monster Vargas had created.

227 glanced to his side as a stratus began to shoot at him. He snarled and grabbed the control panel, heaving it out of its place and swinging it into the officer. He could hear the Stratus's screams but it faded away, his eyes focused on Dr. Vargas as he began to run.

227 shot forward, sprinting on all fours, gaining ground on the man. He imagined tearing him apart. Dr. Vargas skidded into a safe room, and 227 snarled with cruel delight as the puny door shut in his face. How foolish. What good was a door when faced with undeterred rage? He pressed his ear to the door and heard as Dr. Vargas grabbed a gun off of a stand.

Dr. Vargas' experiment heaved against the metal barrier between him and his prey. He couldn't escape. He wouldn't allow it. The door burst open, bullets flying at him. He ducked, moving with incredible speed toward the scientist.

Dr. Vargas reloaded his gun, cursing at the time it took. 227, snarling, slapped it out of his hand and shoved him down.

"I'll kill you, torturer!" he snarled, his voice unearthly, booming as his chest heaved, pupils merely tiny slits against the burning fire of his unquenchable rage. Dr. Vargas scurried back, choking out a whimper.

"Wait, don't! Don't kill me, I beg of you! I need to live! The earth is dying, people are dying, I have to live, if you kill me, people will suffer, the cure to radiation will end, and the world will die. You will have *killed* everyone if you kill me now!" he pleaded, curling away, as sobs shook him.

Zech blinked, contemplating his words, his eyes dilating, some sense returning to him. The monster leaving, Zech returning…

Then, as he stared at the blubbering, pathetic man below him, he snarled, pupils slitting once more, hackles rising as his hatred for this man deafened his ears. No pity filled him. No sorrow.

"If more suffering at your hands, torturer, means the world will live…it is not a world worth saving," spat Zech, lunging forward and sinking his bared teeth into Dr. Vargas's neck; he jerked his head. His tail curled up, hackles rising as he ripped through the skin, blood squirting up and covering his maw, screams filled his ears, but he didn't care.

His teeth let go and he picked the man up, slamming him against a counter as his neck fell limp. His breathing grew steady and his hackles lowered as he stared at the glassed eyes of Dr. Vargas.

Zech blinked and as he took in the gore, his eyes widened and he dropped him. '*Wait…wait.*' He blinked again, his eyes dilating more, to normal and he shook his head. He looked back at the man, blood spurting out and covering his white coat and the counters.

"Wait, no…" whispered Zech. He looked around. Allen...what would Allen say? He remembered the man he had snapped on, the pumping heart that lay on the floor and he fell to his knees.

"What have I done?" he cried, he killed him, and worse...he *meant* to kill him. He realized, as he stared at the corpse, that he had felt no remorse...he had delighted in this bloodshed, he had let himself do this, he had truly been in control. He hit the ground with sorrowful rage but this time at himself.

"I'm sorry, I'm so sorry, no... Allen, I'm sorry," he whimpered. He didn't care for the scientist, he cared for the look on his best friend's face, the look of horror, he saw the day he ripped out someone's heart. His eyes welled with tears and he crumbled, crawling to the body. All the bodies of the Stratus slain by him, and now Vargas, it was all becoming too much for him. He couldn't keep doing this.

Kraken

When the aircraft touched down on the roof of the building, Allen sprang out; he was desperate to save his friend. Maya also climbed out and chased after him. As they ran into the stairwell, they heard an alarm blare and screams echoing through the corridor. Allen looked at Maya with a panicked glance. They both shared the same thought. "What was going on?"

Allen's mind flashed to images of the day when Zech killed a man in front of him, how he begged for forgiveness and sobbed. He ran faster, trying to somehow delay what must have already happened.

The two clattered down the stairs and shoved past fleeing scientists. Where were they coming from? There was a room ahead with a safety door beginning to shut from the ceiling down.

"There!" shouted Allen. He ran for all he was worth, his body and head aching with pain from his injuries, but he paid no mind to them. Maya threw herself to the floor and rolled under just as the door came to a snapping close. They gasped for air. Allen chuckled at their near miss and helped Maya up. It was strangely calm, despite the blaring alarms.

The two made their way down a corridor and turned into the only open door.

There was Zech, crumpled over the mutilated body of a scientist, whose face could not even be made out anymore. Allen took in the blood pooling across the floor. He knew Zech had snapped in self-defense. Slowly he walked to the creature as he sobbed over the body and put a hand on his shoulder; even kneeling, Zech's head reached his chest. Zech looked up at him, his amber eyes widened with fear of himself. Allen smiled sadly.

It would be ok, soon they would be free, and Zech would finally be able to try and rehabilitate himself. Or at least that's what Allen hoped. He felt a twinge of guilt at the fact he had never really had the time to do any of the things he had promised Zech they would help him with. He would make up for that on the surface.

It was Maya who pulled Zech into a hug, and Allen soon joined her after that. Zech let out a soft whimper and eagerly embraced them.

"Let's get you out of here," murmured Allen. They walked out together. Zech pried open the doors and they trudged up the staircase. Allen knew he should've been elated, but truly he was just empty and tired. He wanted to go to sleep for a long time. He was still in shock from what had happened to Veronica, and he truly hadn't processed they were one step closer to liberation. It wouldn't be the same without Veronica. Allen knew out of all of them;

besides Zech, she had been the one who deserved liberation the most.

Zech dragged himself into the aircraft before grabbing Allen and hoisting him in. Maya climbed up on her own and sat with the creature, immediately tending to his wounds, despite the fact they had mostly healed themselves. He still had bullet shrapnel littering his chest.

"Allen..." groaned Zech. Allen was immediately at his side. They stared into each other's eyes with earnestness.

"I'm here," he said, taking hold of Zech's hand. Zech frowned and looked out of the window.

"I don't want to fight anymore," he whispered. Allen nodded. He understood that wish. He would've liked nothing more than to live a peaceful life.

The aircraft began to take off and Damon put it into jump. As he looked out of the window, his eyes widened.

"Ah shit," snarled Damon from the cockpit. Allen perked up- as well as Ricky. That didn't sound good at all.

"What?" Asked Allen as he raced to the front where his father was sitting, face pale, eyes wide. And that's when he saw it. The giant mechanical tentacle of the Kraken. He knew their escape had been far too easy!

"I need someone to fly this thing! I'm going to try to ward it off at least!" Damon shouted. Allen gasped at the command.

"Hey, not one of us knows how to fly one of these machines...if only, if only Ronny were here, Christ!" He swore, his voice cracking. Damon set his jaw, shaking his head.

"It's not too hard. Anyone can do it," he said. Ricky pulled himself up off the ground and hobbled to the cockpit.

"Let me have a go-"

"-what!? Ricky, you're hardly in the condition-"

"Yeah well now you know what you've been putting me through," snapped Ricky. The two best friends stared at each other, and Allen smiled at him, despite the heaviness of his heart. Ricky ruffled Allen's hair before he plopped himself into the Captain's chair. He observed the buttons and levers before shrugging. They didn't have time for a tutorial.

That point was highlighted when the great tentacle clasped its long tendril around the ship and began to pull it quite easily towards the sea.

Ricky spat out a deluge of all his favorite swear words as Damon raced to the craft's gun pit.

Maya wrapped her arms around Zech as he let out a distressed yelp. Ricky brought one of the heavier levers down, and already could feel the force of the engines working double time as he turned up the speed.

Damon readied the guns, his heart racing as he began firing at the ginormous mech. Its tentacle swooped towards them. He could hear screaming from both sides of the city and they pushed him to fight harder.

This was the first time the kraken had breached, this was the first time it had to, but why? Why was the judge so determined to extinguish them? Didn't she already have Veronica? What more could she take from him!? Was she that power hungry? Was this an example to the people behind the fence? Well, he wouldn't let her have it. He wouldn't let her have one more victory over him.

The kraken's tentacles disturbed the water into great waves, the ship lurching back to the sea. They were going to drown!

It's one giant eye stared at Damon, as if it had zoned completely on him and he gulped. His brow creased, and he scowled. He wasn't going down, not when he finally had his son back, not after living years alone with nothing but a vague hope to keep him going. Not after losing Veronica! The white-hot heat for vengeance and freedom focused him to overcome the beast.

He was done living under the fist of a tyrant. He doubled down, trying to attack the kraken's weak spots, the mech towering over even the highest buildings, it was impossible, but he had to do it!

Damon's head whipped back, seeing stars for a moment of confusion as the ship careened forward. He glanced down, the kraken was submerging, steam blowing out as the waves engulfed it. The tentacle was the last, like a final wave goodbye.

He frowned, gaining his senses back and as he watched, the screams died down, replaced by a calm that sent chills down his spine. They had let them go…

Ricky let out a triumphant whoop as the ship shot forward and he flew it far from the city. Zech howled with excitement.

"Oh my God! Allen! Did we just win?" He asked. Allen's eyes were wide as he tried to process what they were doing; their ship was slipping further and further away from the city by the second. Had they really escaped? Could they even call this a victory? They had left Veronica...Ricky was broken, Zech had lost his mind and temper too many times to protect them. He felt empty, drained. He just wanted to sleep. He looked at Ricky who was staring up at him expectantly. Allen sighed and collapsed into the co-pilot's seat. He owed everything to his friends.

"Ricky...thank you, thank you for staying with me 'til the end," he said softly. Ricky smiled sadly at Allen and clasped his hand.

"I wouldn't have had it any other way, ya pox," he grinned. Allen wished he could pull him into a hug, but he knew better than to put any unwanted pressure on those broken ribs. The two merely shared a respectful gaze.

"Allen, who's the old man?" He asked in a whisper as Damon marched out from the gun pit. Allen looked over at him and groaned.

"Well luck would have it that the universe traded out Ronny with...well, with my old man," he murmured. Ricky's eyes widened in utter shock and disbelief, but he didn't even have time to process what Allen had said before he left him alone with his thoughts in the cockpit.

Damon swept his son into a tight embrace, and Allen was too tired to fight against it. Truly, he didn't want to fight him either.

Allen didn't want to let go, he breathed a sigh of relief, closing his eyes. Despite his anger at the man, he felt nothing but an intense love that had been stored in the trenches of his mind. The last time he had been embraced by his father had been ten years ago.

He frowned slowly; he knew it wouldn't be the same. His dad wasn't there, and even though he was here now, he knew there would be a gap they would have to refill.

"This is a good restart," he murmured. Damon glanced down at him, knowing exactly what he meant.

"I agree, and I swear Allen, I'll never leave you again, you'll always have me around to help you. You know, it's ironic," he said.

"How so?" asked Allen. Damon chuckled wryly, glancing out the window as he thought about his response. It was too ironic, it almost made him mad.

"We're back where we started, we were never together in *heaven* and yet, we're here going right back to the surface again," he said. He frowned, some heaven that was. Allen wrinkled his forehead in thought.

"Let's be honest, Magnus city was never Heaven." The two shared a look of respectful understanding before Allen frowned and looked away. "...I don't know if I'll ever forgive you...but I want to try and start over," he muttered. Damon and Allen exchanged a shared glance of bitter sweetness, before Allen sat back, leaning against Zech, who was sprawled against the floor. He had already fallen into a deep, much needed slumber. The two, father and son, lay there in silence.

LOOSE ENDS

Maya stared out the window as she sat beside Ricky in the cockpit. She was deathly silent, her mind adrift, thoughts blown away by the wind that soared past them as they dove deeper into the night. The glow of the moon was the only thing to guide them.

Ricky started as she sniffed, glancing at her with a raised brow. He turned back to the night sky.

"Are you ok?" he asked after a long moment. Maya glanced back at him. She shrugged absentmindedly.

"I don't think any of us are really ok. I feel terrible that we just left Veronica behind…but the Judge...she had her, and we're just a bunch of kids. I'm surprised we even got away." Ricky merely listened to her, gazing out at the night sky as her soft voice filled his ears. He nodded along to the words she said, his lip curling as what happened to Veronica played on repeat in his head. He didn't think he could forgive himself for leaving her.

"And not only that, but everything I worked for is gone...don't get me wrong, I loved all of this, the excitement... It helped me grow back into my own skin, y'know? I just, all I wanted was to help people, to save people...I had a plan to work in the Medicum in the Fence, then I could be with you all, and with my dad...I was so close to being a real doctor...it sounds stupid," she turned to him, her eyes wide in fear and a hint of regret.

"It's not stupid. All I wanted to do was build mechs and become an engineer, you think I don't miss that? But guess what? Just because you're not an esteemed surgeon up there in those crystal towers, doesn't mean your career is over, it doesn't mean you're not a real doctor," he said, the concept making him chuckle a bit. She turned to him, a hint of hope lighting her eyes.

"We'll need you; we'll need me! Our dreams don't end after Magnus, in fact...on the surface, they're gonna need you more than anyone in Magnus ever will." He nodded firmly at the statement, believing it genuinely with every fiber of his being. Maya smiled at his words and tucked a strand of hair behind her ears, sitting back with the rekindling of hope.

"You're right Ricky… yeah, kudos to the nerds," she said with a smirk. Ricky grinned, holding his hand up for a high five, which she graciously took. Her hand missed, accidentally hitting his face. He winced, groaning as he held his stinging cheek.

"Oh! I'm so sorry!" she cried, crawling over to him to see if she hurt him. He waved her away, shaking off the tingling pain.

"I'm fine, I'm fine, don't worry about it!" he grumbled, blushing a bright red as Maya burst out laughing, sitting back against her seat.

Damon walked in, with a questioning look on his face at their giggling. They looked up at him, hushing at the presence of their mysterious savior.

"I'm coming to take over so you kids can all be together. I figured you all need time to debrief...good job you two, you did well," he said, a twinkle of respect in his eyes. Maya and Ricky glowed at the compliment, before getting up to sit on the deck.

Zech hugged his knees to his chest, playing the death of Dr. Vargas in his mind over and over. He tried to forgive himself, he tried to remind himself that Allen was not mad, and that he had been right.

His brow furrowed; he never wanted that to happen again, he never wanted to blink back into consciousness only to return to blood and screams. He had done it too many times. His ears lowered as his thoughts grew darker. What if he killed Allen? Or Ricky, or Maya? He would never forgive himself if he snapped on them.

He let out a shaky breath, glancing at his friends. He growled low in his throat at the missing Veronica. It just wasn't right, everything was wrong, their victory was hollow without her laughter and enthusiasm and bravado.

Zech had also not forgotten just how painful every step of the way was. He was exhausted, but plagued with nightmares that wouldn't let him sleep any longer. His friends lay huddled together, and Zech caught the glisten of a tear roll down Allen's cheek. The two locked eyes, as if searching for the other's deepest secrets.

"Hey Zech, come over here," Allen cajoled. He glanced over at the group and smiled halfheartedly. He wanted to say no, he wanted to keep thinking, but...thinking only led to sorrow.

So, he crawled over to his best friend, letting his head rest on Allen's chest. His eyes closed at the pleasantness of Allen's companionship.

He couldn't keep dwelling on it, or else he would only feel worse, and Zech wanted nothing but to feel happy. He never wanted to do what he did again. He couldn't change the past, but he could change himself for the future. He would control himself, he would unlearn the savageness, just like how he learned to read and talk. He wouldn't kill again; he wouldn't allow himself the chance.

He looked at Allen, then to the rest of his friends. The absence of Veronica was a hole in his heart, but he couldn't deny the pleasure of having his other friends there with him. He loved them. They were his family. The thought made him smile. They loved him too, they wouldn't let him snap any longer.

"Don't leave me again, ok? I don't like being alone," he said, his eyes wide with sorrow. Allen looked down at him, the group slowly nodding. Maya smiled softly.

"Don't worry we'll never let anyone take you again, we're free now," she whispered, going to sit beside him. Zech smiled, wrapping an arm around her. Ricky chuckled at the fox, smiling brightly. Everyone gave their enthusiastic agreements.

"We're here, I'm here, and Maya's right, we're free," Allen whispered, his eyes growing heavy. The friends lay there, huddled in the ship, darkness engulfing them as slowly, the heaviness of the pain of that night, and the countless nights before washed away. All the hungry, sleepless nights spent in the Fence. All the Scandals, gang wars and disgust. All the rumors, and toxicity. The sun would set on those nights. For tomorrow was a new day.

CHECKMATE

Heavy footfalls echoed through the empty hallways, the flowing grey robes leading the way. The judge entered her office, her eyes hard and cold as she stared out the window, overlooking the entire city.

"Your honor...we had them...why would you let them go?" asked Matias. The judge glanced at him, her brow creasing.

"I'm not wasting my time with them right now. Those criminals came from the ghetto, and so the ghetto will pay. I want you to flood that wretched place with chimeras and gorgons, if anyone steps out of line, if anyone even *speaks* about mutiny, I want them dead. Understand General?" she spat, sliding into her seat with liquid grace. She smirked and the two looked at a drugged Veronica who stumbled in behind them, her eyelids heavy.

"Besides...I have what I want," she said with a nod at the girl. Matias narrowed his eyes. He had been fond of Veronica, and he felt absolutely vile standing with this woman.

"Ma'am...we can't just terrorize our civilians...ghetto or not, they're people...I'm, I've already helped you destroy a child," murmured Matias, his eyes glued to the floor in regret. He wished it could've gone differently, he wished he had taken Veronica away, joined her when she had offered, now as he looked back on it.

The judge turned, sensing his hesitation and she chuffed, unimpressed at her general's lack of enthusiasm.

"They were young adults, not children, and they deserve the punishment of any adult...but I digress. Do as I say, I don't want one street to go unsupervised in the Fence...and I couldn't care less about those stragglers, right Veronica?' she asked firmly, narrowing her eyes at the man. Veronica nodded absentmindedly, not listening, but obedient to the one who spoke to her. The Judge smiled from the sick pleasure she derived from the submission of her enemy's daughter. Matias frowned at the exchange.

"This is sick," he mumbled, shaking his head in regret. The judge scoffed, turning her chair to face the window. The moonlight put a faint halo around her face as she thought.

"Will you turn against me too? Just like that Lieutenant? You know you will not be as lucky as them," she said, her voice shaking with anger. Matias stared at her with fear, before nodding slowly.

"Of course, your honor...we will send out the mechs this instant," he said, bowing his head and turning away, wanting to get as far away as possible from this woman, from this courthouse. The Judge turned, stopping him with a small wave of her fingers.

"And Matias...tell your husband that I wish him well...have a good night," she said softly. Matias shuddered, but nodded firmly, entering the elevator. As the doors closed, the Judge nodded.

Her silver eyes stared intently at the black sky and the corners of her lips lifted only slightly. She looked back at Veronica, who stood motionless and almost lifeless in the corner of her office, a sullen, dead look on her face, a spittle of drool sliding down her chin.

The Judge hummed in delight; she turned to her chess board that sat upon her desk; her white queen knocking over the final barrier.

"Checkmate," she whispered, before standing. She beckoned for Veronica to follow her, and the girl did as she was told, stumbling after her master. The Judge's robes flowed gracefully behind her. She was a silky, silvery lion on the prowl as she returned to her chambers. A lioness who was now on the hunt.

The moonlight caught a glisten off of the white queen, before a cloud passed over; darkness falling upon the office.

ACKNOWLEDGMENTS

Writing this book has been a journey filled with the ups and downs and twists and turns that come with creating. This three-year ride has been rife with procrastination, endless research, and then sudden bursts of productivity at two o'clock in the morning! These characters have been a part of my life for so long that it almost feels like they're real. Then of course, there were the real people who lifted me up and supported me through this adventure. I couldn't have done it without the help and encouragement of:

My mother, who was always there, lifting me up, pushing me to be the best version of myself, and giving me tips on how to make my world bigger and better. She is the rock that keeps me firm when the wind might blow a bit too hard.

Shelley Rubenstien, my editor and friend who worked tireless hours to fix all the times I repeated the phrase "he rose a brow."

Gabriel Bara, my closest friend and biggest fan who cheered me on and read my drafts. He was a big part of my creative process and honestly, "Reckless Skies" wouldn't be the story it is if it weren't for his influence and constructive criticism.

My good friend Kai; it was through her and our time writing together from when we were very young that the character of Allen was created. Which launched my book into existence!

I would also like to give a big thank you to all the people who made the technical aspects of making this book a physical object possible. Thank you, Franziska Haase, for the amazing book cover and her patience; you brought my artistic visions to life in a way I could never dream possible. I also want to thank the team at Ingramspark who made my dreams of becoming a published author a reality. Lastly, I want to pay my respects to the dozens of authors who inspired me and taught me how to refine my craft.

Of course, the true last person I want to thank, and I know, it's gonna sound cheesy; you. Thank you for seeing this and thinking, "Hey that looks cool" and then choosing it. It's the readers that truly make a space for writers to exist. You have my love and gratitude.